COME RAIN OR SHINE

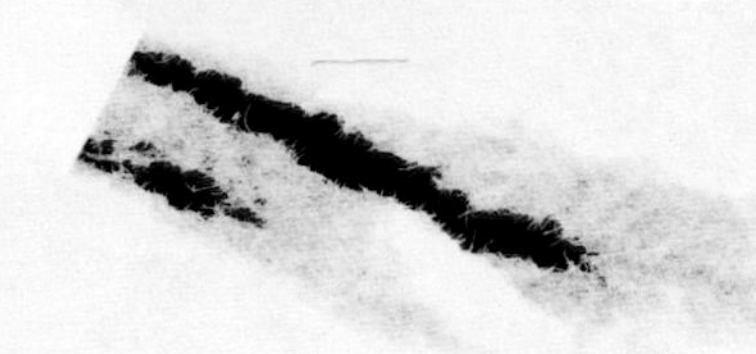

Also by Susan Sallis

A SCATTERING OF DAISIES
DAFFODILS OF NEWENT
BLUEBELL WINDOWS
ROSEMARY FOR REMEMBRANCE
SUMMER VISITORS
BY SUN OR CANDLELIGHT
AN ORDINARY WOMAN
DAUGHTERS OF THE MOON
SWEETER THAN WINE
WATER UNDER THE BRIDGE
TOUCHED BY ANGELS
CHOICES

COME RAIN OR SHINE

Susan Sallis

BANTAM PRESS

LONDON • NEW YORK • TORONTO • SYDNEY • AUCKLAND

TRANSWORLD PUBLISHERS LTD
61–63 Uxbridge Road, London W5 5SA

TRANSWORLD PUBLISHERS (AUSTRALIA) PTY LTD
15–25 Helles Avenue, Moorebank, NSW 2170

TRANSWORLD PUBLISHERS (NZ) LTD
3 William Pickering Drive, Albany, Auckland

Published 1998 by Bantam Press
a division of Transworld Publishers Ltd

A catalogue record for this book is
available from the British Library.

0593 043561

Typeset in 12/13½pt New Baskerville by
Hewer Text Composition Services, Edinburgh.

Printed in Great Britain by
Mackays of Chatham plc, Chatham, Kent.

For my family

[illegible]

There had been a chocolatory [illegible] in the [illegible] ever since [illegible] some few [illegible] [illegible] working until [illegible] [illegible] [illegible] [illegible] [illegible] Markham – Mr Edward [illegible] [illegible] father [illegible] long after [illegible] [illegible] there [illegible] were [illegible] [illegible] [illegible] and [illegible] [illegible] Queen as clearly [illegible] [illegible] could also produce [illegible] [illegible] and [illegible] from their [illegible] [illegible] the [illegible] [illegible] [illegible] [illegible] and [illegible] [illegible] [illegible] in the air [illegible] [illegible] [illegible] [illegible] of years. The [illegible] [illegible] Americans, on [illegible] [illegible] Markhams leapt gratefully [illegible] [illegible] by 1938 they needed [illegible] [illegible] staff: they needed [illegible]

Edith Manners and [illegible] [illegible] [illegible] for twenty years. They [illegible] [illegible] had been [illegible] – along [illegible] [illegible] with a kind of [illegible] [illegible] [illegible] and [illegible] the [illegible] [illegible] Son, and opened [illegible] [illegible] had [illegible] their [illegible] [illegible] [illegible] along the [illegible] [illegible] [illegible] enough, and Evelyn [illegible] [illegible]

Markhams

There had been a clockmaker's in Birmingham's Corporation Street ever since Joseph Chamberlain was mayor in 1873. But it was not until the new Queen Elizabeth came to the throne in 1953 that the business expanded into jewellery. The brothers Markham – Mr Edgar and Mr Delano – took over from their father not long after the war had finished; they had inherited their precise ways from the 'old man' and could screw in an eye-glass and examine the tiny workings of a Rolex or an Omega as closely as Sam, their old clockmaker. They could also produce intricate and wonderful designs – a skill inherited from their artist mother. Between them they crafted the diamond tiara, necklace and drop earrings they called the Coronation Suite, which was presented to the young Queen – and graciously accepted. They replicated it in marcasite and exhibited it in the shop window and at various Chamber of Commerce gatherings. They could also now display a royal coat of arms. The workshop was a hive of industry and the Americans, on the way to Stratford-on-Avon, swooped. Markhams leapt gracefully into the new Elizabethan age and by 1958 they needed more staff; they needed a new kind of staff; they needed younger staff.

Edith Manners and Evelyn Hazell had been at Markhams for twenty years . They had been engaged by the old man and had been ruled – along with the clock- and watch-making staff – with a rod of iron. All through the war they had regularly sandbagged the shopfront against blast fire-watched with Sam and opened for 'business as usual' after the raids. They had outlived their immediate families and appeared to be alone in the world. 'Markhams is my family now,' Edith said smugly and Evelyn, older but more innocent, nodded and spoke of 'the boys' – meaning Mr Delano and Mr Edgar – like a proud nanny. They were not going to take kindly to an influx of staff.

When Mr Delano suggested that Edith should concentrate entirely on dealing with the invoices, she said, 'But what about our letters, sir?'

Mr Delano rubbed his chin nervously. 'My brother has suggested we take on a young lady fresh from a Swiss secretarial school. She will be able to deal with the foreign correspondence.'

Edith drew in her mouth until she was lipless. 'Do I know her, sir?'

'No.' Mr Delano avoided her eyes. 'But neither do I. Mr Edgar has known her since she was a small girl. She finishes at Berne this summer and will doubtless join us in the autumn.'

'I see.' Edith said no more. She was loyal to both brothers, but it was a fact that Mr Delano was always in the shop whereas Mr Edgar acted as a kind of agent and was only visible at odd times. He was something in the Chamber of Commerce; he was chairman of the local Rotary Club; he was often seen in local theatres or dining at hotels; he 'put himself about', as Edith said.

It was Mr Edgar who recruited Prudence Adair. Her mother, the Honorable Mrs Adair, had been widowed since just before Pru's birth and she had a string of male escorts who surrounded her with a kind of courtly love. Mr Edgar was one of these, but, unlike many of them, he was genuinely fond of young Pru. When she was on holiday from her boarding school he would insist that she came along on picnics, was included in tennis parties and bridge evenings. She was tall and gawky and very good at knocking things over: her mother's drinks, vases of flowers, once a whole shelf of books. She was black and blue from a variety of bruises; the sight of her getting in and out of a car was pathetic.

She told Edgar she wanted to do something, but she did not know what. Nursing? She would probably kill her patients off. The law? She had an excellent brain and had been chairman of her school debating society. But that did not appeal either.

'I wouldn't mind making pots,' she said, smiling her wide smile.

Her mother made a face. 'Too messy, darling. And you don't need to do anything. You're beautiful and you have lots of money – your darling daddy left heaps in trust, you know. You'll marry well and have a simply lovely time.'

'Oh, Mummy!' Pru rolled her grey eyes almost back into her head. Her mother shrieked, Edgar laughed. But he could see that Constance Adair was right: Pru was beautiful in her way. She would be ideal wife-material once she had learned to control her movements. There seemed no escape from her destiny.

'What about a secretarial school?' he suggested. 'They'd teach you business basics. And you could be someone's secretary while you think about what you really want to do.'

Pru and her mother both wrinkled their noses. Edgar said, 'These schools do things like fashion and deportment. After all, a good secretary is often a hostess at business meetings.'

'I should probably knock everything over,' Pru said gloomily.

'Don't you see, dear girl, that is exactly what these finishing places do. They teach you how to move around without knocking things over. They polish up your second language – French, I suppose. You have a good brain, Pru. It's full of facts. A finishing school would teach you how to use those facts to your advantage.'

Pru was cautious. But really there seemed nothing else to do, so eventually she was sent out to Berne for two years. There, she 'polished' her French and German and learned the knack of repulsing Italian suitors; she took a great many dancing lessons where her tutor explained to her about 'personal space'; she learned about food and drink and clothes and hair. When she came home she seemed taller than ever, very elegant, very assured, yet strangely apart, almost distant. Her mother's life seemed unbearably trivial to her, yet she acknowledged that her own was probably worse: her mother, after all, chaired many charities and used her social life to further their interests. Prudence – for some reason she was not clear about – still shunned the social life. She had had no reason to turn down Mr Edgar's suggestion that she become a secretary at Markhams but she viewed it without enthusiasm. However, she liked Edgar, and Mr Delano seemed just as nice. She told herself that in spite of her reservations she would put her heart and soul into this job. She took up her post in the autumn of 1958.

She settled in immediately and with hardly a ripple. She deferred to Edith with great tact and when Mr Delano complimented her on her work she said, 'I have an excellent teacher in Miss Manners.' Edith discovered that she could keep an eye on the invoices properly now and find time to 'go to the front' as they called the showroom. Both she and Evelyn liked Pru from the start. There was an inbred graciousness about the tall, elegant girl that put everyone at their ease. They knew from the outset that she would never lose her temper, that she was discretion itself when she dealt with any of the correspondence, but especially when she typed Mr Edgar's private letters. When clients came up to the office to see the brothers, she put them at their ease. The Americans adored her, though none of them asked her for a date like they did Natasha Barkwith.

Natasha arrived a few months before Prudence. She dropped out of her History of Art degree course in Sheffield and took her very successful social life with her into her parents' home. Luckily her father belonged to the same Rotary Club as did Mr Edgar and was able to arrange a position for her at Markhams. Natasha had an allowance from her grandparents and so was able to take a very small salary and the title of 'designer in precious stones' at Markhams.

The post suited her very well. She did not enjoy hard work and soon drifted out of the workroom and into the showroom. With her cloud of dark hair and enormous brown eyes she looked like a youthful Hedy Lamarr; Mr Delano realized that her more public presence was an asset. He encouraged her to model the jewellery she designed. The sight of Natasha Barkwith wearing a diamanté choker as a Suzanne Lenglen headband was startling in the middle of the afternoon. Younger people came to the shop. And more Americans.

Better still, Natasha liked Pru, recognizing in her a maturity Natasha herself would never possess. She enjoyed shocking Edith and Evelyn with her succession of 'dates'. And there was Maisie. Maisie who was like the rabbit in *Alice in Wonderland,* constantly scurrying everywhere, at everyone's beck and call. Maisie adored Natasha. Natasha enjoyed that too. In fact she was hardly ever bored.

Maisie Jenkins had been Mr Delano's contribution to the extra staff. Quite simply, he inserted an advertisement in the *Post,* and when Maisie's application arrived he was charmed with her round script and her honesty.

'I wish to apply for the post of filing clerk in your office. I have never filed anything but I am very willing.'

He had interviewed her with two other girls. She was small and blond and blue-eyed: Edgar would tell him he was a pushover for a pretty face. Perhaps Edgar was right. It would be pleasant to see Maisie Jenkins's face around the office. He asked her if she would mind keeping the stoves up during the winter – coals had to be brought from the cellar, the ashes riddled each morning. Her face beamed.

'I would love that more than anything!' she said.

He was surprised, but when the winter arrived he realized she had probably never been so warm before. She made tea at regular intervals and though her filing was haphazard her delight at being on the staff shone around her like an aura. No-one told her off. She washed up hygienically in the cupboard next to the lavatory; she polished the clock glasses, the brass along the edge of the counters, Mr Delano's office. What did it matter if she took nearly an hour to find a file? The world was changing and girls who were enthusiastic about the more menial jobs that cropped up in a shop like Markhams were few and far between.

Maisie never spoke of her private life. Only Pru knew where she lived and Pru was a very private private secretary.

Rachel Strang was the fourth recruit. She was Pru's understudy. She could have had Pru's job had her father been quicker off the mark. He was a member of the Chamber of Commerce and – for a time – very much admired by the Markham brothers as being 'a true patriot'. He was a man with an eye to the main chance and knew that an office grounding at a place like Markhams would stand his daughter in good stead. But the position of private secretary had already been promised to Prudence Adair. So Rachel dealt with letters for the home market while Pru had the interesting stuff: the export trade. At one time Rachel seriously considered tripping Pru up as she descended the stairs from Mr Delano's office, but, like everyone else, she was extremely fond of Pru so that was out of the question.

Rachel was short and as strong as her name. She had a head of thick straw-coloured hair and pale blue eyes and in her neat grey suits and white blouses she looked efficient and capable. But not attractive. She was ambitious. Markhams was only a starting block. She had always wanted to be a secretary. Her mother, in a fit of jealous rage, had once pronounced that secretaries were the real power behind the throne. Rachel wanted power. But she wanted friendship too and the other girls were all friendly.

Occasionally they would spend a Saturday together enjoying the pursuit that the pre-war generation had enjoyed: walking. They would catch a train to Barnt Green and 'do' the Lickey Hills. Another train would take them to Worcester and then Malvern Link and from there they would hike to the highest peak. 'Only ten feet off being a mountain?' Maisie squeaked the first time they did it. Pru stood looking over Worcestershire, the wind blowing her skirt close to her body, her hand shading her eyes in a way that Maisie thought made her resemble a Greek goddess. Natasha, exhausted and therefore irritable, said, 'For God's sake, stop looking like some ancient mariner, Pru, and let's get down into Great Malvern and have some tea!' And Pru, laughing gently, linked arms with Edith and led the way back down.

They all knew they were happy. They also knew that it would not last.

One

It was Natasha's mother, Mary Barkwith, who mooted the idea that the staff from Markhams should meet again. A reunion. Natasha had returned to England from the States in the spring; she had brought her daughter Hilary with her and enrolled her at Chudleigh School as a weekly boarder. She did not mention her divorce for some time. When Hilary announced that she wished to spend the summer holidays in Maine with her father, Natasha had taken her back to the apartment in New York. Mary Barkwith had hoped very much that Natasha and Harvey Nolan would patch things up and she would receive a phone call to say that Natasha was also spending the summer in Maine. But Natasha returned home alone, and was obviously unhappy. It emerged that Mary Pressburger, Harvey's secretary, had been invited to Maine in Natasha's place. Mary Pressburger was the very serious Other Woman. The thought of her frolicking with Harvey – and therefore with Hilary – made Natasha feel so ill she had run from it and come home to her parents' house at Nortons Heath in Warwickshire, where, it seemed, she might quite easily die of boredom.

In order to alleviate the dullness of life at Thatch End, she had already arranged a brief affair with Ron, the plumber who was working on her father's latest craze: a swimming pool in the garden. She had tried to make it torrid. In her mind she had called him her 'bit of rough' – he might well be something to tell Harvey about if ever they saw each other long enough for one of their almighty rows. But Ron had eyes like her old spaniel, Ferris, and had seemed determined to fall in love with her. She finished with Ron, and then there was nothing: a sort of limbo.

Mary Barkwith said, 'Darling, I am *not* trying to get rid of you! But you've made it all too plain that bridge and tennis are not for you—'

'I play them all the time back home,' Natasha informed her mother bleakly. She knew only too well she wasn't fitting in with anything in Nortons Heath.

Her mother said acutely, 'That's when you're with Harvey, darling. Don't you remember how Ida Wainwright was? For years? She just had to work her way through it.'

'Mummy, Ida was widowed! Her husband died!'

'She was bereft. And you are bereft. She had to learn to live on her own. So do you. In some ways it's more difficult for you.'

'Because I know Harvey is living it up with Mary Pressburger?'

Mary looked distressed. She made an obvious effort to rally both of them. 'Listen. You've always kept in touch with Pru—'

'Christmas cards.'

'And letters. You know she's living in that commune in Cornwall. You've got an address. And you could send a letter to Rachel care of the House.'

'With a capital aitch?' Natasha snorted a laugh. 'She'd kill me!'

'Well, see what Pru says.' Mary sighed deeply. 'Darling. Can't you see that you're in between two worlds? Go back to the old one – hear what has happened to Pru and Maisie and Rachel and Evelyn and that other dear old soul . . .'

'Edith,' Natasha supplied with deeper gloom. Edith had told her once that she would come to no good. She was right. Of course. As usual.

Pru's voice had not changed; it was deep, slow and hesitant.

'I think it would be good,' she said consideringly. 'How long? Lunch? Weekend? And where?'

'I haven't given it a thought.' Natasha was phoning from her father's study where she could watch the gardeners who were now landscaping around the pool. None of them had

Ron's broad shoulders and narrow flanks. They all looked like starving hippies. 'I suppose if you and I could foregather over – say – a week, it would give the others the opportunity to come when they had the time.'

'Sounds sensible.' Pru made some noises. It became apparent she was looking through a diary. 'Um . . . let me see . . . yes. I could manage the last week in August. How about you?'

Natasha turned sideways to look at her reflection in the heavily framed mirror at the side of her father's desk. She was still darkly attractive even without make-up; but since arriving in England at the beginning of the summer a line had appeared either side of her mouth. Both lines turned down towards her chin. She made a hideous grinning face at her reflection and forced the lines almost up to her eyes. That was no better.

Already the idea of a reunion was going cold on her. She thought of Pru, willowy, beautiful, subtly mysterious, who had suddenly gone native in Cornwall. If there had been an unhappy love affair or a death or . . . anything . . . Pru would never say. And in spite of – or perhaps because of – Pru's terrific reticence, Natasha knew she ought to be likewise. British dignity and all that sort of stuff. And the whole point of seeing Pru would be to offload her own peculiar state of affairs. Pru had always held everyone at arm's length and Natasha could tell from her voice that she had not changed in this.

She said heavily, 'Well, any time suits me. Hilary and I are living back home now. She goes to Chudleigh Girls. Boards in the week. She's spending the summer with her father. Not back till mid-September.'

Pru said, 'I see.'

'Yes.' Natasha made another face and then turned away from the mirror. 'I expect you do. Never mind, huh? Next question – are you in touch with any of the others?'

'You sound so American!' Pru laughed her deep, amused laugh. 'Well, I saw Maisie two years ago. And she keeps in touch with Evelyn.'

'What about Edith?'

'She died. Two years ago. I went to the funeral. That's how I know where Maisie is. She was there too.'

Natasha said violently, 'Oh God!'

'Listen.' Pru abandoned her diffident tone and became suddenly forceful. 'I'm not sure about Rachel, but I think this would be a good time for you and me and Maisie to meet. And as a matter of fact, there is somewhere we can go. Not a hotel – I couldn't stand a hotel, could you?'

Natasha thought of hot showers and cooling fans and a bar where they knew how to mix a proper martini. 'No,' she sighed.

'I've inherited a house! I don't know a thing about it. And anyway I don't want it. I'm going to sell it eventually. But it will be ideal for us to have a little hol. Our old stamping ground, too.'

Natasha opened her eyes. 'Not the Malverns?'

'Yes. We can take the train to Malvern Link like we used to and get a taxi. I think it's about four miles. Too far to walk – with luggage. What d'you say?'

Natasha remembered their rambles in the high hills on the edge of Worcestershire. She bit her lip. She and Harvey had done their exploring there too. Was it quite the place in which to forget him?

Pru said, 'I've been scurraging around through my address book while we talked and I've just come up with Rachel's number. If I ring Rachel, will you do Maisie? She'll know about Evelyn. And there were those two temps—'

'We don't want any of the temps. Just the six of us. Sorry, five.' Natasha turned to the mirror again. She had been biting her bottom lip and could see an ooze of blood. She had been biting her lip a lot since the divorce. There were times when she actually hated Harvey. She said, 'I'm not sure about me contacting Maisie. I haven't seen her since I came home to have Hilary and she was in the middle of a rather passionate affair–'

Pru interrupted. 'I know about that. But that's fifteen years ago and she went back to her husband.'

Natasha said, 'She went back to her husband because of me. That was the trouble. Pru, I don't want to contact her, can't you—'

'She'd always do anything for you,' Pru swept on, apparently not hearing. 'Her number is Lennox 4050. And her married name is—'

Natasha said grimly, 'Davenport. I'm not likely to forget. He made all those glass units for the shop – that's how he met Maisie. And anyway, my father built a factory for him.'

'Well done, Nash!' Pru sounded like the head girl at Natasha's old school. 'And I'll make sure Rachel turns up. She thinks she's running the Liberal Party. I'll put her wise!' She laughed so that Natasha could not voice any more objections, then went on more seriously. 'I'll ring you with directions and so forth. I'll have to organize someone local to go in and polish the place up a bit.'

'So you'll be in touch?'

Pru said she would be. Then she said she'd have to go because she was on kitchen duty and it was nearly lunchtime. She put down her receiver. Natasha swivelled her father's chair and made another face in the mirror. Edith gone. And Maisie . . . Did she feel betrayed? She replaced her phone and said aloud, 'Damn!'

The door opened and Mrs Mayhew came in. She was the Barkwiths' cleaner. She held out a man's sock as if it were a dead toad.

'Found this under your bed,' she said.

Natasha took it. She would have liked to tell Mrs Mayhew that her brief fling with Ron the plumber had finally ended before she took Hilary back to the States three weeks ago, which meant that Mrs Mayhew had not cleaned under her bed in all that time. But it wasn't worth it.

She beamed. 'Thank you so much, Mrs Mayhew,' she said. 'Could you possibly pop it in the bin for me? One sock isn't much good to most people, is it?'

She picked up the phone and dialled the Lennox number before Mrs Mayhew could open her mouth again. At least the woman had forced her to do Pru's bidding though it was a fruitless mission; Natasha knew that Maisie would not accept any invitation from her.

She half hoped one of the Davenport household would pick up the phone. But of course it was Maisie. The voice was the same; the childish lisp, the slight Brummie accent she had tried so hard to lose.

'Lennox 4050. Maisie Davenport speaking.'

'Maisie.' Natasha swallowed. 'It's me. Natasha.'

There was a scream of joy from the other end. 'Nash! My God! It can't be you! You live in America!'

'Came home last Christmas. I got Hilary – my daughter, you know – into Chudleigh. That's my old school.' Natasha couldn't believe it; had Maisie forgotten what happened fifteen years ago?

'I remember Hilary. She was about four weeks old when I saw you last.' There wasn't a trace of bitterness in the childish voice. Natasha turned her father's chair right round and stared at the door behind which Mrs Mayhew was banging about with the vacuum. Maisie said, 'Listen. Can I come and see you? No. Better not. Edward isn't keen on me going out alone. Come here. Can you? Will you?'

'Better still. Pru's got a house. In the Malverns. She wants us all to meet up. Last week in August. A grand reunion. What do you say?' Blurt it out. Get rid of it.

There was a hesitation from the Davenport end. Maisie was going to turn down the invitation. Natasha had known she would, but it hurt all the same. Suddenly she wanted to see Maisie again. She wanted Maisie to like her still, to expiate all that guilt.

Maisie said slowly, her accent stronger, 'You see, the thing is, Nash, Edward likes me to be at home. With him and the children.'

Of course. He must have found out about Maisie's affair with Tom. He'd never risked it happening again. But dammit, that was fifteen years ago.

She said heavily, 'How many children, Maisie? I seem to remember you had two.'

'Yes. I was expecting then – I didn't mention it. Then I had another two. Five altogether.'

Natasha was horrified. 'Five children? Maisie! You've had your work cut out!'

Maisie lisped lightly, 'Mark is nineteen and Jess eighteen now.'

'Grown up.'

'They're both at Edinburgh. They wanted to be vets and that was the place to go, it seems.' She paused and added, 'They like animals better than people.'

Natasha frowned. 'Yes. Well. Lots of us are like that.'

Maisie's voice quickened. 'The last two are still at home. Edward said they could go to a day school.' She laughed. 'It would give me something to do.' She almost hiccoughed in her eagerness to tell their names. 'Simon and Ian. Simon is fourteen and Ian is thirteen.'

Natasha's frown deepened. 'Maisie! *And* you've left out the middle one! She must be almost the same age as Hilary. So you had three children in three years!'

'Yes.' The laughter had gone. 'She was a boy, actually. Tom. He's at boarding school. Like the older two.'

Natasha felt her heart contract. Tom. That had been the name of the man. Tom. Tom McEvoy. Suddenly a lot of things Maisie had said began to connect.

She said urgently, 'You've got to come, Maisie. We need to talk. Properly.'

Maisie accepted instantly that Natasha understood. She said in a small voice, 'It's no good, Nash. I'd love to come but Edward won't allow it.'

Natasha was appalled. She said, 'Listen. I'll come and talk to him. Persuade him.'

She heard her own words. They were almost the same as she had said before when she had talked Maisie out of running off with Tom McEvoy. She stopped speaking and gnawed at her lip.

But Maisie did not seem to make any connections; she certainly made no objections either.

'Well, you could try, I suppose.' Her tone became self-reproving. 'Don't get the wrong idea, Nash. Ted is a wonderful man. Really wonderful. It's just that . . .'

'He's possessive?' It sounded like an insult but Maisie accepted the word almost gratefully.

'That's all it is. A lot of people who are insecure are possessive. Aren't they? And he's old-fashioned too. A wife's place . . . all that, you know.'

'When shall I come?'

'Let me pave the way. Tell him you're home. I'll ring you. OK?'

Natasha replaced the receiver again and sat still, looking down at the desk. She thought of Tom McEvoy. She'd been right; he wasn't good enough for Maisie. Even without Natasha's persuasion, he would eventually have dropped her.

Even so . . .

The door opened and Mrs Mayhew stood there flourishing the sock.

'Found another one!' she announced triumphantly. 'Inside your pillowcase this time!'

Natasha forced another grin. 'What a relief! Thanks, Mrs Mayhew. Could you put both of them in the laundry basket? Daddy will be so pleased!'

She waited until the door closed before swivelling the chair so that she could look in the mirror again. She ran her fingers through her hair so that it stood out from her face. The way she had worn it when she was twenty-five; when she was beautiful; the mid-Sixties. Tom McEvoy had not stood a chance. But, as it turned out, neither had Maisie.

She noticed that her bottom lip was bleeding again and her eyes were too bright. She thought: poor Maisie . . . she must have told her husband about the affair; she must have told him about the baby. Natasha vaguely remembered Ted Davenport and his assiduous courtship of Maisie in the shop. And her father had told her things about him too.

Natasha bit her lip again as she worked things out. Tom McEvoy's child must have been born the winter after she'd had Hilary. A year later there had been another baby. And a year after that, another. She said aloud to the mirror, 'Poor Maisie.'

Two

Maisie was obsessed with the idea of the reunion. After Nash phoned, she went straight to Mrs Donald, the cook-housekeeper, who knew all about everything and apparently understood.

'Nash is an amazing girl,' she explained, producing an old and faded snapshot. 'If anyone can persuade Ted it'll be Nash.'

Mrs Donald studied the photograph carefully. She was making Mr Davenport's favourite fruit cake and continued to stir it gently with her other hand.

'Or . . .' she said judiciously, 'she might put him off entirely.'

Maisie thought about it and nodded. She was not frightened of Edward Davenport; she had known when she told him the truth about her third pregnancy that he would punish her for the rest of her life. She accepted that that was just; it was hard, but it was just. And his punishment included the possessiveness Nash had mentioned, and Maisie did not mind that. She knew she was what he called 'a hopeless case', and his all-pervading presence in her life stopped her being hopeless.

Mrs Donald handed back the snapshot and began to scrape the cake mixture into its prepared tin. She passed the spoon to Maisie for her to lick clean and said, 'If you were to ask him, he might say no, but that would be that. If he thinks you've put your friend up to anything . . .' She passed over the empty mixing bowl for Maisie to scrape out and opened the oven door. They had never openly discussed Edward's violence – it hardly ever erupted these days – but Maisie knew exactly what Mrs Donald meant.

She said loyally, 'Oh, I don't think so. But it might be

better for me to talk to him. Yes. I think you're right.' She flashed Mrs Donald a smile. 'As always!'

Mrs Donald flushed slightly. She was older than Maisie by ten years, her dark hair swept Brontë-like over her ears and into a knot halfway up the back of her head. Her features were not classical enough to take this severity and when she first arrived, not long after Tom's disastrous birth, Maisie had thought of her as another Mrs Danvers from the film she'd seen of *Rebecca*. But then, when Ted had come upon Maisie breastfeeding Tom, it had been Mrs Donald who intervened and took one of the blows on her face.

Maisie had expected her to resign immediately, but she had not. Her involvement in the family row had seemed to make her one of the family. The bruise on her high cheekbone had highlighted her dark eyes, giving them some kind of light and life. Until it faded she was beautiful and tragic. And Maisie, still childlike with her mop of golden curls and her china-blue eyes, looked on her as the mother she could not remember.

Mrs Donald laughed to cover her embarrassment. 'Get along with you,' she said, just like a mother might do.

Maisie laughed too. 'It would be so lovely to see them all again. Rachel is married to a politician now – it was what she always wanted. And Nash has got the most gorgeous husband, Harvey Nolan – he's terrifically rich – American.' She giggled. 'I always remember realizing he was serious about Nash. We'd gone for one of our tramps in the hills and he just arrived – I mean, it was obvious he'd followed her, but as far as we were concerned he just popped out from behind a hedge! Nash's face was a picture! Up till then he'd just been one of our American clients – he made passes at her in the showroom all the time because she modelled jewellery for him. But they all did that. And then, quite suddenly, he was smitten. It was amazing – he was everywhere. There was no way she could stand against him – not that she wanted to, I'm sure.' She stopped giggling, remembering that Nash was quite capable of standing against any man if she wished to. Not everyone was like Maisie. Maisie, who had not been able to make a stand. Ever.

Mrs Donald finished washing her hands and went to the roller towel.

'She probably fell head over heels in love with him,' she said as if reading Maisie's thoughts. 'Like you did with Mr Davenport.'

Maisie nodded vigorously and took the bowl to the sink to wash up. She still did the washing-up and other mundane jobs just as she had at Markhams. She enjoyed them. If she'd made Ted's cake, she'd be on pins in case it wasn't just right.

Mrs Donald said gently, 'He'll be home for lunch today. Why don't you tackle him then. Get it off your chest.' She did not add that she would also be at lunch, whereas this evening, after supper, she always went to her own room to watch television. Edward Davenport had never been violent in front of Mrs Donald since the incident when he had roared, 'Breastfeeding? You never breastfed Mark or Jess! This one is special, is he? This one must have the best!' And had torn the baby from her and almost thrown him into his carrycot. But Maisie had never blamed him: she should not have confessed about Tom McEvoy. She should have kept it a secret just as Pru had told her to do.

She said heavily, 'Yes. All right. Lunchtime.' She held the mixing bowl under the hot tap to rinse it and added, 'What is for lunch, Mrs Donald?'

Mrs Donald hesitated. The doctor had suggested that Edward ought to lose some weight and she had been producing salads for lunch. He hated salads.

She said, 'I'll do brains on toast and plenty of afters to fill him up.'

They smiled at each other and Mrs Donald went for her summer jacket to drive to the village in her own little car and call at the butcher's shop.

Maisie looked across the round table in the breakfast room and thought how handsome Ted was. More so than when she had first known him when he had just inherited his father's rundown factory, and came to Markhams to convince Mr Edgar that new shopfittings would double their display area besides being more convenient and 'classier'. Mr Edgar had visibly winced at the word, but when Ted produced sketches and did complicted mathematical problems in front of Mr Edgar – then and there – he was impressed.

'The man knows his business,' he said to Mr Delano later.

'He's pushy,' Mr Delano objected.

'He's a member of Rotary. He organized the last charity drive.'

Mr Delano did not mind this kind of discussion in front of Pru who did all his Rotary correspondence and was as discreet as a clam, but Rachel Strang was hovering by the door with a message and he knew full well she would report back to the other girls.

'All right. If you think he should refit the showroom, I'm quite happy about it.'

Ted had done all the measuring himself and had accepted many a cup of tea from Maisie's small hands. She recognized his strength of will; she knew from the beginning that it would be useless to stand against that. When he asked her to go out with him, she did not like to say no. When he insisted that she should sleep with him, she knew that in the end she would give way, so she said yes immediately. When she became pregnant with Mark she had been eternally grateful to Ted for marrying her. And, really, there was no reason to stop being grateful. Not really.

He looked up from his plate and caught her looking at him.

'Know me next time, will you?' he asked, sounding just like the boys who had chased her years ago in the playground of Chamberlain Street School.

She flushed guiltily. 'I was just thinking . . . you haven't a grey hair in your head. You . . .' she felt his eyes hard on her, pressing almost physically '. . . you're still very goodlooking.'

'What are you after, Maisie?' He liked the compliment; his voice was jocular. It was unfortunate that she did in fact want something and now it would sound false.

'Nothing.' She held his gaze for as long as she could and then picked up her glass of water. He laughed.

'Come on. Out with it. You've seen a dress? A pair of shoes?'

That was unfair. She rarely bought clothes. Before her sterilization he had bought things for her himself. Mostly underwear in which she dressed up in the evenings. She had liked that. It made her feel so special. Now, since she was barren, their lovemaking was infrequent. She understood that too.

'It's just that . . . I had a phone call this morning.'

Jocularity faded. 'If Tom is whining again about his school, let him whine. He's got to realize that life is not a bed of roses, even when you go to the most expensive boarding school in the whole damned universe!'

Maisie shook her head, unable to speak. The thought of Tom, homesick, made her so unhappy she never could speak, not even to Tom.

Edward lifted his brows. 'Not Simon's bloody headmaster? God, Maisie! I knew we should have sent them packing as well! Just because you were all broody and couldn't have any more kids, I agreed to them going to a day school! And look what it's done for them!'

Mrs Donald came back into the breakfast room trundling the trolley ahead of her. There was summer pudding, a sorbet and a cheese board. She began to relay the table.

Maisie said in her small sibilant voice, 'It's not Simon. And actually, Ted, they're both doing ever so well. Simon's art work is quite amazing.'

Ted said, 'Art! He'll probably want to go back to the hippy days of the Sixties or something just as useless. Heaven knows where he gets all that from.'

Maisie recalled the mid-Sixties when she had met Tom McEvoy. He had wanted her to throw up everything, leave her husband and children and just take to the road with him. She might well have done – again unable to say no – if it hadn't been for Nash. Perhaps . . . she should have gone with him. She thought of Tom's birth and then the violence of Simon's conception and his birth less than a year later; and then again with Ian another year later. And it would have gone on except that something went wrong and she had the sterilization in 1970.

She said, 'Anyway, it wasn't anything like that, darling. It was from someone I used to work with in Markhams. Natasha Barkwith. D'you remember Natasha?'

'How could I forget any of them? Interfering little bitches. Don't think I never knew that they tried to talk you out of marrying me.'

Mrs Donald put a plate in front of him and pushed the puddings and cheese in a semicircle around him like a palisade.

Maisie was genuinely astonished. 'Why on earth would you think that? They thought it was wonderful for me – Rachel – I remember Rachel actually saying she was green with envy!'

Partially mollified, he cut a piece of cheese. 'That stuck-up Prudence Adair never liked me. And the other one—'

'Nash? She was always for it.' Maisie let her tongue run away with her. 'My God, Nash was *always* for it! If it hadn't been for her—' She stopped suddenly, realizing where she was going.

He said grimly, 'If it hadn't been for her you'd have left me back in Sixty-five – is that what you were going to say?'

She forced a laugh. 'You know full well I would never have left you. I will never leave you.' She looked into his dark, veiled eyes, tried to hold them in a gaze that would convince utterly. They knew each other's pain, understood things the world never could. She wanted to make contact at that level, just as she had done so often . . . before. And just for an instant it worked because he said shortly, 'I know that,' and then looked away.

There was a short pause. She knew this was her opportunity to ask him about the reunion, but hard on the heels of what had been nearly a declaration of her total commitment to him, it seemed manipulative. He forced her to continue.

'Well, what about the phone call from the Barkwith girl? No . . . Nolan now, isn't it?'

She swallowed. 'Fancy you remembering.'

'Her father did the plans for the new factory. I heard quite a bit about the precious Nolans. The apartment in New York – view of the Empire State – holiday place in Maine – money, money, money, that's all they think about.'

It was such an unfair accusation that again Maisie was silent. Edith had always 'kept tabs' on Natasha's new life in the States, and it had been obvious that though Harvey Nolan made a great deal of money in a great many ways, he used it to enjoy life. Ted made money too; making money was definitely his driving force. But there the similarity ended.

Maisie sighed and Ted snapped, 'What?'

She said without apparent relevance, 'I miss Edith.'

'Edith Manners? The one who died last year? That old biddy?'

'She was always fond of me. Kept in touch. Actually she died two years ago. She was a kind of—'

He was suddenly contrite. 'Mother? Surely not?'

She smiled, accepting that Edith had not been maternal. 'I was going to say a maiden aunt. And she wasn't that old either. Fifty-four it said in the paper.'

'My God. I remember her in the shop back in 1963. She seemed old then.'

'Well, you know. The black dresses.'

'Yes.' They actually smiled at each other. Mrs Donald gathered up dishes and went out of the room.

Maisie said, 'Nash was ringing about a get-together. Evelyn and Rachel. Maybe Pru if she can be spared from that commune place. What do you think?'

He lifted his shoulders. 'Why not? You could invite them here for a lunch or something.' He wrinkled his nose. 'Must admit I can't see Prudence Adair here somehow.'

'I don't think she'll come. Not when she knows I might be there.' Of course they were going to stay in Pru's house so that was a ridiculous thing to say. And anyway, she was no longer afraid of Pru. It was all forgotten, all done with.

'Well, you'd have to be there if it was your lunch.' He grinned, then frowned. 'I thought you two got on like a house on fire.'

'It sort of drifted away. She was, well, superior to me. Obviously.'

He was angry on her behalf. 'What rubbish! Frumpy old maid like her, superior to you! What did she say to you – was there a row?'

'No, of course not. It was a feeling I had, that's all.' In her eagerness to turn the talk away from Pru, she blurted, 'Nash thought we might go walking in the Malverns. Like we used to.'

He became wary. 'You'd be out all day. You'd have to go early in the morning . . .' He noticed Maisie's sudden flush and said, 'Hang on. Are you planning to stay overnight in a hotel or something? Talk till midnight? All girls together? Run down your husbands – discuss your sex lives – oh no, my girl! That's not going to happen!'

She managed another laugh. 'Of course it's not! As if I would discuss any of my private affairs with people I haven't seen for fifteen years!'

'Fifteen years?'

'Well, of course I see Evelyn. Quite often, because she is lonely now that Edith has died. But—'

'I remember you went to see Natasha Nolan after she'd had her kid. I know she talked to you. Christ, how you can bear to see her again, I don't know!' He cast his eyes to the ceiling, then looked at her. 'But you saw Prudence Adair as well? And Rachel Strang?'

'They came to Thatch End to see baby Hilary. It was only natural—'

'So they all know about Tom? Christ – I was the laughing stock of Markhams, was I?'

She gave a cry of despair. 'Of course not! Oh, Ted – you know it wasn't like that!'

'You said yourself you wouldn't have come back to me if it hadn't have been for Natasha!'

'That's not true! That is just not true! I would never have left you, Ted! I've told you over and over again how bitterly I regret . . .' She put her hands to her face. 'Ted it was a mad fling. I'm sorry. I've tried to show you how sorry—'

He stood up and she thought he was going to come around the table and strike her. She stayed erect in her chair, her hands still over her face, refusing to cower.

He stood so close she could smell his familiar smell. She longed to put her arms around him and tell him that it was all right. But she knew from past experience that it would be the wrong thing to do.

At last, when she was at screaming point, he said heavily, 'It's no good talking, is it? It's always there and always will be.'

'Oh my God. Ted, I'm so sorry!'

'I'm going back to work. Just one thing. You will not be seeing your old colleagues. Not ever again. Is that clear?'

She took her hands from her face. He had moved to the door. His anger had solidified into a hardness she recognized. It had been better when his temper had flared and he had hit her. There were reconciliations then.

She nodded slowly. It didn't matter. It really didn't matter.

He said, 'Good.' And was gone.

After they had cleared lunch, Mrs Donald, silently sympathetic, said, 'Are you going to the cricket match this afternoon, Mrs Davenport?'

'Cricket match?' Maisie shook her head to clear it and then nodded. It was the last day of the summer term at St Martins where Simon and Ian went to school, and they always had a cricket match to wind up the school year. 'Of course. I'd almost forgotten.' She glanced at her watch. 'I'd better change.'

'Shall I drive you there?' Mrs Donald offered. Edward Davenport had never agreed to Maisie taking driving lessons.

'No. No thank you. I'd like to walk.'

Maisie went upstairs and changed into the frock she planned to wear for the boys. It was sky blue with large white daisies printed on a heavy linen. The boys were both going through the stage of ignoring her unless it was absolutely necessary to acknowledge her, but she knew they liked the daisy dress.

She walked slowly down the short avenue of elms that led straight onto the Birmingham road. Ted liked the accessibility of the big house on the A38 yet it meant that they rarely had casual callers. Schoolboy friends could not drop in for a game of football on the immaculate lawn. When Maisie went to Edinburgh to stay with Jess she loved the way her daughter's room was always filled with people. Ted preferred to put up at a hotel and take Mark and Jess out for meals. 'Their places are like railway waiting rooms,' he complained. Maisie laughed. 'Not a bit, Ted! Nobody speaks in railway waiting rooms!' And he had laughed with her and agreed. 'Babel, then,' he amended. 'Thank God for one-four-eight.' That was the number of their house; it had no name.

Maisie touched the gateposts as she went through; they were metal so it was not a conventionally superstitious act but a personal thing; if she touched certain objects she would return to them. She remembered touching the filing cabinet at Markhams, warding off possible dismissal. She had wanted to stay there for the rest of her life like Edith and Evelyn. In the end she had resigned in order to marry Ted and have Mark, but that was even more wonderful than Markhams.

And it still was, of course. She had gone hopelessly wrong with her lunchtime negotiations – as usual. She smiled wryly to herself. She was disappointed about Malvern; but she had half-expected it anyway. What made her cross – with herself – was that she had also scuttled the opportunity of having the girls for a meal at one-four-eight. Somehow she had put them all in the light of interfering Nosey-Parkers, and nothing could be farther from the truth.

She passed Dr James's house and recalled his kindness about the sterilization. She had told him again and again she didn't mind, five children were quite sufficient, but he must have known what it would do to Ted. She sighed and shook her head and leaned over to touch his lemon verbena and send a heady scent around the dusty laurel hedge. She moved on, smiling in spite of everything. After all, she had the children and Ted, and she had managed without the girls for fifteen years. And it had been a shock to see Pru at Edith's funeral. Yes . . . she had almost forgotten the difficulty with Pru. Maybe it was all for the best.

Inside the school gates she saw two or three women whose boys had gone to primary school with Simon and Ian. They walked across the asphalt to the playing fields, talking about special coaching for university entrance exams. They could well afford it. 'I look on money spent on educating Adrian as money in the bank,' one of them said didactically. Maisie nodded. It was early days for Simon and Ian, but Tom was another thing. He was fifteen and unhappy; he was not going to do well in exams. He missed his brothers badly. If only he could come home and go to St Martins with them, it might help. Now *that* was something worth fighting for. She might bring it up this evening. After one of his spats, Ted was invariably contrite – not that he would ever admit it. But in the old days he would massage her neck for her and they would make love. These days he might bring her flowers and chocolates. She promised herself that if he did that this evening she would talk about Tom.

Simon ran over to her after his innings.

'Mum, don't wait. Ian and me have volunteered to do some clearing up. We won't be home till about six. OK?'

'OK.' She smiled. She would have an hour alone with Ted before supper. She began to work out cogent arguments for Tom starting the autumn term at St Martins.

She was almost back home when one of the cars coming towards her began to flash its lights. She stopped, frowning. It wasn't Ted, in any case Ted used his horn rather than his lights. It wasn't Mrs Donald.

And then the indicator went on and the car drew into the middle of the road – daringly rather than dangerously – and Maisie could see a cloud of dark hair and the kind of sun top that could be worn by only one person she knew. Her pleasure swamped all the other feelings of the day. She had expected another phone call or a letter. Nash had phoned this morning and was here now!

'Nash!'

'Darling!' Nash parked against the flow of traffic and received a blast from someone's horn. 'Hop in and remind me where you live – I must have passed it – I remember a forbidding rank of elms—' She pulled Maisie into the car, hugging her at the same time. She smelled of lavender. She had always worn flower perfumes. Maisie had thought she was wonderful. Still did.

'You'll have to turn somewhere.' She was giggling like a

schoolgirl. Nash always made her giggle. 'There's a roundabout just up here.'

'I know. I've been around it twice . . .' Nash was looking in her mirror and spoke to the reflection there. 'Are you going to wait for me . . . no? Then you're an utter bastard!' Maisie's giggles accelerated with the engine note. 'But you are going to wait?' Natasha continued. 'You darling man!' She blew a kiss out of the window and rejoined her line of traffic. They swept around the roundabout and back to one-four-eight. 'Oh yes, of course. I saw the elms without leaves and now they're all glorious . . .' They swept around the front of the house. 'It's still a grim old pile though, Maisie. Why don't you get Ted to move out to the Lickeys somewhere? Barnt Green?'

'Oh, I'd love it. I could join the WI and things.' Maisie felt young and helpless again. She turned and studied Natasha. 'Oh my God. You're even more beautiful. Look at you – wanton and wonderful!'

'Maisie!' Natasha giggled now. 'What a thing to say! How did you know about my plumber?'

'What?'

'Nothing. Now. Before we go in, feed me my lines. Have you mentioned the Malvern week to Edward?'

'Yes.' Suddenly Maisie could not tell Natasha that Ted had given it the thumbs-down. Thank goodness he was still at the factory otherwise Nash might well be sent packing. She said, 'He's thinking about it.'

'*Thinking* about it? As if you're a good little girl or something!'

Maisie said defensively, 'It's not like that. The boys will be home for the long holiday. If Jess comes, so well and good. She would cope. But if not . . .'

'So it's up to you really, is it?'

'I suppose so.'

Natasha stared at her for a long moment. Then she said, 'Tom will be home, I suppose.'

'Yes.'

Natasha bit her lip. Maisie could see this was a habit; a little bubble of blood appeared. 'So. That makes it hard for you, darling.' Natasha shrugged. 'Maybe just a couple of days then?' She looked into Maisie's china-blue eyes and added quickly, 'Just a day would be better than nothing. Pru particularly wants to see you.'

Maisie felt a little nerve jump in her stomach lining. She said, 'I'll have to see. Listen, why are we sitting here? Come on in and Mrs Donald will make us some tea and you can show me some snaps of Hilary.'

Natasha said wryly, 'And you can show me fifty of Mark and Jess and Tom and Ian and Simon.'

Maisie was delighted. 'You've remembered all their names!'

'Yes.' Natasha raised her brows, perhaps surprised by herself. 'Yes, I have, haven't I? This whole reunion thing must be more important to me than I realized.'

'And to me,' Maisie said earnestly, leading the way into the cool of the house. 'Since Edith died I've thought so much about our time together at Markhams.' She went into the sitting room and they both made themselves comfortable on the sofa. 'D'you know, Mr Delano and Mr Edgar have hardly changed. Ted took me in to choose an anniversary present and they had us up in the office for sherry and biscuits – the girl who brought them in was very smart and efficient.'

Natasha laughed. 'They were both born elderly, weren't they?' She opened her bag, took out a cigarette case and began the business of lighting up. 'I wonder if they're queer?'

'*Queer*?' Maisie was horrified. 'What a dreadful thing to say, Nash! Especially as Mr Edgar is in love with Mrs Adair!'

'Nothing ever comes of it though, does it?' Nash snorted smoke through her nose like a beautiful dragon. 'Could be a jolly good cover-up.'

They dallied with that idea, then the idea that Evelyn might marry Mr Delano, then how Rachel had so amazingly married her Liberal Member of Parliament.

'I mean, he was married already,' Maisie said. 'And I thought she wanted to be the power behind the throne, not alongside it!'

'She probably found out that her father was sleeping with his secretary,' Nash said casually. She leaned forward. 'Oh, Maisie, try to come to Malvern. It would be great. We can gossip into the small hours and walk all day and eat like pigs – oh do come. It won't be at all the same without you.'

'Of course it will,' Maisie demurred.

'It won't. Honestly. You were always the one who bound us together. You were the kid sister none of us had. We knew life had been hard for you and we sort of bonded together to make it better.'

'Did you?' Maisie flushed with pleasure. 'Well, it worked. I was so happy at Markhams. Nobody ever grumbed at me when I couldn't find a file or spilt the tea or something. Oh it was wonderful.' She laughed. 'I modelled myself on you, Nash.'

'The funny thing was, you were slightly older than we three. Yet you still look so young – like a kid.'

'It's my hair. It won't sit down.' Maisie felt embarrassed. She hated being the subject of conversation. 'Listen, I'll go and round up some tea. Put your legs up.'

'Say you'll come!' Natasha held out dramatic pleading arms as Maisie stood up. 'Please Maisie dear. Please—'

'Oh . . . stop it!'

But Maisie wished she could go. How wonderful it would be to be . . . well, herself again. She sighed and went into the kitchen. There was no sign of Mrs Donald, she must be having a lie-down. Maisie laid a tray and made a pot of tea and then, unexpectedly, heard a groan.

She froze and listened so hard her ears began to hum. It came again and it was from Mrs Donald's room. With her heart in her mouth she moved swiftly and silently down the passage. Were there intruders? Was Mrs Donald tied up in there, unable to move, unable to do more than groan?

The door was tightly shut and Maisie was wary of opening it on to, perhaps, a burglar. She went back to the kitchen for a chair; placed it gently in front of the door and stood on it to look through the transom.

After perhaps ten seconds, she got quietly off the chair and took it back to the kitchen. Then she carried the tray back into the sitting room and put it on the low table by the window.

'I've been thinking,' she said carefully as she poured the

tea. 'I'll telephone Jess – make a point of asking her to help me out. She won't mind. And I'll come to Malvern for the full week.'

Natasha sat up on the sofa and stared, astonished. 'My God! I never thought you would! Oh terrific – well done, our Maisie! Well done!'

Maisie passed her a cup of tea and sat down by the table. She wondered whether to ask Nash if she could come and stay at Thatch End until then, but decided against it. There was too much to do, too much to think about. And Tom would be home tomorrow.

She said, 'I think it will do us all good. Like you said. And the Malverns will be cooler.'

'Yes.' Nash stared over the rim of her teacup. 'Has something happened, darling? No, don't answer that. Just come to Malvern and we'll tell each other. Everything. What do you say?'

'I say – marvellous.' And Maisie smiled.

Three

Prudence had taken Natasha's call in the conservatory of Telegraph House. She did not immediately ring Rachel; she was on gardening shift this morning and had been in the middle of picking raspberries for this evening's meal. She stood for a moment staring through the patterned glass at the enormous view, absorbing it without really seeing it, letting it soothe her as it always did. Her grey eyes, narrowed against the sun, seemed gradually to pick up the colour of the sea and sky; they glinted as if she were suddenly excited, and she closed them momentarily, trying to regain her usual calm. She had not removed her straw sunhat and her long fair hair straggled beneath it, mingling with the frayed weave, indistinguishable from it. She wore jeans and a man's shirt; the svelte figure turned out by her Swiss secretarial school had long gone.

The thought that she might be seeing Maisie again filled her with piercing joy in the front of her mind, grey foreboding at the back. Pru always thought of her head being in two sections; the front was the part which revelled in the sea and the sun and picking raspberries and being part of this small community. The back was different. The back dealt – or rather, did not deal – with things that were unbearable. And Maisie's fear of her was completely unbearable.

She rubbed the palms of her long hands against the sides of her jeans and turned purposefully for the door. Meg Simmonds, on indoor duties because it was 'that time of the month', paused in watering the plants.

'Are you leaving us, Pru?'

Meg was often ill and got no help from the medical profession, who saw the community as a problem. She was always told to 'get out and lead a normal life'.

Pru shook her head. 'Not for long. It's this house of mine, Meg. As you know it's up for sale and I need to go and see it – sort things out. I might meet some old friends there. They could help. Perhaps.'

'Worcestershire, isn't it? Will you drive?'

'I haven't thought. Probably.'

'I could come with you. Help you with the driving. It's a long way.'

Pru had no difficulty in saying frankly, 'My dear, thank you. But these friends are from a long time ago. Before this.' She waved her elegant hand around the conservatory.

Meg nodded and said, 'Of course.' They all had their old lives to contend with now and again. Sometimes it helped to have support from the others, sometimes it did not. Pru's mother always acted as if everyone at Telegraph House were unclean in some way. Support from any of them would have been seen by her as aggressive.

Pru smiled, 'They're not like my mother. At least, I don't think so.'

Meg smiled too. 'You read my mind!'

Pru opened the door and held aside one of the heavy grape-laden vines. 'Probably. It's one of the joys of belonging here.'

She walked slowly back to the fruit enclosure, thinking about the community and all its blessings. It was a haven for Pru, a haven from life with Mr Delano or Mother; certainly from Maisie. But havens were temporary. Outside the community, outside this house perched on the cliffs above the entry to the first underwater cable to America, was another life. It was dangerous, its highs nearly always followed by lows. But it was exciting and real. Pru shivered slightly in the blazing sun and pulled her straw hat over her ears as if she were cold.

She began to pick again, never squashing the fragile fruit, and she thought of Markhams and the six of them who had become friends as well as colleagues. Would they be able to pick up that friendship after so long? She had not seen Nash or Rachel for fifteen years and Maisie had been very wary of her at Edith's funeral. Pru had looked covertly but carefully at her as she bowed her head during the service; there had been no bruising that she could see. But then, Maisie was draped in scarves ears up to her ears. Neither of them had been able to have more than a few words with Evelyn, who was completely grief-stricken. Maisie had said in a low voice, 'Don't worry, I'll keep in close touch with her.'

They knew so little of each other any more. Three spinsters and three married women. Two with children. And now, Edith dead. And Nash divorced. And Maisie still in thrall to one of the three men who had been kind to her. And the only one who had stuck by her.

She flinched slightly as a small thorn from the raspberry cane went into her thumb. She straightened and sucked it out vigorously, wanting it to hurt. And the back of her mind came to the front unawares and she remembered fifteen years ago, going to see Natasha's baby and talking properly to Maisie . . . probably for the last time.

She remembered saying, 'Leave him! For God's sake, leave him – stand on your own feet for once in your life! Men aren't the answer to everything – your bloody brother or your awful husband or this . . . Tom McEvoy . . . whatever his bloody name is!'

That was when Maisie began to look frightened, because Pru never swore. 'You don't understand, Pru—'

'Of course I understand! I had access to the personal files, remember! I'm the only one who understands!'

Maisie blanched and Pru had been forced to reassure her. 'Don't worry, I tore up that bit. Not even the Markham brothers knew. Don't look like that – please, Maisie!' She tried to put a long arm around Maisie's shoulders but Maisie dodged as if from a blow. Suddenly Pru knew that she had done that before.

Pru said quietly, 'Does he hit you? Does Edward Davenport hit you, Maisie?'

Maisie ignored that. 'He knows. Ted knows. Ted understands and forgives me. He's loyal and true. He'll never leave me. I shall tell him about Tom McEvoy and the baby and he'll, he'll . . .' she began to cry.

Pru waited, breathing deeply. When the storm had passed she repeated emphatically, 'Either you must leave him. Or you must never tell him about this hippy medical student. Do you understand me, Maisie – are you listening?'

'Of course I'm listening. It's you who is not listening! Ted and I – we're honest with each other. Yes, he'll be angry – I deserve that, don't I? But he'll always be loyal – he won't leave me—'

'And therefore you cannot leave him,' Pru said drily.

Maisie hiccoughed on her tears. 'You make it sound like a punishment.'

'It is. That is exactly what it is. You don't love this man – you didn't love this Tom McEvoy nor Roly.'

'I've got two children by Ted! They're beautiful and clever – how can I leave them?'

'You'd bring them. To this house I've got in Cornwall. It's wonderful, Maisie. A few like-minded people are already there and others will follow. We shall be self-supporting – grow our own food, maybe make our own clothes. Weaving . . . I'm going to be a potter. I've always wanted to be a potter!' She saw the change in Maisie's face and asked gently, 'What have you wanted to be, Maisie?'

'A mother,' Maisie said simply.

'Well then. Bring your children and come with me. The new baby will be born in the house, she – he – will belong to all of us and yet will be solely yours.'

Maisie said slowly, 'Ted would not allow it.'

'Let me talk to him. Go and pack. Now. When he comes in I will tell him.'

'No.' To Pru's amazement, Maisie was suddenly very calm and assured. 'No. It's not what I want, Pru. Nash showed me what I want. I want the same as she wants. The very best for the children. Security and comfort. Nice holidays.' She shrugged slightly. 'I know it sounds money-grabbing but when you've had nothing—'

'Don't compare yourself with Nash. She's had everything she ever wanted.'

'You're jealous,' Maisie said wonderingly. 'My God. You are – you're jealous. Were you in love with Harvey Nolan?'

Pru let out a mighty laugh at that. 'No,' she said emphatically. 'But perhaps I am jealous. You've always admired Nash, haven't you? And Nash dissuaded you from going off with your hippie. But you won't let me persuade you to come away and live in Cornwall. Maybe I am jealous.'

Maisie laughed uncomfortably. 'Don't be silly, Pru.'

Pru shrugged and said lightly, 'Yes, it is silly. I love you and you love Nash.'

And Maisie said, suddenly relieved, 'Oh . . . here's Ted now! Don't worry about me, Pru. You wouldn't understand. We're very much in love.'

Whether she had meant to wound, Pru would never know. But it wounded.

Rachel's voice on the other end of the phone was crisp yet defensive. Pru assumed that she was protecting her husband from unwanted callers. Duncan Stayte was a Liberal Member for somewhere in the East Midlands. Pru frowned, trying to remember. It had been in Rutland but since Rutland disappeared it was . . . Leicestershire perhaps?

'It's Pru. Pru Adair. Markhams. D'you remember?' She felt strange about this call. It was not being made from the conservatory but from the small lobby outside the dining room. People could hear if they wished to. They had all left their 'old lives' behind them, and when they cropped up, as they did from time to time, it was always an intrusion.

Rachel's voice changed and squeaked with pleasure. 'Pru – how could I forget! I modelled myself on you, remember! How are you?'

'Very well. What about you?'

'Worn to the bone. But loving every minute.'

Pru smiled at someone as they passed by with an enormous dish of raspberries. 'Isn't that wonderful? You have got exactly what you always wanted. And more.'

'Yes.' Rachel tinkled a laugh down the wires. 'The power behind the throne and in front of it!'

Pru did not know how to respond to that. She cleared her throat and began to tell Rachel about the house in Malvern.

'It was bequeathed to me by one of Mummy's boyfriends.

I think they worked it out together. Hoping I would come back to the Midlands and live there.'

'And won't you?'

'This is my life now, Rachel. I've got a pottery in the cellar. My pots are one of our income sources. We're almost entirely self-supporting, you know.'

'How . . . marvellous.'

'Yes, it is. It really is.'

Rachel made an effort to understand. 'A sort of retreat? A refuge even?'

'Yes, in a way.'

'But . . . it doesn't sound very exciting.'

'Excitement is where you find it, don't you agree? To stand and watch the sun drown in the sea is more than just exciting. It becomes a spiritual experience.'

'And there is no . . . well, quarrelling? Surely people get on each other's nerves . . . even the six of us did sometimes. At Markhams.'

'We talk each evening. Anything that has happened to hurt or offend us in any way is discussed. And healed.' It sounded a bit pi. Prudence laughed. 'All that business about experiencing pain to know what pleasure truly is . . . that's rubbish. I've proved it.' She squeezed against the wall as a trolley of used dinner plates went by. 'You should come down sometime, Rachel.'

'Oh no.' Rachel was quick off the mark. 'No, it's not for me. You were always one on your own, Pru. You had a sort of calm solitariness even when the shop was heaving with customers and Mr Delano having kittens.'

That had been the Swiss school. They had taught Pru how to control herself physically; to hold her awkward limbs still, to keep her thoughts to herself. She remembered the Swedish gym instructor. 'You are in your own space bubble. No-one must intrude. Within that space you are safe. Do you understand?' She had understood very well. When you knew you were different from everyone else, you needed your space bubble more than ever.

She said, 'Yes. You needed to keep calm at Markhams. Mr Delano could become almost . . . hysterical . . . at times.' And she smiled because although that was another thing right at the back of her mind, when it did crop up it never hurt. In fact as the years went by it became funnier and funnier. Mr Delano had not been tall like Mr Edgar, which meant his balding head barely reached Pru's ear. She had merely had to hold out her long arms and brace the palms of her hands against his shoulders. She could see him now, flailing helplessly to get near her. 'Just let me hold you, Miss Adair, I adore you – I'm offering you marriage and—' Poor Mr Delano. He should have known her Swedish gym instructor.

Rachel said, 'I did wonder at one time if you and he might make a match of it.'

'Rachel!' But Pru was laughing. 'He was twenty-five years older than me and five feet six and he had about three hairs on his head!'

'Yes. And if your mother had agreed to marry Mr Edgar, it could have been awkward!' They were both laughing helplessly. Pru had forgotten that Rachel had made her laugh. It would be good to see her.

She said, 'Listen. Nash rang. Between us we're cooking up a reunion. A Markhams reunion. This house of mine is in the Malverns where we used to go. Remember?'

'Oh yes!' Rachel sounded unexpectedly nostalgic.

'Last week in August? I shall be going down beforehand to get it ready and Nash will want the full week. You could come when you were able.'

'Ah. I'm not sure. I'll have to look in the diary. Can you hang on?'

'Not really. Other people might want the phone. Listen. Come if you can. How's that?'

'Yes. OK.' Rachel paused then added, 'I will make a real effort, Pru. I'd love it. It's just that . . .'

'I know. Other commitments.'

'Is Maisie coming?'

'Don't know. Nash is dealing with Maisie and Evelyn.

'What about Edith?'

'She died. Two years ago.'

'Oh my God! I didn't know! Oh, Pru.'

'Yes. It makes it more important somehow, doesn't it?'

Another pause. 'Yes. It does.' Rachel drew a trembling breath. 'Give me some directions. I've got a pen and pad right here.'

Pru told her where the house was then she rang off. Meg was hovering nearby and they changed places. Meg murmured something as she dialled a number and as Pru went back into the dining room she heard her anxious voice say, 'Mummy? Oh I'm so glad it's you . . .'

She finished her meal and helped with the washing-up, then drifted into the sitting room where the others were already discussing what had happened during the day. Four of them had taken goods and produce into Truro to various outlets who bought their stuff. Two others had dealt with a blockage to the cesspit and had arranged for the sewage lorry to empty it the following week. The cooks needed supplies of flour and were still pushing for a cake stall once a week.

'We don't want people coming here,' Pru objected as she always did.

'They wouldn't come anyway.' It was Meg, appearing from the lobby, her small face set in lines of pain. 'The villagers are scared stiff of us. The only people who would come are tourists visiting a different kind of zoo.'

Everyone looked at her because the outburst was so uncharacteristic. She remained standing, holding onto the back of one of the armchairs, her knuckles white.

Pru said, 'What has happened?'

Meg said, 'I've just telephoned my mother. My father has agreed to have me back home.' Her lower lip trembled. 'I'm leaving Telegraph House.'

There was an outcry. People had left before, but usually after a short trial period. Meg was one of the originals. She bowed her head over the chair back and began to cry. Pru, still standing, went to her and held her close.

The babble died down. Someone stood up and indicated her chair. Pru led the weeping girl to it and crouched by her.

'Talk to us, Meg.' Pru's calm and gentle voice was infinitely reassuring. 'We're sad that you have come to this decision – help us to understand.'

Meg controlled herself with difficulty. 'Sorry. Sorry, everyone. I was only eighteen when I came here. Now I'm thirty-two. I can't imagine being anywhere else.' She forced a watery smile as she looked round at them. 'This is my home.'

Several voices asked her why she was leaving in that case. Pru said, 'If it's something at home you don't want to talk about, then all right. You know you can come back when it's sorted out.'

Meg was suddenly very calm. She said, 'I'm going to tell you, then I'm going to bed. Tomorrow I'll ask one of you to take me to Penzance for the train home. I don't want to talk about it. I'm sorry but that's how it is.' She took a breath. 'I've been to see a specialist. I've got cancer of the uterus. I thought I wanted to die here. And then I found I didn't.' She smiled. 'That's it.' She turned to Pru. 'You were the one who bought the house and got us started. When my father turned me out, this place was . . . everything. Thank you, Pru.'

She got up amid an awful silence, and left the room. Someone half-stood and Pru held out her hand. 'Don't. In the morning she might talk again. Let her rest.'

They all looked at each other. Margaret James, who had dealt with the problems at the cesspit, said, 'Everything else seems pretty pointless. Anyway, we'd finished talking, hadn't we?'

'I think so.' Pru looked around. 'Does anyone want to say anything?'

'Only that this is bloody awful,' said Marion Jeffort, the cook.

They all nodded. Nobody made a move. The ringing of the phone made them all jump. Pru hurried into the hall to answer it; it could be Meg's mother.

It was Natasha.

'Darling, is that you? You'll never guess. She's coming! I didn't think she would. I went round this afternoon and spent hours there! Only just got back home!'

In spite of what had just happened, Pru could not help a small jump of pleasure. Maisie. Maisie was coming to meet her. Perhaps she was no longer afraid.

She said, 'I'm glad. But, Nash, I can't stop now—'

'I must just tell you how amazing it was. She'd been to a cricket match at the school and was walking home and I picked her up. Same old Maisie – thrilled to death to see me, but immediately I mentioned the reunion she was as wary as a cat. We got indoors – absolutely gorgeous but horrible. You know what I mean. But that doesn't matter because Maisie loves it. Still cautious, still fending me off . . . I was absolutely certain she wouldn't come. And then she went to get us some tea and lo and behold, complete change. She must have talked to that Mrs Donald – the cook-housekeeper woman. They're quite close. She said she'd come. And then – even when the awful Ted arrived home and obviously saw me as Jezebel in person, she took not a scrap of notice. It was amazing.'

Pru frowned in the direction of the stairs, wondering whether Meg could hear her. 'It does sound unlike Maisie. I only hope that when you left he didn't take it out on her.'

'You mean . . .?'

'That's what I mean,' Pru said grimly.

'I don't think so. The boys came back and we all had supper together. And she telephoned her daughter, Jess, and then young Tom . . . she sort of . . . almost ignored Ted. It was . . . well, amazing!' She paused. 'They don't sleep together now. She took me up to her room to see some photographs of Tom. It was just her room. And there was a lock on the door.'

'Really?' Pru glanced at the stairs again then turned her back. 'Are you going to pick her up? She doesn't drive.'

'She's going on the train. Like we used to. She liked the idea of that. I said I'd go with her but she said, no, just her and Evelyn. She's going to see Evelyn. She's kept in touch since Edith died.'

'I gave you directions to the house, didn't I?'

'Yes. And I passed them on to Maisie. She said she'd take a taxi from Malvern Link.'

'Rachel's coming too. So that's about it.'

'Yes.' Natasha laughed. 'I haven't felt so excited since . . . well, since my last row with Harvey, I guess!'

'Oh, Nash.'

'Oh . . . shoot!' said Nash.

Pru replaced her receiver and glanced back. Meg was standing at the top of the stairs. Pru walked slowly up to meet her. Meg put her head on Pru's shoulder. They walked down the landing together.

Four

Rachel put down the phone and stared across the expanse of parquet floor to the coloured glass of the front door. Duncan's office was to the right of the door so that official visitors did not have to tramp over Rachel's Chinese scatter rugs. It wasn't a big house because their real home was Charnwood Court in Leicestershire, but it was home to Rachel; for ten years she had worked here as Duncan's secretary. Besides, although Duncan had private funds, since decimalization money values had gone mad and this house was fairly economical to run.

It was in an interesting area and handy for Pimlico tube station. If she went upstairs to the sitting room above Duncan's office she could just see the cylindrical humps of Battersea Power Station on the other side of the river. And the Embankment was five minutes walk away. Yes, it was a pleasing house and a pleasing area. So very much nicer than Charnwood where she felt lonely and out of place.

Miss Chambers came out of the small converted breakfast room holding an enormous bunch of letters for Duncan to sign. She had been chosen by Rachel, so she wasn't pretty; she had a noticeable moustache and her hair, though thick, was iron grey and would never 'go right'. She complained often about it, picking at the bits that stuck out and making it all much worse. Rachel knew that if she went to a decent hairdresser she could be tinted and cut into the latest shape. But she never told Miss Chambers that.

She hurried across the parquet now, holding out her arms. 'I'll take those in. Mr Stayte has a visitor.' As Miss Chambers had welcomed the visitor and taken in a tea tray soon afterwards, this information was redundant and practically insulting. Rachel had found it very hard to cease being Duncan's secretary and become his wife. She wanted it both ways: the power behind the throne and in front of it. Luckily Miss Chambers was not interested in power and relinquished the letters with a grateful smile.

'You might as well get off,' Rachel said as a reward. 'I'll do the post if you could leave out the envelopes.'

Miss Chambers looked suitably grateful and disappeared into her office. Rachel tapped lightly on Duncan's door and went in immediately. The visitor, a PPS who occasionally gave Duncan snippets of information which were supposed to be important, was leaning on the big table in the window looking at some c.v's. Duncan was at his shoulder. They were both sniggering and jumped guiltily at her entrance.

'Sorry, darling.' She smiled at them both. 'Hello, Douglas.' Privately she called the PPS 'Judas' . 'I've sent Miss Chambers off early. Here are the letters for signature.' She put them on the desk and approached the table. There were, of course, photographs with the c.vs. The one on top of the pile was of a woman aged about forty, with the severe hairstyle and dark suit of someone wanting to be taken seriously. Her face belied the style. Her eyes had gleamed with an inner amusement as she stared at the camera.

'Candidates for the vacancy at Stour?' Rachel asked. Stour was a neighbouring constituency; if the woman in the photograph got the seat she and Duncan would be seeing a great deal of each other. Rachel moved the photograph to look at the one beneath. This one showed a middle-aged man. She smiled fleetingly up at Duncan. 'The floaters are more likely to go for him. Solidity. Reliability. Old-fashioned values.'

For an instant a flash of annoyance lit Duncan's dark eyes. Then he smiled back at her and said smoothly, 'Thank you, darling.' He went to the desk. 'As Miss Chambers has already left, there's no hurry to sign these. Will you leave them with me for an hour while Douglas and I finish our discussion?'

She should have accepted her dismissal and left with silent dignity. That way it would put Duncan in the wrong and he would apologize to her over supper and they would go off to the theatre as if nothing had happened. But she could not leave it there.

'All right. But don't forget the post goes in an hour. I'll need them before then if I'm to get them ready.'

She picked up the tea tray so that Duncan had to open the door for her. She gave him another of her fleeting smiles as she passed him, but he did not respond. When she had been his secretary he had called that intimate look 'the will o' the wisp smile' which Rachel, always conscious of her sturdy build, had enjoyed very much.

She carried the tray into the kitchen. By the time she had washed up the bone-china cups and saucers, she had escalated the small exchange into a deadly insult and was fuming. She dried the china carefully and replaced it on the shining shelf of the dresser. She began to mutter.

'I give my whole life to that man! He couldn't – wouldn't – have got his blasted seat in the House if it hadn't been for me! Does he remember how I flogged around Soar Tops – all those villages and hamlets, always raining – telling people how caring and marvellous he was? And nothing's changed since we got married! I still canvass, work on his speeches with him, practically write them!' She went back into the hall and into Miss Chambers's office. The envelopes were stacked in a neat pile awaiting the signed letters. She put them to one side and began to go through Miss Chambers's drawers methodically as she had done so often before. She knew there would be no evidence of anything clandestine, but by now it had become an obsession. When she had finished, she sat in the swivel chair and turned it slowly back and forth, unconsciously soothing herself. If Duncan allowed Judas to persuade him into opting for that female candidate with the come-to-bed eyes, she knew her own life would become miserable. He had swapped wives once; he could so easily do it again. She never forgot that.

Rachel felt the swivel chair jar beneath her and knew she had disconnected the thread again. She got up quickly and turned the chair upside down. Last week when it had happened, Duncan had completely unscrewed the stand from the seat and then carefully screwed it on again. But this time it was properly wedged. She muttered a curse and gripped the seat between her knees while she put pressure on the screw. She could always complain to Duncan that the chair was worn out and she had merely sat on it to assemble the envelopes . . . but he might comment on the fact that it did not seem to happen when Miss Chambers sat upon it. And Rachel needed no unspoken criticism of her escalating weight.

She jerked the chair legs and the burred thread released the wing nut at last. She righted the chair and sat on it gingerly just as Duncan brought in the letters. She could sense his annoyance as the door opened and was deeply thankful that the chair was apparently all right.

'Look here, Ray,' at least he wasn't using her full name; that always boded badly. 'I wish you wouldn't so obviously interfere when Douglas is around. OK, he's a good friend to us, but if he can blab to me about what happens in Government circles, then he can just as easily blab to someone else about what happens in our Party.'

'Darling. Sorry.' She could feel the chair teeter and held her breath for an instant. 'It was intended as a comment. That was all. I'm more likely to be objective perhaps . . . nearer to the ordinary voter. And quite honestly, darling, the man's photograph said things like stability, trustworthiness . . .'

'But he looked blimpish, Ray. Can't you see that the voting public now want something else from their representatives? They want intelligence – Sally Worthington has got a doctorate in political science, for God's sake.'

'I wonder how she got that!' Rachel could not resist saying it although she knew as she closed her mouth that it left her wide open. Duncan did not hesitate.

'You can't get university honours by sleeping with anyone, Ray!' he snapped. And they both knew exactly what he meant. Rachel felt her defence mechanism spring into action.

'It takes two, remember.'

Duncan put the letters down and stood watching her as she checked addresses and began to insert them into envelopes. Whether he noticed that there was a slight tremor in her fingers she did not know, but he said wearily, 'Don't let's argue again, Ray, please. We've been married almost five years. We should be able to relax now . . . even take each other for granted. Just a little.'

It was the very thing she could not do. He would never

understand that of course because, given half a chance, he would take her absolutely for granted. And he shouldn't. She stuck down the final envelope with a bang of her fist. He really shouldn't. She ran the house, still did most of his secretarial work, was constantly by his side when it came to diplomatic occasions, press conferences, the lot. She had managed to steer his divorce and their marriage into the realms of romance instead of anything clandestine; she pretended to get on famously with Joy, his first wife, and the girls, Rebecca and Janice. 'We simply did not know what had hit us,' she said helplessly if the subject had come up. It never did now. And Joy had remarried, thank God, and the girls were abroad somewhere . . . but she never took anything for granted. And neither should he. How he would cope now without her she simply did not know.

She tried one of her fleeting smiles. 'Sorry, darling. I can't – never will be able to – take our love for granted. It's . . . it sounds corny . . . it's such a precious gift.'

He would have scooped her up and kissed her then, only the chair chose that fatal moment to collapse. She sprawled on the sage-green carpet and when he started to laugh she wanted to burst into tears.

He hauled her to her feet but did not kiss her.

'Oh, Ray . . . you really will have to lose some of this puppy fat.' He patted her buttocks fondly but it was no consolation. She gasped, 'The chair is faulty—'

And he said, 'Never mind. We'll order another one. You can do it. Choose one that will take you as well as Miss Chambers!'

She leaned on the desk with one hand and gathered the letters with the other. He was already at the door.

'I'll have my bath while you're at the post, Ray. We should eat early if we're going to the theatre. Are you organized?'

'Yes.'

When had she not been organized?

'What are you wearing?'

'The blue off-the-shoulder.' Blue was Rachel's colour.

'Haven't you got a bolero thing? It will go colder this evening.'

'It's got a matching stole.'

'Good.'

She left the house still near tears, convinced he was getting at her because of her plump shoulders and arms. She would wear the black dress; the one with the deeply scooped neckline and three-quarter sleeves. It was longer too. Her legs were still sturdy.

Somehow the evening did nothing to allay their abrasiveness. Rachel felt unusually sensitive about taking her bath while Duncan was around. She finished in the kitchen and put the new potatoes in an insulated dish and the salmon and salad on the sideboard while Duncan, distinguished in a dinner suit, had a drink and glanced through some catalogues. When she came down in her black dress he made no comment except to pass over the catalogues. They were of office accessories. She laid them aside but did say while they were eating, 'I think a typing chair with a deep back would be best, Duncan. Miss Chambers needs some support – she is becoming quite stooped.'

He raised his brows. 'My God, she's still in her thirties! I shall be getting a bad name for the way I treat my secretaries! Married two of them and aged the third!'

She hated it when he talked like that, absolutely hated it. And it was a shock to hear him say that Miss Chambers was still in her thirties. Rachel knew that, of course, but she had never told Duncan, and Miss Chambers looked so much older than Rachel herself.

She ignored the first jibe and said, 'How do you know Miss Chambers's age?'

He looked astonished. 'Well, her c.v. of course.'

'Oh. Yes.' She laid down her fork and drank some wine. 'Honestly, Duncan, I do wish you wouldn't talk like that about Joy and myself. It's not . . .'

'Nice?' he supplied, smiling. 'Oh come off it, Ray! We both know it's the sort of thing people say. If we say it ourselves and laugh at it, it can't hurt, can it?'

She agreed, though without conviction. It still hurt her.

It hurt more when they arrived at the Aldwych to find they were meeting Douglas Maccrington and his latest girlfriend. Her name was Isadora something and Rachel immediately thought of her as Iscariot. Judas and Iscariot. It helped to get her through the smiles and handshakes and the immediate pairing of Douglas with Duncan, Isadora with Rachel. They sat through a revival of *My Fair Lady* with an interval for gin and tonics. Duncan was his usual smiling self and when they all shared a taxi afterwards he said, 'I do like something I know. It frees me to enjoy it properly.' Somehow that was like a stab in the back too. She had hated the whole evening, the sheer boredom of seeing something she had seen half-a-dozen times before with two people with whom she had nothing in common . . . and Duncan had thoroughly enjoyed it.

They alighted outside the house; there were still streaks of red in the sky and the river was busy with traffic. They leaned back into the cab to say goodnight and Isadora whispered, 'Let's meet up again. Let's play tennis or something.'

Rachel said, 'Lovely,' and withdrew sharply as if Isadora might drag her back into the cab by force. And then, before Duncan could put his key into the front door, while the cab was only just pulling away from the kerb, the door was flung open and silhouetted in the light was Joy, her red hair all over her shoulders, her sobs surely audible for miles.

'Oh, Dunc! I'm so sorry! But you did say if ever I needed you – Oh, Dunc, what shall I do? I've left him! I've left Lucas! I couldn't stand his philandering any longer! I've got nowhere to go—' Somehow she was in Duncan's arms and Rachel was standing behind him on the bottom step quite unable to get past into her own house. And Judas's head was outside the window of the cab, his ears practically flapping.

'Rachel, how can I apologize . . . I'm so terribly sorry. I simply went to pieces – well, you saw.'

It was an hour later. Rachel thought longingly of her bed with its crisp linen spread and the pillows plumped feather-light next to the open window where any breeze from the river would cool her overheated body. She longed to get out of the black dress which seemed to have shrunk during the evening, and into her lace and satin nightie with its matching negligee. She looked – and therefore felt – better in a nightie than in any other garment.

She said, 'You know you're welcome to the guest room for tonight. But really, Joy, I don't think it's a good idea to ask Duncan to talk to Lucas. If this sort of thing gets in the newspaper – you know how careful Duncan has to be.'

Joy's mouth turned down and shook slightly. She said, 'You mean he can't take another scandal like the last one?'

'Joy, listen, please—'

'No. You listen to me! Just for once!' Joy was suddenly hard. Her mass of red hair had been tied back severely at some point and now looked like a warrior's helmet, the fringe almost meeting her bronze brows and eyes. Her cheekbones looked sharply pointed in the shadowy light from the wall lamps, her generous mouth was a long thin line.

'You owe me a lot of favours, Rachel. A lot of favours. You were determined to have him, weren't you? He was my husband and your boss, and you made him so reliant on you he couldn't live without you – isn't that how you did it? How you are still doing it?'

Rachel was appalled. She had wanted Duncan and she had wanted the status of being his wife, but for a long time now she had truly believed the propaganda they had put out, that the love between them was all-consuming, sweeping everything before it like so much flotsam; wife, daughters, reputation . . . Joy's words reminded her how determined she had been.

She flinched back and put a hand up as if to ward off a blow. 'Joy . . . it wasn't like that! We didn't want it to happen – it just did! Surely you could see that? I hated what it was doing to you and Becky and Jan – I felt responsible—'

'Dammit, Rachel, you *were* responsible – make no mistake about that. And I'm not bitter about it, not really. I've been happy with Lucas. But I want you to help me now. If you do it – give me shelter and comfort –' she grinned, cat-like, 'then it will be all right. Solidarity. That's the name of the game.' The grin disappeared and for a moment a look of genuine pleading came into her eyes. She said, 'Lucas has always been jealous of Duncan – it's my fault, I've made sure of it. My life with a Liberal Member. You know the sort of thing.' Rachel knew. 'If I can phone him from here – get Duncan to intercede – he'll toe the line again. He'll be round here on his knees. I know it.' She tightened her lips, wagged her head and said cajolingly, 'Come on, Rachel. God, it's not much to ask, surely? Can't you let him off the lead just this much?'

Rachel turned and walked to the window. Duncan was in the kitchen making tea – because Joy had wanted tea! There was nothing she could do about this, not really. Duncan would see it as his duty to look after Joy. And he would want it kept quiet, so Rachel would be expected to do the covering up, keep the whole thing going. And there would be interviews with the prospective new candidates . . . Sally Something with the bright, ironic eyes and the man Duncan thought was blimpish. And Joy watching her all the time; watching her running around the place like a scalded cat, overeating in the kitchen when she thought no-one could see her, making herself indispensable as a wife just as she had done as a secretary in Joy's day. Because, basically, Joy was lazy. She had let Rachel do all the work, she had even let Rachel sleep with Duncan . . . It was unbearable. It was almost as if the whole thing had been engineered by Joy. Instead of . . . surely instead of . . . by Rachel herself?

Rachel knew suddenly that she had to get away; she was older now, she could not go through all that again. And she thought suddenly of Pru and the phone call. She thought of the calm swoop of the Malverns and the small town where Elgar had lived and worked.

She turned and smiled. 'Duncan is not on any lead, Joy. As a matter of fact, I was going to tell him tonight, I've arranged to meet some very old friends. A reunion. He'd be managing without me in any case.' She let the smile grow. 'I didn't quite know how to tell Duncan – as you say he does rely on me rather a lot. However, now you are here . . . no problem.'

It was almost worth it just to see Joy's face. She'd heard of dropping jaws but never seen one. It was not pretty. She nodded sympathetically. 'It will be hard work, yes. But you won't mind, will you?' She made for the door just as Duncan entered with the tea tray. 'Darling, I'm off to bed now. Joy and I have been talking – she will tell you all!' She gave him one of her will o' the wisp smiles as she passed him. 'Things will work out fine. Don't worry.'

She knew he would. She knew that in many ways she was indispensable and Joy had proved that she was not. And then there was the constant fear of what the press might find out. She smiled as she got ready for bed. She would go to Birmingham tomorrow and stay with Nash until they could go to the Malverns together. Let them all stew in their own peculiar juices for a while. She slid into her nightdress and smoothed it over generous hips. Perhaps in the next three weeks she could lose some weight.

But when Duncan came to bed she wondered whether it was worth it. He sublimated all his worries in almost an hour of lovemaking. And afterwards as they lay practically steaming in the air from the open windows, he bemoaned what he called her desertion.

'I shall have to go up to Charnwood or something. You can't leave me here with my ex-wife, Ray! It'll get out – it will look as if you've left me! And anyway, Miss Chambers won't be able to cope without you.'

'Once you've got her a new chair, she will manage very well,' Rachel said comfortably. 'I'm sorry, darling, but I've already made these arrangements. I was going to tell you tonight but you and Judas were having such a lovely time I didn't want to spoil anything.'

He groaned and rolled onto her again and she responded enthusiastically as she always did. It was when she had threatened to withhold her sexual favours that he had finally divorced Joy, and married her. She never forgot that for almost two years he had slept with her and Joy, so his needs must be fairly pressing. She made sure he would not need anyone to replace Joy.

Much later, when he was sleeping fitfully and she could hear Joy moving around the kitchen making herself more tea, she wondered whether she might have dug a pit and neatly fallen into it.

Five

Evelyn Hazell had made a rare visit to the hairdresser. She had taken the advice of the beauty consultant in her magazine to pamper herself. The hairdresser had trimmed off the lump of hair she called a bun, shaped it, permed it so that it would hold that shape but not frizz and told her no-one would believe that she was an old-age pensioner now.

Certainly Evelyn, at sixty-seven, was a pensioner, but the adjective 'old-age' took away some of the joy of the occasion and she had to continue to pamper herself with a long cool bath and tea in the garden.

She finished her scone, waved away a wasp, and looked around the small pristine lawn with some satisfaction. She mowed it once a week and weeded its border meticulously. Facing her was the potting shed made to look like a Swiss chalet, behind her were the French windows of her dining room and, on either side, behind fence and trellis, were similar bungalows and gardens owned by people in the same situation. The bungalows were arranged around a patch of grass which the warden called 'the village green'. Mr Lavington in number ten had placed his granddaughter's plastic ducks in the middle of it and called it the village duck pond. Edith had thought it was very funny, so Evelyn had thought so too. But the warden had said brightly, 'Are we getting childish, Mr Lavington?' and no-one had laughed again because the sheltered village was owned by a private company who could recommend nursing care for anyone they thought might lower the tone. And that meant the asylum – though it wasn't called that now, of course.

Evelyn opened her eyes and sighed. However much she tried to keep Edith out of her thoughts, she always came into them somewhere. Ten years younger than Evelyn and with a sense of fun Evelyn envied, she had bridged the gap between the age groups at Markhams. Mr Delano and Mr Edgar and Evelyn at one end, Natasha, Pru, Rachel and Maisie at the other.

When Evelyn applied for a bungalow Edith had been aghast.

'You're only almost fifty-eight, Eve! They're all in their dotage!'

But she'd been delighted for her friend eventually. Especially when she found out about the cancer.

'I like to think of you here, safe and cosy, when you leave Markhams.'

'Don't talk like that, Edith!' Evelyn had been terrified by the whole process of Edith's illness. She could not bear to admit it would lead to death.

'Don't be silly, Eve. I only said how glad I am that you will be comfortable and cared for once you retire!' She smiled. 'Not only that, either. That chap in number ten will keep you on your toes. My God, you might even marry him!'

'Edith, stop it this minute! Mr Lavington is seventy years old and deserves our respect.'

'Our respect is not what he wants though,' Edith said with that wicked twinkle. And Evelyn had just shaken her head helplessly, not knowing what to say. When Prudence Adair had left Markhams in 1966, Edith had returned to the office to do Mr Delano's typing and it was rumoured that some of his obvious adoration for Pru had been directed towards Edith. She had said once to Evelyn, 'I might be a spinster, Eve, but I'm not an old maid, you know.'

And now she was dead and there was a stranger doing the typing in Mr Delano's office and all those lovely old times were gone for ever.

Except for Maisie, of course. Maisie dropped in to the little bungalow by the village green about once a month, bringing flowers and chocolates and news of her five children. When Evelyn had flu just after her retirement, Maisie found her way around the tiny kitchen and made small delicious meals to tempt her back to life.

'I know how you feel,' she had said sternly. 'But you are

not going to join Edith just yet. I still need you and I won't let that happen!'

And Evelyn had smiled through her tears and said it was the fluffiest, lightest scrambled egg she had ever seen. Because she couldn't talk about Edith. And if it had been possible, she would not have thought of her either.

She sighed again at the hopelessness of keeping Edith out of her head and ran her fingers through her new curls as if to brush her out. That made her fingers smell most unpleasantly of the stuff they had put on her hair, so she struggled out of her deckchair and went inside to wash up. Then she looked through the *Radio Times* to see if there was anything on television worth watching. And then, when there wasn't – and much to her annoyance because it meant she wouldn't sleep that night – she had a long nap and woke to find it getting dusky. So she found her tape of Viennese waltzes and inserted it into the player and as the familiar strains of 'The Blue Danube' filled the small sitting room, she smiled happily. She had never been to Vienna and would not go now, but she saw it in her mind with such clarity she was certain she had visited it in a previous life. The Ringstrasse with the high-stepping horses and the cavalry officers in their blue-and-gold uniforms. And carriages filled to capacity with ladies all wearing silk and big hats and some using lorgnettes and making for the Prater Park with the river encircling it. Then quite suddenly the huge ballroom of the Hofburg opened before her and she was whirling down its length in the arms of . . . Mr Lavington? No, not today; Mr Delano. He was the better dancer. She negotiated the door into her small hall and wrapped her arms around her shoulders as she one-two-three'd towards the front door. And as she reached it the bell rang.

She stopped as if shot, her arms crossing her breast religiously, her fish-blue eyes wide with apprehension. She felt as if she had been caught out; if it was the warden would she guess that Evelyn had just come from the Hofburg and was overdue for 'nursing care'?

She opened the door and almost sobbed with relief. Maisie stood there.

Maisie pushed past Evelyn – there was only just room in the tiny hall for that – and made straight for the sitting room. She was lugging a holdall. Evelyn was about to shut the door and follow her when it was pushed open again and a man deposited a case on the mat. 'Five-fifty,' he said laconically. Evelyn glanced over his shoulder and saw a taxi and realized he was the driver. She reached for her charity bag which she always kept behind the door so that she would not have to go purse-hunting when people came round with collecting boxes. It was full of small change. She glanced helplessly in the direction of the sitting room but Maisie did not reappear. She counted out five pounds and fifty pence with some difficulty. The man sniffed; he could see there was nothing left for a tip.

Evelyn closed the door at last and replaced her empty charity bag. Her hands were trembling. They would have been trembling anyway with the flustering task of finding the money, but they were trembling twice over; she knew something was horribly wrong with Maisie.

She lugged the case away from the door and went into the sitting room. Maisie was sitting in one of the two armchairs, her mobile face quite wooden. She was wearing a very pretty blue dress covered in white daisies. Strappy white sandals made her feet look even smaller than they were, her hair was not so curly as usual and was falling untidily over her forehead. Suddenly Evelyn could imagine Maisie as a much older woman; hard and much too self-contained. She was, after all, forty. No longer the zany young junior who had dashed around Markhams trying so hard to do everything right. Maisie looked up and smiled slightly.

'We're going on holiday, Evelyn! Isn't it exciting? Courtesy of Pru – you remember, Pru Adair? Of course you do, silly me. Nash came to see me this afternoon to tell me that Pru has got a house near Malvern Link somewhere. And we're all going to meet up there – the five of us! Like old times!'

Evelyn said fearfully, 'How are we going to get there?'

'Train. Like we used to. Don't you remember our wonderful days out rambling over the hills?'

'That was over fifteen years ago, Maisie. I was in my early fifites then. I can't ramble any more.'

'You and me will stay in then. We'll do the cooking and the cleaning. It'll be great fun to housekeep from scratch, won't it?' Maisie was still smiling rallyingly and she spoke as if coaxing a child.

Evelyn said, 'But the shopping . . . food . . . Neither of us can drive a car. How shall we get the shopping in?'

'We'll manage. Nash will do it for us . . .' Maisie's tone changed as her smile died. She said desperately, 'You must come, Evelyn. I can't go if you don't come. I thought it would be all right with Nash – she would be there all the time so I wouldn't have to be by myself with Pru. But Nash was there this afternoon when . . . she probably knows – she's so worldly-wise – she probably knew years ago! And I can't bear it! And I have to go – I can't stay – and if you're there it will be all right!'

Evelyn expected her to cry; she waited for her to put her head on her knees and sob like the little girl she had always seemed to be. But there were no tears. She put her hands towards the unlit gas fire as if she were cold and said almost normally, 'D'you think we ought to have a cup of tea?'

Evelyn gripped her shaking hands together and said, 'Yes. That would be nice,' and made for the kitchen. She stood by the tiny work surface staring at the kettle and shelf of crockery, and felt a tide of panic starting in her feet and beginning to come up her legs. Inside her head she screamed, 'Edith, why isn't it you here? Something awful has happened and you could deal with it and I can't!'

And as if by magic she felt the tide ebb, first to her knees, then her ankles, then out through her toes. The trembling stopped. She could almost hear Edith saying, 'You silly old dear. I am here. I've never really gone. I'm in you now. So we'll deal with it together. All right?'

And Evelyn said aloud, 'All right.' And she reached for the kettle, turned on the tap and filled it, plugged it in. Then a tray and a cloth . . . drawer. Then the rose-patterned china . . . some biscuits. The kettle was boiling. She pushed her head around the kitchen door and called out, 'Leaf?

Or teabags?' It was such a relief to hear Maisie give a small laugh.

'Dear Evelyn. Leaf, please.'

Which meant the silver strainer and a slop basin. And those paper napkins from Christmas; the holly berries were so cheerful. She carried in the tea tray and in her head Edith said, 'Make everything as normal as you can. We don't want any nervous breakdowns here. Your house is much too small!'

Maisie said, sounding surprised, 'You've got a lovely smile, Evelyn. I've never really noticed before.'

'Well . . .' Evelyn clattered cups onto saucers and began the ritual of pouring. 'I've just had my hair done, you see.'

Maisie did not say, what on earth has that got to do with your smile. She just nodded and took her tea and held the cup to her face so that the steam warmed it. If the day just gone hadn't been so hot, Evelyn would have thought she was feeling cold.

Evelyn said, 'Tell me about Nash. We've had no news of her for ages, have we?'

Maisie focused her gaze through the steam and took a deep breath. 'She's divorced from Harvey Nolan. She and Hilary came home last spring. Hilary went to Chudleigh – the school Nash was at – but didn't like it. She wanted to go back to the States and spend the summer with her father in Maine – apparently they do that every year. So Nash took her back. Then came home again and was most unhappy. Her mother suggested the reunion. Nash rang Pru and, as it happened, Pru has this house in the Malverns . . .' She looked up. 'I've already told you this, haven't I?'

'Not about the divorce. I'm sorry.' Evelyn swallowed and said bravely, 'So when are we going?'

'You'll come? Oh Evelyn, thank you! I couldn't face it alone. They're so . . . you know . . . strong. It's strong to get divorced even, isn't it? And Pru – giving up her worldly possessions and living in a commune . . . and Rachel is practically prime minister.' She stopped because Evelyn was laughing and Evelyn so rarely laughed.

'Rachel, prime minister indeed! The country would be even worse off if that was the case!' Evelyn sobered and leaned forward. 'Has it occurred to you, Maisie, that you are the strong one? Bringing up no less than five children? Nash has a daughter, certainly, but I can't see her having much of a hand in bringing her up. And Pru, Rachel, Edith and I . . . well.' But she didn't look stricken about it, she smiled encouragingly.

Maisie looked at her, then sighed sharply and slumped in the chair, suddenly relaxed. She began to sip her tea. In between, she told Evelyn what she had seen in Mrs Donald's bedroom. Evelyn flinched and looked as if she might be sick.

Maisie said earnestly, 'I know Nash has put up with her husband's infidelities for years. But it's different for Ted and me. It's not . . . the act.' She shook her head. 'It can't be that because you see, I have been unfaithful to Ted.' She shook her head at Evelyn's expression. 'I'm sorry. This is all a bit much for you, isn't it? But I have to tell someone, and I'd like it to be you. Nash . . . Nash would . . . well, be angry, or dismiss it, or something. You never judge. I always noticed this when Edith was alive. She was so quick – and funny – with her judgements. But you never were.'

'Oh, Maisie.' Evelyn almost cried. 'It's only because I'm so . . . wishy-washy!'

'No, you're not. You must have known that Tom was not Ted's son? Edith must have guessed and said something to you.'

'I'd forgotten,' Evelyn said truthfully. She forgot a great deal these days.

Maisie sighed again, finished her tea and put the cup on the tray. 'Oh, this is so lovely. To be here. I've telephoned Jess and she will be home tomorrow to take care of things. I don't have to worry. Except for Tom.'

'Could he come to Malvern with us?' Evelyn suggested.

'I don't think he'd want to. He worships Mark. They play golf and things . . . Anyway, the holiday at Malvern doesn't begin for two weeks. And I've forgotten where Nash said the house is.'

Evelyn said, 'Well, that's all right. We can telephone Pru. There's probably a phone at her community-place-thing. And in the meantime you can have my bed and I'll blow up that air bed and put it in the dining room – you know, the one you gave me for sunbathing.'

'I'll blow it up and I'll sleep on it. Just for tonight. But I can't stay here, Evelyn. I've left a note, but once he controls his anger he will look for me and this will be the first place.'

'Are you that frightened of him?' Evelyn asked, some of her fear creeping back in spite of Edith's strength.

Maisie gazed thoughtfully at her sandals. 'I used to have a dream – before I met Tom McEvoy. It was such a strange dream because there was no pain, no fear, even. It was that Ted was eating me.'

Evelyn gave a cry of horror.

Maisie nodded, 'I know it sounds like a cross between Dracula and cannibalism. But there was never any blood – it was as if I were made of bread. Or cake. I mean, it was funny really. He came up to me, smiling, loving, and just took a mouthful out of my shoulder. And I let him. I knew he had to do it. And I watched him eat my whole arm . . .' Her voice was escalating and Evelyn reached over and took her hand as if dragging her back to reality.

Maisie shook her head and lowered her voice. 'It's all right. Once I met Tom and had that crazy week with him, I decided to go back to Ted. Nash told me it was the best thing to do. And Rachel – well Rachel was adamant. But I was going to go back anyway. You see, that's the whole thing about Ted and me. Loyalty. Whatever happens we are loyal to each other. That's why I don't cringe when he hits me. Because I know it's his way of, of, eating me!' She laughed and hysteria was there again. 'And anyway, he wouldn't have hit me half so often if I hadn't told him that the baby wasn't his. I should have taken that guilt with me to the grave. But at the time I saw it as proving something. Our honesty with each other. Our loyalty – there's that word again.' She sobbed. 'And all the time he and Mrs Donald . . .'

'Don't think about it, my dear. Blot it out of your mind.' Evelyn wondered if it was a good thing that Maisie's control had snapped. She waited for the storm to pass, which it did very quickly.

Maisie said calmly, 'But I didn't dream that dream any

more. That's all I wanted to say. It's something Tom McEvoy did for me . . . and Tom has continued to do for me.' She gave a watery smile, 'I am not edible!'

Evelyn could not smile back. She had known Maisie's husband was domineering and possessive, but she had assumed that Maisie was quite happy to be dominated. She had not known that he resorted to physical violence. And the dream . . . the dream was too horrible to be funny.

She said sadly, 'When he came to the shop and took such an obvious shine to you . . . we were all so pleased . . .' She patted Maisie's hand. 'We should have been more vigilant. You had no-one else. Edith and I . . . we should have had a word with him. Or something.'

Maisie said, just as sadly, 'It would have made no difference, my dear. Except perhaps to alienate him so that I could not have kept in touch with Edith and you. No . . . I couldn't believe my luck. When I left home and got that bedsit in Aston and then the job at Markhams, I thought I was in heaven. I didn't want anything else. I would have stayed there all my working life and been happy. But there was Pru . . .' She shook her curls at Evelyn's raised brows. 'A little misunderstanding, but I was oversensitive. And then Ted came along. I thought he'd drop me like a hot cake when I told him I was pregnant. But he didn't. He got a special licence . . . it was so romantic, you must remember that.'

'I remember that.' Evelyn took a deep breath. Edith had always maintained that Maisie had had to get married, but to hear it spoken aloud by Maisie herself made it spring into perspective. She realized something that none of them had. 'You never loved him, did you? Gratitude isn't love, Maisie. You never loved him properly.'

Maisie shrugged. 'What is love – I don't know, do I? Tom wasn't love either. I love my children. I do know that.'

'Yes. Yes, you have the children.' Evelyn sat back thankfully. It wasn't all horror. Maisie had her children.

There was a silence. After a while Evelyn leaned forward again and poured more tea. She sipped it slowly. There was so much to think about; she must not interfere but she had to help.

She said, 'So you have to fill in two weeks? And then we can go to Malvern for a week. What then?'

'I don't know.'

'Have you got any money?'

'No. We never had a joint account. Nothing like that.'

'I've got some in the house. I can get some more tomorrow.' Evelyn frowned. 'You are leaving him? For good? Are you?'

'I don't know that either. I don't know anything really.'

'Well of course not. You need time to think.' Evelyn's frown deepened. 'We can't really afford a hotel. Stay here with me, Maisie. I'll say I've not seen you. I won't let him in.'

'You don't know him, Evelyn. Tomorrow I must go somewhere else.'

Evelyn had a brainwave. 'Your brother! You had a brother, didn't you? Is he still living in Birmingham?'

Maisie frowned. 'I think so.'

'I'll get the telephone book. Jenkins. Your maiden name was Jenkins. Lots of those. What was the initial?'

Maisie bit her lip, then said, 'R. R for Roland.'

'Right.' Evelyn was not a bustler but she bustled into the hall for the directory and settled down with it and a pencil in evident satisfaction that they were halfway to a solution.

Maisie said in a small voice, 'He won't want anything to do with me, Evelyn. I – I ran away, you see.'

Evelyn forgot that she must not interfere. 'Then he'll probably be delighted to hear you are still alive!' she said and ran her thumbnail down the list of Jenkinses in the book. And, as if surrendering her will yet again, Maisie said nothing.

Six

Rachel said, 'I know what you mean about Pru. But I was never conscious of any mystery. Just bloody superiority!' She laughed to take the sting out of her words. 'I suppose knowing Mrs Adair was an Honourable and that Pru had gone to Switzerland . . . oh and Mr Edgar worshipped at the Hon's court . . . it was a bit demoralizing for me.'

'Christ, Ray, your father was some wheeler-dealer in international affairs – we were in awe of *you*!' Natasha remembered suddenly that a journalist had uncovered some dreadful things about Mr Strang. He had had a finger in the Nigerian Biafran conflict back in Sixty-seven. Selling arms? Spying? Had he even gone to prison? She went on quickly, 'Wasn't he the reason you wanted to be secretary to some famous person? And you've done it!'

The two women were on the lawn at Thatch End, watching the newly completed pool being filled. Rachel had telephoned the previous Saturday and requested what she called 'asylum'.

'I'm longing to see you all, of course, but I desperately need to get away, full stop. Could I come to you, Nash? Would your mother mind? I'm completely out of touch with Maisie and the other two. Pru is living in some commune . . . I expect you feel out of touch too, don't you? We could catch up together. What d'you say?'

'Well, I know Mummy won't mind. And Dad is . . . well . . . he takes his line from her. So . . . why not?' Natasha had been surprised. As Rachel had said, they had gone their separate ways for fifteen years. However it seemed she was chosen by default anyway. 'Yes, do come. As soon as you like. I'll see to the guest room so that Mrs Mayhew doesn't kick up a fuss – she's our help and no help at all as far as I can see.'

And Rachel had arrived today, Monday.

Now she stretched luxuriously in her deckchair and said in response to Natasha's compliment, 'Yes. I know. But it's been hard work, Nash. And it's getting harder.'

Nash had thought Rachel might alleviate the boredom of the next two weeks but already she felt a yawn collecting in her throat. Whether she wanted to or not, she was going to hear all about the life of a politician's wife.

'I don't get it,' she said, purposely giving Rachel an opening on the grounds that the sooner she began the sooner she would finish. 'After all, Duncan's never likely to be part of an actual government, is he? I mean we all know that the Liberals are the safe option for the voter who doesn't know or doesn't care.'

She closed her eyes, prepared to relax away the next half-an-hour's Party political broadcast. Nothing happened for a while. Then Rachel said hesitantly, 'If I tell you something, Nash, will you swear never to breathe a word of it to anyone? Anyone. Harvey or Hilary or your mother – anyone.'

'Oh for Pete's sake, Ray. You don't honestly think I ever – but ever – talk politics, do you?' Nash opened her eyes and looked across at Rachel's deckchair, hoping against hope that she was about to disclose another political scandal like the Profumo affair. That would be something to help with the boredom.

Rachel was apparently convinced. She leaned across the gap between them and lowered her voice. 'I happen to know that there's a great deal of unrest among the leading members of Labour. We think . . . we're sure in fact, that there will be a breakaway quite soon.'

She looked at Natasha significantly and sat back in her chair.

Natasha stared at her. 'Is that it?'

'Isn't it enough? A major Party crumbling before our eyes?'

'What's it got to do with the Liberals for Christ's sake?'

Rachel was astonished. 'Don't you see, Nash? A breakaway Party couldn't stand alone! There will have to be some kind of union with the Liberals. Our chance at last.'

For two pins Natasha could have said, 'So what?' But then Rachel might feel she needed conversion and the next two weeks would become impossible. She smiled slightly and shook her head. 'Sorry, Ray. I don't believe it.' And she too sat back in her chair and waited. Now what would come out? Could Rachel possibly be having an affair with a high-ranking socialist? It was hard to imagine. She had put on a lot of weight and her legs, stretched out from her chair, would only be attractive on a rugby field.

Rachel said, 'I can assure you it's true, Nash. One gets to hear things—'

'Rumours. We have them in the States too. They say Ronnie Reagan will be the next president – you know, the cowboy actor.'

'This is not a rumour.' Rachel sighed and leaned forward again. 'I might as well tell you – none of it means anything to you so it's safe. We have an insider. Duncan gets him perks. Anyway he likes Duncan and Duncan pretends to like him. He's a PPS.'

'What the hell is that?'

'Secretary. To a Minister. Of the Crown.' Rachel was sounding huffy now. Natasha assumed an expression of respect. Rachel mollified, went on, 'I know it's awful, but it happens. I call him Judas.' She giggled suddenly. 'His latest girlfriend is called Isadora. I think I shall call her Iscariot.'

Natasha said, 'I'm impressed. I thought you might be going to tell me you slept with someone and they talked in their sleep!' She giggled but looked hopeful.

Rachel flushed deeply. 'I suppose you are referring to me sleeping with Duncan while he was still married to Joy.' She held up her hand at Natasha's protests. 'I admit it.' She turned to Natasha again and her eyes were very bright. 'I can only assure you, Nash, that I've never slept with anyone but Duncan in my life. I knew . . . immediately . . . he was the one for me. If he'd lost his seat in that election of 1970, it would have made no difference. I was in love with him. And I have been ever since.'

Natasha stared incredulously. 'You mean . . . you actually mean . . . you haven't slept with anyone but Duncan Stayte?'

'Certainly.' Rachel looked defiant. 'What I did was bad enough. Sleeping with him while he was still married to Joy.' She flung her head back and closed her eyes. 'I deserve to be punished for that.'

'Punished? What are you talking about? My God, Rachel, you sound like the Middle Ages! You were not responsible for his divorce—'

'I was actually.' Rachel spoke quietly now. 'He didn't seduce me. I seduced him.'

'And he let it happen. And anyway, honey, one seduction doesn't make a divorce. He could've sacked you. Told you he loved his wife . . .'

'I wouldn't let that happen. I told him I was pregnant. If that had come out it would have finished him. The lesser of the two evils for Duncan was to go along with my version of events – we had been swept madly away on the tide of love and he felt it only fair to his wife and children . . . you know.'

Natasha's boredom had flown. She sat upright looking down at Rachel whose face was the colour of her rugby legs, an unhealthy mottle of whites.

'What about the baby?' she asked after a long pause.

'Baby? Oh the pregnancy you mean. There was no baby. But by the time I had my miscarriage, the split with Joy had happened.' She sighed deeply. 'Actually it made the romantic bit more convincing. Duncan put it like that. He said a baby would have made the whole remarriage thing look . . . pragmatic.'

'So you would have had a child of . . . what? Five years old by now?'

Rachel opened her eyes and squinted irritably against the sun. 'There was no baby! Don't you understand? I tricked him. He wouldn't have married me – he could've weathered the storm of people knowing I was his mistress – there's a certain cachet to that. But I had to be his wife, Nash. Surely you understand, I couldn't be like Miss Benson . . . no-one was happy with that situation. My mother took an overdose – did you know that? And Miss Benson looked more and more like a prostitute – I couldn't have taken that.'

'Who the hell is Miss Benson?' Nash asked.

'Eric's secretary. The one poor Denise called the power behind the throne.'

Natasha said wildly, 'And Eric? And Denise?' She closed her eyes, suddenly understanding. 'Of course. Your parents. You always called them by their first names, didn't you?'

'He preferred it that way. And she . . . wherever he went, she followed.'

Natasha heard the contempt in Rachel's voice and felt a thrill of pure horror. She thought of her own parents with a sudden rush of gratitude; they had always been there for her. That was the trouble with Harvey; he never was.

Rachel said, 'If only she had stood up to him. When he saw that she never would, he made life hell for her. He was like that. A sadist. That's why he . . .' Her voice trailed off.

'He what?' prompted Natasha, practically agog by now.

'Nothing. As a matter of fact Eric taught me a lot. She did too, in a negative way.' Rachel laughed. 'How not to be. He was the positive, she the negative.' She laughed again and said with heavy significance, 'To be and not to be.' She sat up. 'Trouble is, Nash, I'm not sure that what I've done now – leaving Duncan like this – is positive or negative! And I suppose I won't know until I get home.'

'You haven't exactly *left* him, Ray. Two and a half weeks, that's all. And think of all you'll have to tell him. We'll pool all our news and you can give him an unexpurgated version.' She made a face. 'He'll be so glad you're normal, he'll never stop counting his blessings!'

'Yes.' Rachel closed her eyes against the sun and tried to relax. It was impossible to detail all the small things that had happened over the past year . . . the broken typist's chair was just one. And then the arrival of Joy with her red hair and the two children in the background. Who, of course, were Duncan's children as well. She felt herself tensing up in the chair. Should she go straight back home now? Or should she sit it out in the hope that life in Pimlico would become impossible without her guiding hand?

'Tell me about Maisie,' she said, making an effort to be positive.

So Natasha told her the little she had gleaned about Maisie, which, after all, was mainly about Maisie's children.

'Something happened,' she concluded. 'She was the same old Maisie, trying to please everyone. I was certain she would back out of the week in Malvern. And then, quite suddenly, when she brought in the tea, she was different. Sort of . . . flat. And very definite. Anyway, I am so glad she is coming. I always felt, afterwards, I shouldn't have sent her back to that Edward Davenport. At the time it seemed the only possible thing to do. She must have forgiven me by now.'

'Oh you were for her going back too, were you?' Rachel squinted upwards momentarily. 'I was too. Surely there was nothing to forgive. She'd have been crazy to throw in her lot with that hippie. She had money and position . . . she would have lost those –'

'It was the children. She would have lost Mark and Jess too. That was what worried me.' Natasha bit her lip. 'And the man, Tom McEvoy, he was incapable of the kind of devotion Maisie needed. The sort of devotion which, incidentally, Edward Davenport was giving her in a domineering sort of way. I was justified in doing . . . what I did.'

Rachel nodded drowsily. 'I think I was too. We had Maisie's best interests at heart.'

Natasha frowned and closed her eyes too. Of course, Rachel had no idea what Natasha had done to prove to Maisie that she couldn't throw in her lot with Tom McEvoy. And Natasha herself had no idea what Rachel had done. She worried her lip, tasting her own blood. And suddenly thought: poor Maisie.

Rachel, in the no man's land between being asleep and awake, knew she had been completely justified in her actions. Always. Because they had stemmed, every solitary action, from when she was fourteen: still at school, worshipping Eric as she always had done, slightly scornful of her mother who seemed so ineffectual. It had been a day in early summer, not so warm as today because of a breeze that was almost a gale as it swept across the golf course of Barnt Green and rattled the ivy on the red-brick house. A day when Miss Benson had been closeted with her father in his study and the phone had kept ringing . . . it must have been 1953 because Eric had taken her and Denise to a cocktail party in Canonhill Park to celebrate the Coronation just the week before, hadn't she seen the Markham display there? The wonderful diamond Coronation Suite laid out on black velvet; the opulence of it all. Yes, because it was then that she had said to Eric, 'That's where I'd like a job. Markhams.' And he'd said, 'Done.' Just as if she were one of his customers sealing a bargain. And he'd added, 'You'll have to play your cards right though and keep stumm.'

Rachel frowned in her semi-sleep and wondered whether Eric had thought she already knew about him and Miss Benson. She hadn't. Not then. But a week later, on that blowy day, when Eric had finalized his very special deal with an envoy of Colonel Gamal Nassar of the Free Officers Group who had overthrown Egypt's King Farouk the year before, then she had known.

She had been outside while all the phoning was going on; Miss Benson's, 'Would you mind holding the line please' floated through the open window and was whipped off to the 16th hole by the strong breeze. And then her father's whoop of joy had alerted her to his success. Money. There would be heaps of money now. She could just remember when she was nine or ten and the Korean War had begun and Eric had sold some of his army surplus to the Koreans, whether North or South Korea she never knew, but she remembered all the money rolling in then. A new car for Denise, a week in London doing all the shows, party dresses and toys, Miss Benson's perm and fox fur. It was the same now. He emerged from his office, incandescent with triumph, swept her off her feet and waltzed her back into the house. He set her down in the kitchen and gathered Miss Benson into his free arm.

'Denny still out?' he asked Rachel, breathless now, panting. Rachel nodded, laughing, carried with him as she always was.

'Good-oh!' He kissed Miss Benson full on the lips. You could tell it wasn't the first time, they were both expert at it. 'We can celebrate properly.' He sat Miss Benson on a stool next to Rachel and went off to the dining room and the new drinks cabinet. It was not the first time Rachel had tasted whisky, Eric insisted she had some at Christmas and birthdays, but it was the first time she had enjoyed it. Eric poured a second glass for Miss Benson. 'No more for Ray, Eric, really.' Miss Benson liked Rachel.

'She can share mine.'

He held his glass to her lips. She was giggling helplessly. He said with feigned surprise, 'Look at that! Greedy little so-and-so! She's drunk my drink – I'll have to have another!'

Rachel must have passed out. When she opened her eyes she was lying on her bed. The familiar ceiling swam above her: her room had been a nursery when the house was built in 1900; it had a fireplace with a brass-railed guard and in each corner was painted some kind of sprite creature. She had always loved them and called them Dozy, Happy, Doc and Sneezy. Now they looked horrendous, like gargoyles leering down at her. She rolled over to the edge of her bed and was sick on the carpet. The sick smelled of whisky. She groaned and said aloud, 'I'll never touch that dreadful stuff again!' And she rolled back and just lay still waiting for the nausea to pass. When it did she crawled off the bed and went in search of Eric. He would have to clean up the mess because she certainly could not. And it must be cleared before Denise got back from Birmingham otherwise there would be hell to pay. She could just imagine the scene. 'I don't care if you sold the whole British army to this Mr Nasty or whatever his name is! It's no excuse for making your daughter drunk! You are the most irresponsible man I have ever known! Calling that tart your secretary! Oh yes, she's the power behind the throne all right! I know that! And I don't count, do I? Not that I'll ever divorce you – you need not think that! I've earned my share of your carpetbagging! And I'm going to have it. You can bring in a troupe of Bluebell Girls for all I care! You won't get rid of me I can assure you . . .' and so on. And her father would say, 'Christ Almighty, woman! Loads of girls have left school at fourteen and are earning a living! Ray needs to grow up – that's all she's doing – growing up!'

Rachel went woozily along the landing to her mother's room, just to check she wasn't back yet. She opened the door, leaning on it, swinging into the room. And there was Miss Benson on her hands and knees, stark naked and her father the same, rogering away for all the world like their old dog Winston when he mistook someone's leg for a bitch. Rachel gazed, not knowing whether to laugh or scream or be sick again. And then her father looked up from where he appeared to be biting the back of Miss Benson's neck, saw her there, grinned and winked.

Rachel closed the door and went downstairs for a bucket and floorcloth.

She had often wondered, after that, why the incident had bound her and Eric closer than ever. She realized when she was older that he had quite enjoyed her voyeurism; he often kissed Miss Benson in front of her and once he had stood behind his secretary while she was on the telephone and slid his hand inside her blouse, laughing aloud when her voice wobbled on the edge of hysteria. Rachel remembered watching and laughing too. So she must have enjoyed the voyeurism too. It was somehow all part of that bargain they'd made at the Coronation exhibition. The bargain was not mentioned again but she watched him edging closer to the Markham brothers, finding out about them, looking for weak spots. He never did, but when he was runner-up in the Businessman of the Year award in 1958 he hailed them familiarly as 'fellow exporters'.

'I understand a lot of your stuff goes to the States,' he beamed, one arm around Rachel's shoulders, the other at Denise's waist. 'I've got a deal on there at the moment.'

Mr Delano nodded smilingly in a way Rachel was to know much better. She heard him say to Pru once, 'A nod and a smile costs nothing and gives nothing away, my dear. I think you know that.'

Mr Edgar said, 'Pleasure to meet you, Strang. I remember the support you offered to our armies during the Suez crisis.' He shook his head. 'The United Nations slipped up there.'

Eric shrugged, smiling rather like Mr Delano. 'Ah well. Win some, lose some.' He had lost a great deal during the Suez crisis but was making up for it now in Algeria.

'It was a question of national pride. You upheld that, Strang.'

Eric's smile became modest. Rachel wanted to laugh. She might well instruct him later on the true meaning of national pride. He would suck in his cheeks as he listened to her and then whisper in her ear, 'But it never bought anyone a nice red sports car, did it, my darling?'

Mr Delano coughed and asked, 'Did you say you are exporting to a firm in the States?'

Eric pressed Rachel's shoulders significantly. 'Yessirree!' He laughed at his own imitation which was execrable. 'By the name of the Alabama Spoon and Fork Company.' He laughed again and no-one knew whether he was joking or not. Mr Delano smiled and nodded and Mr Edgar asked what happened to the knives and Eric said he did not deal in weapons any more and then everyone laughed. Rachel, who knew that Eric was actually doing a deal with Algeria, not Alabama at all, moved slightly so that her father would realize she was in on the whole joke. He then introduced her – 'My one and only . . . helps me out when my secretary is overworked' – and then, provokingly, 'My wife, Denise. The power behind the throne,' – then they moved off.

'That's how it's done, baby,' he said in a low voice. 'Contact has been made. Softly, softly. OK?'

'OK, Eric.' She smiled up at him. She was eighteen then and had shed most of her puppy fat. She knew she looked good in her plain grey flannel suit with pearls at her throat, and black court shoes making her legs look longer and slimmer.

Denise was appalled when they explained to her later that one day soon she would be working in a shop.

'A shop girl!' They were in the Bentley going home along the A38. 'Are you crazy, Ray?' She turned in the front seat and looked back at Rachel. 'Who will you meet at Markhams, for God's sake! Shop people, that's who! You're going to be married to someone who is someone, my girl – not a man you meet in a bloody shop!' She turned back and addressed

Eric. 'Get rid of Miss Rosa Benson for Christ's sake! Take on Rachel – she could do just as good a job – take her around with you, show her off.'

He said, 'I've thought about it. But I'd rather she didn't get involved in some of my deals. I'd prefer her to be quite separate from the family, actually. And she needs experience, good solid experience. She'd get a great deal at Markhams – it's the sort of family firm that counts when you're looking for other jobs.' He slowed to go through a water splash. 'A good reference is what Rachel needs. Then I'll get her something special.' He caught her eye in the mirror. 'OK, baby?'

'OK, Eric,' she said again.

'What do you mean – right away from the family?' Denise asked querulously. 'She *lives* at home for God's sake!'

'I thought a flat. In Birmingham. A mews flat where she can keep her car . . .'

Rachel smiled while Denise started to cry and to ask what would become of her all alone in Barnt Green when Eric and Miss Benson were travelling the world. Rachel cut her out, just like Eric did, and thought about what her father's words actually meant. Eric thought of Markhams as an apprenticeship. For something better. But a good solid foundation to keep her clear of any future trouble. She nibbled her top lip with her bottom teeth. Already, then, he had known that his luck would not always hold out.

As it happened, Pru got to Markhams first, but after her initial disappointment Rachel did not mind too much. She learned a lot from Pru, though privately she thought she was a fool to fend off Mr Delano quite so rigorously. Rachel, remembering Miss Benson, knew that she would have played the game very differently. But Mr Delano never made advances to Rachel; in fact no-one ever did until Duncan. When she saw how Edward Davenport fell for Maisie, how Harvey Nolan, the American, laid siege to Natasha, how Edith could still summon a look of adoration from her old boss, she wondered what was the matter with her. She wondered if her love for Eric had unsexed her in some peculiar way.

It had been a relief when Eric had contributed lavishly to Liberal Party funds and secured a position for her with the would-be member for Soar in Rutland. Markhams had given her experience in some ways, but not in others. Without Eric's help she would not have landed the position of private secretary to a prospective MP.

She had driven to Charnwood House in another sports car; this time bottle green as befitted a supporter of the Liberal Party. And when Duncan Stayte had been elected as the representative for Soar, how she had worked! Her green car had been everywhere, to the remotest farms and to the more built-up areas around Leicester. And when Duncan had got a seat in the general election of 1974, he had shown his gratitude in the way she had wanted.

She stopped her thoughts there. The next eighteen months had probably been the happiest in her life and if Denise hadn't taken that overdose they could have gone on indefinitely. Duncan had felt about his wife, Joy, just as Eric had felt about Denise. She was his wife and the mother of his children, but she took him for granted and she was often tired and fed-up and not in the least interested in his career. Whereas Rachel was entirely on the ball, never tired, kept her depressions to herself and was completely undemanding. His stolen hours with her were exciting. She had learned a lot from watching her father with Miss Benson; her small stocky frame had an allure too. She was rarely ill and very strong.

But then Denise killed herself and Rachel knew that there was no such thing as a happy romantic triangle. She had to have Duncan all to herself.

She did not want to think about that; she certainly did not want to dream about it. She sighed and moved her head from side to side on the rough canvas of the chair, telling herself she was not asleep and she had perfect control over her thoughts.

And then, through the red mist of the sun on her closed eyelids, she saw Natasha's shape getting out of her chair and heard her say loudly, 'Oh no! Oh my God! Wake up, Ray! It's that bloody husband of Maisie's! It's Edward Davenport! If he's going to blame me for persuading Maisie to—'

Rachel, totally confused, opened her eyes, immediately screwed them against the sun, and saw Natasha in her ridiculous shorts and suntop, moving gracefully across the lawn.

'Edward! It is you, isn't it? Have you brought Maisie to see us?'

Natasha had dozed too and had her own dreams; at first, disconcertingly, of Ron the plumber.

She imagined she had relegated Ron to the pinkish, purplish background inhabited by the men with whom she had enjoyed a fling. From the days at Chudleigh School, when she had taken up fencing simply because it meant visiting the local boys' school where she had been seduced quickly by the fencing master, to Tom McEvoy, who had supposedly been in love with Maisie but was in fact in love with the idea of free love, Natasha had enjoyed men. She enjoyed the way they became interested in her; the way they moved closer to her; the way they engineered obvious meetings; the way they said afterwards, 'My God, you're wonderful! The most beautiful, the most exciting, the . . .' The superlatives soon changed. 'What do you mean, you can't see me again? I thought you and your husband had an open marriage? You are the worst kind of woman – unfaithful to everyone.' When she laughed at them they reacted differently. Some walked away furiously, one had tried to strangle her. She had never minded. It showed that she still had power over people . . . actually over most men. Except Harvey.

But Ron had been different. Ron had been tender, careful of her feelings, knowing at first that she was vulnerable after the divorce, but soon wanting to look after her. Wanting to marry her.

He had been involved with installing the swimming pool at Thatch End. Natasha had watched the progress of the pool with a moody kind of interest that lifted her gently to the surface of her boredom then dumped her back into it again, in time with the excavator. Hilary was still finishing the summer term at Chudleigh; she hated it and had already informed her mother she would not be going back there.

Natasha singled Ron out instantly as the only man among the half a dozen or so struggling in the mud who looked in the slightest bit sexy. He had very wide shoulders tapering to narrow hips and a mop of brown curls that reminded her of the American pop singer Hilary idolized.

'Why isn't that man wearing a hard hat?' she asked her father, who had joined her at the window with his morning toast.

'He's the plumber. Just taking measurements. Depths and so on.' Leo Barkwith looked at his daughter. 'Hands off, Nash. Just because you're bored, don't ruin someone else's life.'

She glanced at her father in surprise; he did not usually speak so frankly.

'Well, I am bored,' she said defiantly. 'Right down to my socks. What am I going to do, Daddy? I'm forty-one in December. Is this . . . it?'

'I shouldn't think so. Knowing you.'

She chose to see this as uncaring and squeezed a tear into one eye. 'You don't understand. It's been rough. With Harvey. When I look at you and Mummy—'

'You wanted him. No-one could stop you!'

She wailed, 'I was expecting Hillie! You knew that!'

'I repeat, it was what you wanted. A lever to force Harvey to the altar.'

'I thought I could change him.'

Leo snorted a laugh and unexpectedly she started to weep in earnest, so he put his arm around her and patted her back and told her it would come right in the end. But he had no suggestions to that end and, when he went to the office and her mother was on the telephone, she went and stood by the plumber and asked him what he thought of the pool. In close-up his face was not that attractive; it looked as if it had been modelled in plasticine by an eight-year-old. But it was mobile and not boring. He told her some of the technicalities of installing a pool; he spoke of drainage and filters and heating and pumps. He had pale blue eyes and she held his gaze with her dark ones.

It took a week to smuggle him up to her room. And when she called him her 'bit of rough' he did not like it.

'Call me Ron. And I'll call you Tash.'

'You will not! You will call me Mrs Nolan.'

He laughed at that and she liked him. She put her soul into their lovemaking, hoping to feel as she did with Harvey. And Ron got the wrong idea. He thought she was in love with him and eventually asked her if she would 'tie the knot' with him.

Natasha was basically a kind person, especially when it did her no harm, so she did not let him see that the idea of being married to a plumber was laughable. She kissed him and said huskily, 'Just because my marriage is in ruins doesn't mean I'd break up yours, Ron.'

He was surprised. 'I en't married, Natashy. I 'ad someone once. But it wasn't right and she left.' He propped himself on his elbow and looked down at her. 'If you want, I'll marry you.'

She said, 'Ah . . . Ron. Thanks. But no thanks. Is that all right with you?'

'Well, I'm sorry. Course. You're a smashing woman.'

Woman. Not girl.

She grinned. 'And I'm rich.'

He grinned back. 'There's that too.'

They both laughed and hugged. Like friends. And that's all it had been. A couple of weeks later, Chudleigh's summer term had come to an end and she had agreed to take Hilary back to New York. She half-hoped something would come of it. Ron had made her think that perhaps she and Harvey had had something besides sex. They had laughed too; they had been comfortable together at times. Surely when Harvey found her in the apartment, he wouldn't be able to let her leave again.

That was what Hilary thought too. On the plane she started one of her 'persuasions' as she called them.

'Stay with us, Ma. The apartment is big enough so you won't have to see that much of Harve. We can go shopping every afternoon. The Blums will still be in the city and—'

'And they'll invite you to their place in Maine so you can windsurf with Ruth and Larry and I'll be in the apartment with your father. Thanks a lot. Are you trying your hand at matchmaking?'

Hilary spread her hands. Natasha noticed the purple nail varnish with distaste. 'Listen, Ma. Harve's a shit. We both know that. But . . . he's fun! And the Blums will ask you to Maine too – you can swim every day and lie about and play bridge in the evenings. You'll die if you stay here! I'm not kidding – you'll just curl up and die! You're getting to be boring yourself. If it hadn't been for that workman guy—'

'What the hell d'you mean?'

'Oh, Ma! Nothing gets past Mrs Mayhew.'

'I can assure you, Hillie—'

'Assure your Aunt Fanny, Ma!' Hilary grinned. 'That's an English saying. I don't know who this Aunt Fanny is.'

'It's just disgraceful of Mrs Mayhew to spread that kind of gossip. And to my own baby daughter!'

'I am fifteen, Natasha!' Hilary spoke slowly as if to a child. 'Anyway, I stopped her in her tracks, I can tell you!'

Natasha was intrigued in spite of herself. 'What did you say?'

'I just said – good old Ma, she's found something to pep up this English dulldom.'

'What did *she* say?' Natasha had to smile.

'She said like mother like daughter. Or like daughter like mother. Can't remember now. Doesn't matter. Listen, Ma, stop changing the subject. Let's go home and stay home. *Please*!'

Natasha shook her head, not so much in negation as in bewilderment. She no longer knew what she wanted, how she felt. And amazingly, at fifteen years old, Hilary seemed to understand. She took her mother's arm and hugged it to her.

'I'll have a word with Harvey. Just give it two or three days.'

Natasha snuffled a laugh, trying to imagine this kind of conversation between herself and her mother twenty-five years a go. Or even now.

'OK,' she said weakly.

It hadn't worked simply because Harvey had moved out of the apartment. Mrs Riley, the housekeeper, who did not believe in beating about the bush, informed them that Mr Nolan and his secretary, Miss Pressburger, could be contacted at this number. Natasha and Hilary looked at the series of digits glumly. They both knew the number well; it belonged to the New York apartment of the Blums. So the Blums had nailed their flag to Harvey's mast; they had even accepted Mary Pressburger.

'You went too far this time, Ma,' Hilary said gloomily. 'I might be able to persuade them to invite you to Maine but it sounds as if they're on Harve's side.'

'Don't bother,' Natasha said, gathering the remnants of her pride. 'I never went for Lew Blum. He was always trying to get me into the kitchen.'

'Great. So Mabs will be delighted with Mary Pressburger Not Lew's type.' Hilary screwed up the paper with the Blums' number written on it in her father's handwriting and threw it at the brass coal scuttle which was their waste-paper basket. It missed. 'Oh . . . shit,' she said. Natasha did not reprimand her. She could almost smell her bridges burning inexorably and knew she would have to go back to England and Nortons Heath and Thatch End and . . . Mrs Mayhew.

She said, 'Don't worry about it, honey. I'd have gone back anyway.'

'OK.' Hilary went to one of the windows. The apartment was high enough for her to be able to see along the spine of Manhattan to Battery Point. She thought of the view from her dormitory at Chudleigh. Green. Warwickshire was so green. The leafy lanes of Warwickshire . . .

She said abruptly, 'It must have been when you burned his suits. He could take everything else. But his suits . . .'

Natasha could feel tears in her throat. She said, 'I shall miss you. I hope you have a wonderful time. Larry Blum. Be careful of him. You're only fifteen.'

'It's OK, Ma. Ruth wouldn't let anything or anyone get to her twin brother. They're practically incestuous.'

'What do you know about incest, for God's sake?'

'It's in the Bible.'

'Oh well. In this case I'm thankful for it.'

Hilary laughed suddenly. 'Oh Ma. You're great. Really. Don't let them make you boring, will you?'

'Honey, has it occurred to you that I *am* boring? Underneath it all, I am . . . boring.'

'Don't you believe it! You had me, remember. I'm not going to let you get boring. Not ever.'

Natasha joined her at the window and they stared together. She said in a low voice, 'You're not coming back, are you? I can tell your headmistress that you're not coming back.'

And suddenly fifteen-year-old Hilary was five again and bewildered. 'Ma, I don't know! This is home – this is where I belong – where you belong too. And I love Pop – I can't help it! I know he's terrible and when he's trying to make out like he does – he's so embarrassing! But I still love him. Harvey the Horrible, Ruth calls him, but she still blushes when he looks at her. And d'you know . . . sometimes . . . so do I! Is there something wrong with me, Ma? Am I queer or something?'

Natasha laughed for the first time since Mrs Riley had given her the piece of paper.

'Dear Hillie!' She held out her arms and Hilary rushed into them and sobbed loudly. 'Of course you love him, and of course you're not queer! You're absolutely wonderful because you see all his faults and you still love him – dammit, you *understand* the, the—'

Hilary sobbed, 'The son of a bitch.'

Natasha laughed again. 'Quite,' she agreed in her most English voice. 'And I want all your options to stay open. OK? I won't say anything to Miss Carthew at school. But if you want to stay here, then I shall be happy about that too. OK? I mean it, Hillie. I don't want you blaming me for anything. I want you to be happy in your own way. And if that means—'

'I know, I know. Don't say it again, Ma. Please. I know what you mean and I love you for it, but I can't bear it either.' She straightened, scrubbed her eyes with her knuckles and took a proffered Kleenex to deal with her nose. Then she grinned. 'It's awful being a half-breed, you know. Half American, half English. When I'm looking at the leafy lanes, I think of the

Empire State. And when I look at that,' she turned and glanced out of the window again and her young mouth shook. 'I think of Nortons Heath. Can you do anything about that, Ma?'

Natasha said quietly, 'Not a thing. Except to remind you that your father is very rich and you will be able to see those leafy lanes whenever you wish. Money is . . . so useful.'

'Is that why you went for Harve in the first place?' Hilary asked, her voice even quieter than her mother's.

'I didn't know he was rich. But I knew he was powerful. More powerful than I was. That was why I . . . married him.'

Hilary laughed suddenly, and the tension was gone. She turned and danced across the room. She was so beautiful: rich brown hair and eyes, legs that 'went on for ever' as Harvey used to say. Yes, she was like her mother.

She said gaily, 'You liar! You married Harve because he made you pregnant! And back then, it wasn't so good being a single mother. Wow . . .' she paused by the door. 'I could have been illegitimate. Now that would have been fun!' She grinned across the room. 'I'm going for a glass of milk. What do you want?'

'Tea.' Natasha said, and then sat down suddenly. Hilary thought she was being outrageous and funny. But her words hurt. Natasha did not know why, but they hurt. She had wondered so often – in fact every time she and Harvey had one of their monumental rows about his latest bimbo – whether she would have been just another bimbo if Hilary hadn't been conceived. And yet . . . and yet . . . he had been so delighted when she told him. They had been on the peak of the Malvern Hills . . . quite alone except for a party of hikers making their way back down to Great Malvern and a civilized tea in the Elgar Tea Rooms. His face had broken open somehow so that it was askew. He had breathed, 'Nash . . . are you sure?' and when she nodded he had cupped her face in his big, warm hands and said, 'This is it, honey. This is what we've been waiting for. This makes it . . . real.' And she had felt herself turning to water and had whispered, 'Oh Harvey . . .' Then he had kissed her so tenderly. Then he had turned and yelled down at the knapsacks of the hikers, 'Hey! You down there! Can you hear me! We're having a baby! We . . . are . . . having . . .

a baby! Our union is bearing fruit just like it's supposed to do! Can you hear me?' And she had collapsed laughing and put her fingers over his mouth and he had bitten them and they had clutched each other and sat down together on the scoured hillside. It had been a moment to remember. But, of course, it had gone. Sixteen years before. Like everything that had already happened, it was lost.

She, too, felt lost. She came home and everything was as it had been before. Her mother was on a dozen committees and in between her good works she played tennis and bridge. Natasha also played tennis and bridge in the States and could have gone with her mother and been welcomed. But somehow she couldn't. Whatever she did she would be odd man out. So she did nothing and was even more odd man out. There was no Ron any more and her friends from school had all married and scattered and Hillie was in America with Harvey and Mary Pressburger and the bloody Blums. And Larry Blum would find a way to get away from Ruth and he would seduce Hillie and . . . the whole damned cycle would start again, only worse.

Until her mother suggested the reunion, she had felt like someone in space, whirling around the cosmos without meaning, without purpose. She forced herself to recall the pleasure of hearing Pru's voice, of seeing Maisie and knowing that Maisie held nothing against her. Of seeing Rachel this morning.

Natasha turned her head and opened an eye to see whether Rachel was awake. A gentle snore came from the other deckchair and she wondered whether she too had been snoring. And then there was a crunch on the gravel drive and she turned the other way to see who was coming. And recognized Edward Davenport. As she said later to Rachel, 'There's only one word to describe his condition and that is *fulminating*! He managed to keep a lid on his fury but you could practically hear it bubbling away underneath what he was saying!'

And Rachel, with more perception than Natasha had given her credit for, replied, 'You could smell it too. Brimstone!'

Seven

That Friday lunchtime when Maisie had told him that she would never leave him, Edward had believed her implicitly. For many years now he had known she would not; the time for parting had gone. It could possibly have happened back in 1965 if she hadn't told him the truth – the truth about Tom. But she had bared her soul and asked – not for forgiveness, but for justice. And he had meted out justice ever since. The first time he punished her he wondered if she might run away; he relished the thought, imagining catching her up at New Street station and leading her very gently to the car. Their reconciliations were always satisfyingly emotional and if she ran away sometimes they could be even better. But she never did. She had nowhere to go of course; her foster home had long disappeared with slum clearance and she never wanted to see her foster parents again. Then there were the children. She adored Mark and Jess. And then there was Tom. Once Tom was born, that was it. He made assurance doubly sure by making her pregnant twice more. But really there had been no need. Her devotion was absolute.

He did not feel the need to punish her so often once she had had the hysterectomy. For one thing she had been so frail and sickly then that he might have really hurt her, and that would have meant hospital and Nosey Parker social workers and heaven knew what. Besides, half the joy of punishing her had been the victor's lovemaking afterwards. And there was no point in that any more: she was, to all intents and purposes, barren. Besides, Mrs Donald was well-established by then. There had been that business when she stood between him and Maisie and came out of it with a black eye. Maisie had been terrified that she would leave; even create a fuss.

He had not worried at all; he had seen the look on her face as she turned it towards him. She had enjoyed it.

But that was a relationship completely separate from him and Maisie. Maisie still belonged to him, her love for him was more than anyone could begin to imagine, he could not imagine it himself. It wasn't slavery by any means; it was more a kind of enormous loyalty. She was true to him; she would always be true to him. He assumed it was because he had given her everything she valued most and she could not live without him.

So when she simply disappeared that Friday evening, he could not make any sense of it at all. He had long ago stopped checking to see if she was packing a bag; but she must have done because Mrs Donald looked in her wardrobe and she had taken skirts and blouses and shoes besides a basic change of underwear. She must also have called a taxi at some time because she could not have carried that kind of luggage to a bus stop. By this time the boys were in bed and he woke them both to question them angrily. All they knew was that Mum had phoned Jess and she was coming home tomorrow. And then Mum had phoned Tom at school, but they did not know what she said to him. She had popped in to say goodnight to them . . . yes, she had been a bit odd because she had kissed them both and told them she would see them soon.

'Did she say tomorrow?' Edward had them both standing before him, tousled hair and pyjamas, the picture of bewilderment. They glanced at each other. He seized the fronts of their jackets and shook them vigorously. 'Come on – what did she say? Exactly now!'

Ian starting hiccoughing which he always did when he was nervous. In this case, probably when he was about to lie. Edward shook him again. Mrs Donald said smoothly, 'It's all right, Ian. We think Mummy must have gone to stay with her friend Natasha Barkwith, but we don't want to worry them with a phone call this late. She probably left a note but we can't find it. Did she leave a message with you?'

'No,' Ian hiccoughed. Simon said quickly, 'It's just that, I don't think she *did* say she'd see us tomorrow. I think she just said, "I'll see you soon." Yes, that is what she said. It was all a bit weird. She said she'd loved the cricket match and she'd see us soon. And she kissed us.' He made a face. Ian said, 'She always gives us a kiss. But she sort of drops it on us. Not like this.'

Edward felt at a complete loss. Ian was no longer hiccoughing; the boys were not lying. He released them and straightened.

Mrs Donald took over again. 'She's obviouly gone to the Barkwiths. We shall find a note, or she'll phone.' She glanced at Edward. 'Back to bed, Mr Davenport?'

'Er . . . yes. Of course.' Edward left the bedroom without saying goodnight and waited on the landing. He heard Mrs Donald tucking the boys back in and saying something reassuring. He knew that Maisie had not left a note. She was making some kind of protest initiated by that oversexed hussy Natasha Barkwith. A feminist if ever he saw one.

Mrs Donald came out of the boys' room and the two of them went downstairs and into the sitting room. She crossed straight to the new cocktail cabinet, poured him a whisky which he drank in one gulp.

'I'm not going to phone anywhere tonight,' he said grimly. 'Let her stew. If she's trying to frighten me, she has failed.'

'She'll be home tomorrow,' Mrs Donald said confidently. 'She couldn't live without you. You know that.'

He nodded. It was true. Without him and what he had given her, she had no identity. He followed Mrs Donald to her room and began to undress. There was, after all, one thing he had not given her, yet was very much part of her. He paused in taking off a sock. He wished he knew what Maisie had said to Tom on the telephone that evening.

She did not come back the next day; but the rest of the family did and the house was so full of bags and parcels and cases and children he had no time to follow a train of thought, let alone any investigations.

Tom arrived first in a taxi. Simon and Ian greeted him vociferously and helped him unload his stuff in the big bedroom which entailed a great deal of throwing of clothes and shoes and pillows. And shouting. Tom was the only child to inherit Maisie's hair, and his blond curls made him look angelic which he certainly was not. But compared to Ian's and Simon's wild hysteria he seemed a little subdued this time. And not a bit surprised when Edward interrupted the pillow fight to say, 'Can I have a word, Tom? In my study.'

Edward knew he must be careful. Maisie must have told Tom something because the boy was not in the least surprised by her absence. But would she have been indiscreet enough to swear him to secrecy? The Maisie Edward knew certainly would not; her first loyalty was always, unswervingly, to her husband. But this vanishing act made him wonder if he was dealing with a new Maisie.

He said, 'Everything OK at school, Tom?' He opened a drawer and took out a packet of cigarettes. He lit one and handed the packet to Tom. The boy shook his head but only after a second's hesitation. Edward thought grimly: so he's smoking at school, is he?

Tom said, 'Actually, Mum said something about school.'

'What, last night when she phoned you?' Edward watched the young face through his cigarette smoke.

'No. Just after half-term.' Tom shrugged. 'I suppose I worried her . . . I was homesick. You know. She said she wondered about me going to St Martin's with Si and Ian. She was going to talk to you about it.'

He thought back and realized that she had in fact dropped endless hints about Tom moving to a day school. It was her way of 'talking' to him.

He said, 'It's not such a good school as Luddington. You still want to follow in Mark's footsteps, don't you?'

'Oh yes.' Tom grinned. 'Mum said he'd be home today. That will be great!'

Edward inhaled sharply. So that was what she had said. But how on earth had she explained her disappearance?

'Yes. We shall be a houseful. As usual. Perhaps that was why your mother decided to take a little break!' He rolled his eyes humorously and Tom continued to grin happily.

'Well, Dad . . . you've always gone off on holiday during the summer vac! I suppose Mum thought it was her turn!'

Edward stubbed his cigarette out on the ashtray and kept both hands on the desk. He had never beaten Tom or even given him a quick clout like he had the other boys.

'Quite,' he said, forcing himself to smile. 'Quite. Pity she couldn't hang on just to see you though, old man. I'm sorry about that.'

Tom nodded. 'I know. But it was a sort of emergency.'

'Yes. I suppose so.'

Edward frowned, not knowing where to go next, and Tom, misunderstanding, said quickly, 'Don't worry, Dad. I think Mum said Aunt Edie had a fall or something.'

'Edie? Edith Manners? She died – she's dead for God's sake!'

'Sorry. I meant the other one.'

Edward forced a laugh. 'I thought you must. It was Evelyn Hazell she was worried about.'

'That's right.' Tom saw Simon through the study window. He was holding a football. 'She didn't want you to worry as well – and you knew all the time!'

Edward managed another laugh. 'There's no secrets between your mother and me,' he said.

Tom half turned for the door and then paused. 'Yes. That's true, isn't it? Some of the blokes at school – their parents are rowing all the time. But you and Mum . . . you're the perfect couple.' He waved to Simon. 'OK if I go now, Dad? Si's waiting for a kickaround.'

'Yes. But watch the state of the grass. It's only in that good condition because we're using sprinklers!'

Edward sat down and turned his chair to watch the boys rampaging across the pristine lawn. The perfect couple. Tom was right; that's what he and Maisie were.

He smiled. She was at Evelyn's. Probably sleeping very uncomfortably on the sofa. He would let her stay there till Monday. Part of her punishment.

Jess and Mark arrived in Mark's battered old car later that evening. Jess, the only girl in the family, kissed her father's cheek with what Edward immediately divined as some reserve. He didn't care. Whatever Maisie had said to Jess, it didn't matter. He was ebullient with good spirits, anticipating Maisie's voluntary return the next day with her tail well and truly between her legs. A holiday forsooth! At Evelyn Hazell's ghastly little 'sheltered bungalow' forsooth! He recalled – ages ago – Maisie telling him about the village green and some plastic ducks. He hadn't laughed. 'My God, it takes me back to the old days – the bad old days, Maisie. How can you be so flippant?' Incredibly, she had smiled and said, 'Oh come on, Ted. They weren't that bad, were they? Remember making newspaper boats and floating them on the canal? Mr Lavington hasn't grown up in some ways. He was sending up that awful warden woman, but there was part of him that would have loved her to sink a little pond right in the middle of the green so that he could float his ducks!' He'd said, 'You *must* be getting old if you're remembering the good bits! What about your brother? What about all that?' He'd shut her up well and truly then. Poisoned Evelyn Hazell's little complex for her, too. She'd be hating every minute of her so-called holiday!

Jess said, 'You're in a good mood, Dad! I thought you'd be as miserable as sin with Mum taking a break and me in charge of the household!'

'I've got absolute faith in my daughter's capabilities!' Edward sparked a glance at his daughter. She was so like him; she might even know what was going on. He said unguardedly, 'Your mother will be back tomorrow anyway.'

Jess raised her brows. 'Oh will she? That's good. I thought she said she was going off for a week or two. Some old girls' reunion or something.'

Edward felt his eyes open wide and turned immediately to the window. 'Look at those crazy boys – Mark's as bad as Ian! God, how am I going to put up with it!'

Jess said, 'Dad? What's going on? Why is Mum coming home tomorrow? You're not doing your Hitler act again, are you?'

'What the hell d'you mean by that?' He turned on her, furiously. 'My relationship with your mother – hers with me too – is none of your bloody business! And don't you forget it!'

She stared at him, well used to his temper flares, but sifting this one carefully for clues. She said slowly, 'Has she left you? My God, she has, hasn't she? What have you done, Dad?'

He said, 'Your mother has not . . . "left me" . . . as you so dramatically put it, Jess! She's gone to see Evelyn Hazell – apparently there's a small crisis there. I think she will come home tomorrow. That is all.'

Jess said slowly, 'Right. That is all then. Right. I'd better go and see Mrs Donald, hadn't I? Sort out some menus. Things like that.'

He knew she was being sarcastic. He knew she was unconvinced. But there was nothing he could do.

He said, 'And I'll go and rescue Mark.'

Sunday was a muddle. They had a Sunday lunch but without Maisie to intervene in the bickering, to be overtly interested in what was happening in Edinburgh, to make sure he knew he was in charge of the whole thing, it was hopeless. The boys had their own code; their sentences were never finished, sometimes neither were their words. Edward picked up that 'savvo' they were going to Edgbaston for the 'crick' and Mark was 'shuvving'. Mark left his conversation with Jess long enough to mention that he was taking the boys off for a one-day match in the car after lunch and was that all right? 'Perfectly,' Edward said, grateful for the opportunity to sit silently in the garden and think about Maisie. Mrs Donald stood up to change the plates and her hand touched his. With a sinking heart he knew there would be no thinking time.

Jess said, 'On my last practice, I picked up a terrible bruise on the shin – it was when that cow needed scouring out Stirling way . . . d'you remember?'

Edward said heavily, 'Jess . . . please. We are eating.'

'Sorry, Dad. Didn't think you were listening.' She smiled at him, yesterday's sparky exchange apparently forgotten. But he knew it was not. Jess might not have any facts at her disposal but she had that woman's intuition thing. She did not think her mother would return home that night.

And she didn't.

Edward went into his office on Monday morning very early. The obvious opulence of the new suite above the new factory did not give him his usual pleasure. He remembered Leo Barkwith looking around the completed office floor and smiling as if they were sharing a joke. 'Very over the top, old man,' he had said. 'I suppose the clients like to see your stuff *in situ*.'

Edward hadn't thought of that. Most of the mirrored shelving units, cabinets, computer stations, could in fact be bought from the factory. He had had them installed for his own pleasure. To remind himself constantly of how he had gone up in the world. He had commissioned Leo Barkwith to design the factory for the same reason. He remembered Barkwith's daughter lording it in Markhams way back in the Fifties. Now her father was working for him.

He went through orders and complaints quickly, dictated some letters into the machine and made some phone calls. It was ten-thirty. He left the office and got into his car.

Earlswood was some way out of the city; the drive gave him time to make and discard a dozen plans. In the end he knew he would have to say nothing. In fact he would not have to get out of the car. She would come to him and he would act as if he were picking her up after a weekend with poor little Evelyn. He would be cold and silent during the drive home; he could not begin any kind of punishment while the children were around, but later . . . maybe as late as the autumn . . . And of course she would know it was coming. It would be part of it. The waiting.

He had driven her here before but even so he took a wrong turning in the maze of small estates around the lakes. By the time he drew up, with the green one side and Evelyn's potty little bungalow the other, he was having great difficulty in controlling his temper. It was midday. If they'd gone out for a walk they would be back for lunch. He remembered that Evelyn stuck rigidly to a routine as far as meals were concerned; she had an ulcer or something.

The lace curtain twitched; they were in. He switched off and sat immobile at the wheel, forcing his upper body to relax but tense as a spring from the waist down. Nothing happened. He checked the dashboard clock. Five past twelve. He would wait till ten past then he would leave. Or would he? He no longer knew what to do. By eight minutes past twelve he was shaking. It would serve her right of course if he had a heart attack, but he had no intention of putting himself in her power like that.

He erupted from the car at nine minutes past and almost ran for the front door. It opened before he reached it and Evelyn's body blocked the opening. She was wearing a dun-coloured linen frock and her face and arms seemed the same muddy brown. He thought suddenly of Maisie's daisy frock; and even when she'd been sunbathing her skin was never brown, it was the colour of honey.

Evelyn did not beat about the bush.

'She's not here,' she said in a high, tense voice. 'And I don't like the car parked for so long outside. Please go.'

He was so astonished he stopped in his tracks. Mousy Evelyn was suddenly a lion . . . no, not a lion, a small, tatty but haughty camel.

She began to remove her body from the doorway and close the door. He got his foot inside it just in time. 'I know she's here, Evelyn. I just want to speak to her. That's all. No need to be so protective.' He had to be reasonable, probably everyone in the small circle of sheltered homes was watching him. He said, 'Come on. Be a good girl. I'm her husband and I want to speak to her.'

She did not actually bang the door against his foot, but her body was still in the way. She said with great dignity, 'I am not a girl, Edward, I am a woman of sixty-seven. And I always speak the truth. Maisie is not here.'

'The very fact that you knew I had come for her rather belies that statement, Evelyn.' He pressed close to her and with a small gasp she backed into the narow hall. He raised his voice slightly, 'Maisie, it's me. The children are home and want to see you. Come on – let's get going!'

The silence was thick.

Evelyn turned suddenly and went into the sitting room. He followed closely. She sat down and gripped the arms of her chair.

'Edward . . .' her voice shook ever so slightly. 'I told you I don't lie. I won't lie now. Maisie was here. She's now left. And that is all I can tell you.'

He stared down at her. Her hair was thinning on top and he could see the pink of her scalp. He could crush her head like an eggshell with one blow.

He said harshly, 'Where has she gone now?'

Evelyn looked at the carpet. 'I'm not sure. I don't think she was sure either. Maybe back to one-four-eight. Maybe to other friends.'

He turned and left without another word. She would sit and tremble all on her own for a while, then she would phone Maisie to warn her. That was probably good. Maisie would say to Natasha, 'Oh God, he's coming,' and Natasha would try to talk her into lying low, or facing it out. Maisie could not cope with either of those alternatives; she would either run again or she would go and pack her things and be ready to come home with him.

He was tempted to drive immediately to Thatch End, then decided against it. Time was on his side. He was angry but he was not desperate like Maisie obviously was. Let her go on being desperate. Let her stew as she had stewed since last Friday. If this was some little display of rebellion from her, it had died by now. He tried to tell himself he held all the winning cards; her punishment had actually already started. It was only when he drove through the gate of one-four-eight that it occurred to him the boot was on the other foot. Jess appeared from nowhere and walked alongside the car.

'Any news?' So she was beginning to worry now.

He did not prevaricate. 'She's not at Evelyn's. Probably at the Barkwiths' place. Thatch End.'

He got out of the car and Jess took his arm rallyingly. 'You must stop being so anxious, Dad.' She hugged his arm to her side as if she were comforting him. 'Mum is all right. You don't give her credit for any sense at all. She's having a little break. She doesn't want to tell us where she is – she's giving herself a bit of private life.'

He let himself be led into the house. Lunch was on the

table. Mrs Donald was hovering almost nervously. He could hear Mark from the downstairs bathroom chivvying the boys into washing.

He said, 'What do you mean, private life? We don't have private lives, your mother and me. We're married.'

Jess laughed, drew out his chair and poured him something with ice, pale pink.

'I didn't mean private in that sense. I meant . . . separate. You've got your life at work, Dad. Mum's had her life here and with us kids. Now her friends from way back have suddenly surfaced. She wants to see them. They're hers. Can't you understand that?'

'No. Sorry, Jess, but no, I can't. If she'd talked to me – shared her plans—'

'You would have said no. Other women would argue, even defy you. But not Mum. This is her way of saying a whole heap of things to which you wouldn't listen – you wouldn't even hear.'

Mrs Donald wheeled in a trolley laden with a tureen and soup plates. She began to serve a clear soup. The boys came in and Tom asked Mark about some trip to Bristol.

'Mum said on the phone she'd fix it with you. Did she remember?'

'Yes. She talked to me at mid-term about it. I've got two mates who are getting their field studies done at the veterinary college. We can do the rounds with them if you like.' He glanced at Ian and Simon. 'Sorry, not you two.' He ignored the yells of protest and turned his gaze on Jess. 'I suppose not you either, sis. With Mum away.'

She said, 'I don't see why not. You can cope, can't you, Dad? Si and Ian need a bit of chauffeuring around, that's all.'

Edward felt something like panic. It was as if there was some conspiracy, first of all to make him feel an outsider in his own family and then to desert him.

He said, 'I've been looking after the little perishers for the past fourteen years for goodness' sake.'

They all laughed at that and he almost justified himself – after all it wasn't all Maisie's doing by any means, she couldn't drive and he'd taken the boys to cubs and football matches and judo classes . . . it was one of the reasons he'd wanted them all to go to boarding school. He managed to smile grimly and say nothing. But a new anger was growing inside him, an anger compounded by . . . was it fear? And he realized then that Maisie might well be desperate; Maisie might well feel punished by his absence. But he was desperate too. And it was possible, just possible, that he was frightened.

On the drive down the A38 to Northfield and then the Heaths, and finally Nortons Heath, he deliberately whipped his anger up to cover any signs of desperation or fear. In his head he called her the kind of names his father had called his mother: filthy degrading names that had entered his consciousness at a very early age and coloured his perception of women ever since. He remembered what she had told him about her foster home, her foster father, her brother; he snarled aloud through the windscreen, 'Christ, she probably asked for it!' And he wished that her confidence, which had seemed so touching and trustful at the time, had not drawn him to tell her about his own father. He certainly had not asked for that. But she probably thought they were similar experiences. Hadn't she said once that they were welded together by their terrible childhoods? Yes, it was when she told him about Tom McEvoy . . . she had tried to explain that it had been a moment of madness. 'He could never understand me, Ted. Not like you. Everything has been easy for him – his life has been carefree and . . . and sunny. He would never be able to understand the kind of things we've known.'

And all the time they had shared nothing; not really. Because she had asked for it, and he had not.

He drew into Thatch End and left his car beneath one of the willows lining the drive. It was three-thirty. Leo Barkwith would be at his office and with a bit of luck Mary Barkwith would be playing tennis or bridge or whatever she did on Monday afternoons. He rang the bell; there was no answer. He realized suddenly he had heartburn; his mouth filled with bile and he fumbled for a handkerchief and stood for a moment with it pressed to his lips, cursing the watery soup and the pink iced drink Jess had served two hours before. And then he walked around the side of the house and there, sitting in deckchairs under yet another of the weeping willows, were two female figures. Natasha's dark hair was spread all over the place and her suntop and shorts seemed to reveal more than they covered. The other girl was asleep. She was certainly fair, but . . . he blinked hard. It was not Maisie. It was that wretched woman who had hit the headlines when she ousted her boss's wife and married him herself. He had no time for women like that. He strode towards the chairs.

Eight

Natasha left a note for her parents. 'Ray and I have gone to see Evelyn Hazell. Probably take her out for a meal. See you later. Love, Nash. By the way, I've stopped being bored.'

Rachel still had her green sports car and they took it in preference to Nash's runabout because Rachel was more used to driving on the left-hand side of the road. Both women were soberly dressed in linen suits and blouses, in deference to what they imagined Evelyn would approve of.

'After all, the old girl must be nearly seventy now,' Natasha said as the wind backcombed her hair into an unruly cloud. 'I wonder what it's like to be old?'

Rachel, concentrating on negotiating what amounted to rush-hour traffic, spoke tersely. 'We thought forty was ancient when we were at Markhams, and we're over that now.'

'I feel exactly the same now as I did then.' Natasha wriggled her narrow skirt over her hips and wondered whether she had put on weight since she'd bought it. 'Well . . . in some ways,' she amended.

'I don't.' Rachel squinted in the mirror but not at her reflection. She knew she had changed physically, she took that for granted. 'I used to feel . . . kind of smug then. I knew Eric could fix anything. I just waited for him to do it. I don't feel that any more.'

'Why?' Natasha asked unguardedly.

'Because he's in prison,' Rachel said shortly. 'I thought you knew. It was why Denise killed herself.'

Natasha bit her lip, remembering various snippets relayed by her mother. 'Sorry. I had no idea. Was it in the papers? I was in the States of course.'

'Duncan managed to keep it out of the papers. It wouldn't

have done him any good. I thought he might get rid of me.' She changed lanes adroitly and leaned back. 'That was why . . . it's no excuse of course . . . but that was when I invented the baby.'

'Ah. I see.' Natasha tasted her own blood on her bottom lip. 'I'm sorry, Ray. I suppose . . . in a way . . . I had it easy.'

Rachel shrugged. 'Depends where you're standing, doesn't it? You're a bit on your own now and I'm not. And . . . well, I have got what I wanted. Unless it's disappearing right now while we're talking.' She turned and grinned suddenly. 'Anyway, neither of us have had to contend with Edward Davenport for twenty years, have we? Poor old Maisie!'

Natasha stopped worrying her lip and wondering if things would have been different had she not burned Harvey's clothes; she grinned too. 'He really was dreadful, wasn't he? I thought we managed rather well. When you got up and offered him your chair and a drink of water, I thought he might kill you!'

Rachel shrugged. 'Stupid man. I've seen voters like that. Apoplectic because they think the country's going to the dogs. They stop hearing anything but their own voices.'

'I wondered whether he hit Maisie.' Natasha had another try at anchoring her skirt. 'If she has left him, then good luck to her. But if she's not with Evelyn and she's not with us, where the hell can she be? She doesn't know anyone else.'

Rachel said, 'She could have phoned Pru. She could have gone to the commune. Or met Pru and gone straight to the Malvern house.'

'We'll see what Evelyn says. And then we might have to do some more sleuthing.'

Both women giggled like schoolgirls. Even Rachel's colour was better.

Evelyn had managed to control her trembling and had got herself a sandwich for lunch. She would normally have spent an hour in her pristine garden, but because of Edward Davenport she had gone upstairs to lie down. She was delighted to see the girls in one way; not in another. She only had to look at Natasha to see that her presence meant some kind of disruption, even her hair seemed intent on escaping her scalp. And Rachel . . . she had not known what to make of Rachel at Markhams: the enigma had deepened as time went by and she had read pieces from the newspapers and Edith had passed on bits of gossip.

But . . . they were the same girls who had brightened the darkness of Markhams, who had seemed to herald the future, who had made her scramble through thickets of fern up on the Lickey Hills and who . . . when all was said and done, had made her laugh.

She laughed now as Rachel kissed her demurely and Nash hugged her and snuffled into her neck and told her that retirement suited her.

'Don't give me that!' she said, leading them into the sitting room where so recently Edward had towered above her as she sat in the armchair. 'I've just this minute got off the bed so I'm tousled and dishevelled! Sit down and say you forgive me.'

The two women sat, Rachel in the other armchair, Natasha on the rug. 'What d'you mean, forgive you?' Natasha was still grinning happily. She was unexpectedly delighted to see dear, small, frumpish Evelyn who now seemed to incorporate in her body the cheeky sparrow who had been Edith.

'Well . . . lumbering you with Edward Davenport! I take it that's why you're here?' Evelyn gripped the arms of her chair as she had before. 'I had to say something. I had to get rid of him.' She put her hands in her lap and gripped them with determination. 'I tried to phone you – just to warn you he might appear. But there was no answer.'

Rachel said regretfully, 'We were in the garden. Asleep. It didn't matter, did it, Nash?'

'She—' Natasha inclined her head at Rachel. 'She dealt with him. I can see why she's the power behind the throne, Evie. D'you remember she used to tell us she wanted to be the power behind the throne?'

Evelyn, who knew she was being soothingly indulged, nodded happily.

Natasha did an imitation of Rachel. 'Are you under the impression you are dealing with someone who cares about your domestic problems, Mr Davenport? Because if so, I suggest you go away and think again. If Maisie were here spending the afternoon with us, you would see her. You would probably see another chair, another cup and saucer. She is not here and there are only two chairs and two cups and saucers. Contrary to your last foolish accusation, we have nothing to hide.'

Evelyn clapped her hands delightedly. Rachel said tersely, 'The man is an idiot.'

Evelyn stopped laughing. 'He's not that, Rachel,' she said slowly. 'He is behaving like one perhaps, at present. Because he is so worried about Maisie. But . . . he is not an idiot. When he calms down he will be back.'

Nash said, 'And you're here on your own and scared of him.' She tried to cross her legs, gave an exclamation of disgust at the constricting skirt and pushed it up to her thighs. 'Right. You're coming back with us.'

'No, I couldn't possibly . . .' Evelyn looked away from the expanse of bare leg. 'Your dear mother must have a limit to her hospitality.'

'Rubbish. She'll love seeing you. Daddy will too. And I think we can use the pool tomorrow. Won't that be fun?'

Evelyn thought of last Friday's hair-do. It had already taken rather a beating. Anyway she hadn't swum for years.

Rachel said, 'I think Evelyn's got something, Nash. After all, Maisie's horrible husband will go to Thatch End when he discovers Evelyn's flown the nest. If he finds her there he'll try to bully her and there will be a row . . . not nice for your parents.'

Natasha was silent. Rachel's words made her think of Hillie's name for her father: Horrible Harvey. Certainly Edward Davenport was a horrible husband. Harvey was not horrible in that way. She nibbled her lip again.

Rachel went on, 'Listen, Evelyn, how long does Maisie intend to stay away – did she tell you?'

Evelyn knitted her fingers together. 'She's left him – she's left Edward. And she's got no money. It's . . . difficult.'

'She hasn't left him for good, surely?'

'Oh yes. I think so.'

'Did you try and persuade her to go back to him?'

'Oh no.'

'Well, when we meet up, I shall. It's ridiculous. She's given him twenty years of her life – five children – she won't have a thing, he'll make sure of that. I know a vindictive character when I see one, and he's vindictive!'

Evelyn unlaced two of her fingers. 'She won't listen to you.'

'She did before. I persuaded her to go back to him before.'

Natasha cleared her throat. 'Actually, Ray, it was me who did that.'

'I doubt it. I'm more persuasive than you, Nash.'

Natasha said in a low voice, 'I didn't actually talk much. I told her that Tom McEvoy would sleep with anyone and I proved it.'

'What?' Rachel yelped. 'My God, Nash! You'd got a newborn child – you'd come home to have Hilary – that's why we were all at Thatch End!'

'Hillie was a month old.' Nash dabbed at her lip with a scrap of handkerchief. 'Harvey was . . . living it up back home. I felt I was killing two birds with one stone.' She straightened her legs and pulled down the skirt. 'I'm ashamed – I've always been ashamed of what I did. Maisie appeared to have forgotten all about it when I called on her last Friday. She was so . . . sweet.' She sighed. 'I won't be trying to persuade her to go back to Ted Davenport. I think she should have left him years ago. McEvoy might have been faithful if she'd actually gone off with him. For a time.'

Unexpectedly Evelyn leaned forward and put her hand over Natasha's. She said, 'Maisie would have gone back home anyway, Nash. Nothing to do with you. We talked and talked that night. There were the children, remember. But even more than them . . . she felt this enormous sense of loyalty and duty to her husband. Nothing would have made her leave him. Until now.' Evelyn's colour became hectic. She said, 'I can't tell you everything. But . . . last Friday . . . when she went to get the tea, Nash, she saw something. The housekeeper and Edward were . . . I was going to say, making love. But it was nothing to do with love. It involved . . . things.'

Rachel was wide-eyed. Natasha put her free hand over Evelyn's. 'It's all right, my dear. I've wondered for ages, if he was . . . I think he must be a sadomasochist.' She glanced at Rachel. 'We won't be talking her into going back to him. Hey, Rachel?'

Rachel breathed, 'Oh my God . . .'

Natasha scrambled to her knees, still clasping Evelyn's hand between hers. She leaned into Evelyn's lap.

'Listen, honey. You can't stay here if he's going to come back. He might hit you. Anything. You must come back to Thatch End with us. I'll tell Daddy about it and he'll know what to do.'

Rachel levered herself upright and went to the window as if trying to escape her own thoughts. 'I've got a better idea.' She put her hands on the window ledge with great care; it was full of china ladies. 'We go to Malvern. Immediately. Ring Pru, tell her the situation and drive up tonight.'

'Great!' Natasha shook Evelyn's hand gently. 'That's the answer, honey! We begin our reunion a little earlier than planned! How about it?'

But Evelyn was already shaking her head. 'Maisie is coming back here in three weeks. We're sharing a taxi to New Street. Catching the train. Like we used to.'

Rachel moved one of the china ladies closer to another. 'You know where she is, don't you?'

'Of course. I couldn't have let her go without knowing. She's gone to her brother's.'

Natasha frowned, remembering something from the past, not able to capture it.

'Yes. There was a brother, wasn't there? But she never saw him. Where does he live, Evelyn?'

'I was looking up his name in the directory. And she said it was all right, she knew where he was and she would go there.'

'She didn't phone him?'

'No. We were going to phone then she said she'd just turn up and it would be all right.'

There was a small silence in the room. Then Natasha released Evelyn's hands and stood up. 'Nothing to stop us phoning and leaving a message. We can pick her up tomorrow. OK?'

'Well . . . I don't see why not.' Evelyn sounded doubtful. 'She needed time to think, you see. And she's had the weekend and most of today. Yes. She'll probably be glad to get away.' She rubbed at her knuckles. 'The phone and the directory are in the hall, Nash.'

The two of them went through the book and found columns of Jenkins. Rachel stayed by the window. 'I've got a feeling about this,' she said. 'There's something wrong. She wouldn't have gone off into the blue without phoning first.'

Evelyn said determinedly, 'It was Roland. I remember that. R for Roland.'

Natasha scribbled down some numbers and went out into the hall. They heard her telephoning. 'Mr Jenkins? I wonder if your sister, Maisie, is around? Sorry, I must have the wrong number.' It happened three times, then four. Natasha called out, 'Last one! Cross your fingers. It's bound to be this one!'

But it wasn't. She came slowly back into the sitting room. 'Is there someone who would give her a message when she calls for you?'

Evelyn said, 'She's not going to call for me. Is she? She's gone. She's disappeared.'

Natsha said, 'Oh now, come on, Evelyn. People don't disappear. Especially women like Maisie who have five children!'

Rachel said, 'Who's that funny old duffer out there? He seems to be putting some plastic ducks on the grass. In a row. He must be bonkers!'

Evelyn almost leapt to the window. It was, of course, Mr Lavington.

'Oh my God,' she wailed. 'If the warden sees him she'll have him out of his bungalow before you can say knife. She doesn't like him anyway and this will be the perfect excuse.' She turned to the two women. 'It's a joke, you see. The warden thought that bit of grass looked like a village green which was a bit silly, so Mr Lavington borrowed the ducks from his granddaughter and every now and then he puts them in a ring – as if there's a village pond. It infuriates the warden. She thinks he's getting at her. Which he is. She'll phone the housing association and suggest he's not fit to live alone.'

Natasha wondered how she had the effrontery to feel bored, ever. She said, 'May I ask him in, Evie? For a coffee or something.'

Rachel said, 'If the Libs get in, you know, that sort of thing couldn't happen. There has to be decent security of tenure in these places otherwise the whole concept becomes meaningless.'

Evelyn said, 'I've got some sherry in the sideboard.' Her eyes were suddenly bright and there was colour in her face. 'Tell him to bring his ducks with him, Nash.'

Mr Lavington thoroughly enjoyed the sherry and the company of the three women. He sat back in Evelyn's armchair and told them his latest plan for making the place look as if people lived there as well as died there.

'I've gone over her head . . .' he was referring to the warden, a lady he did not like apparently. 'By the biggest stroke of luck I've had since I backed Red Rum, it turns out my son drinks with one of the directors of the housing association.' He grinned. 'It's not much of a lever but it's enough. Young Sam, my son, is a good sort. Doesn't come to see me often so he's got a bit of a conscience about me. And he likes his pint. He agreed with me entirely about the pub.'

'Pub?' Evelyn asked faintly.

'A village pub. We've got a green and the church isn't far away, but we haven't got a village pub.' He grinned at Evelyn. 'Don't worry, lass. Not the sort of place where people come out rolling drunk night after night. Think of it as a meeting place. We should have a residents' association – but where should we meet? A little pub is what we need. Skittle alley at the back, p'raps.'

'She won't allow it,' Evelyn said, her voice a thread.

'Then she must resign and make way for someone who doesn't treat us like cattle.' Mr Lavington blew out his cheeks.

'My God, if she could give us all a pill to make us sleep till we die, it would suit her down to the socks! She doesn't see us as people. She sees us as numbers, units, sheep—'

'I think it's a great idea,' Nash put in from the garden chair she had placed carefully in the grate because there was no room anywhere else. 'There could be pub meals too – then if you're not up to cooking—'

Rachel intoned, 'This sort of situation simply would not arise under the Liberals.'

Evelyn said doubtfully, 'But the warden . . . perhaps she's relying on her free bungalow . . . we don't know her circumstances or anything about her.'

Mr Lavington leaned forward and clapped his large hand on Evelyn's knee. She jumped. 'That's the reason for the ducks!' he said happily. 'Now do you understand?'

'No,' she admitted.

He spread his hands with a kind of innocence. 'I'm wearing her down, Miss Hazell. I'm a thorn in her side. She's tried to get rid of me – I expect you knew that – and she can't. I'm not certifiable yet by any means. By the end of the summer, if my son's friend puts it to her tactfully, she will see that a pub will, in fact, get rid of me.' He leaned back again and looked around beatifically. 'I like my pint.'

Natasha looked at Evelyn. 'And if he's having his pint, he's safely tucked up somewhere. He's not a loose cannon.' She smiled encouragingly. 'It's rather a splendid idea, don't you think, Evie? You could go over once or twice a week and have a gin and tonic with him. You used to like a g and t after our rambles. Didn't you?'

'Oh, Nash . . .' but Evelyn was smiling tremulously.

Rachel actually laughed. 'I think you'd make a jolly good politician, Mr Lavington! Any chance of recruiting you to the Liberal Party?'

'No fear. I've been Labour all my life and that's how I'll leave it!' Mr Lavington said stoutly.

Natasha and Evelyn laughed and found they could not stop. Mr Lavington sat back, pleased with his social success. Rachel smiled tightly, shaking her head. And then the phone rang and everything stopped.

'It's him,' Evelyn whispered. 'Oh my God . . .'

Rachel said, 'I'll deal with him.' She began to ease herself between the garden chair and Mr Lavington.

Natasha hissed, 'Try to make certain he doesn't come bothering Evelyn again, tell him my father will talk to the police—'

'Don't worry.' Rachel inched out of the room and they heard her pick up the phone. Then her voice blossomed. 'Maisie! Is it you? It's Rachel here – Rachel Stayte – Rachel Strang that was! Nash and I are here with Evelyn. We've been so worried . . .' Natasha leaned over and took Evelyn's hands. They smiled at Mr Lavington who was looking extremely intrigued. Rachel's voice rose. 'Listen, Maisie – don't ring off! Evelyn would like a word. We're thinking of going to Malvern early and we'll pick you up and . . .' Another pause. 'Well, all right. If you really think . . . Nash has got the address.' She called back into the sitting room, 'Nash – the address of Pru's house?'

Nash, infected by the obvious urgency of Rachel's voice, shouted, 'Prospect House, Malvern Minor. We can fetch her. Any time.'

Rachel said, 'Did you hear that, Maisie? Repeat it then . . . go on. Yes. OK. Listen, just have a word with the others—' her voice cut off abruptly and then they heard her replace the receiver. She reappeared in the doorway. 'The money must have run out. I could have got her number and phoned back. Obviously her brother isn't on the phone.'

Evelyn said, 'Never mind. At least we know she's with him and she's all right.'

Nash nodded. Mr Lavington said, 'Perhaps I'd better be off. Thoroughly enjoyed talking to you ladies but—'

Nash said slowly, 'I've got an idea. Would you help us, Mr Lavington? You're a born schemer – that's obvious – and we need someone like you.' She gave him one of her full smiles and he smirked back.

'No need to flatter me, lass. I'll help you any way I can. For Miss Hazell's sake.'

Evelyn blushed and put a hand to her hair.

Natasha said, 'It's simple really. Would you change houses with Evelyn? Just for tonight?' She ignored a whimper of protest from Evelyn and swept on. 'We'll tell you all about it. You see we all used to work together. At the jewellers in Corporation Street. And we thought we'd have a reunion this year. One of us has got a house in the Malverns – we used to go there on weekend rambles, you know the kind of thing.' Natasha got to her knees, the better to dramatize the whole story. Her big eyes opened wide then narrowed to slits, then became utterly reasonable as she spoke of Maisie's bid for freedom. 'What we'd like to do really is to find her and keep her with us – just guard her from this awful husband. But she's chosen to go to her brother's – we've never met him. In fact it's all rather mysterious—'

'The whole thing sounds a mystery to me, lass. You say this friend of yours, Maisie, she's been ill-treated? There are places for battered wives, you know.'

'She won't admit she's been battered.' Rachel took over. 'She's got this terrific loyalty to her husband.'

'Very commendable. Pity more of you young women haven't got it.' Mr Lavington looked down to where his collection of plastic ducks lined the fireplace. 'Yes. Well. I don't know about all this marital strife. I was always taught to keep out of domestic quarrels. But if this blighter is worrying Miss Hazell, then of course I'm only too glad to be here. Reception committee like.' He leaned forward. 'What d'you say to all this, Miss Hazell?'

She swallowed. 'It's an imposition, Mr Lavington. But it would solve our problem. I can go and stay with Natasha and Rachel, but if he comes looking for me there, there will be a fuss and it seems unfair on Natasha's parents to inflict . . . This would solve the problem very well. If you didn't mind.'

'If there's any trouble from him, he'll get as good as he gives,' Mr Lavington rumbled aggressively.

'We don't want trouble though.' Evelyn clutched at his gnarled fingers, then released them, embarrassed. 'Sorry. Sorry. It's just that . . . it's not just the warden. It's the other tenants. I don't want to be the subject of a lot of chatter.'

'Of course not, Miss Hazell.' The old man's face softened. 'You're what my late wife would call a real lady.'

Evelyn blushed again but said firmly, 'Well, I don't know

about that, I'm sure. But if this whole thing can be quietly done, I would be grateful.'

After a few additional plans were laid, Rachel went to make more tea; Natasha and Evelyn went to pack an overnight bag and change the sheets on the bed and Mr Lavington returned home to do the same. Evelyn was twittering by this time.

'My dear, nothing like this has happened to me before! When dear Edith was fit and well, she used to tell me the most amazing things about some of the clientele at Markhams – and her neighbours! I didn't always believe her, but now . . .'

'She would enjoy all this.' Natasha flapped a sheet over the single bed. It looked unutterably lonely.

'Yes. She would. But not at poor Maisie's expense.'

'No.' Natasha paused in tucking the sheet. 'Evie, d'you think Maisie really would have gone back to Edward Davenport? You know, even if I hadn't . . . done what I did?'

'Yes.' Evelyn looked up from an open drawer. 'But, Nash . . . you shouldn't have done it. Just because your husband behaves badly doesn't mean . . . you shouldn't have done it.'

'I know.' Natasha thought of Ron and sighed. 'It's funny, Evie. Sometimes, because of this boredom thing, I splash about. And I must do a lot of damage.'

'Yes, dear.' Evelyn smiled. 'It's a good job we all love you.'

Natasha said, 'Oh . . . Evie . . .'

That evening Edward Davenport knocked on the door of Evelyn's bungalow. The dismissal he had received from Rachel Stayte had not calmed him and Jess's advice to 'leave Mum alone for a bit' – which was exactly what he had intended to do – had been like a red rag to a bull. On the drive over, he had thought of Evelyn's undoubted vulnerability with great pleasure. He intended to put the fear of God into her. He wanted to know where Maisie had holed herself up, but, as well as that, he wanted to frighten Evelyn out of her wits.

It was something of a shock therefore, to have the door opened by an elderly gentleman with whiskers and very blue, very fierce eyes staring at him from beneath two shelves of white eyebrows. This man was holding three plastic ducks in one hand. Ever since his father had been taken away to an asylum back in the early Fifties, Edward had shunned any sign of insanity. He took a step backwards.

'Yes?' said the old man in the loud voice used by the deaf.

'This is Miss Hazell's bungalow,' Edward said.

'It is. She's not here.'

Edward was not used to being shouted at. He frowned and summoned his anger. 'And where is she?'

'Gone to her sister's. Wales. Took her down to the train and said I'd clear up here.' The old man stared deeply into Edward's eyes. 'Ill,' he said.

'Ill? Miss Hazell's ill? She was fine this morning! I saw her this morning.' Edward heard his own voice, blustering, almost bleating.

'C'llapsed. I was seeing to the duck pond.' The plastic ducks were poked under Edward's nose. 'Heard her call. She'd fainted right away.'

'Oh . . . well . . .' Edward stared at the ducks, fascinated. It was as if the silly old duffer wanted to give them to him. He was obviously as mad as a hatter. 'D'you know when she will be back?'

'Never. Shouldn't think. Warden don't like us here if we're ill.'

'I see.' Edward took another two paces backwards. 'Well. Thank you. Thank you so much.'

He got into the car and Mr Lavington watched him drive away and then picked up the phone. 'I'm all right if you're all right,' he replied to Evelyn's effusions. 'And we don't know if he'll be back. Let's leave it like it is, shall we?'

'All right. And thank you so much, Mr Lavington. You've been – and are being – such a comfort.'

She could not see him, but the old man's face coloured more vividly than hers had done earlier.

Nine

Tuesday was not quite so hot; the heat mist that had been evaporating before ten each morning hung around until the three women were driving through Worcester. The Severn, winding around the cathedral, appeared to be steaming and as they took the road out to Malvern, two o'clock boomed sonorously from the tower. 'Like the knell of doom!' Evelyn said from her seat next to Rachel. At the last minute she had not really wanted to come with the other two. Natasha still seemed to be the crazy girl she had been back in Markhams; Rachel just the opposite, very set in her ways . . . and so grossly overweight and odd in a sunhat that appeared to have come from the Malaysian jungles. And it had been hard to leave the bungalow, now scented with Mr Lavington's pipe tobacco. She was afraid she might miss the next scene between him and the warden. But then . . . there was Edward Davenport. So she had told herself how wonderful it was to be seeing old friends again, and allowed herself to be tucked up in the open car next to Rachel.

Natasha leaned forward and shouted into the wind, 'Not for us though. No doom and gloom for us! We're off on holiday! For three weeks – yes?'

'Rather!' Rachel echoed with determination. Like Evelyn, she now had her doubts about the wisdom of what she now saw as 'an escapade'. Duncan had phoned her at Thatch End last night and said Joy was driving him mad and when was Rachel coming home. If this thing with Maisie had not blown out of all proportion she would have gone then and there. However, as she seemed the only one capable of dealing with Edward Davenport, she had loaded up the boot of her car, kissed Mrs Barkwith with genuine affection, shaken hands with

Leo Barkwith and wondered how on earth people lived in the country. And this was not proper country, not compared with Charnwood. She shivered; she had put up with Charnwood for years until Duncan got his seat. And Joy had always loved it. She had a sudden terror that Joy would persuade Duncan to go back there for the summer.

Natasha was the only person who appeared to be on top of the world. She was looking forward to seeing Pru again, of course, but it was more than that. Maisie's awful situation might well prove to be Natasha's purpose in life. Last night, lying in bed unable to sleep, she had made extravagant plans for the two of them. Perhaps buying Pru's house and filling it with Hillie and Maisie's children; perhaps Hillie would fall for the eldest boy – was it Mark? And he could become a country vet and Hillie would be his nurse . . . rather like that thing on television. It would be at once secure, safe, and yet exciting too. And all that business with Mr Lavington and Evie. Couldn't she matchmake there too? He was a rugged old type, just right to protect Evie. The way he had dealt with Edward Davenport must have been super. He had made them all laugh that morning. 'Thought I was barmy, he did,' the old man had chuckled. Natasha sighed and sat back, pleased with herself because in a lot of ways she had engineered this whole thing and Hillie certainly would not think England was boring when she heard about it. The emerging sun warmed her closed lids and a delightful languor flowed through her. She had not felt like this since . . . since Harvey. Suddenly, unexpectedly, she felt tears behind her closed lids. If only she hadn't burned his stupid clothes!

Rachel changed down to take the long avenue which led to Great Malvern. Above them the enormous undulating hills gradually became substantial. The sun shone on the bare humps and eiderdowns of trees and picked out white cottages and a church spire. Suddenly they were driving through the town; the terraced streets and parks were just as they remembered from years before. Not English at all; Swiss or Austrian. Natasha sat up and began to exclaim. Evie smiled, recalling that she had bought a lovely tweed skirt in that delightfully old-fashioned department store. Rachel realized suddenly that this was the only place where she had felt entirely free of Eric and Denise and Miss Benson. She slowed to a crawl. The abbey was on their left. They looked over the roof to the tranquillity of the gardens behind it. Then they continued on the upper road, passing Malvern Link before they knew it. After some hesitation at a junction, they took a small road which led through a pass to the other side of the hills. Herefordshire. It spread before them, already smelling of apples and cider.

'I think we're right,' Rachel said. 'Didn't you say Pru told us to keep going west until we came to Bryn's Farm?'

'Never mind if we're on the wrong road completely!' Natasha sat up on the back of the seat. 'My God, this is worth seeing. Breathe deeply, girls. That air is coming from the estuary and the Atlantic and the Scillies and . . . home!'

Evie said, 'Home?'

'America.' Natasha closed her eyes again. Hillie was in Maine now. Right now.

They took the left fork and trundled along a narrow road which appeared to girdle the shoulder of the hill. Worcester Beacon was on their left, the peak rearing above them, a benevolent warning of their own insignificance. The lane became narrower with mud tracks like tramlines. Rachel muttered something under her breath and the car bounced over a rock and slithered back into the ruts with protesting squeaks from the tyres.

'What happens if we meet something?' Evelyn quavered.

'We reverse for half a mile,' Rachel replied grimly.

They passed a sweep of barrenness dotted with sheep, then the road looped into a copse of trees and when they emerged into the sun again, a farm was just below them, the one-storey building huddled into the hillside as if pushed there by the prevailing south-westerlies.

'Damn!' Rachel applied her brakes. 'It was the wrong road. This is a dead end.'

Natasha sat up on the back of her seat again and looked down. 'It's the farm, I think. The one Pru mentioned. Bryn's Farm, was it?'

'But the road *ends* there!' Rachel repeated slowly as if

to a child. The strain of driving affected Rachel badly at times.

Natasha shielded her eyes with one hand. 'I'm not sure it does. Anyway drive into the farmyard and let's make some enquiries, for Pete's sake!'

Evelyn fiddled nervously with her headscarf, hoping the two of them weren't going to get scratchy. Rachel let the clutch out with a jerk and they leapt forward and Evelyn felt her neck crick ominously. Natasha almost fell back onto the boot.

'Steady the Buffs!' she called out humorously, remembering that Mr Delano had rallied them with those words in the old days. Then they were at the farm gate and someone was lumbering forward to open it for them. A line of geese appeared from behind the house, waddling frantically, honking. Evelyn shrank back.

The man swung with the gate and bellowed, 'You Miss Adair's party? Came down's morning to warn me you wuz coming.'

Natasha was delighted at being proved right. 'So we're heading in the right direction?' Rachel eased the car through the gate and waited while the man closed it again. He was a typical hill farmer, small and wiry. He reminded Rachel of the root of a tree. And Duncan was the proud foliage above. Between them they represented all that was good in the country. Her eyes watered. After all they were in Elgar-land. Hope. Glory.

Natasha was handing over money. Americans. They thought you had to pay for everything. But it made the farmer smile.

'I'll let you out the other side,' he said. 'Then you follow the grass track and it leads you right to Prospect.' He put one side of his buttocks on the boot and banged the side of the car with a mud-encrusted wellington boot. 'Off we go.' He hung on to the folded canvas of the roof, lifted his feet and turned to squint at Natasha. 'Miss Adair said one of you looked like Elizabeth Taylor. That must be you, miss.'

'Natasha Nolan,' Natasha introduced herself then indicated

the others. 'Miss Hazell. Mrs Stayte.' She liked Pru's description of her; and it must still hold good even though Pru had not seen her for fifteen years.

'I'm Bryn. Mrs Bryn's in the house. You'll like Prospect. It's all right in the summer. No good in the winter.'

'Who lived there before Pru had it? Miss Adair.'

'Her uncle did own it. And let it out to a madwoman.'

'Madwoman? Oh my God.'

'Not hopping mad, you understand. She thought she were another composer – music. You know. Wandered around the hills absorbing the essence. That's what she told Mrs Bryn. I'm absorbing the essence, she did say. Funny old girl. Died two year ago. It been empty since then. No other tenants wanted it. Too remote like.'

'What about shopping?' asked practical Rachel. 'Where do we buy groceries?'

They had crossed the farmyard accompanied by the geese. Bryn got off the car to open the far gate. Rachel surveyed his regulation jeans with their myriad studs and hoped gloomily he hadn't scratched her boot.

'Miss Adair phoned through to the missus. We got enough stuff to feed the five thousand. She picked it up when they arrived yesterday.'

'They?'

'Two of 'em. Miss Adair and Miss Simmonds.'

'But . . . they weren't expecting us then.' Rachel was already driving through the gate and Natasha had to turn so that she was almost kneeling on the back of the seat.

Bryn, misunderstanding, said, 'Told you. There's enough for a Sunday School treat! And the missus will be going into the town tomorrow anyway.'

Natasha waved as the car bucked over a bump and she sat down unceremoniously. 'I meant, they weren't expecting us,' she said to the back of Rachel's head. 'That's why there are two of them. She had invited another house guest until we turned up in a fortnight's time.'

Evelyn said, 'We're imposing. Aren't we? Changing plans like that—'

Rachel said, 'You're always talking about imposing on

people, Evie! For goodness' sake! Pru was capable of asking us to wait, surely?'

Evelyn said firmly, 'We should have waited, Rachel. Leaving suddenly like that – what was the point of it?'

Rachel spoke slowly again. 'The point, Evie, was to get away from that obnoxious man who was frightening you half to death. And not to involve Mr and Mrs Barkwith in the problem.'

Natasha stuck her head between theirs. 'Listen, girls. We're here now. And Pru can cope – you know very well she can cope with anything. So just relax and enjoy the view.'

The silence simmered. It was almost four o'clock and the sun was at an angle of forty-five degrees, beaming intensely onto this side of the hills. Evie moved her chiffon scarf to protect her forehead and Natasha finger-combed her hair into more thickness. Rachel, dour in her bush hat, drove grimly along the grass track defined merely by previous tyre tracks. It would be hopeless if it rained; they would be cut off. Natasha suddenly voiced this fear with some excitement.

'Say, girls, just imagine if it rains – a real good thunderstorm – phone lines down, tyres skidding on this wet grass . . . we'd be marooned! Like characters in an Agatha Christie!'

Evelyn made a faint noise. Rachel, whose imagination was far more pedestrian than Natasha's, told Natasha, curtly, to shut up. And then they rounded a fold in the hill and turned sharply to avoid a stream which was gurgling along one of the ancient seams, and there, a quarter of a mile ahead, sitting by the water completely out of place, was a four-square, two-storeyed house, looking like a child's drawing, with a shallow-pitched roof, a door in the middle flanked by two windows and three windows along the top.

Natasha felt her spirits descend. 'Have you ever seen such an ugly building?' she said. 'My God. No wonder Pru wants to sell it.'

'She never will.' Rachel felt the car lurch towards the stream; she righted it quickly and put it into first. 'Who would want to live here? Who could *get* here?' The wheels gripped on gravel, the semblance of a driveway. They drove sedately to the front door.

'Oh dear,' said Evie. 'I have this feeling. We shouldn't have come. Pru wanted time to get the place shipshape for us.'

'For goodness' sake, Evie! If you say that once more . . .' Rachel was already clambering out of the car, stiff after the drive, shaking her slacks into position. She had worn them to hide her legs but wondered now if they made her look bigger than ever.

Natasha swung herself lithely over the side and went to help Evelyn. And from the side of the house a girl appeared. She wore khaki shorts and a man's shirt tied at her waist by the tails. Her feet and legs were bare and dripping. Her dark hair was held off her face by a rubber band. She looked about eighteen.

'Hello.' She came forward, smiling, drying her hands on the seat of her shorts. 'I'm Meg Simmonds. I've been stacking bottles in the stream to keep them cool. There's no more room in the fridge and we're not sure how good it is anyway.' She paused but no-one said anything. The three of them were stunned at her youth; they had imagined Pru's companion to be the same age as they were themselves.

Meg licked her lips and her smile became nervous. 'Pru is making up the beds. We've had the mattresses and blankets outside all day, making sure they're aired. You know. She's just . . . seeing to them.'

Rachel recovered herself and remembered she was a Member's wife.

'Rachel Stayte,' she said, holding out her hand. 'Sorry, I'm all hot and sticky from the drive.' She indicated Evie who was standing by the bonnet now, slightly bent as if unable to straighten herself. 'This is Evelyn Hazell. And Natasha.'

'Hi,' Natasha said easily. And Evelyn made an effort to unlock her cramped limbs and said, 'We're pleased to meet you, Miss Simmonds.'

Meg smiled normally again as she shook hands all round. 'Call me Meg, please. Pru has been telling me about you and I am going to call you Nash and Evie and Ray like she does. If that's all right?'

They fell over themselves to reassure her. And then, thankfully, a head appeared through an open upstairs window and Pru's well-modulated voice called a greeting.

'I'm just coming. I can't believe this, can you? Getting together again after all this time . . . it's marvellous!'

She did not wait for a response and by the time Rachel had opened the boot, she was among them, laughing, hugging, smelling strongly of camphor, indefinably changed from a young woman into an older woman, but still Pru, statuesque, different, but beautiful.

'Evie . . . my dear. You've got lots to tell me. Nash said on the telephone that you're an unsung heroine. But not for long because we're going to sing like mad!'

Rachel said, 'If you could grab Evie's bag, Pru . . . and could Meg give us a hand with some of Nash's stuff? Heaven knows why she wants her tennis racquet, for goodness' sake!'

'Leave that!' Pru's voice was suddenly authoritative. 'Leave it in the boot for now. Meg . . . why don't you put the kettle on? The kitchen will be the only quiet place for a while. I'll get this lot sorted.'

Meg smiled briefly and melted away. Rachel raised her brows at Natasha; the youngest of them and she was spared from the donkey work.

Natasha said, 'She seems sweet, Pru. From the commune?'

'Yes.' Pru humped Evie's bag over one shoulder and took her case in the other hand. She said, 'We've got plenty of cold drinks but I thought tea and scones by the stream might be rather nice.'

There was a small silence, the other three all recognizing that the subject was being changed. Then Evelyn said, 'Like one of our picnics. D'you remember how you four would always swop sandwiches? Edie would have liked me to share hers too, but I never would.' She took Natasha's tennis bag before Rachel slammed the boot. 'I wish I had now.'

'Don't bother with that . . . oh well all right then.' Natasha fell in by her side. 'You must tell Rachel and me about Edith,' Natasha said. 'We did not know she was even ill. She always seemed so strong and healthy.'

They went through the front door. A staircase met them, taking up a lot of a narrow hall which ran from front to back of the house. The door at the end was open and they could see the hill rearing up behind it and hear the stream rushing past. On the left was an open door showing a room full of light. The doors on the right were firmly shut.

Pru jerked her head. 'The sitting room is nice. It runs the length of the house and has windows front, side and back.' She jerked again. 'Dining room and kitchen that side. Both a bit dark and grotty. But usable.' She began to climb the stairs. 'Four bedrooms above and a bathroom. Come on.'

Rachel said, 'Look. I don't want to be a pain in the neck. But I'd rather not share. A broom cupboard will do so long as it's to myself.'

'No-one has to share.' Pru stopped on the landing and put her load down. 'Meg and I are together. That leaves three rooms for you three.'

'What about when Maisie arrives?'

'Meg will be gone by then. She can share with me.' Pru indicated the doors along the landing. 'I'll leave you to sort yourselves out and go and help Meg with the tea things. Take your time.'

Natasha caught her arm. 'Hang on a second, Pru. What's with Meg? When the farmer guy, Bryn, when he mentioned a Miss Simmonds we imagined someone from your place. Your commune, community, whatever you call it.'

Pru was already three stairs down. She glanced at Natasha's hand, then up at Natasha, smiled, patted the hand and removed it, then said, 'But she is. She was a founder member. She's been at Telegraph House for fourteen years. Now she is leaving. I'm going to drive her to her home tomorrow.'

Natasha's eyes widened incredulously. 'Fourteen years! But she looks about eighteen!'

'She's thirty-two,' Pru's smile widened. 'Our lives are so simple . . . no stress . . . some of us tend not to age.'

She continued on her way and Natasha turned to the other two. 'Well, I can't believe it!' And then she grinned. 'Perhaps we should join!'

But Evelyn said soberly, 'It hasn't worked for Pru. Her hair is very grey. I didn't notice it in the sunlight – she simply looked fairer than usual.'

Rachel nodded and immediately turned to the room in the front of the house. 'No difference, is there?' she said, thrusting her bag ahead of her to block the door.

'Only that the back bedrooms are bound to look out on the hill.' Natasha grinned at Evelyn. 'I think I'd vote for her, wouldn't you, Evie? She knows all about the main chance!'

Evelyn said immediately, 'I don't mind a back bedroom.'

'Neither do I.' Natasha went up and down the landing looking into the rooms. 'Pru and Meg seem to be in the one back bedroom, so I'll go in the other. The bathroom is between you and me, Ray. And the stairwell between you and the others, Evie. Is that OK?'

'Of course. Whatever you think, dear.'

There was a general sorting of bags. Natasha called along the landing that her bed was 'mighty hard'; Rachel discovered a nest of woodlice behind some torn wallpaper. Evelyn pottered about quietly and after a while Natasha heard her singing. She stopped shaking out clothes and putting them on hangers, and listened. Evelyn obviously had no idea she was humming; the tune sounded vaguely like a Sixties number sung by the Mamas and the Papas. Natasha closed her eyes for a moment. The sound of the stream rushing along the side of the house complemented the song. She was back on her first holiday with Harvey: California . . . oranges and lemons simply growing . . . the warmth; the huge land one side, the huge Pacific the other. The surf . . . right outside the beach house. She had been very pregnant and had walked along the sea inside the crook of Harvey's arm and talked nonsense about wanting her baby born in the waves . . . a water baby. She remembered Harvey saying, 'Hey. Honey. We dragged ourselves out of the sea billions of years ago. Why go back?' And she had spouted some nonsense about progress having nothing to do with going upwards and onwards, but completing a circle. How he had loved it when she came out with stuff like that. 'My wonderful girl-woman,' he had called her.

Pru's voice spoke from the doorway. 'All right, Nash? Enough hangers?'

'Yes. Plenty.' Natasha looked at the heap of clothes still not accommodated. 'Well . . . it doesn't matter anyway. We're going to be living in shorts and tops.'

'Don't rely on the weather.' Pru came into the room and began to hang dresses over blouses and tuck them into the heavy old wardrobe. 'Don't you remember how the storms would come sweeping in from the west even in midsummer? Doesn't matter so much if you're on the Worcestershire side. But this side gets the full force of them. I remember coming here with Mummy and Eustace. We could hardly stand against the wind. And on the second night we heard this ghastly rending noise and we came out onto the landing and looked down and the stream was rushing right through the hall and out of the front door!'

'Oh heavens!' Natasha laughed with her though it did not sound funny. 'I just hope that doesn't happen this time. And who was Eustace? What a gorgeous name!'

'He's the "uncle" who left me this place. One of Mummy's many. You know. They were all darlings. I suspect, actually, he was gay and used Mummy as a very useful cover.' Pru went to the window and looked at the face of the hill. It rose steeply here and then rounded off and peaked again at the Hereford Beacon. 'Mummy's always been good like that. Terribly openminded. I'm very lucky.' She spoke emphatically as if convincing herself, and Natasha pushed Harvey out of her head and came around the bed to stand by her friend.

'Is anything wrong, Pru?'

Pru grinned sideways at her, almost naturally. 'I'd forgotten how damned sentient you are!' She resumed her sightless stare and took a deep breath. 'Yes, there is. I came in here to tell you anyway. You can pass it on and then, perhaps, we shall be able to make Meg's evening here something special.'

There was a silence. Natasha said nothing; waited. Pru cleared her throat and spoke very matter of factly. 'Meg has cancer. That's why she's going home. To die. She let me drive her here . . . she wanted to see this place. And when she heard you were coming early she wanted to see you too. I'm allowed to take her home tomorrow too . . . somewhere near Chester. Her father owns a bookbinding business. And then . . . and then I probably won't see her again.' She lifted her shoulders. 'That's her wish and obviously I have to respect it.'

Natasha stood rigidly, staring, as Pru was staring, at the bare face of the hill. It was one of the few times she did not know what to say. For fully half a minute the two of them were side by side, joined by the awfulness of Pru's disclosure. And then Natasha turned and put her arms around her friend and her head onto the wide shoulder and Pru turned in to her and held her and murmured.

'I'm so sorry, Pru.' Natasha's whisper was a thread. 'How dreadful . . . how ghastly . . .' A sudden tremor shook her and she clung harder to Pru's shirt.

Pru's murmur strengthened. 'Don't be frightened.'

'It's just . . . oh for a moment there I imagined how it would be if it were Hillie.'

Pru laughed quietly. 'I meant . . . don't be frightened of me. Of us.'

Natasha drew away. 'I'm not. Of course, *I'm* not religious but I'm glad you are, honey. Both of you. You need any comfort you can get.'

Pru's arms dropped to her sides. 'What makes you say that? How do you know that we are religious?'

'Well, the commune of course. That's what it's all about, surely? Living the good life?' She shrugged. 'Am I being simplistic? Sorry, but that's what I call being religious.'

Pru smiled slightly and went towards the door. 'We're not a religious community, darling. Some of us believe in God. Some of us don't. We're quite a mixed bunch. Except for one thing.'

'What's that?' Natasha was frowning, trying to understand.

Pru turned her smile on the vivid dark face silhouetted against the window.

'We're lesbians, Nash. I thought you knew. When I bought Telegraph House, it was still socially unacceptable. Now things are better, I supposed. And we stay together as a family.' She could not see Natasha's expression but she could imagine it and her smile widened. 'You can tell the others. Or not. I'll go and see if they're sorting themselves. And then we'll have tea by the water and you can tell me exactly what has been happening over the past weekend.'

The door closed behind her. And Nash continued to stare at it.

Ten

The next morning Pru loaded the boot of her Ford Sierra with Meg's belongings. They did not encourage possessions at the commune and there were just two bags: one containing Meg's clothes and the other a few books, pictures and a collection of mugs Pru had made for her over the years. The car, one of three owned by Telegraph House, had been used by the market gardeners and still smelled damply of earth. Pru went back into the house and emerged with pillows. She padded the passenger seat with care and pulled down the sun visor. She had heard Meg in the bathroom during the night being sick.

Natasha came out to say goodbye. She wore a man's silk dressing-gown, wine red with white spots, tied tightly at the waist. Her hair appeared to have a life of its own.

'I think the others are still asleep. Evelyn got up about six and made a pot of tea and we sat in her room watching the light come around the Beacon. Then she and Rachel went back to bed.'

'And you didn't.'

'No. I had a lot of thinking to do.' Natasha smiled whimsically. Pru noticed her bottom lip was blistered.

Meg appeared in the doorway and held onto the jamb. Pru went to her and supported her. The small, childish face was damp with sweat. She said, 'I'm all right, Pru. Honestly.'

Natasha came to her other side. 'You're not all right,' she said. 'Let us take your weight. *Then* you'll be all right.'

Between them they got the slight figure settled on the pillows. Meg put her head back and closed her eyes. 'I'm sorry,' she whispered. 'So sorry.'

'So are we, dearest. So are we.' Pru dropped a kiss on the

waxy forehead. 'Try to sleep. It'll be bumpy but at least the springs are good on this old tub.' She straightened, closed the door and turned to Natasha. 'Thank you, my dear. You being here . . . it would have been marvellous anyway. Now it is terribly important. For me.'

'For me too.' Natasha looked through the window. 'Will she be all right, Pru? She seemed fine last night. I didn't say anything to the others because poor Evelyn would have gone all peculiar. But she seemed . . . well . . . healthy.'

'It's the vomiting. It exhausts her. She might get a second wind as the morning goes on. Try not to worry, Nash. I'll be with you tonight. Late I expect.'

'All right. Take care.' Suddenly Natasha reached up and drew Pru's head towards her. 'I think I've taken it all in now, Pru. And I'm not frightened in the least. You're still Pru Adair. Aren't you?'

They both laughed and Natasha kissed her very naturally and then let her go. Pru got into the car, started it up and drove carefully down the gravel driveway and around the bluff. She glanced in the mirror before the house disappeared from view. Natasha had taken off her dressing-gown and was waving it above her head like a flag of victory.

Meg said faintly, eyes still closed, 'Did she tell them?'

'About your illness? No. She probably will during the day and if not I will this evening. If they'd known they would have all come to wave you off, my dear.'

'I meant . . . did she tell them about us? About Telegraph House?'

'No. And I don't think she will.' Pru glanced anxiously sideways as the car took a molehill under its offside wheels. 'She thinks she is shallow. She is not at all. She can deal with the knowledge that I am different. She probably thinks that Ray and Evie could not.'

There was a long silence. They came to the farm and as there was no sign of the Bryns, Pru got out and saw to the two gates. The geese honked at the car; somewhere a dog barked. And then the silence was there again until they reached the road junction.

Meg opened her eyes and shifted slightly so that she was sitting up.

'How do you know so much about people, Pru?' she asked.

'They're not people. They are old friends. We knew each other as you do when you are young and you work together. We . . . simply accepted each other.'

'You know other people too. You understand them. I think you even understood that awful man they were talking about. Edward Davenport.'

'Oh yes. I understand him very well.'

'His poor wife . . .'

'Maisie. But you see, my darling, Maisie knows him – has always known – him very well.'

Meg opened her eyes, shocked. 'Are you saying that Maisie wanted to be ill-treated?'

Pru shook her head. 'I've no idea, Meggie. But I do know she needed him. She had ample opportunities to escape him but she never did. He, he assuaged . . .' she laughed at her own words, 'he assuaged her guilt.'

'By punishing her?'

'Yes.' Pru negotiated a farm tractor in the middle of the High Street. The little town was coming to life. Shopkeepers were pulling down sun awnings and window cleaners were at work. 'That's so naive, isn't it? But yes.'

Meg waited until they were through the town and gliding down the long avenue of trees. 'That's how it will be for me, you know. At home. Not Mummy. And no-one will say anything of course. But I know Daddy will think I'm being punished for my lack of self-discipline.'

Pru laughed aloud, tipping her head back, her throat long and white against the tan of her face. 'That's one thing I don't get from my mother. She's never been hot on self-discipline.'

'You make up for it though, in lots of ways.' Meg lay back and closed her eyes. 'Oh, Pru, I'm sorry to be leaving you. Will you be all right?'

'You're not leaving me. You're part of me. That won't change.' Pru's laughter died. She tightened her mouth against a tremor. Then said, 'I think what you're doing is right. You must give your parents this time.'

'Yes.' Meg settled her small body among the pillows. 'I am so comfortable. So warm. Would you mind if I slept?'

'Oh my dear girl . . .'

'When you get back . . . there's a letter under your pillow.'

Pru squeezed her eyes tightly shut for a moment and then opened them wide. Meg was already asleep. Pru murmured, 'Thank you.'

Back at the house Natasha found bacon and eggs and cooked a proper breakfast. She was not a domestic type and it took a long time but she was proud of the result: hot plates, cold orange juice, toast and marmalade. She yelled at the foot of the stairs that breakfast was absolutely ready and she wanted customers pronto.

Evelyn came down, twittering, clutching the early morning tea tray. 'I can't believe it's eight-thirty. I haven't slept this late since . . . well, I simply can't remember. I'll wash these up, dear and—'

'Dump them in the sink. There are enough clean ones. Where's Ray? If she's wasting time in the bathroom everything will be spoiled.' Natasha heard herself with some amusement. She sounded like Mrs Mayhew.

'I'm here.' Rachel came down the stairs yawning prodigiously. 'I hardly slept through the night, then we had that cup of tea and I went out like a light!'

'We can sleep out in the sunshine. We've got all day to ourselves and I suggest we do nothing. Absolutely nothing.'

Evelyn settled herself before her breakfast with obvious anticipation. 'That doesn't sound like you, Nash,' she commented, cutting her bacon into bite-size pieces because of her dentures. 'You're always on the go.'

'We could have a walk later, perhaps.' Natasha buttered some toast. 'I feel the last few days have been so packed with incident we need time to think about them. We can do our long tramps when Pru gets back. And when Maisie arrives.'

'If she arrives,' Evelyn added gloomily.

'She'll arrive,' Natasha said, with more confidence than she felt. 'She needs us. And we need her. Especially Pru. She'll arrive.'

Rachel said, 'I shouldn't eat this cooked meal. I usually have a crispbread and some fruit.'

'Well there's no fruit and no crispbread.'

Rachel grinned, 'Didn't mean to sound ungrateful, Nash. It's really good. We need not eat lunch anyway.' She looked around. 'Don't tell me they've gone already?'

'Pru and Meg?' Nash pushed her plate aside hardly touched. 'Yes. They left at seven-thirty. Pru wanted to get Meg home before the real heat of the day.'

'She's very protective of the girl, isn't she? All that fussing last night about getting enough sleep!'

Natasha said flatly, 'Meg's got cancer. Terminal. I shouldn't think it'll be very long now. She's going back home anyway.'

Evelyn and Rachel stopped eating, mouths full, eyes wide with shock.

'Oh my God!' 'Dear Lord!' They spoke in unison.

Natasha said soberly, 'She was in a bad way this morning. Apparently she'd been sick in the night and was exhausted. I just hope Pru can cope.'

Evelyn said, 'Pru can cope with anything. She was wonderful at Edith's funeral. I couldn't have done without her. Maisie too. They were both marvellous.'

'Oh Evie . . .' Natasha showed distress for the first time. 'I wish I'd been there too.'

'Oh no, dear.' Evelyn began to chew again. 'It wasn't your type of thing at all.' She realized she was eating and stopped again. 'That poor girl. She seemed so interested last night. When we were talking about Maisie and Edward.'

Natasha took a piece of toast and said nothing.

Rachel said, 'I'm surprised Meg didn't stay down in Cornwall. I suppose the parents could have gone down to be with her. Usually those sort of communities look after their own.'

'What sort of communities?' Natasha asked, staring at her toast.

'Well, you know. The spiritual, do-it-all-yourself type.' Rachel forked a piece of bacon into her mouth. 'That's why she looked so young. I've noticed it before in people with terminal illnesses. They sort of . . . revert.'

Evelyn said, 'Poor little scrap. It's just too awful. And there we were making Edward Davenport into a joke. And all the time she knew her days were numbered. I'm glad she decided to go back home. It's not a natural life really, is it? Living together and sharing everything. I mean, I'm so thankful for my little bungalow and my independence.'

'It depends.' Natasha glanced quickly from one to the other and then started to butter her toast. 'What suits one person, doesn't always . . . oh my God, I'm sounding more like Mrs Mayhew than ever!' The others looked at her uncomprehendingly. 'Our daily. She's full of sayings. Signs. Portents. Ghastly woman.'

'She seemed OK to me,' Rachel said, finishing off the last of her breakfast. 'Probably told you a few home truths, that's why you don't like her!'

Natasha forced a laugh. 'She'd faint if she knew I'd cooked a proper breakfast, certainly!' She sat back, apparently making up her mind about something. 'Listen. Let's try not to talk about Meg any more. Until Pru comes back and tells us . . . what she decides to tell us. Agreed?' The other two sighed and nodded and Natasha went on briskly, 'Well, that's that then. Who's having the bathroom first?'

It was inevitable that Rachel should be the first. And that Evelyn should be next. Natasha washed up with a kind of resignation, cursing without rancour when she splashed her dressing-gown which was one of Harvey's best and which she had purloined rather than burned. When she had carefully put away the last dish, she studied her reflection in the misted old mirror above the sink. The blister on her lip had burst, probably because she had bitten it hard during breakfast. But the rest of her face remained stubbornly beautiful despite her being sleepless all night.

'It's no good, Nash baby,' she said. 'If you're going to turn into a saint, you have to accept you won't look any different!'

She slid out of the dressing-gown and put it in a bowl to wash it. It would dry in this glorious sunshine and perhaps stop smelling of Harvey. She did not know whether that was good or bad.

Edward looked across the table at Simon and Ian. He had never liked Wednesdays in term time because Maisie invariably had the members of the Parent Teacher Association around for meetings, or fund-raising or something. On Wednesdays her mind was elsewhere; not on him. But that was term time. This was the first Wednesday of the long school holiday when she should be here performing what he always thought of as her 'juggling act'. She did not even realize she was performing it; she simply thought of her job as 'keeping everyone happy'. But he could make it harder or easier for her by a twitch of his eyebrow. If she said, 'Darling, we thought of going for a picnic which means we won't be in for lunch and probably late back this evening. Will you be all right?' And when he frowned, she would add quickly, 'Could we have an early lunch here and a long afternoon out?' And then one of the children would moan that if they missed the early train they would have to wait until mid-afternoon for another one. And that was when he would grudgingly agree to them being out all day. Usually it was enough to receive her gratitude, but sometimes he even went so far as to say, 'Well all right. But you owe me one. Don't forget.'

This Wednesday was quite different. Not only was Maisie missing from the breakfast table, but Mark, Jess and Tom were too. They had been up at the crack of dawn to drive down to Bristol before the holiday traffic got under way. The house had been filled with their bustle for a frantic half an hour, and then had gone strangely silent.

So Edward stared at his youngest sons and felt the empty house pressing around him and wondered what the hell he was going to do.

Mrs Donald came in with toast and a large bowl of fluffy scrambled eggs. The boys, suddenly released from their father's attention, whooped and reached and subsided in one fluid action. When Edward did not roar at them about their manners, they began to help themselves rather more sedately. Mrs Donald sat down and poured tea.

'And what are you two up to this morning?' she asked brightly. 'Cricket of course, we all know that!' She shot an arch look at Edward. 'But where?'

'Archer's dad is taking us to Edgbaston.' Simon grinned smugly. 'He's a member. We can go in the hospitality tent and everything.'

'Are you going to be a damned nuisance to everyone?' Edward asked.

'Course not.' Ian, usually the quiet one, was suddenly indignant. 'Mum came with us last year with Archer's mum. We know what to do, don't we, Si?'

'Yeh.' Simon kept a weather-eye on his father. 'But last year, Mum treated everyone to lunch. You know, kind of repaying them for taking us. And she's not here this year.'

'Well I'm not handing over that kind of money,' Edward's face darkened suddenly as he wondered where the hell Maisie had got the money to pay for six lunches. He knew what she spent down to the last penny. Or thought he did. Jess had made such a thing about Maisie and her 'holiday' and her 'privacy'; and all the time she must have had secrets by the sackful. Was there another man? Christ, could there possibly be another man? He said furiously, 'You'd better tell Archer the truth. That your mother has walked out on you!'

Both boys suddenly stopped eating in mid-chew. Mrs Donald said quickly, 'Come on. Your father's teasing you. You know your mother would never leave you.'

'Well, she's not here!' Edward laboured on heavily. 'I don't see her. Do you? And where is her cup and saucer? Is she under the table perhaps?'

Simon recommenced chewing and spluttered a crumbly giggle. 'Dad. We're teenagers, you know!'

Mrs Donald laughed too. 'I expect her cup and saucer are on the breakfast table at Thatch End. Let's hope they're making a fuss of her. A real rest. That's what she needs.'

Edward listened to her trying to make this nightmare into something normal. Anyone would think she was genuinely fond of Maisie. She couldn't be . . . they were arch rivals. Surely she would be hoping Maisie would not appear again and she could step into her shoes? He shuddered at the thought. The joy of being with Mrs Donald relied on Maisie also being part of his life. Maisie was fair and child- like and good. Mrs Donald was dark and deep and not good. Without Maisie as the other side of the coin, Mrs Donald was . . . wrong.

Breakfast finished and she chivvied the boys upstairs to get ready.

'I'll take them over to the Archers and be back by ten,' she said, stacking plates expertly. 'You could go to work late.' She gave a sideways smile.

He said, 'I'm going to work now. I'm meeting Leo Barkwith. We shall be lunching out so don't bother with anything.'

Mrs Donald accepted that without question. But at the door she suddenly said, 'The sooner Mrs Davenport comes home, the sooner we can get back to normal!'

It was almost funny. Except that it wasn't.

He decided on a man-to-man approach with Leo Barkwith. He waited until they had finished discussing a possible extension to the factory to include a glazier's shop, then suggested lunch at a small pub near Rackham's where there was a measure of privacy. The weather was glorious. They took a taxi and walked the last few yards. The sunshine would be too much later on; but at midday it was still fresh and there was a quality to the air that made Edward feel anything was possible. He would find Maisie and they would live a really normal life without Mrs Donald and without any more punishment. She was still so beautiful and he would take her out and about and people would envy him for her sweetness. Yes, that was Maisie's quality: sweetness. He longed for it.

Barkwith ordered sandwiches.

'Sorry, Edward. Mary and I have the house to ourselves tonight and she's going to do a slap-up meal. I have to do it justice.'

'You've had a full house. Yes.' Edward was forced to order sandwiches also; he had been hoping to have a good meal and so avoid dinner alone with Mrs Donald. 'The girls have gone now, have they?'

Leo nodded. 'Departed. Yesterday. For two or three weeks I think. It will do them good getting together again after all this time.'

'Yes.' Edward's mind was buzzing. He remembered Maisie saying something about the Malverns. No need to take it any further; there could not be that many hotels in the area. He'd just phone each one until he found a Mrs Davenport. He abandoned the man-to-man approach and began to talk expansively about his children. All five of them.

'You've got a grandchild so you're still in touch with today's generation,' he pontificated, leaning back in his chair. 'Always on the go. So much energy.'

'Hilary has certainly got that.' Leo Barkwith thought of his streetwise granddaughter and smiled affectionately. 'What I really like about Hillie is her sense of humour. She takes a potentially tragic event and flips it over so that you see the funny side of it.' He chuckled. 'I expect Maisie has told you that Nash has divorced her husband. Before she did so, she incinerated his clothes. And he's a vain man.' He shook his head. 'I know it sounds ghastly but Hillie had us rolling in the aisles. Even her mother laughed.'

Edward's opinion of Natasha Nolan sank lower still. The thought of Maisie cohorting with her and that superior Prudence Adair, not to mention the MP's wife, made his blood run cold.

'I dare say,' he replied. He thought about it. 'I believe Maisie laughs quite a lot with our children.'

'Well . . . naturally.' Leo finished the last of his sandwich and stood up. 'I really have to go, Edward. The new project is most interesting and I'll let you have some plans within the next few weeks.' He shook hands. He wondered why he felt sorry for this tough-looking, rough diamond of a man. Nash had said he was 'ghastly' but then Nash said that kind of thing. He seemed to be coping very well all on his own with his family home for the summer.

Leo said impulsively, 'The next couple of weeks will fly by, old man. And at least Maisie is catching up with her family as well as her friends.'

Edward stayed where he was for some time, rubbing his knuckles where Leo had gripped them hard and sympathetically. Family. Leo had said she was with her family. And she certainly was not at home with her real family where she should be. So . . . where was she? In Malvern with her friends, or somewhere else? Edward narrowed his eyes. She had not seen her brother since before her marriage. Twenty-two years at least. And she had never wanted to see him again. He was the real reason she had run away and found her own bedsit and applied for jobs.

Edward felt a headache coming on as he tried to recall everything Maisie had ever said about her foster parents; about her brother. The father had used his belt on her, but he had used it more often on the brother. So why had she fled from all of them – not just the foster parents, but the brother as well?

When the incipient headache became full-blown, he got up, paid the bill downstairs and asked for a phone directory. He made a list of the same numbers Rachel had phoned on Monday evening; then he added the addresses. He must not forewarn her with a telephone call; he must surprise her; turn up as if he had known all the time where she was.

He returned the directory and went outside to call a taxi.

Rachel found some deckchairs in the coal house; Evelyn made some punch using some of the bottles in the stream, Natasha gave up the idea of a bath and lay in the stream in her nightdress and then let it dry on her in the sun.

'You'll get rheumatism,' Evelyn prophesied. 'In fact rheumatic fever probably!'

'Oh the voice of doom!' Natasha intoned. She smiled beatifically into the sun, eyes closed. 'That was a marvellous experience, Evie. You should try it.'

Evelyn moaned and shuddered. Rachel said, 'Your hair looks like a bush.'

'Now that's more to the point.' Natasha opened one eye. 'Are you still any good with hair, Ray?'

'I don't know. It's years since we used to give each other home perms.'

'You can have a go this evening. If you've still got the knack, you can do all of us. Each evening.'

'Promises, promises,' Rachel said with one of her rare flashes of humour.

Evie said, 'I don't want anyone to do mine. I get it done at a very nice salon and I can keep it going in between perms.'

'Good old Evie.'

The girls slept in the sun, ate a sandwich for lunch and slept again. About four o'clock they went inside to assemble a meal for Pru's return. A tin of soup, salad and cold meat. Evelyn offered to scrape some new potatoes and Rachel went to look for early blackberries. Natasha yawned her way upstairs to take off her nightie, fold the crisply dry dressing-gown and put on shirt and shorts. Her bed looked inviting; she could have crashed out on it then and there but the phone rang from the landing extension and she hurried to get it before Evie had to dry her hands and answer it below.

It was Hilary, as clear as if she were in the next room, shouting unnecessarily.

'Mom? Nash? Is that you?'

'No. It's the wicked witch of the north. Is it you?' Natasha replied.

'Yeah. How's it going?'

'Great. And very, very interesting.'

'Damn. Damn. I wanted it to be dreadful so that I could persuade you to join us. Horrible Harve and the Pressburger have gone. The surf is wonderful. Mabs says it's no fun without you.'

'Hey. I thought she was on Harvey's side.'

'Well she is. But she's not on the Pressburger's side at all.'

'I think the English reply to that is – what a turn-up for the books!'

'Mom, please come over. I need you.'

'Honey . . . I need you too. But it's kind of difficult at the moment. There's a helluva lot going on here. I'll tell you all about it one day.' Natasha bit her lip. 'I think I'm needed here, darling. Properly needed.'

'D'you think I don't properly need you?' Hillie's voice became tragic. 'Ma . . . listen. I'm falling in love with Larry Blum. And if you're not here to keep an eye on me I think I'm going to sleep with him.'

'Sweetie, if you intend to sleep with Larry Blum, then my presence would not make a scrap of difference. My God, whenever have you taken any notice of me?'

'Nash – I'm fifteen for God's sake! I need a chaperone!'

'You've got Ruth. She won't let you get within three feet of her twin brother and you know it. Now stop emotionally blackmailing me and tell me how you are.'

There was a short silence then the young voice said sulkily, 'As a matter of fact, I'm fine. I won the windsurfing championships yesterday and Larry is green with envy and won't speak to me.'

Natasha started to laugh and Hillie practically spat down the phone, 'Thanks for the sympathy!'

'You have it, my darling. And I'm so proud of you I could just stand here and melt. And I bet Ruth is your best friend, isn't she?'

'Oh sure. She loves it that Larry hates me. I tell you something, Ma. That little joke we had about the incest could be true. It's just not natural the way she adores him. I mean, he's not adorable. He's just not in the least little bit adorable!'

'No. I rather agree with you there.'

'Ma, please come over. Or let me come to you. It's awful here. I can get on a plane by myself – shall I? Say yes – please, Ma – say yes!'

Natasha frowned and bit her lip almost through. 'Honey . . . I feel dreadful saying this . . . but no. Not yet anyway. It's a tricky situation here. Maisie has disappeared and her husband turns out to be a wife-beater and he's after her. And Pru's friend is dying of cancer . . . and Rachel is scared her husband is going back to his first wife. And Evie might be having a romance with another pensioner . . . I'm the only one who is stable! So that will tell you what kind of trouble we're in!'

There was another little silence. Then Hillie said, 'It's a funny thing, Ma. You're sounding like you used to be. Interested in everything. You know, *keen.* Enthusiastic. Maybe if you'd stayed like that, Horrible Harvey wouldn't have . . . gone.'

'What are you saying, baby? That the divorce was my fault?'

'I don't know. Perhaps there were other ways of dealing with Harvey's bimbos. Other than driving them into insane asylums. Having those screaming rows. Burning his clothes.'

'That was only because Pressburger was serious. The others . . . and I never drove anyone into an insane asylum, honey. Be fair!'

Hilary was suddenly defeated. 'Maybe it was Harvey then. I don't know any more.' She sounded about ten years old, lost, 'I only know I want you both. At the same time. Even if you scream and he shouts and you throw things and he throws them back.'

'Oh, Hillie. What sort of parents have we been?'

'The only ones I want,' said the little voice. And the phone went dead.

Natasha found she was weeping. She hung onto the landing banisters and lowered her head before the storm. And then from outside came the sound of a car engine.

She flew down the stairs and reached the Ford just as Pru switched off the engine. She had nothing on her feet and the gravel was painful. She held the driver's door open.

'Was she all right? Are you all right? Pru, I was so sorry . . .'

Pru got out stiffly and stood in the late sunshine, flexing her hips and shoulders. She said, 'It's all right. I didn't stay. There was quite a bit of silent animosity coming at me from the father. I talked to the mother – about Meg's medication and things. And it was her . . . she didn't mean to be insulting. Or hurtful.' Pru hung her head and tried to laugh. 'It was funny I suppose.' She looked up. 'I feel sick, Nash.'

'What? What was it?' Nash put her arms around the narrow

waist. 'Lean on me, Pru. What did she say? Surely she – they – were grateful that Meg had been happy with you all those years?'

'She said – God, I don't know how to tell you. She asked me if I had done anything to Meg. To start this thing in her uterus. Like . . .' she hiccoughed, '. . . like syphilis is spread. That's what she said.' Pru's body was shaken by a sob. She clutched Natasha's shoulders. 'Nash, it's not like that. We *care* about each other! We don't indulge in – in sexual . . . *antics*! That's for perverts like Edward Davenport!'

'Yes, my darling. Yes. I know.' Nash propped Pru against the car. 'Come on now. Don't let the girls see you like this.' She fished in the pocket of her shorts. 'Here. Let me dry your face. Come on. You need a good night's sleep. You've done what you had to do. What Meg wanted you to do. Her mother spoke from complete ignorance, Pru. You must forgive her. Come on now.'

Rachel appeared around a corner of the house, her basket brimming with blackberries. 'Pru! Didn't hear the car!' She came closer. 'Are you all right? Oh of course you're not! Nash told us about Meg. How absolutely rotten . . . come on in. We've got supper almost ready.' She put down her basket and took Pru's other arm. 'Come on, old girl. Come and have a bath and get changed. We're here. We'll look after you.'

That started Pru weeping again. But at least this time she smiled through her tears. They took her inside and let Evelyn exclaim over her. Natasha ran her bath. They found towels and wrapped her up afterwards.

Natasha said, 'Would you like my dressing-gown? It's silk and rather posh.'

Pru smiled. 'Thanks, Nash. But it's not going to fit me, is it?'

'Yes.' Natasha ran and fetched it and flapped it out. 'It's a man's actually. I like them enormous. And I washed it this morning.'

Pru sat, resplendent in Harvey's spotted dressing-gown. She told them about the journey she had made. And then she said, 'I must have been a bit delirious. Heat or something.

I thought I saw Edith. I came back through the centre of Birmingham . . . old times' sake, you know. And there she was. Following this woman. I got the impression she was, sort of, protecting her.'

Evelyn wavered. 'Edith? Oh my God!'

'Of course, it wasn't really Edith.' Pru shook her head. 'I wish I hadn't mentioned it. It was just so vivid. I had to tell you.'

Natasha said, 'And she was following someone? Keeping an eye on them?'

'Yes.'

'It wasn't Maisie by any chance was it?'

They were all electrified. Pru laughed. 'Certainly not. To tell you the truth I didn't notice much about the woman. It was the Edith lookalike that startled me.'

'But you knew it was a woman?' Evelyn said, her voice still shaky.

'Yes.' Pru frowned, thinking back. 'Someone much older than Maisie though.'

Rachel laughed. 'What a lot of nonsense! We know Maisie is staying with her brother and will be joining us as soon as she can get away.'

Natasha shook her head. 'We don't actually *know* any of that, Ray.' She turned to Pru. 'And Maisie is no longer young.'

'She looks it though, doesn't she? Remember I saw her at Edith's funeral. She still had that schoolgirl look about her.'

Evelyn said, 'Actually . . . when she was with me . . . something she said or did . . . I remember thinking that if she went back to her husband, she would look hard . . . she had lines around her mouth. Just for a minute, she did look much older.'

Natasha said, 'What was she wearing, Pru? This woman. Can you close your eyes and just see a colour perhaps?'

Pru did close her eyes and after a while she opened them and smiled. 'Something totally unsuitable actually. A sort of mutton-dressed-up-as-lamb look. A frock. Blue . . . white spots. Not unlike this dressing-gown.'

Natasha looked across at Evelyn. 'I wonder if she changed

last Friday night, before she came to you? She was wearing a blue dress then. White daisies.'

Evelyn had a hand to her throat. 'Oh my God . . . what is happening?'

Natasha said firmly, 'I don't think it was Edith. I don't believe in ghosts. But I think Pru saw Maisie.'

The girls were silent. Then Pru put down her coffee cup and stood up.

'I'm going to bed, girls. If it was Maisie she was heading for the station. In which case, she will get a taxi at Malvern and be here in a couple of hours. And I simply must sleep. Forgive me.'

They nodded. And then they began to clear away the supper things. It seemed almost too mundane. But there was really nothing else to be done.

Eleven

Maisie did not arrive at Prospect House that evening, nor during the night, nor the whole of the next day. The four women told each other they were revelling in doing nothing; they could not go for a walk, 'In case Maisie turns up,' said Rachel who no longer enjoyed walking. It was too hot to cook and Natasha's housewifely splurge had disappeared as fast as it had come. Apart from washing their smalls and hoovering the ground floor, they spent their time in the faded deckchairs by the stream. They talked occasionally. They wondered aloud about Maisie and reminded each other that they must ask her if she was walking down Corporation Street at four-thirty on Wednesday afternoon. Evelyn was convinced that Pru had seen Edith and that she would bring Maisie to them eventually.

'I like to think she's with us still.' Evelyn smiled into the sun, feeling somehow that if Edith was looking after Maisie then obviously she would still be looking after her special friend, Evelyn. It was most reassuring. Edith would not think the business with the warden and Mr Lavington was petty; she would actually enjoy it. Somehow, Edith was taking the anxiety out of a great many things.

Pru said, 'It was just an illusion, Evie. Because I was worried and upset. I shouldn't have told you.'

'I'm glad you did!' Evelyn nodded happily. 'It makes such a difference. We simply do not have to worry. About Maisie. About anything really!'

'Well that's all right then!' Natasha glanced humorously at Pru then looked around her. 'Edith! Where are you? We need sandwiches and coffee! It's almost suppertime.'

Evelyn was shocked. 'Nash! How could you? It's not a laughing matter!'

'Sorry. Sorry, Evie.' Natasha pulled a penitent face. 'I'll get us something. Cheese? There's some ham left if you prefer.' She took orders on her fingers and added, 'Come on, Ray. Give me a hand. Let Pru and Evie sleep for a while.'

They both protested but Natasha made urgent signs with her eyebrows and Rachel struggled out of her chair and joined her.

'What?' She accepted the cheese dish and grater and put them on the kitchen table. 'Did you want to have a word?'

'Only that Pru is more upset and tired than she's letting on. I think Evie's . . . *simplicity* will be good for her. Just for half an hour or so.'

'Simplicity? Oh, the idea of Edith as a guardian angel. Yes. Strange, I didn't see Pru as being that kind of religious. You know, metaphysical and things.'

'No. Nor me.' Natasha made two cups of instant coffee and passed one over. She lit a cigarette and put two pills in her mouth.

'My God.' Rachel stared. 'What are you doing? Is that some kind of drug? And I didn't know you smoked!'

'Well, I do. And I take drugs. And I need them both just at the moment.'

Rachel was really shocked. 'I thought we were all so relaxed together! I thought we'd left our worries behind.'

Natasha drew deeply on her cigarette. 'Have you?' she asked directly.

'Yes. No. Oh God, I don't know. I tried to ring Duncan last night and there was no answer. I left this number and a message on the machine. He hasn't rung back.'

Natasha said, 'My daughter needs me. And I had to tell her she couldn't have me. Not for a while. It hurt.'

Rachel sat down opposite and picked up her cup. 'And poor old Pru . . . She must be horribly distressed to conjure a ghost. And Edith Manners's ghost . . . of all people.'

'Or ghosts,' quipped Natasha with a grin.

'The drug's working, is it?' Rachel asked disapprovingly.

'Oh for God's sake, Ray!' Natasha stubbed out her cigarette. 'I hardly ever smoke, and the pills were aspirin!'

'Really?' Rachel relaxed as Natasha nodded. 'Well, thank the Lord for that. We all rely on you, you know!'

'*What*?'

'We do. Your sense of humour – or sense of the absurd. Whatever.'

Natasha, spurred by the praise more than she would have been by criticism, stood up and began to assemble some sandwiches.

She said, 'Funny. You're the capable one. MP's wife. And you make things happen. You always wanted to be a personal secretary to someone important. And you were. And then you fell in love and . . .' She stopped talking, remembering some of the things Rachel had told her about her marriage to Duncan Stayte.

Rachel fetched the carving knife and cut a pile of sandwiches into neat triangles and began to arrange them on a dish in between tomatoes and cucumber slices.

'Quite.' She shrugged her substantial shoulders. 'I made that happen, didn't I? But Duncan didn't mind. Not too much. He might be getting fed-up with it recently. You know, he finds fault.' She began to tell Natasha about the typist's swivel chair. And then about the possible candidate for the next-door constituency up in Leicestershire. 'Oh, lots of little things. I don't know if they add up to a row of beans or not. He keeps referring to what he calls my puppy fat.' She rubbed her shoulders self-consciously. 'I'm not so much fat as solid. I take after Eric of course.'

Natasha said, 'Well, I can see that would hurt. Mind you, better if he calls it puppy fat, rather than weight.'

'Yes. But Joy, his first wife, is rail-thin.'

'Oh. And she's with him now?'

'Yes.' Rachel found she was practically mimicking Nash and gnawing at her bottom lip. She said, 'The thing is, Nash, she, Joy, just adored Charnwood. The house is enormous and there's things like horse-riding and beagling . . . I hated it.'

'I can imagine.'

'We haven't been back there for ages now. It's much better to be seen in London – he goes up for surgeries and things. Keeps in touch. But then his actual workplace is the House.

I'm always telling him that. Douglas Maccrington – Judas – couldn't keep in touch for one thing.'

She piled the tiny sandwiches too high and they fell onto the cucumber. Natasha watched her re-erect them and said slowly, 'And you think Joy might have taken him back there? That's why he's not answering the phone and ringing you back?'

'I can't think of another reason.'

'No. It's the most reasonable. And it's not so bad, is it, Ray? If he's going to have to put up with his first wife for a time, better to be out of the limelight, surely?'

'I suppose so.' Rachel finished with the sandwiches and gave her fleeting smile to Natasha. 'I suppose what's really bugging me is my lack of control over all this. I couldn't do a thing when she turned up. She was all distraught and turning to Duncan as the father of her children – an area in which I am inexperienced!' Her tone became dry and acid. Natasha laughed. 'I know it sounds hilarious now, Nash, but it wasn't. Honestly. I knew that night that I couldn't put up with it. There wasn't room in the house for the two of us.' She shrugged. 'I don't know whether I thought Duncan would come running to me . . . I don't know anything any more. Only that everything is out of my hands.' She looked utterly defenceless. 'Completely out of my hands,' she repeated.

Natasha, cast in her new role of pseudo-strength, did not know what to say. Pru saved her from failure by poking her head in at the window.

'Never mind supper for the moment. Come and see the sunset,' she commanded.

They made for the kitchen door and, on the spur of the moment, Natasha reached out and put her arm around Rachel's shoulders. Rachel favoured her with one of her peculiar half-smiles and said, 'Thanks, Nash.' And Natasha, marvelling with the others at the blood-red sunset in the west, thought how strange it all was because since meeting Harvey she had felt like a pawn in his peculiar game of kiss and be found out, and now, out of the blue, she had some kind of power.

Pru said gently, 'Are you all right, Nash?'

Natasha nodded and laughed. 'Yes. Actually, honey, against

all the odds, I am all right.' She reached for Pru's long fingers. 'You can try leaning on me. Just a bit. And if you want to.'

Pru laughed too, pleased. 'I'd forgotten what a joy you always were, Nash.' She looked across at the other two who were standing on the bank above the stream, trying to focus a pair of binoculars. 'Thank God things worked out like this.'

Natasha nodded. 'Hear, hear,' she said. And then, 'Oh my God. Look to your right. Have you seen anything so pastoral since you were a baby?' Because around the bluff was plodding a shire horse and sitting across its broad back was Bryn the farmer.

They all went to meet him and to make a fuss of the horse.

'I'm not stopping, ladies.' He looked down on the four of them. Ill-assorted lot, they were. 'Thought I'd better tell you. Someone was after you. Earlier. Drove up from Brum, apparently. After an elderly lady who I thought must be you, miss.' He nodded at Evelyn who puckered her lips in case he might be taking a liberty.

'He didn't arrive,' Pru frowned up into the sunset. 'We've been sitting outside all day and would have seen – or heard – a car.'

'I sent him packing. You tole me you wanted to be by yourselves, miss – ' he now nodded at Pru ' – so I said as 'ow 'e'd got the wrong directions altogether. That the farm was a dead end. Nothin' after. 'Sides, he was after five ladies, not four.' He lifted his shoulders. 'I thought you'd know who it was and if you wanted to get in touch you could. But . . . he were a wrong-un. No two ways about that. I didn't want him disturbing the peace.'

Pru was still bewildered; the others knew who it was. Evelyn said shakily, 'A man on his own. Strong-looking? Dark?'

'Aye. Thought you'd know him. Sorry if I didn't do the right thing.'

Nash said fervently 'You did the right thing, Mr Bryn. Thank you. Thank you very much.' She glanced at Pru. 'It's Maisie's husband. Edward Davenport.'

'That's it! He left his name. Mrs Bryn reckoned that were a bad sign. Reckoned he didn't believe me.'

‘O–oh,’ quavered Evelyn. ‘Is there another way of reaching the house?’

‘No.’ Bryn laughed. ‘Don’t you worry now. Anyone who wants to see you has got to come through the farmyard. Or tramp down from the Beacon. And I don’t reckon he were the tramping sort.’

‘And he was alone?’ Nash was frowning. Ted Davenport appeared to have given up too easily. ‘He didn’t have a woman with him? Our age. Curly fair hair?’

‘That’d be his wife. He said she had fair curly hair. But no-one were with him. Not unless she were in the boot!’ Bryn laughed easily, pulling on the bridle so that the old horse turned, stamping, and immediately set off. ‘And I don’t reckon this is a gangster film, is it, miss?’

Pru called, ‘Certainly not, Mr Bryn!’ She laughed. ‘I’ll come and see Mrs Bryn first thing tomorrow. She said she’d do our shopping for us. Is that still all right?’

‘Aye. Certainly. It’s nice to ‘ave someone living here after all this time.’ He turned in the saddle. ‘You ought to stay on here, miss. You could make them pots you were telling us about. Plenty of shops’d buy them, you know.’

Pru laughed. She glanced at Evelyn and then put a long protective arm around the cardiganed shoulders. ‘Evie. What is it? You look as if you’re seeing ghosts!’

‘It’s Maisie,’ Evelyn looked up into the grey eyes and clutched at Pru’s arm as if to keep it in position. ‘Oh Pru, you didn’t see him! He’s a dreadful man! What if he’s murdered Maisie? What if she really was in the boot of his car?’

‘Darling!’ Pru led the older woman back to the chairs and sat her down. ‘For goodness’ sake! As if he’d come here to show us!’

‘He could have been covering himself! If he . . . did it . . . yesterday. He could pretend he was still looking for her. I saw a film once – just like that. In fact the murderer was so mad, he genuinely believed he *was* still looking for his victim!’

‘Oh I don’t think Edward Davenport is mad, Evie. Just very angry. And Mr Bryn has put him off our scent. Please try not to worry about him. Or Maisie.’

Natasha and Rachel crowded around reassuringly but Evelyn was temporarily past reassurance. 'I don't see how I can stop worrying about Maisie, girls. I gave her twenty pounds which was all I had in the house. She had a taxi – that must have taken most of the money.'

Nash said, 'Aren't you forgetting, Evie – she telephoned us. On Monday evening. She was with her brother.'

Rachel spoke sharply. 'Listen, Evie. Just because that old farmer chap makes a joke, you're reduced to a pulp! You've got to stop it! I agree Ted Davenport must be a swine and a bit of a nutcase too. But Maisie has lived with him for twenty years. Whatever he's done, or not done, she's still in one piece! She chose to stay. She can cope with him. If he has caught up with her, it's much more likely she sent him packing with a flea in his ear, and he came here to blame it all on to us!'

Evie glanced up, her pale blue eyes still anxious but respectful of Rachel's authority. 'Oh . . . yes, you're right, of course. I'm a stupid old woman!' She held up her hand at the chorus of protest. 'You don't know me. I pretend. A lot of the time, I pretend things.' She managed a laugh. 'D'you know, when Maisie arrived last Friday evening, I was in the ballroom at the Hofburg in Vienna! I was dancing! With Mr Delano!'

Everyone laughed obediently except Natasha. She said, 'Oh, Evie. How marvellous. To be able to escape into your other world must be . . . wonderful.'

Evelyn looked surprised, then nodded. 'It is. But I never tell anyone in case the warden reports me to the housing committee!'

'Well you don't have to worry about that any more.' Nash grinned. 'Mr Lavington's son sounds a power to be reckoned with. I think he'll sort out the warden, don't you?'

'Oh yes!' Evelyn said fervently.

'Meanwhile . . .' Natasha stood up and went to the edge of the stream. 'If it's still hot like this tomorrow, we'll make our own pretend world. I'm going to dam up the stream.' She pointed. 'Across there. It'll build up against these steep banks and we can have an overflow . . . here.' She moved downstream and pointed to a spot just below the kitchen window. 'So we shall have a pool . . . well, how big? Twelve by twelve, would you say? And at least six feet deep!'

Rachel was unexpectedly enthusiastic. 'It would be wonderful to be able to swim, Nash. Can it be done?'

'No reason why not. We can pretend we're in Hollywood. Own private pool. Perhaps Warren Beatty will call for coffee.'

'You won't want me to get in, will you?' Evie asked, smiling tremulously because they were all so kind.

Natasha and Rachel shook their heads, but Pru said, 'Of course you will get in, Evie. You were quite a good swimmer. I remember we went to Northfield baths once. You did a classic breaststroke!'

'Edith said I looked like a worried mallard!'

'Edith couldn't swim.' Pru kissed the permed hair gently. 'Come on, Evie. Don't promote Edith to the status of a saint. She was anything but.'

Evelyn waited until the other two were scrambling around in the water choosing suitably sized rocks for the dam. 'But you do think she might be keeping an eye on Maisie, don't you?' she asked Pru who, after all, had started a religious community.

Pru straightened and stared at the still glorious sunset. 'I hope so,' she said.

Later, she ensconced Evelyn in the sitting room in front of the nine o'clock news which flickered in black and white on the old television set, and spoke to Rachel and Natasha in the kitchen.

'I don't want to worry Evie all over again.' She poured hot water into a glass and added glucose. 'But I rather think Maisie would not turn to her brother.' She sat at the kitchen table and sipped slowly on her drink. 'I cannot tell you my reasons for saying that. I had access to Maisie's personal file, obviously. Mr Delano told me things. And then . . . when we came to see you, Nash . . . after Hilary was born . . . Maisie and I talked.

She explained to me – or she thought she explained to me – why she was going to tell her husband about Tom McEvoy – and her new pregnancy. I advised against it, and I offered her another solution. Life with me at Telegraph House.' Pru laughed shortly then finished her drink and stood up. 'She was disgusted and frightened.' She shrugged. 'I didn't think she would be able to face me again. I still don't think she will turn up here. But I also think – I'm almost certain – that neither will she go to her brother's.'

Rachel was completely bewildered. 'What are you talking about, Pru? Maisie adored you – we all adored you—'

Natasha said, 'You told her that you were a lesbian.'

'Of course.'

Natasha nodded. 'She probably thought Ted's ways were . . . "jolly manly". Or something.' She too laughed shortly. 'Christ. What a mess.'

Rachel said, 'The community . . . it's a lesbian community?'

'Yes.' Pru rinsed her glass and began to polish it. 'I'm not about to explain. Or to make any kind of excuse. I opened Telegraph House for women like myself. So that we could lead normal lives.' She replaced the glass in the cupboard with a click. 'That's it.'

'Well . . .' Rachel frowned. 'So what? This is 1980 for God's sake!'

Pru sat down again, suddenly. 'Thanks, Ray.' Suddenly she put her hands to her face and made a sound of complete despair. 'I thought . . . after Maisie'reaction . . . I didn't think any of you . . .' She looked at Natasha and smiled through a waterfall of tears. 'But you weren't frightened, Nash. And Rachel thinks I'm . . . *normal*!'

Rachel said, 'Oh, Pru . . . come on. You don't have to cry about it.'

Natasha put her arms around the wide shoulders and held the fair greying head to her ridiculous suntop. 'I think she's crying for Meg. And for Maisie,' she said. And Rachel too, sat down, with a thump.

At last, when Natasha had seated herself and Pru was explaining the efficacy of hot water and glucose, Rachel said heavily, 'Well, we can't comment on the likelihood, or not, of Maisie going to her brother's. So . . . what are we going to do about her?'

Pru looked agonized again and Natasha said hastily, 'Listen, both of you. Before any of us knew Maisie, she was looking after herself. She got the job at Markhams, she skivvied around there like a lunatic, loving every minute, earning every penny. She was . . . streetwise. She can look after herself. Really. There's nothing we can do, so I suggest we do just that. Nothing.'

Rachel did not look comforted, though she nodded when Pru nodded. Then she said, 'I'm going to go and sit with Evie for an hour before bed. I take it we don't share any of this with her?'

Reluctantly the other two nodded.

Just after dawn that day when the streets were still empty, Edward Davenport left one-four-eight and drove across town to Aston. He had done his planning carefully; in that time before Mark, before marriage, Maisie had mentioned Chamberlain Street. The playground there had been a place of terror for her after her brother had left. All the boys had tried to herd her behind the coke pile outside the furnace room; she had escaped by the skin of her teeth so she had never known what would happen if they'd got her there. But Roly had told her later. Roly had told her in order to protect her; all it had done was to frighten her. She had hidden in the stationery cupboard most days, missing her school dinner, eventually fainting away during the afternoon art class. She had made it sound comical, but both she and Ted had known it was not comical. In order to escape his father's belt, Ted had hidden for three days under the floorboards in the small room his father used as an office. And not very long after that he ended up in hospital and old man Davenport, carpenter and psychotic, had been committed. He had died and left his rundown cabinet-making business to Ted.

But if Maisie had ended up in hospital, her foster father would have had the perfect justification for beating her. After all, she was wayward. She slept with her brother.

Ted tightened his lips at the thought of what must have

gone on in that house somewhere near Chamberlain Street School. And he had actually thought it bonded him with Maisie. She had been so convincing as she painted herself the innocent victim. And all the time . . . all the time, she had been a whore. He had no doubt at all that she would go back to her roots now. For one thing she had nowhere else to go, and for another . . . it was what she would do. Unexpectedly a snippet from one of the psalms came into his head . . . something about a dog returning to its vomit. He smiled grimly as he negotiated the narrow streets which had been taken over by immigrants. A mosque ballooned from the tenements. He hated it. He hated . . . everything. But he was certain that, at last, he was on the right track. All he had to do was find the right house.

There was, of course, a Patel's. And it was open. He parked right outside on double-yellow lines and went inside. He put a twenty-pound note on the counter and looked into the fathomless dark eyes of one of the legion of Patels.

'I'm looking for my brother-in-law,' he said, directly. 'Roly Jenkins.'

It was almost too easy. The Asian face broke into a wide smile. 'Roly the plumber?' He nodded in time with Edward. 'I show you his work. Splendid it is. Splendid.' He lifted the flap on the counter and Edward followed him willy-nilly past sacks of peculiar-smelling cereals or spices or something. They were in a kitchen, brand, spanking new with mock-oak cupboards, gleaming white surfaces, a baby in a high chair and a woman in a sari. 'Splendid?' asked Patel.

Edward had not waited for so much as a cup of tea before he left this morning; he began to feel lightheaded. 'Splendid,' he agreed.

'You want him to work for you. Then he will. Most certainly he will.'

Edward backed himself against a humming dishwasher. The baby offered him a spoonful of something disgusting. 'It's just . . . we've lost touch, you see. I don't know exactly where he lives.'

Patel beamed again. 'The same house. His parents were there and now he lives there. His wife—' He spread his hands and turned his smile inside out. 'Gone many years. He is alone.'

'Not now, he isn't,' Edward said without thinking.

'Yes, sir. I do assure you. He lives alone.' Patel looked earnest. 'He is a good man.'

Vibrations from the dishwasher echoed in Edward's stomach and he wondered if he felt sick. 'And the number of the old house?' he asked.

'Same as before. Nineteen. Nineteen, Chamberlain Street. Which is named for Joseph Chamberlain, do you know?' Patel smiled proudly. 'Nothing changes around here.'

The irony of this statement was not lost on Edward. He fumbled his way out of the shop, refused to take back the twenty-pound note and then changed his mind. Once on the pavement, he breathed in the city smell with relief, then got in the car and moved off, though Patel was mouthing that number nineteen was 'a few steps only'. Edward drove past it and parked outside a house that boasted an acacia tree in its tiny front garden. He glanced at the clock on the dashboard. It was seven-thirty. He needed to be early. He needed, if possible, to catch them in bed. That would be a triumph indeed. He suddenly knew what Maisie's punishment would be: he would divorce her, get custody of the boys, Tom included, and consign her to her incestuous lover for the rest of her life.

He almost ran up the path of number nineteen – Patel still waving at him happily – and pushed at the door hopefully. He was ridiculously disappointed to find it locked, though he had known it would be. There went his hope of finding the two of them in flagrante. There was no side entrance; just a solid cliff of houses extending from Patel's to the mosque at the end of the street. He swore. Then tapped on the glass. Then seized the knocker and tried to lift it. It moved half an inch with a hideous creaking sound. He pushed it back down where it gave the faintest click. He swore again.

Above him a window opened and a man's head appeared. The man was obviously wearing pyjamas; his hair was tousled. But he was only half the act.

'Yeh?' He sounded amiable. 'Emergency?'

Edward nodded furiously. He hardly knew what he was doing any more. 'It's my wife!' he said hoarsely.

'Pipe?' The man injected a note of patience into his voice. 'Which pipe would that be then?'

Edward shouted 'Wife!' at him and the man looked puzzled then said, 'Hang on. I'll be down.'

Edward leaned against the side of the tiny porch and closed his eyes for a moment. Tilting his head like that had caused him to feel dizzy. He clutched at the sooty wall and felt the rough angle of the brick bite into his palm. He swore again.

The door opened and the man was there wearing dungarees, pushing his fingers through his hair. He had curly hair. Like Maisie's. He was unlike her otherwise except that he wore one of her typical expressions. Kind? Indulgent?

'Better come in. I'll get my kit and we can go round to the van together.'

Edward said, 'I've got the car—'

'Then I'll follow you.' The man, Maisie's brother, Roly Jenkins, led the way down the narrow passage and turned left into a room that would once have been called the front parlour. He pulled a pair of trainers from under a chair and sat down to put them on. 'Tell me where it is and what happened. If there's much flooding I can do a temporary repair.' He looked up and smiled slightly. 'Don't worry. The insurance'll cover the damage.'

Edward was beginning to know the feeling of powerlessness. It swept over him again now and he sat down abruptly on the edge of another chair. 'I don't think so,' he said.

'Where is it?' Roly Jenkins finished tying his shoes and looked up. 'Come on, man, we're losing precious time. Where is the burst?'

'It's my wife,' Edward repeated helplessly.

'Yeh. They do tend to go over the top. It'll be clean water. She's no need to—'

'I'm looking for my *wife!*' Edward said desperately.

The man's face opened blankly. 'What do you mean? I'm a plumber, man! Has someone had you on? I'm not a counsellor—'

'She's disappeared.' Edward tried to make his brain work.

This was not the way to go about things. He said, 'Where is *your* wife?'

The man Jenkins said, 'We got divorced. A long time ago. I en't got no wife, mate. And if I did have one, you couldn't have her!' He had tried to make a joke and he laughed at it himself. Edward stared at him.

'You've got someone upstairs,' he accused. 'And I think it's my wife!'

'Oh my God.' Jenkins stared at him disbelievingly. 'A nutter. What have I done to deserve this. Nice sunny Thursday in August, the whole of Birmingham to choose from and he has to come here.'

Edward began to gather his wits. 'Don't you pretend you don't know what I'm talking about!' He stood up. He was not as tall as Jenkins but he was broader, more powerful. 'I know about you and Maisie! I've always known! She told me when I met her first, over twenty years ago! She had to run away from you then! And now she's run away from me and I want her back! She needs to be punished – d'you hear me – she needs to be punished!'

Jenkins sat where he was, his jaw agape. 'Maisie? D'you mean Maisie Jenkins? My Maisie?'

Edward roared at that and Jenkins held up a hand. 'I haven't seen Maisie since the day she left here. I knew she'd go one day . . . and she did. That was that.' He stared up at Edward who was now as red as a turkey cock. 'You're married to her? She's left you?' He too stood and viewed Edward from another angle. Then he said heavily, 'How long have you been married to her?'

'I told you. Twenty years. We've got five children – big house – I've given her everything she could possibly want—'

'And she left you. What else did you give her – besides those thing?'

'What d'you mean by that?'

'She wouldn't leave without a good reason. Especially if there are children. Oh Christ . . . poor Maisie . . . what did you do to her?'

Edward felt his feet move as if he were dancing on the spot. 'None of your blasted business!'

'She used to take regular beatings from our foster da. She stuck that . . .' Jenkins frowned. 'What have you done to her? Not just beaten her – dammit, the poor kid is used to that. You've done something else!'

Edward howled. 'I want my wife! I know she's upstairs—'

Suddenly Jenkins took him by the shoulders and turned him around. He forced his arms halfway up his back and frogmarched him out of the parlour and straight up the narrow stairs. Then they went on an inspection of the three bedrooms and the bathroom. No-one else was in the house.

'Satisfied?' he asked Edward who was now gibbering with frustration. He began to shove the older man ahead of him down the stairs. They both stumbled and nearly went headlong. 'I want you to go now. I'm not going to hit you because I'd probably be the one who ended up in court. But I don't want to see your face again. Is that understood?'

He marched Edward to his car and made a mental note of the number. Edward drove off erratically and Roly Jenkins watched him go. And then propped himself under the acacia tree and thought. If only Maisie had come to him. If only . . .

Edward drove without knowing where he was going. When he found himself on the Worcester Road he made a sound between clenched teeth that sounded like clashing gears. And then he was gibbering again, but this time it was the helpless gibbering of a child. And tears spurted sporadically down to his unshaved chin. He had done something he had promised Maisie never to do: he had contacted her brother, Roly. But what was worse than the broken promise was that he had found, not a monster, but a decent man who had probably loved Maisie very much. Just as Maisie, more than probably, had loved him. He breathed deeply in an effort to put an end to the silly childish chatterings; his breath came out as a groan and for an instant he closed his eyes. The blast of a horn snapped him back to some kind of sense. He jerked the car to the left and drove past a signpost to Upton upon Severn. And then he was on familiar ground. He had driven Maisie here in the old days, when they were first married and

Mark and Jess were still babies. Once or twice, that was all. She had thought he was wonderful, taking the children off for an hour or two while she 'rambled' with the girls from Markhams. Those were the days before Mrs Donald when he had known that girl in the Shambles in Worcester. She had been too young, of course, and there had nearly been trouble. It was safer – and better – with Mrs Donald.

He took the car along to Malvern East, through the woods and the tiny hamlets and the churches and pubs. He wondered what would happen if he came face to face with Natasha Barkwith. Or Nolan. Or whatever her name was. He might be able to knock her down and call it an accident. He thought with some satisfaction of bending over her in the roadway and saying, 'This is what comes of taking my wife from me.'

In one of the openings which the footpaths took to the Beacons, he reversed the car and drove back the way he had come. It occurred to him that his fantasy might well materialize into reality. Supposing Evelyn Hazell was not in Wales at all? Supposing she and those two hell cats from Thatch End were in fact staying somewhere in Malvern already? Might they have Maisie with them?

He drove carefully into the narrow, crowded street of Great Malvern and pulled into a pub car-park to think. It was ten-thirty. They might come into this place to do some shopping. They might be staying at this pub. Or the one up the road. Or at the Link. He did not know what to do. A glance in the mirror showed him looking swarthily wild. If he went from hotel to hotel enquiring for them, he could easily get into trouble. And after that humiliating business with Roly Jenkins he wanted no more trouble unless he chose it himself. He fumbled in the map pocket and brought out a handful of road maps. He looked at the area with something like despair. He could search for years and not find them. Or he could just . . . meet them. Rambling, drinking coffee in the Elgar Tea Rooms . . . anything.

He crumpled the maps into a heap on the passenger seat and closed his eyes. His head was aching; every bone in his body felt fragile, as if it could snap under its own tension. He struggled to relax, breathing deeply again, tasting the salt of his tears on his lips, hating himself but hating Maisie more.

At last he managed to surrender himself to some kind of fate. After all, he was in the right; Maisie was his wife and she had deserted not only him but the whole family. If there was any justice at all he would find her – or one of her satanic friends – by simply driving around. That was what he would do. He would drive up and down for two hours. If nothing had happened in that time, he would go home.

Bryn's farm was his first attempt at allowing fate to steer a course. He cursed aloud when he saw the lane was a dead end but drove on to the gate where Bryn was doing some fence repairs and enquired if his wife and friends had passed that way.

'What do they look like?' Bryn asked, his sheeplike gaze taking in the expensive car and the gangster's face.

'There would be five of them,' Edward felt a glimmer of hope at the question. 'One elderly woman. The other four in their early forties. My wife is blond. Curly hair.'

Bryn answered truthfully, 'No. No-one like that, sir.'

'Well, has anyone been this way this morning?' Edward asked, his voice sharpening with irritation.

'Not a soul. Few sheep. No yoomans.'

Edward reversed with some difficulty – Bryn made no attempt to open the gate. Then the car, already dust-laden, ground its way through the cow parsley and back to the main road. Edward had already had enough of leaving any decisions to fate. It was not his way; he made his own destiny. He drove back through Great Malvern and on to the A38. He tried to put Maisie out of his head and think of Mrs Donald. And he would phone the Bristol number Jess had left with him, and tell her to get back home and do what her mother had asked her to do: look after him.

Twelve

Langford Veterinary Hospital was an enormous compound cut off from the village by a high stone wall. Inside it had the feeling of another village; there was a clock tower, and the stables and outbuildings were grouped around it cosily.

The three Davenport children had been visiting various farms in Somerset with Mark's friend, Stephen Ford. It was the end of the day and they had come back to Langford very slowly, following a horsebox containing a sick mare. They parked Mark's car thankfully and watched as some students emerged from the main building to help unload the mare.

Tom said, 'If I were a sick animal, I think I'd like to come here. It seems so homely.'

Mark laughed indulgently but Stephen nodded. 'There's a lot in that. We've got a psychology department here and their findings suggest that animals are very much influenced by their environment. Their actual housing. I met a farmer over in Exmoor who puts photographs around his cowshed. Reckons he gets a better yield.' They all laughed but then Mark said, 'How I hate that word "suggested" when it's used scientifically! Exactly what does it mean? Science should never suggest. It should state, define, confirm. Never suggest!' He made the innocuous word sound blasphemous and Jess laughed.

'Don't put Tom off for ever,' she begged. 'His first view of that breech birth this morning can't have done much for his enthusiasm.'

Tom, who had in fact been admiring the architecture of the school to take his mind off some of the sights he had seen, grinned at his sister. 'I keep thinking of when you mentioned scouring a cow or something, d'you remember? In front of poor old Dad?'

'She did it purposely,' Mark said.

Stephen demanded to be enlightened about the scouring and Tom did so with great enjoyment. Stephen Ford was older than Jess and Mark and in his final year at veterinary school. He was working in a local practice for the summer holidays and returned to the hospital each evening. Even Tom could see he had taken a shine to Jess. It made the two days' break down here even more interesting. Tom was only a year older than Simon but this year he was beginning to find personal relationships rather intriguing.

Mark said, 'Dad is slightly narrow-minded, Steve. His view of everything comes through Mum's eyes. She's gone off with some old mates of hers and he really doesn't know how to deal with us – the family, I mean.'

Jess looked up at her brother, surprised. 'D'you know, I think for once in your life you're right, Mark.' She glanced sideways at Tom. 'So you're right too, Tom. It is a case of poor old Dad.'

Mark said comfortably, 'Oh, he'll be OK once she's back.'

Jess said nothing. Tom turned to Stephen Ford, 'Our mother is a very kind person. She has gone to look after her aged friend.' Even to his own ears that sounded wrong; he was not surprised when everyone laughed.

Stephen said, 'You make her sound like someone out of a Victorian novel, Tom! Remember, I've met her once. Blond curls and dimples. Not a bit Victorian.' He looked at Jess. She was dark, like a Cherokee with her single plait and high cheekbones. She must take after her father. But she was not narrow-minded.

Jess, only too conscious of Stephen's gaze, felt herself heating up. She had intended keeping her suspicions to herself but to cover her confusion she said suddenly, 'I wonder just where Mum has gone. She certainly is not at Evelyn Hazell's place. Dad went there to find her.'

Mark said, surprised, 'I didn't realize he was looking for her.'

'Well he went to Earlswood where Evelyn lives. And he went to Thatch End where the Barkwiths live. No luck. I rather think Mum's pal, Natasha, sent him home with a flea in his ear. He wasn't happy when he got back.'

Mark was bewildered. 'Well, where the devil is she, then? Mum's never done this before – just disappeared!'

Tom felt a small quiver in his diaphragm. Jess put a hand on his shoulder. 'She hasn't disappeared – not like that. Idiot.' She made a meaning face above Tom's head. 'Apparently one of the other people from that shop – Markhams – has inherited a house. Malvern, Mum said. She must have gone there.' She grinned at Tom. 'A reunion. That's what they planned.'

'But—' Tom was not reassured.

'Listen.' Stephen stopped in front of the stable block where he had a room. 'D'you want tea and toast? Then I could take you to see that goat farm I told you about. Or we could go swimming at Weston. Come on, it's your last night!'

Jess kept her grin in place. 'I vote for swimming. What d'you say, Tom? I reckon you've had enough of our four-footed friends for a bit, haven't you?'

Tom let himself be jollied along for then, but as they were collecting their swimming things he said, 'Shall we go home through the Malverns? We might see something of Mum and her friends.'

And Jess said jokily, 'Good wheeze!' and then shook her head ruefully. 'Sorry. Yes. We'll do that, Tom. I keep forgetting you're sixteen soon.'

'So do I.' Stephen looked at the three of them. 'Funny. You three always seem young to me. Must be because of the sheltered existence you led. Boarding school and so on.' He ran, cowering, to the car and they all settled into it, laughing almost naturally.

It was when they were on their way home the next day that the subject of their mother's 'disappearance' cropped up again. Tom had a wakeful night to think about it and went straight to the crux of the matter.

'If Dad is looking for Mum, then he doesn't know where she's gone. And she would never go anywhere without telling him.' He leaned forward in the back seat and looked first at Mark's profile, then Jess's. 'What does it mean?'

Mark said heavily, 'I'm asking that question too. What do you know, Jess?'

Jess shrugged. 'I said to Dad, it's nothing world-shattering. And I still think it's nothing important. But certainly I agree with Tom, it's not like Mum.' She sighed. 'I suppose they must have had a row. A blinder of a row too. And Mum's gone off with her friends without leaving a forwarding address.' She made a face. 'I just hope she can enjoy herself. Knowing Mum she's sitting around feeling guilty.'

'Well if we can find her, we can tell her Dad's OK,' Tom said doubtfully.

'Yes.' Jess turned to look at him. 'We haven't got much chance of finding this house though, Tom. The Malvern Hills cover a rather large area. There are cottages and houses dotted around all over the place.'

Mark said, 'No other info? She just told you she was going to Malvern?'

Jess said hesitantly, 'She didn't exactly say she was going. She said her friend had inherited a house there and they were planning a reunion. And could I possibly cope at home.'

'Mrs Donald does most of the stuff at home anyway,' Tom commented.

'Except where we're concerned. Mum does all our stuff.'

Tom said stoutly, 'Well, we can manage, can't we? If she needs to get away that badly . . . we can manage.'

'Sure we can,' Mark said heartily.

But then Tom said, 'I just wish we knew where she *was*!'

And, surprisingly, Jess echoed, 'So do I.'

But their detour through and around the Malvern Hills did not help. Jess told Tom how their mother had brought them here when they were young. For picnics, hide and seek, rounders and then cricket. Tom could not remember. He thought it looked like a foreign country. And somewhere in it, his mother was lost to him.

* * *

The weekend flew by. Natasha was unexpectedly brilliant at constructing a dam to hold back enough water in which to swim. The steep banks lent themselves to the project; she organized everyone into collecting the large flat boulders she needed and buttressed each layer carefully, leaving an empty space at the nearside bank so that the water did not build up too much pressure before she was ready for it. Muddy and unkempt, dressed in cut-off jeans and a bra top, she waded back and forth, collecting the stones supplied by Rachel and Pru and piling them carefully into position.

Pru was amused; the others were delighted to see her laugh as she held a part of the wall against imminent collapse.

'It's all very well for you!' she gasped, water spilling over her shoulders. 'Just sitting around watching! Nash, you're the architect! Come and archi!'

Nash removed some stones from her overflow. 'We've got to lower the pressure again. Just for a while until we're more certain of the dam.'

'Lower it, lower it!' gasped Pru as the water reached her chin.

Rachel plunged in alongside Natasha and took the stones from her. Evelyn bleated helplessly. The water level began to subside and, to their delight, when they looked up at Evelyn she was peeling off her tights and her pleated skirt lay neatly folded by her shoes.

'Come on, Evie!' Natasha said. 'Let's make a human chain – take that flat stone from Ray – don't just drop it, honey! We shall need it later!'

'Sorry, Nash.' Evelyn was gasping. 'This water's damned cold!'

They howled and Evelyn smirked too as she got used to the temperature. Rachel said, 'Oh, if Mr Lavington could see you now!' Evelyn smirked again; the girls laughed louder.

Natasha said, wonderingly, 'We're having a good time, girls. Wouldn't you say?'

'Nothing like hard work for helping you over hurdles.' Rachel spoke with unaccustomed humour, then promptly slipped and fell into the deeper water. The next minute they were all leaping and splashing like eighteen-year-olds again and it was only Pru's voice, raised to concert pitch that broke through the babble.

'Phone! Someone . . . I can't go otherwise Nash's wonderful wall will collapse—'

Evelyn said, 'Oh Lord! Suppose it's that man!'

Rachel said, 'I'll go. It'll be Duncan for me.'

They all waited while Rachel sprinted up the bank and into the house and they must have been tense because when she called back, 'Nash – it's for you! Your daughter!' they all subsided, smiling. Natasha might be anxious for her Hilary, but at least it wasn't Edward Davenport on the line, and Meg hadn't died and Duncan hadn't decided to go back to Joy.

Natasha stood in the narrow hall dripping water onto the threadbare carpet. 'Darling, are you all right?'

'Sure. How about you? Has your Maisie turned up yet?'

'No. But we're not going to worry. She still thinks we're not getting together until the last week in August. She'll turn up then.'

'Good. Listen, Ma. You weren't joking. Larry Blum is a complete shit. And Ruth must be too because she probably started the whole thing. I just can't hang around and watch that going on with Mabs Blum thinking they're so perfect and I'm crazy because my parents have split up. My God, you and Harve are normal compared with the Blums – I mean normal, Ma! Even Mary Pressburger seems—'

'Honey, stop.' Natasha was getting cold in the sunless hall. She looked down at her bare and muddy feet. She could hear the others, outside, a sudden scream of laughter as part of the dam no doubt gave way again. But in her head she could almost see Maine and the tennis courts and hear Mabs saying, 'Anyone for bridge?' She thought, surprised, I would hate that now. Something has happened to me . . . I would just hate it. She said flatly, 'I am not coming over there. I mean it, Hillie. I am so sorry you're finding it difficult—'

'Ma, have you forgotten what we talked about already? Incest! That's what it is, Ma! I'm not kidding! I've practically stumbled over them a coupla times. I can't take it, Ma!'

Natasha sighed. She knew that Hilary got her sense of drama from her. Wasn't this why this whole Maisie thing was so intriguing? But it was hard to deal with at such a long distance. She said soothingly, 'Hillie. Have you tried talking to Ruth?'

'No! She gives me the creeps. I don't want to talk to her again.'

'OK. Is your father back there for the weekend?'

'Yeh. Otherwise I couldn't have . . . done . . . what I've done.'

Natasha felt a familiar sense of doom. 'What exactly have you done, Hillie?' she asked very calmly.

'Never mind that, Ma. I just wanted you to understand the situation. You do, don't you?'

'I know it's hard for you, baby—'

'Good. Well, that's great. That's excellent.' Natasha heard her daughter take a breath. 'Listen, I've got a cab waiting here. I need some directions. I've got the phone number and I know it's Prospect House, East Malvern. But he wants to know a bit more. Before he'll take me.'

Natasha squeezed her eyes shut and opened them again. She was still in the hallway and through the window by the front door the gravel track meandered alongside the stream to that first bluff.

She said, 'Honey. What are you talking about? A cab? Where do you want the cab driver to take you?'

Hilary sounded impatient. 'To you, of course! To this Prospect House! He can get to Worcester – piece of cake apparently – ' she put on a cockney accent. Natasha recognized bravado when she heard it.

She dropped her voice to one of sepulchral calm. 'Hillie. Where are you speaking from?'

'For God's sake, Ma! Heathrow Airport, of course. And this cab – taxi – is ticking up like crazy—'

'*Heathrow airport*!' Her scream must have been heard outside because the background of laughter ceased suddenly. 'You're in England? What the hell are you playing at, Hilary? You wanted to go home for the long vacation and I took you back and your father was going to take you down to Maine where we've been before and you've been perfectly happy—'

'Ma . . .' Hilary's voice was suddenly very young. 'Ma, please listen. Please. I thought I wanted to be with Harve – you know all the fun things – all that stuff. England – Grannie and Grandad and even the new pool . . . it seemed boring and awful. And anyway, Ma, I thought I could patch things up between you and Pop somehow. And then that didn't work and you went back and . . . Ma, I miss you. I'm sorry. But it's done now and I'm here and I want to be with you as soon as I can.'

Natasha heard her own breathing. There was a sound behind her and when she looked round the other three were there, muddy and dripping like she was herself. She summoned a weak smile and made a gesture with her hand.

'How – how did you manage it? My God, they'll send for the police—'

'I left a note for Harve. Of course. One of Lew's colleagues had flown out with some business papers and was going back. He gave me a lift. Some private airport. I got a taxi to J.F.K. There was a cancellation . . . oh you know. It wasn't hard, Ma.'

Natasha sobbed. 'Anything could have happened. You're fifteen, Hillie!'

'Well, it didn't. I'm here. This is me. Hello?'

'Don't be sassy.' Natasha snapped, furious now. 'What did you do for money?'

'I borrowed one of Harve's cards.'

Natasha made a moaning sound. 'That's theft, Hilary! Haven't you got any moral sense any more?'

'How can it be theft? He'd have *given* it to me if I'd asked him! Only he might not have let me leave. So I borrowed it. I'm not going to *keep* it, Ma! I'm not that dishonest!'

Natasha felt she was losing her grip. 'He'll stop it!' she wailed. 'And anyway English taxi drivers won't look at cards – not from a young girl!'

'He wouldn't do that. I explained in my note that I'd use it just for necessities.' Natasha made a sound of despair. A taxi from London to Malvern, a necessity? Hilary went on quickly, 'Anyway, I knew the problem about cards in Britain. So I got a load of cash from one of the dispensers in J.F.K. I asked the cab driver if he minded dollars and he said not a bit.'

Natasha made another sound. She realized that Pru and the others were close. She leaned forward and put her forehead on Pru's shouder. 'Forget the taxi. He could kidnap you. Anything. I'll come and get you. I'll be two or three hours – I'm not sure – but—'

'Ma. Will you calm down? I am coming in the cab. Now.' Hilary spoke slowly, enunciating very precisely. 'Whether you give me directions or not, I am on my way. OK?'

'No. Not OK. Get the cab driver to the phone. I'll give him directions myself.'

'Can I trust you, Ma?'

'In this, yes. In other things, I'm not sure.'

Hilary snuffled a laugh and for the first time Natasha realized she was weeping.

She lifted her head from Pru's shoulder and said, 'Pru, I'm so sorry. Hillie is coming here. Do you mind very much?'

Pru's smile was instant. 'So long as you don't decide to go back to Thatch End with her until September . . .'

'Does anyone else mind?' Natasha looked at the other two who both shook their heads, smiling. Evelyn murmured something about a chip off the old block.

A male voice – with a cockney accent – spoke into Natasha's ear. 'The young lady says you want a word? You're 'er mother, she says.'

'I am. Now listen. She's my only child. She's just arrived from the States. I want to see her as soon as possible – but not too soon – drive carefully! Can I trust you?'

'She's asked me to bring 'er up to Worcester. You can trust me to do that. She's a fare just like any other fare as far as I'm concerned—'

'Well, not as far as I'm concerned! She's fifteen years old—'

He interrupted, obviously shocked at that. 'Fifteen d'you say? I got a fifteen-year-old girl. She don't look like this one.'

Natasha said hurriedly, 'Probably on the plane it was better to look . . . I hope she hasn't tampered with her passport.'

'Well if she has she's got away with it.' The driver sounded resigned. 'Listen, lady. I'll bring her home. Tell me where to come and I'll 'ave 'er with you in a couple of hours. Sounds as if she needs a bit of parental guidance. Can't say fairer than that.'

Natasha took a breath to say more, then let it go. She began to give careful directions. At the end of them she asked to speak to Hilary again.

'If there's any difficulty, just ask him to stop at the nearest phone box and ring here. I can meet you anywhere. Is that understood? You can reverse the charges.'

'Of course. That's what I did this time. Rachel agreed to take my call.' Natasha made another sound, rather like a yelp and Hilary said, 'Oh, Ma . . .' and gave a husky laugh. Then said cheerfully, 'What are you doing – what were you doing when I rang?'

'Building a dam,' Natasha said with resignation.

'Oh, Ma! How – how – excellent! Leave some for me to do!' And the line went dead.

Everything seemed to be ticking over fairly well when the three older Davenport children arrived home. On Saturday Jess kept a sharp eye on her father and saw he was 'going downhill' as she put it to Mark. The mealtime conversations were as noisy as ever but both Edward and Mrs Donald seemed to be in a world of their own. Simon and Ian had been kicking around the house for two days and reported to Mark that Dad had been at the office from before breakfast until late at night. Mrs Donald had provided food and clean clothes, otherwise they had looked after themselves. They were delighted to see Jess: they wanted a mother figure. Jess felt the responsibility like a weight. Mark took his share, entertaining them with tales of country life in Somerset. But everything was different now. Jess puzzled about it as she hoovered and dusted and tidied up after the five of them. Her mother had been absent before she and Mark and Tom had gone to see Stephen but things had not been like this.

And then, on Sunday evening, Mrs Donald dropped her bombshell.

It was six o'clock and Jess had joined her in the kitchen

to help with the supper. She said, 'Dad has gone for a drive but he said he'd be back by seven. Is that OK?'

Mrs Donald shrugged. 'It doesn't matter to me. I'm the housekeeper.'

Jess looked at her in surprise but there was no acrimony in the voice. It was just a statement. And Jess knew that it was true. Mrs Donald was 'fond' of Mum and took her cue from Mum about how to look after Dad. But she was not one of the family. She had been with them for thirteen years but she was still just the housekeeper.

Jess said awkwardly, 'Well . . . how is Dad? Eating OK? Simon and Ian were saying he's putting in some very long hours at work.'

'Why don't you ask him?'

Jess began to feel most peculiar; like an inquisitive visitor. 'I have. But he seems . . . well, you know . . . in a gloom. I suppose he's worried about Mum.'

Mrs Donald placed a huge bowl of salad on the tray. 'As far as I know all he's done is search for your mother.' She looked up. 'I'm not staying, Jess. Obviously your mother's not coming home. I always thought . . . I didn't realize how much she did around the house. I can't manage on my own.'

Jess was appalled. She had thought the atmosphere was bad; she had thought her father was gradually withdrawing into himself. It appeared that they had all reached a precipice without knowing it. She tried to speak in a reasonable voice.

'You're quite wrong about my mother, Mrs D. I don't know how many times I have to say this. She is taking a much-needed break. She will be back. And now I'm here I can help you. There's absolutely no need to leave us for the sake of a couple of weeks, surely?'

'You don't understand, Jess.' Mrs Donald took an enormous breath; the whole effort of speaking seemed almost too much for her. 'Your father is a violent man. I am afraid he might have . . . hurt your mother.'

Jess knew she should be furious; she should order the woman out of the house. She was on the point of doing so, and then did not.

Mrs Donald said, 'I am very fond of Mrs Davenport. I couldn't stay here without her.'

Jess simply stared. There was a sinking feeling in the pit of her stomach. She tried to work her mouth to ask . . . all sorts of things. In the end all she could say was, 'But . . . I love him. He's my father.'

'So does she. Love him. Or she did.' Mrs Donald shrugged. 'Something happened.' She turned away as if losing interest. 'Anyway, I can't live with him if she's not here. And that's that.'

Afterwards Jess was to remember that her words were inappropriate. At the time all she could say was, 'He's smacked us of course. When we were younger. But . . .'

'He won't touch any of you. Unless it's Tom.'

'Tom? Why Tom? As far as I know he has never punished Tom. Not once.'

Mrs Donald shrugged. 'He knew she'd go if he did.' She was cutting bread and buttering it now. 'But she went before Tom got back from school. So that's not it.'

Jess stared down at the loaded tray. Little memories rose inexorably to the surface of her mind. Mum wearing dark glasses in the middle of winter. The broken wrist that time, and a garbled account of a fall. But her father had actually teased her about both injuries. 'I knock her about . . . didn't you know?' and he had kissed her and laughed. And Jess was almost certain that her mother had laughed too.

She said flatly, 'I don't believe it.'

Mrs Donald said, 'When he came home on Thursday he'd been driving all day. Looking for her. Down Aston way where her brother lives. In Malvern where she was supposed to be going with her friends. He was frantic.' She piled the bread and butter on a plate and brought it to the tray. 'I asked him how he'd got on. And he knocked me to the ground.'

Jess gasped. 'Oh God.'

'It wasn't the usual . . .' Mrs Donald seemed to check herself. 'It was . . . out of character—'

'Of course it was,' Jess said wildly.

'But I can't risk it.' She picked up the loaded tray decisively. 'I'll tell him tomorrow and leave on Tuesday.'

'Where will you go?' Jess wailed.

Mrs Donald smiled grimly. 'My mother is still alive. Probably be glad of a hand.' She made for the door and turned her back to push it open. 'He's been good to me. I want to make that clear. But . . . he needs both of us. And if she's gone then I must go.'

Jess wailed, 'I don't understand . . .'

Mrs Donald had one more bombshell to drop. 'You four will be all right. But watch out for young Tom. If what I hear is right, your grandfather ended up as mad as a hatter. Could be your dad's going the same way. So . . . just watch out for Tom.'

Jess found herself wailing at the door as it swung back and forth. Tom . . . why Tom? And what had happened to her grandfather? His name was never mentioned. He had died aeons ago, in a hospital somewhere. She sat down suddenly on a stool.

'What is happening?' she whispered. 'My God, what is happening?'

Her father came in at seven o'clock; he seemed mildly pleased to see them though he was even quieter than usual. Mrs Donald served the meal without fuss as she always did and the babble between the younger boys was normal. Jess had been longing to get Mark to herself and tell him what had gone on in the kitchen just now, but as the meal progressed she wondered if she had imagined a lot of the exchange with Mrs Donald. It was her prerogative to leave one-four-eight when ever she wanted to: her reasons for doing so had seemed clear-cut at first . . . after all she wouldn't have lied about being knocked down, would she? But then later, there was some confusion. All that business about Edward needing his wife and his housekeeper . . . it had been more than that . . . what exactly had she said? And if she had been knocked down, wouldn't she have called the police? And all those dire warnings about Tom. Tom was the apple of his father's eye. Sent to boarding school like his older sister and brother; whereas Simon and Ian were kept at home. She shook her head: she did not know what was happening. Or if anything really was happening.

'Headache, Jess?' Mark asked.

'Yes. I think I have.' She tried to shoot a humorous look at the boys. 'Not used to all this racket.'

He said in a low voice, 'Try not to worry. I'm sure everything will be back to normal soon.'

She widened her smile. 'What is normal?' She glanced at Mrs Donald's closed face then at her father picking at a bread roll. A sudden thought came into her mind, to be instantly dismissed. Mrs Donald was so . . . unattractive.

She shook her head, 'Perhaps what we thought was normal wasn't really normal at all.'

Mark said, 'Come on, old girl. You're going all doe-eyed about Steve. That's what this is all about.'

She shook her head again. 'I hadn't thought of Steve or those two wonderful days for at least an hour!' But she felt better for the reminder and smiled, remembering how he had looked at her. She said, 'Everything will be all right.'

'That's what I just said!' Mark rolled his eyes.

It was difficult to know whether Edward had been following this, or any of the other conversations around the table, but at this point he stood up suddenly and left the room.

Tom called out, 'Dad, there's a pudding! Mrs Donald has made ice-cream!'

Mrs Donald actually smiled. 'Your father doesn't like ice-cream, Tom. He's going for a walk in the garden. Let him have a bit of peace.' She began to gather up the salad plates. She seemed released by Edward's departure. 'I nearly always make a pudding with your father in mind.' She smiled again. 'But there are five of you and I know you like my strawberry ice-cream.'

Simon and Ian cheered loudly, which covered the fact that the other three looked startled by her unaccustomed explanation. She waved aside any help from Jess and carried the tray to the kitchen.

Jess said inconsequentially, 'We've always thought this was normal because we haven't known anything else. Suppose it's not a bit normal. If you remember, Steve thought we were . . . well, unusual . . . because we'd been to boarding school. I mean, it's all relative, isn't it?'

Tom said, 'There's not many families around with five children. That's one unusual thing.'

Simon said, 'And we're pretty close in age.'

'Mum always wanted a big family,' Mark maintained. 'Nothing wrong in that. If she hadn't had the hysterectomy, I reckon we might be six. Or seven.'

Ian and Simon looked surprised. Jess went on as if thinking aloud. 'Mrs Donald is . . . odd. And Mum herself – she's never worked – she's given her life over to us and to Dad.'

'Mainly Dad,' Mark said.

Mrs Donald came in with the tray again; this time loaded with sundae dishes. She smiled slightly at the obvious silence. 'So you've told them?' she said to Jess.

'No. Not yet.' Jess clapped her hands theatrically at the strawberry-topped puddings. 'Oh goodie. Thanks, Mrs D.'

'Told us what?' Mark asked.

'Nothing. I'll go into it later.'

Tom said, 'Mum's coming home! That's it, isn't it?'

'Not yet.' Jess waved her spoon at her brother. 'For goodness' sake, Tom! How many times have I told you, they are having a reunion!'

Mrs Donald's smile became indulgent. 'I'm leaving, Tom. I told Jess before supper. I can't manage without your mother and that's that.'

'But she'll be back!' Tom bleated.

'I don't think so.' Mrs Donald tucked into her ice-cream with evident enjoyment.

Tom looked wildly at Mark, then at Jess, who shook her head very slightly and started to eat as well. Edward came back into the room. They all glanced at him and then quickly away. His face had a cadaverous look they had not noticed before.

He went to the drinks cabinet and poured himself a whisky.

Tom quavered, 'Dad. Mrs Donald says Mum isn't coming home.'

Edward turned quite slowly and stared at the housekeeper. Jess thought; oh my God, she's enjoying this. She's done this before . . . tortured him . . . deliberately.

'What do you know?' he asked hoarsely.

'Only what you know.' She finished her pudding and pushed the dish away from her. 'It happened before, didn't it? Wasn't it a hippie then? Perhaps she's found him again. Tom's dad. Seems only right he should know his proper dad.' She laughed.

He threw his glass at her. It skittered along the table. Ian moved sideways and it flew between the two boys and onto the carpet. It did not break. The smell of whisky was everywhere. He advanced towards Mrs Donald. 'You know nothing about Maisie, do you? You . . . whore! Do you think that I have any feeling towards you – anything in the slightest—'

She hissed, 'Why do you sleep with me then? Is it because Maisie won't do what I do for you? Won't—'

Jess moved at last; she grabbed the younger boys and hustled them out of the room. Ian was hiccoughing loudly; Tom was white, his blue eyes enormous. They heard Mark say loudly, 'Dad! Stop this. Now! Mrs Donald – get out – just leave. Ring for a taxi and go!'

'I was going anyway. Ask your sister. I already told her I was going.'

Edward continued to advance towards her and now his arms were outstretched. Jess, glancing over her shoulder, knew he was going to take her by the throat. Amazingly she stayed where she was, still smiling. And then Mark was standing in front of her, taking his father's hands and turning them as if Edward had suddenly gone blind and needed a guide. They moved towards the sofa.

Jess shut the garden door on the boys and went back.

'Come on now, Mrs D. I'll help you pack.'

The strange thing was, Mrs Donald did not want to leave the room. She sat there looking at Edward, still smiling slightly.

'I think your father is having a nervous breakdown,' she said. And she laughed again as she stood up at last.

The taxi bumped into view and began to grind up the gravel towards the house. Farmer Bryn, forewarned on the telephone, stood on the old-fashioned running board giving directions and making comments. The four women could hear Hilary's voice coming through the open window.

'Wow, this is wonderful, Mr Bryn. Like a foreign country somehow. No wonder that musician chap wrote all those stirring bits.' She carolled a few bars of 'Land of Hope and Glory'. Mr Bryn said, 'Yes, miss.'

Hilary, in a determined effort to break through his phlegm, said gaily, 'D'you know, I was probably conceived up here somewhere! Harvey and Nash did their courting in these hills!' Natasha uttered one of her yelps of annoyance; Pru and Rachel grinned; Evelyn buttoned up her face. And Farmer Bryn said, 'That so, miss?'

And then the taxi came to a halt and Hilary emerged, heartbreakingly beautiful, and stood still, looking at her mother across twenty yards of gravel.

Natasha murmured, 'Oh God. What shall I do with her? She's going to be so . . . disruptive!'

And then Hilary said, 'Ma . . . oh, Ma . . .' and began to run. And Natasha went to meet her and the next instant they were weeping in each other's arms while Pru told the driver that there was a meal and a chair waiting for him indoors.

'I love you, Ma,' Hilary sobbed. 'I'm so sorry. I can't help it! I love you!'

'And I love you too,' Natasha said, unreservedly.

Thirteen

Sam Lavington woke early as usual and waited for six o'clock to boom out from the church tower behind the estate. He made it a rule not to get up before six; half-past five was uncivilized; six o'clock was simply early. He did not really enjoy the enforced lie-in, it was when he did his serious thinking which was not always a cheerful process. On the other hand it gave him time to shift his cramped limbs around the bed and make sure they were all working. During the day he seemed able to control his thoughts. They skittered around such things as food and washing-up, gardening and keeping himself shipshape. He did not permit anything very deep to cross his mind during the day; his plans for reorganizing the estate often preceded an afternoon nap, also how he was going to make Miss Hazell's life a bit more interesting. But during those early mornings he thought of how old he was . . . another two years till eighty . . . and how old Young Sam was . . . fifty-two, was it possible? And that meant that Bessie had been dead just over thirty years. He sighed. It couldn't have been easy for Young Sam to celebrate that first birthday without his mum; and it would have to be his twenty-first. Life was a sod at times.

He shifted slightly, feeling cramp tightening his calf muscles. Toes up towards the ceiling . . . that was better. Of course duvets had their uses; if he was strapped in with a sheet the way Bessie had always made the bed, he wouldn't be able to point his toes anywhere except down. He had noticed Miss Hazell had a duvet. She was such a lady, so neat and precise, old-fashioned values though she couldn't be seventy yet. But then again in other ways, she wasn't a bit old-fashioned. Going along with those crazy friends of hers. He smiled, wondering how they were all getting along together. It would be good to see her back in her bungalow; he'd enjoy hearing all about it, having a bit of a chat. And he could make a story out of his confrontation with Edward Davenport. Nasty bit of work he'd been.

His calf muscles released themselves and he relaxed, smiling wider. Miss Hazell had taken his mind off matters of death . . . She was part of this getting-old business and people-dying business; but she was also part of something else. A future. An interesting future.

He did not wait for the church clock, but swung his legs out of bed and sat for a moment getting his bearings. Then he leaned forward and twitched the curtains aside. Not quite such a lovely morning but not bad. No wind anyway; he didn't like wind; rain he could take, but wind, no. He glanced sideways at the mirror which hung above his chest of drawers. He looked awful; a stereotypical old man. He had a bit of hair but not much and his mouth went right in so that his large nose became larger. He took his teeth out of their glass and slid them into his mouth and immediately looked better. Thank God for that. He wasn't vain – at least he didn't think so – but he was fastidious and proud of it. He liked clean bed linen and pyjamas, a shower every day, and often a shave twice a day if he was going to the pub to see Young Sam. It upset him to see himself looking so . . . face it, man . . . old. He couldn't expect someone of not-yet-seventy to want to be with a man who looked over a hundred. Yet she had seemed pleased enough to see him last Monday. Miss Hazell. It had a nice ring to it. And she had a nice look to her. Her bungalow and everything in it was clean and neat. Like herself really. She was no beauty but she was trim and . . . and good. Like a nice apple. Not that he intended to bite her . . . his grin came again. Perhaps one day he could tell her that. Make her laugh. Perhaps.

He got up and began the business of the day and halfway through his shower the church clock struck six. He was at least twenty minutes ahead of schedule. Well . . . just this once he'd go along to that twenty-four-hour garage on the main road and get himself a paper and read the blasted thing from cover to cover. He made a face in the steamy mirror: that would kill at least ten minutes! He grinned. He was feeling quite witty today.

At midday he realized he was half an hour behind schedule. He said aloud, 'If that's not sod's law, I don't know what is.' He went into the kitchen to scrape a couple of new potatoes and fry a rasher of bacon. He promised himself an hour's weeding on the allotment this afternoon and perhaps a full day's gardening tomorrow. Sitting around reading silly newspapers was wasting his life, and he did not know how much of that he'd got either. It was no surprise when he ran the knife along his thumb knuckle and fetched blood: it was that sort of day. He wound his handkerchief around the thumb, finished scraping, lit two gas rings and went for the bacon. The doorbell rang.

'Bugger it!' he muttered. 'If that's old Thomson wanting to borrow my drain rods again, I'll tell him to hang on to them and I'll ruddy well borrow them back when I want them next!'

He turned off the gas jets and shuffled down the hall like the old man who had looked out of the mirror this morning. Two years off eighty and he was supposed to look after the whole estate. He opened the door, frowning fiercely, and then stopped frowning. A girl stood on the step. A girl of about sixteen, seventeen. Dark hair, long plait.

She said, 'Mr Lavington?'

'Aye.' He was cautious. These market research places were sending them out younger than ever these days.

She said, 'My mother is a friend of your neighbour. Miss Evelyn Hazell.'

And then he knew. She was a beautiful girl and her father was downright ugly, but there was a likeness.

He said, 'Ah?' If her father had sent her he wasn't going to make it easy for her.

He saw her swallow. She had a long throat and you could see it contract. She said, 'We . . . I . . . my brother and I . . . we wondered if there was any way we could get in touch with Evelyn. A phone number. Or something.'

She wore blue denims and she suddenly put her hands in her pockets as if she didn't know what to do with them. He stared at her. She was as tall as her father but with none of his bulk. She wore a check shirt and he could see the bones of her shoulders through the cotton. He looked past her and saw a car at the kerb; no-one else in it. Even so, she wasn't old enough to drive it, so where was her father?

He sighed heavily, thinking of his potatoes and bacon. 'You'd better come in,' he said and led the way into the sitting room. He sat down on the window-seat he'd made and indicated the one easy chair. He always did this. People thought he was being polite but in fact it put them in the light and made him into a silhouette.

He said, 'Miss Davenport, isn't it?'

That got her. Her big eyes opened wide and she said, 'Well, yes. How did you know?'

'I've met your father and you're like him. Where is he?'

'At home. We live in Edgbaston.' Her hands were out of her pockets and were twisting away on her knees.

'You're too young to drive. Who brought you here?'

'I'm eighteen. I've already done a year at Edinburgh. Training to be a vet.'

He raised his brows. 'Most girls these days look older than they are. You don't.'

'Don't I? I never think about it.' She shrugged and added irrelevantly, 'I've got four brothers.'

'Yes. That Natasha said there were five children.' He sat back. 'Well, you're looking for Evelyn Hazell who you think will know the whereabouts of your mother. What made you come to my house?'

'My father came to see you. Last week.'

'Yes but I wasn't here. I was looking after Miss Hazell's place.'

She nodded. 'But he said you had some plastic ducks. And there were some plastic ducks on your lawn. So I thought . . .'

He nodded. 'Fair enough. You're doing some detective work for him. All I know is Miss Hazell went off with her sister to Wales. Sorry. No other information.'

She bit her lip. 'The thing is . . . Mark and I . . . my brother who is also at Edinburgh . . . we went off last Wednesday to see a friend in Bristol. We took Tom. That's our other brother . . . next one down. We got back on Friday. And things weren't too good. And then on Sunday our housekeeper left. And Dad . . . I think he's having a nervous breakdown. I don't know much about it. Everyone seems to think Mum has left him – he thinks that now. But – ' she swallowed again and then coughed ' – he seems to hate her now. He just wants to find her to, to, punish her.' Tears suddenly enlarged her eyes. 'He's been to her brother's house in Aston and she wasn't there and the brother was . . . was . . . a bit violent I think. So he hates the brother. And he hates you. And he really, really hates the Barkwiths because they must have a phone number or something to get in touch with Natasha, but they won't give it to him – I expect Natasha told them not to –'

Sam said gruffly, 'She did.' He leaned towards her and handed her the pristine handkerchief from his breast pocket. She blew her nose fiercely and pressed the linen to her eyes.

'You know all about it, don't you? You think he's wicked and evil – we think he probably does hit Mum, but she's never said anything and she seemed to be really happy with him . . . and if Tom . . . if Tom . . .' she started to cry properly and he could not hear what she said.

'Look.' He spoke loudly because she was making little moaning sounds into his handkerchief. 'Look, I don't want to cause you any upset, miss. I'll tell you what I know. It won't help you, but then . . . it might.'

She controlled herself with difficulty, blew her nose again and said, 'Please. Call me Jess.'

So he did. And he told her exactly what had happened the previous Monday evening and how Edward Davenport had frightened little Miss Hazell half to death and how Miss Hazell and her two friends, one of whom was Natasha Barkwith, had confided in him. And how they had gone to Malvern to their other friend, the very next day, and he had slept in Miss Hazell's bed and she had slept here, in his, and he had fended off Edward Davenport when he turned up.

He said, 'I'll admit to you, Jess my girl, I enjoyed it all.

Being taken into their little plan like that. Life can get a bit dull around here, you have to do something to pep it up. That's why I keep ducks!' He grinned at her expression and shook his head. 'I'll tell you about that another time. But last week, it was something different. Nothing I'd worked out myself. Just a bolt from the blue. And they asked me to help out.' He puffed out his cheeks comically. 'I felt like a knight in shining armour! I can tell you that!'

He'd made her smile at last. She really was beautiful. And hopefully not a damned fool like her mother either.

She said, 'But they didn't know where Mum was?'

'With her brother. She phoned. She was with her brother.'

Jess shook her head sadly, 'I don't think so. Dad isn't easily fooled and he had a word with the local shopkeeper too. Mum is quite distinctive. If she'd been around she would be noticed.'

'Well then, she's in an hotel somewhere. She'll be turning up at the end of this week, you see. There's going to be five of them up there. They've got a house. They'll be having high jinks – just you wait and see.'

'The thing is,' Jess said, 'I don't reckon Dad will . . . manage . . . that long.'

Sam said stubbornly, 'He'll have to, won't he?'

'You don't understand. There's been a row.' She hiccoughed loudly. 'He said . . . he said he was going to kill Tom.'

'Tom? That's the brother next to you?' He saw her face as she nodded and said reassuringly, 'Fathers say things like that, my girl. They don't do it. Not to their own kids.'

She said something and then hiccoughed again. He said, 'What?' and she said too loudly, 'Tom's not his son!' then she put her hands to her face and started to weep again.

He removed the first handkerchief which was balled on her lap, and went into the bedroom to fetch another one. On the way back he diverted into the kitchen and lit the gas under the kettle. It was what women did: made tea. Back in the sitting room her sobs had reached the shuddering stage. He gave her the clean handkerchief, told her about the kettle and sat down again.

She gasped, 'I'm so sorry, Mr Lavington—'

'Call me Sam,' he suggested.

'It's just that Mrs Donald said he was going mad like our grandfather and when I asked him about it he said – he said—'

'Take it steadily, my girl.'

'His father hit him – all the time – and then, so badly, they put him in an asylum and then he died.'

Sam thought about that then said, 'So he takes it out on his wife and hits her.' He took a breath. 'Who is Mrs . . . whatever-you-said?'

'She was our housekeeper.' Jess finally dried her eyes and had another blow and said coherently, 'I've got a feeling there was something between them. Something quite horrible.'

'Forget that for now.' He got up and went into the kitchen and made a pot of tea. 'Let that brew a bit, we don't want to drink dishwater.' He stood before her, looking down. A straight middle parting ran from forehead to crown and the hair was sort of gathered up somehow before it was plaited. He said, 'You think his only hope is to have his wife back so that he can hit her again?'

'*No*!' It was a cry of anguish. 'We wouldn't – Mark wouldn't allow that!' She calmed herself very obviously. 'Mark is with him now. Mark has been quite terrific. He got rid of Mrs Donald. And he stopped Dad from . . . doing anything to her. And I think he's been talking to him most of the night. But we don't know what else to do. If Mum will just come and see him, it might . . . help.'

'Hmm.' Sam thought about it, then went into the kitchen and poured two mugs of tea. 'I've put sugar in whether you take it or not. Give you some energy. There's biscuits in that tin. Try to eat a couple of 'em. I bet you haven't had any breakfast, have you?'

'No.' She accepted the tea and, like her mother, put her hands around the mug as if to warm them. 'We had supper last night and Mrs Donald had done ice-cream though she knew Dad didn't like it. And then she said something about Tom. And Dad went for her and she, she, really enjoyed it all. It was terrible. She's fond of Mum. And of us.' Jess shook her head despairingly. 'There's something we don't understand about it all. It's so frightening. Everything was all right . . . even when Mum wasn't there. We all thought she was having this holiday in Malvern and we were OK with that – she rang me to see if I could manage. Well of course I could . . . there wasn't much to do except make the boys wash their hands and make their beds and clear up a bit. And when I asked Dad if it was all right to go with Tom and Mark to Bristol, he seemed fine. I knew he was worried about Mum . . . I suppose I didn't want to go into it much.' She sipped her tea gratefully. 'I kidded myself that everything was quite normal. And then I began to wonder what normal was. And then – then it sort of blew up last night.'

Sam opened the biscuit tin and thrust it under her nose. She took a digestive and dipped it into her tea. He could not believe she was eighteen; she looked younger by the minute.

'I rang Mrs Barkwith first thing this morning. I couldn't tell her about Dad of course. I just said I wanted to talk to Mum urgently and could I have the phone number of the Malvern house and she said Mum wasn't there anyway and then she said she had to go.' Jess finished her biscuit and swallowed. 'She was trying to get rid of me. It was obvious Natasha had said she mustn't give out the address or phone number. And then I thought of you.'

'Well, I'm glad you did, my girl. Though I'm bound by a promise too. But I've thought of a way round it. So have another biscuit and then I'll phone the number I've got and you can come and talk to Natasha. That way you won't know the number. Is that all right?'

'Oh yes. Thank you, thank you, Mr Lavington.'

'Sam,' he said as he went into the hall.

'Sam,' she repeated obediently.

She spoke to Pru; Natasha had gone into Malvern with Hillie to buy a swimming costume.

'Hillie?' Jess queried.

'Nash's daughter.'

'I didn't realize she was with you.'

Jess heard laughter in the deep voice. 'Neither did we!' Then the voice deepened more. 'Jess, Mr Lavington says he hasn't given you this number. Don't get the wrong idea, my dear. We thought your mother needed a bit of space. When she arrives we'd like her to feel she's still got space. Do you understand?'

'Of course. It's what I told Dad last week.' Jess felt completely helpless. 'It's just that all sorts of things have been happening and I do need to talk to Mum.'

'She's not here. Can you talk to me instead?'

Jess had just told the whole sorry tale to Sam Lavington. She had a feeling it would sound worse the second time and she still felt a sense of loyalty to her father. On the other hand, this wasn't Natasha, described by Maisie as 'crazy and beautiful'. This was Pru Adair who had abandoned the rat race of life and put her money into a sort of retreat in Cornwall.

Jess said bleakly, 'I think my father is going mad. And the only person who can help him is my mother.'

There was a little silence. Then Pru said, 'I see.' Another short pause. Jess waited for the easy reassurance, the brush-off. Pru said, 'Is he dangerous?'

Jess let her breath go into the receiver like a gale. She began to talk. It was easier when no-one was there in the tiny hall. She put in details she hadn't told Mr Lavington. She blurted, 'He might easily have attacked Mrs Donald. And that was what Mrs Donald wanted! It had happened before – you could tell! It was awful – just awful! But Mark ordered her out and I helped her pack . . . she's gone.'

Pru said quietly, 'I think you had better bring Tom up to us. I think he might be at risk.'

Jess stopped breathing. 'So it's true. You know all about it.'

'Yes. The three of us knew already. And now Evie knows.' Pru's voice changed, became businesslike. 'Bring him into Malvern, Jess. We'll meet you there. Outside the Elgar Tea Rooms. Can Mark come with you?'

'I'm not sure. The other two boys can't really cope.'

'Then you come on your own. Try not to worry. What time can you be in Malvern?'

'I'll go home and get some lunch for them. And . . . four o'clock?'

'Ideal. Tell Tom to bring his swimming trunks, will you?'

Jess put down the phone. A house with a swimming pool. Lucky old Tom.

Hilary and Natasha had bought swimsuits all round. Hilary's was a bikini and Evelyn's had a skirt. The others were more or less regulation. They undressed almost immediately and put them on. The weather was not quite so hot, but it was quite warm enough to try the new pool. They splashed around ecstatically until Natasha's wall began to collapse at the worst pressure point. Rachel and Natasha scrambled around it and started to pile stones frantically. Hilary floated on her back, bobbing against the wall like a cork, laughing uncontrollably. Evelyn got out and stood on the bank, towelling herself and shivering slightly. Pru joined her. She had not wanted to tell the others about Jess's phone call while Hilary was around, but suddenly she realized that they were all in this particular mess together and if Tom was going to be joining them Hilary might have to be his friend.

She called, 'Girls, Evelyn and I will go and cut some sandwiches for lunch. As soon as you've shored up the gap, come on in. I have to go to Malvern this afternoon and I want to talk to you first.'

Natasha screamed, 'Hillie! If you don't come and give us a hand – this minute – I'll send you back to Maine tomorrow! Is that understood?'

Hilary said, 'I was coming anyway. And that bit of blackmail is absolutely pointless because I wouldn't go.'

'What would you do, Hillie?' Rachel thought Hilary was a great improvement on Joy's daughters.

'I'd do a Maisie!' giggled Hilary.

'For God's sake don't let Evie hear you joke about Maisie,' Rachel advised soberly.

And Hilary, who was as sensitive underneath her brashness as was her mother, said just as seriously, 'Don't worry, I won't.'

They packed stones assiduously until Pru called them for lunch, then splashed muddily to the makeshift shower which Evelyn had rigged up at the corner of the house: a length of hosepipe coming from the kitchen tap. Then they towelled vigorously and went indoors to find shorts and shirts and even sweaters. It was good to gather around the kitchen table where the cooker was still giving off some heat. Natasha had brought in some pasties and Pru had baked potatoes to go with them. Hilary warmed her hands on her potato and closed her eyes ecstatically, 'Isn't this great?' she asked. 'It's a shame there are all these mod cons. We ought to have a wood stove and have to collect our own fuel. And pump water from an underground spring.' Everyone looked at her and she sighed. 'That's the trouble with being with you oldies. You've got no imaginations! Even Larry Blum knew how to pretend.'

Natasha looked at Evelyn and started to laugh. 'Little does she know, hey, Evie?' She looked sternly at her daughter. 'Have *you* ever danced in the ballroom of the Hofburg in Vienna? No? Have you ever made a pool before from a stream, like the Swiss Family Robinson? No? Then kindly rethink your previous statement!'

Pru intervened in what was obviously a normal mother-and-daughter conversation. She wondered how Natasha could stand the constant cut and thrust of life with Hillie, and probably, in the past, even more so, with Harvey.

'Listen you two. It's obvious that Hillie is going to miss having any younger companionship. But that might well be changed this afternoon.'

Natasha could not miss a chance for another dig. 'Not *more* extras? This reunion is supposed to be for *us*!'

Hilary stuck out her tongue. Pru put her hands over her ears and said rapidly, 'Phone call from Jess Davenport. Speaking from Mr Lavington's hall back in Earlswood.'

She had captured her audience. There were gasps all round. Hilary said, 'I thought no-one knew where you'd gone?'

'Don't be an idiot,' Natasha advised briefly and for once, seriously. 'Grannie and Grandad had to know – I swore them to secrecy. And Mr Lavington had to be in on it.'

Pru removed her hands. 'Well, obviously your parents refused to give Jess our number. So she went to see Mr L.' She stared across the room; she looked older than her forty years. 'Maisie's children are having a dreadful time. That housekeeper has left. And it sounds as if Edward Davenport has flipped. Mark was staying with him while Jess tried to contact us.'

Rachel said acutely, 'She thinks if Maisie goes back he will be all right.'

'Yes.' Pru sighed. 'She realizes that it might not work like that. That he might try to kill her. But meanwhile it is all she can think of. Poor kid.'

'So you had to tell her we can't help?' Natasha was looking intently at Pru's face. The large grey eyes were unseeing. 'And you invited her up here?'

Pru sighed again and came back to her surroundings. 'It's worse than that. This housekeeper woman let the cat out of the bag about Tom. She did it – Jess thinks – so that they could keep an eye on him. Apparently, Edward has never touched Tom because he knew that if he did, Maisie would snap. But Maisie is not there now. And Edward seems to have gone mad.'

Hilary drew in a sharp breath. Pru used the words deliberately as if wanting to shock them all. She had succeeded.

Evelyn said, 'I wouldn't believe this could be happening. Except that I've seen him. Yes, I think he has gone mad. Oh my dear Lord. What are we going to do?'

Rachel said, 'We should go down there. All of us. Have him sectioned.'

Natasha said slowly, 'Perhaps . . . perhaps he needed both women. That Mrs Danvers-type, silent and deep and terrible. And Maisie, sunny and open and . . . innocent.'

Pru said, 'Maisie is not innocent, Nash. And she is not open. And if both women appeared together on his doorstep, I think he would try to kill them both.'

Hilary gasped again. She leaned over and took her mother's hand. 'This is serious, Ma? Not like you and Harve?'

Natasha looked at her and then, quite suddenly, smiled. 'No. Not like me and Harve. Is it?'

Rachel said, 'Do we go down there, Pru? What did you say to Jess Davenport?'

'I've asked her to bring Tom and meet me at the Elgar Tea Rooms in Malvern. I propose we have Tom here until Maisie turns up. And I think a couple of us should go back to Edgbaston with Jess and see what the position is there.'

Rachel, Evelyn and Natasha all spoke at once. 'Of course.'

Pru hesitated. She looked at Evie. 'Obviously Evie can't go. And . . . I'm sorry, girls, but I must be get-atable on the phone. For Meg.'

Natasha said fervently, 'Obviously. Hillie will look after Tom. Ray and I will go back with Jess. How does that sound?'

'Ma . . .'

'It will be for a few hours probably,' Natasha said swiftly, pressing Hilary's fingers hard. 'And you've got a job to do. I'll tell you about Tom while Pru goes to fetch him from Malvern. It's terribly important that you make a place for him here. It won't be easy probably – I don't know what sort of boy he is. But it's up to you, Hillie.'

'Is this as important as getting you and Harve back together?'

'Yes.'

'Then . . . OK.'

Pru smiled at last. 'I hope you know how good you are together,' she said in a ghastly American accent.

'We do,' Hilary said instantly and seriously. And then looked at her mother. 'Don't we, Ma?'

Pru thought how odd it was when the small girl looked out of Hilary's sophisticated face.

Natasha leaned across the corner of the table and pecked Hilary on the nose. 'Of course we do,' she said quietly.

And then they immediately made plans. Pru would meet Jess and Tom by herself. Hopefully she would be gone just an hour. She would bring them both back to Prospect House so that Jess could see Tom settled in. And then Jess and Natasha would drive back to Birmingham, followed by Ray in her sports car.

Evelyn said, 'What will you *do*, my dears? You've got no . . .

right. I mean he can just order you out and there's nothing you can do about it.'

Natasha shrugged. 'Have to play it by ear,' she said not meeting Hilary's dark eyes.

Rachel put a hand on Evelyn's and patted it gently. 'I think one of us should go in alone. As Jess's "aunty" if need bc. He hates me but he won't throw me out immediately because he'll think I know where Maisie is. By the time I've smiled and smiled and had a cup of tea and been introduced all round . . . well, then we'll play it by ear.' She nodded at Natasha. 'You can wait in the car.'

Hilary said, 'With the engine running.' And they all laughed.

While Pru was away they cleared up their laundry, made a pile of sandwiches and tried to decide where Tom would sleep.

Evelyn was adamant. 'He's not used to sleeping alone. At school he's in a dormitory and at home he sleeps with Ian and Simon. And he knows me. Maisie used to bring him to see me when I lived in town with Edith. And then after I moved to the bungalow he would always come during his holidays.'

Hilary listened in amazement. 'How old is this kid?' she asked her mother.

'About six months younger than you,' Natasha said levelly. 'And I don't want any cracks. And neither does he.'

'OK, OK. I didn't realize this whole thing involved baby sitting.'

'Hillie. Stop it.'

Hilary managed to look ashamed. 'Yeh. Sorry. At least neither you nor Harve have ever wanted to kill me.'

'Don't be too certain of that.'

Hilary did not laugh. After a moment she said intensely, 'Ma, you've got to see him. Apologize for burning his stuff. I know all about everything, but you're so – so – *right* – for each other!'

'I take it you are talking about your father?' Natasha shook her head wryly. 'Maybe I'm like Maisie, hon. I need some kind of loyalty.'

Hilary said desperately, 'Not total, Ma. Remember Ron the plumber? From what Mrs Mayhew said—'

'Hilary. Stop. You don't understand, honey, even though you think you do. Just drop it. OK?'

There was a long pause. Hilary said, 'OK. But if ever you bump into him – you know, a party or something – will you just talk to him? Just talk. Please?'

Natasha nodded, though she knew that it was very unlikely that she would ever see Harvey Nolan again. Her heart almost failed her at the thought. And then Rachel was calling from upstairs and she went to join her.

Fourteen

Tom had barely spoken since that terrible scene with Mrs Donald. He knew exactly what was happening; the whole thing was so completely logical, and fitted so well with various small events in his memory, that there was no moment of confusion or even rebellion. He had always been closest to his mother; now he knew why. His father had often treated him politely, as a visitor; now he knew why. There was only a year between him and Simon and another year to Ian and they had always been a trio, yet he had been sent away to school and they had not; now he knew why. But most importantly, he had always felt different from the others. Always. He was like his mother physically, like his brothers in many ways because he had been with them for always. But there was a part of him that had none of the conventionality of the Davenports. He adored Mark and thought he wanted to be a vet, but the three days in Bristol had shown him otherwise. He adored his mother and when the other two went back to school, and he had her to himself for an extra precious week or so, he thoroughly enjoyed doing all the domestic things with her. Shopping, cooking, going for walks, visiting old Edith and Evelyn . . . just for a week or two. And then he was back at school, away from it all, on the touchline of the world as it were. Because that was what he wanted to do really: see the world. Travel. Not to any particular destination. Just to move. So in a way it was a relief to understand completely and at long last, why he was different; why he was odd man out.

What was confusing was how he felt about his . . . what was he . . . stepfather? Edward. Ted, as his mother called him. Ted, according to his mother, was a wonderful father. He was the universal provider: home, food, expensive education and all that went with it. And compassionate. Maisie had told all her children how compassionate Ted was. He would forgive anything because he loved them.

Tom, sitting by Jess in Mark's car, chugging along the A38 towards Worcester, knew that this image of Ted had always puzzled him. The one thing they were all quite certain about at number one-four-eight was that Ted Davenport's benevolence relied on his domination of them. He dominated his wife, he dominated his housekeeper. Until they went to Edinburgh he had dominated Jess and Mark. When Mark had suggested that a reliable car would be the best possible Christmas and birthday presents he and Jess could wish for, Ted had frowned prodigiously. 'How will you earn that?' he asked. 'You'll never be around to do any jobs.'

'They're wonderful with the boys in the holidays,' Maisie put in eagerly. 'And you can well afford it, Ted.' Tom realized now that his mother rarely said '*we* could afford' anything. Ted was the breadwinner.

He had laughed. 'Oh yes. I can afford it.' He looked humorously at his wife. 'And I guess you'll earn it for them, won't you?'

She had flushed and shaken her head slightly. Tom had known what his father meant. Like Jess he was now remembering all kinds of things, small pieces of the jigsaw that fitted together to make a picture he had never seen before.

And now Ted appeared to have 'flipped' as Ian put it through his hiccoughs. And it must be serious because Jess was getting Tom out of the way; taking him up to Malvern where his mother was supposed to be turning up magically at the end of the week.

They were in Ombersley Road and the cathedral loomed ahead. He read out road signs to Jess and she manoeuvred the car adroitly into the correct lane.

He wound up his window. 'It's colder, isn't it?' He was shivering.

'Yes. But it's still a wonderful day.'

There was a long silence, then she said briskly, 'We're going to meet Pru Adair in Malvern – I remember her.

And then she'll lead us to the house. It's quite remote apparently.'

'How will Mum find it? She's hopeless at finding places.'

'She'll have a taxi and the taxi driver will find it.' They passed the signpost to Upton-upon-Severn. She said quietly, 'We've been through all this before, Tom.'

'Yes.'

'I know this whole thing is like a nightmare. Try to push it away – don't think about it. Once Mum is with you, she'll explain and it will seem all right.'

'I'm not . . . you know. Upset or anything. It makes it so . . . understandable. I mean, if Mum slipped up . . . whatever you like to call it . . . it explains why Dad was horrid to her sometimes.'

'Yes.' She did not want to think about that. And the other boys . . . Simon and Ian. How had they come about? Had Dad had to . . . force her? She shuddered. Then remembered Mum had had her hysterectomy after Ian's birth and shuddered again.

She said, 'I'm going to pull over a minute, Tom. I feel a bit queasy.'

She pulled the car on to the verge and switched off, then she sat still and breathed deeply.

He said, 'Listen, sis. I know I shouldn't but I can drive. D'you want me to take over?'

'Shut up.'

'What?' he was startled. He'd always been able to say anything to Jess. 'Oh God. I called you sis. I'm sorry.'

She turned on him, blazing. 'I am your sister! You're my brother. But . . . but I'm also Ted Davenport's daughter! Can't you see . . . can't you see what it's like for the rest of us? He's mad! And we're his children!'

Tom was shocked out of his stillness. He stared at her and at last said, 'It'll be all right. When Mum comes. It'll be all right.'

She said bleakly, 'Yes,' and switched on again.

They negotiated the long avenue of trees and turned left for Great Malvern. The small town spread out before them, the terraced streets and railed walkways, the leaping hills beyond. In spite of himself Tom exclaimed with pleasure. 'Oh Jess – can't you stay? We could explore . . . look, they go on for ever!'

Jess did not even reply; the town consisted of one main street and the tea rooms were down a level in one of the pretty squares by the abbey. She drew into the car-park of a pub and switched off.

'We'll walk down,' she said briefly. She was unaccountably nervous. She knew her mother had been rather in awe of Pru Adair and wondered what she had let Tom in for.

Then a voice called 'Down here!' and she looked over the railings and saw a tall, grey-haired woman in slacks and shirt sitting at one of the tables grouped on the pavement. Her legs were resting on the wall of a raised flower bed in an attitude of studied relaxation. She waved a long arm.

'That's her,' Jess said with certainty. She preceded Tom down a short flight of stone steps and went forward, hand outstretched.

'Miss Adair. This really is kind of you. I expect it's a storm in a teacup, but we did not know quite what to do.'

'We're in the same boat.' Pru stood up and drew Jess towards her to kiss her cheek. 'And Tom. You won't remember me. Well, I don't remember you really, but you are so like your mother.' She pumped his hand as if congratulating him. 'This is great. Something really nice coming out of something really awful.'

Jess was grateful that they did not have to pretend nothing was the matter. She sat down where Pru indicated and Tom plonked himself next to her.

Pru said, 'Shall we have a cup of tea? Ice-cream? Cakes?'

Tom shook his head and Jess said, 'May we have a cup of tea at your house, do you think? It might . . . ease us in. A bit.'

Pru laughed. 'You will be practically force-fed at the house. I left the others tidying frantically. The house is right by a stream – quite a rushing stream because of the hill. We've dammed it back to make a deep pool where we can swim. But of course it's awfully muddy and though we've got a system for washing ourselves off before we go inside the house, it's all a bit makeshift. In fact everything is pretty basic. Hope you won't mind, Tom.'

In spite of himself, Tom brightened. He had imagined a luxury villa with a heated pool. This sounded much better.

'It's just very good of you to have me,' he managed to say.

'Not a bit of it, Tom! Nash and Maisie are the only two of us who managed a family. It's good to see that family. You are all part of our reunion, you know.'

'Well, if – when – Mum turns up, it will make it better,' he admitted.

'Meanwhile you and Hilary will get on really well. It'll be good for her to have someone her own age.'

Tom eyes widened in horror. 'Hilary? A girl?'

Pru looked startled and then laughed quickly. 'Didn't I mention it on the phone? Hilary is Nash's daughter and she was in the States with her father. She got homesick for England – and for Nash of course. And she turned up on Sunday.'

Tom looked at Jess. 'You didn't say anything about a girl,' he accused.

'No. I didn't realize . . . she arrived of her own accord? I mean . . . what about money and plane tickets and things?'

'She borrowed money. From her father.' Pru took her feet from the wall and stood up. 'My car is in the car-park behind the Lamb and Flag. I'll fetch it and drive to the pub and then we can set off. Straight through Malvern Link and keep going till you come to a T-junction. Then left. Anyway I shall be in front so that's all right.'

She took the steps to the higher level, waved and crossed the road. Tom said, 'It's bad enough with four women. Now there's going to be a girl! I can't cope with this, Jess. What am I going to do?'

'Tom, it's only until Friday. Please. You know it's better to be out of Dad's way.'

'What if Mum doesn't turn up on Friday?'

'How many more times? She just will!'

'I'll phone every day. And I'll use a code name. Who shall I say?'

Jess tried to make her brain work. 'I don't know,' she said.

'I'll say Steve. I won't say, I'm Steve . . . I'll just say, it's Steve. Then I'm not exactly lying.'

'Oh, Tom.' Jess could have wept quite easily. It was all so dreadful. And he had chosen Steve's name; the most reassuring he could think of at the moment.

Suddenly he became the comforter. 'Cheer up, sis. I'll be OK. You know that. I'm not bothered by some American kid. It'll be something to make Mum laugh, won't it? Me having to look after some homesick Yank!' He swallowed. 'Just be careful. Get Doc James into the house. Mum thinks he's wonderful. See what he says about it all. You could invite him over for a drink . . . just see what he says.'

'Yes. That's a good idea.' Jess looked up. 'Oh, there's Miss Adair now. Come on, let's go.'

They went back to Mark's car and clambered inside it. Pru flashed her lights and started off up towards Malvern Link. Sedately they followed.

If it had not been for her single term at Chudleigh, Hilary would not have been able to cope with Tom at all. As it was, she knew that there were girls of fifteen in the world who had no idea what was going on. All she had to do was to extend that description to include boys.

As soon as Jess and her mother had disappeared around the gravel track, closely followed by Rachel in her sports car, Hilary had turned to Tom as instructed, and said, 'What would you like to do before supper? Did you bring any swimming trunks? We could have a swim if you like.'

Tom looked longingly in the direction of the cars and said, 'It's a bit cold, isn't it? And shouldn't we help Miss Adair and Aunt Evie with the meal?'

Hilary wanted to call him a wimp, then remembered how she'd felt with Larry and Ruth. It was no fun being an outsider. She said, 'I think they'd like to be on their own for a bit.' She glanced at the sky. 'How about a walk then? I haven't had time to do much exploring. Let's take an hour and see what we can find.'

Tom said nothing; his gaze descended from the horizon to his trainers. He stood there.

Hilary had to work at being sorry for him. She counted to ten then said briskly, 'I'll grab a sweatshirt and tell the girls what we're doing. D'you want a jacket?'

He looked up at her. His eyes were intensely blue. And it was obvious he hadn't heard the suggestion about a walk. He said, 'The girls?'

'I know. It's weird, yeh? That's what they call each other and they've got me doing it too!' She laughed and went back into the house. Her sweatshirt was on the newel post which was a good thing because she had a feeling that with time on his hands Tom would wander off. She ran into the kitchen. 'Just taking the dog for a walk,' she said to Pru and Evelyn who were clearing up the tea things.

Evelyn looked up uncomprehendingly. Pru said reprovingly, 'Hillie. Don't be unkind.'

Hilary said, 'Don't worry, Pru. I'll get used to him and he'll get used to me, I guess.' She tied her sweatshirt around her waist by the sleeves. 'He calls you Miss Adair. And he calls Evie, Aunt Evie.'

'Hillie!' Pru said warningly.

Evelyn said, 'I've always been Aunt Evie to him. Maisie has no other family, you see. Well, I suppose there's the brother . . . I never knew about him.'

'Listen. I'd love to stay and chat but he might disappear if I don't grab him!' Hilary made her exit, grinning at the two women who were forced, unwillingly, to grin back.

Tom stood exactly where she had left him, gazing back down the road as if he expected the cars to return at any minute. She said, 'Let's go to the farm, shall we? Look at some sheep? They're kind of soothing.'

She started off, crunching on the gravel with great deliberation. After she had taken half a dozen steps and given up on him coming with her, she heard him begin to walk. He dragged his feet, even the sound of him moving spelled uncertainty, unwillingness. She thought, fleetingly, of Larry

Blum and his sheer energy. And Ruth too. She wondered if there was anything between them; certainly Ruth loved her brother far too much for her own good. She muttered, 'He's a selfish, spoiled brat!'

Tom, surely too far behind to hear, said, startled, 'Spoiled? Sorry . . . I didn't quite hear . . .'

She kicked at the gravel while he caught up. 'I was thinking aloud. Three days ago I was still in Maine. Windsurfing, body-surfing. All that kind of stuff. It's . . . well, sort of . . . different, here.'

He said fervently, 'Yes. Like being stood on your head.'

She said, surprised, 'Sure.'

He stood beside her; apparently that was the end of the walk. She decided to stick it out – no words, no movement. She counted to ten, then past ten up to twenty. And then she could stick it no longer.

'OK, you win. What now?' she said.

'Win?' He had that half-baked look again. 'Was it a game?'

'Oh for crying out loud!' She flung her head back and looked at the grey sky. 'You stood still, so I stood still. You didn't speak, so I didn't speak. Now I've speaked – sorry, spoked – sorry, spoken . . . you see how you've got me all of a which-way? So I guess you've won whatever game you're playing.' He continued to look bewildered, so she said flatly, 'Shall we go in? Watch telly or something?'

'I thought we were going for a walk?'

'Oh. Did you? Now there's an idea.' She pretended eagerness. 'Tell you what, Tom – shall we go for a walk?'

His eyes were so blue it almost hurt to look at them. Then they crinkled at the edges and he laughed. 'You're a bit of a case, aren't you? Are all American girls like you?'

She puffed a sigh of relief. 'So we're not in a laugh-free zone?' Then she grinned too. 'No other girl is like me, Tom Davenport. And don't you forget it!'

And Tom, suddenly and completely unexpectedly, felt the skin on his body and face shiver and contract slightly. He said involuntarily, 'Oh . . . oh God!'

'What? What is it?'

'I don't know. What do they say – a goose walked over my grave?' He shook his head. 'I don't know.'

'Your mom? Your dad? The fact that you're a bastard?'

He shouted another laugh, shocked this time. 'You don't believe in dressing things up, Hilary.'

'I'd love it if it was me. I'm nearly a bastard of course. I was conceived in these 'ere 'ills, you know. I've been trying to live up to it ever since.'

'Well, it's not that. Part of it was that all that seemed to go away. I felt as if the world was suddenly opening in front of me. I've always wanted to travel. And it was as if – this walk – was the start of an enormous journey.'

She nodded sagely and then skipped ahead of him and called back, 'It's simple. You've fallen in love with me. Life will never be the same again. Everywhere you look I'll be there. And, by gum, you'll have to run to catch me!' And she broke into a run as she spoke.

He stared at her flying figure. The shoulder-length hair beat time on her shoulders; the khaki shorts and aertex shirt were more like a schoolboy's uniform than feminine wear; the pumping brown arms and legs moved as regularly and easily as pistons.

He shouted, 'You're terrible, Hilary Nolan! You're a terrible woman!' But by then he was running after her and when they came full-stop to the five-barred gate which led into Bryn's farmyard, they were both laughing uncontrollably.

He waited until they were breathing almost normally then he said, 'There's a sort of combe over there. You can't see it, can you? But it's there in a dip of the hills. If we were invaded you could live there and no-one would find you. The hills sort of fold over you.'

She was astonished. 'How do you know?'

'Oh . . . Mum and me . . . we'd come up sometimes when the others were at school. Mum loved it up here.' He frowned earnestly. 'That's why she will turn up. On Friday. I'm sure of it.'

'That's what everyone keeps saying. And now you. As if you're all trying to convince yourselves.'

Tom nodded. 'It is a bit like that. We're worried, you see. Ian has hardly stopped hiccoughing since Sunday.'

'It's only Monday today,' Hilary said.

'Yes, it is, isn't it? It seems ages since Dad . . . since . . .'

'Since everything turned upside down,' Hilary supplied.

'Yes.'

'You'll get used to it. Look at bats.'

He smiled. 'Yes. Look at bats.'

She asked curiously, 'Do you think you did just fall in love with me?'

'I don't know. I've never fallen in love.' He saw her face. 'I like you. I think I could like you very much. You're very unusual.'

'Yes. But I have to work at it and sometimes it's very tiring.' She looked at the shiny pitted wood of the gate and ran her thumbnail along a groove. 'But however unusual I get, no-one has ever fallen in love with me.'

'I expect you're so damned unusual they get frightened.'

She thought about this. 'You could be right. Are you frightened?'

He laughed and shook his head.

'Not even when I called you a bastard?'

'Not frightened. A bit surprised. People – the family I mean – they're so embarrassed about it. No-one has mentioned it. Yet it was so obvious. Mrs Donald spoke about it deliberately. So that Dad would go for her. And he did.'

'When I called you . . . that . . . did it hurt you?'

'No. You made it sound quite important and special.'

'Good.' She turned and leaned her back against the gate. She was delighted to see that her breasts pushed the aertex up in a highly provocative way. 'Now,' she said. 'You'd better tell me everything.'

'But you know, surely?'

She shook her head. 'Why has Ian got hiccoughs? Who is Mrs Donald? What – *exactly* – did she say? Is your father really so awful – he frightened Evie to death apparently. Are you in love with Jess?'

'Hell's bells!' He looked at her wildly. 'Jess is my sister!'

'She's your half-sister. And she is more than just pretty. She is really beautiful. And she must be clever if she is going to be a vet. The family I was staying with in the States, they've got twins. Larry and Ruth Blum. And she is in love with him.'

'Codswallap!' he said rudely. 'You've got sex on the brain, woman! I'm not going to say another word if you keep dragging sex into everything!'

'Sorry! Sorry, Tom!' She stood away from the gate so that her shirt hung straight down. 'Let's walk back and I won't say another word. But we're in this thing together, aren't we? All of us. So I really do need to know everything.'

He looked at her and sighed. 'I think you're enjoying it really. But OK. It'll be a kind of relief to talk about it in detail. I suppose.'

They fell into step across the springy grass. He started with Ian's hiccoughs, described Ted Davenport in some detail and as fairly as he could. He admitted that he was glad he was at boarding school and possibly that was the main reason for not seeing what was going on right under his nose. Then he began to talk about his mother and how she was always there between him and Ted Davenport. How her whole life was centred around her husband; how strangely grateful she was to him. And how intensely loyal.

By this time they had rounded the bluff and the four-square house was visible at the end of the gravel drive. It was the glowing windows of the house that made them both turn and look towards the sunset.

Hilary breathed, 'Nash brought me out to look at it last night. She said if I didn't like it I could get on the next plane back to the States.'

Tom said, 'There's such a lot of sky. There has to be to make room for all those colours.'

Hilary made a funny snuffling sound then snapped, 'Dammit! What makes me want to cry when I see this blasted country?!'

'Does it make you homesick?'

'I don't know what it is. It's deadly dull here usually – I mean without Dad so many things are dull. But it kind of seeps under my ribcage somehow.'

'I'm sorry.' He sighed. 'Funny, isn't it? You seem to be a father missing. I'm two fathers and a mother missing.'

She looked at him gloomily. 'Is that all we've got in common?'

'No. We're part of a reunion. We must have loads of things in common.'

They walked again and she began to brighten. 'When your mother has turned up and everything is OK back home, will you try to find your father? Your real father? I could help you. It would be like a quest.'

He looked at her sideways but she knew it. It was as if those blue eyes burned her skin. 'I don't know,' he said. 'I should think . . . probably . . . that Mum and me will have to set up house on our own.'

'Oh. Gosh. No more boarding school then?'

'I'll have to get a job.'

'And you wanted to travel.'

'Yes.'

'Well, listen, Tom. You never know what is going to happen. That's what makes everything so exciting. So don't get depressed. OK?'

He grinned. 'I did feel depressed. I felt shut up inside myself. I don't now.'

'Because of me?' she asked hopefully.

'Definitely because of you.' He looked at her warningly. 'But that does not mean I'm in love with you. OK?'

She said meekly, 'OK.' But her dark eyes gleamed.

They went into the house, past Pru who was on the phone in the hall and straight through to the kitchen where the lights were on. Supper was laid on the big deal table: an enormous pile of bread and butter surrounded by platters of cold meat, hard-boiled eggs, a jar of pâté. Evelyn was straining a saucepan of new potatoes. Tom sat down, smiling at Hilary.

'Funny things might be happening everywhere else,' he commented. 'But . . . somehow . . . here . . . well, *this* is normal!'

And from the hall Pru's voice, firm and unusually authoritative said, 'Duncan, we haven't met. But you must realize that I am not in the habit of telling lies. Rachel is not here.

She and Natasha have gone into Birmingham on an errand. I am sorry I cannot go into details but it is quite a personal thing. She might be home later, she might not return until tomorrow. But she is not refusing to come to the phone to speak to you.' There was a pause and then Pru said in a more conciliatory tone, 'Of course I appreciate your anxiety. Listen. Immediately she steps over the threshold I'll ask her to phone you. Meanwhile all I can do is to assure you she's fit and well. Sorry . . . did you say happy? Yes, she's very happy. We are all happy to be together again after so long.'

Pru replaced the receiver and appeared in the kitchen doorway. Hilary giggled. 'I haven't heard you do your head of the community voice before, Pru.'

Evelyn said, 'Was that Rachel's husband?'

Pru said, 'It was. In quite a state. Things are not going very well without Rachel at the helm apparently.'

'That will please her,' Evelyn commented, decanting the potatoes into a vegetable dish and putting it on the table.

Pru smiled. 'Well at least poor old Duncan isn't worrying you, Evie.'

'No.' Evelyn sat down and smiled all around. 'I do feel safe here. Even without Rachel and Nash . . . it's having you, Tom. And Hilary. Yes, that's what it must be.'

Hilary said, 'It's a bit like being under siege, isn't it? If only we had a drawbridge—'

Tom said, 'Perhaps we could lay some traps along the drive. You know, like Swiss Family Robinson.'

He was a little overwhelmed when they all looked at him and smiled.

Pru said, 'Well, I think you must be part of the reunion now, Tom!'

Hilary said, 'Our knight in shining armour!'

He blushed and took a hard-boiled egg. He suddenly realized he was starving.

Fifteen

As the A38 took them through Northfield, Natasha showed uncharacteristic signs of nerves.

'Keep Jess well in your sights,' she said. 'Once we get onto the Edgbaston stretch, the right turn into Maisie's place is quite difficult to spot.'

'No problem.' Rachel was used to driving in London. 'I'm just worried about Jess being on her own. One of us should have gone in her car. She's had a long time to think – and believe me, driving on your own is a sure way of thinking!'

'We did offer. She obviously wanted to be by herself. It would have been tricky – to talk or not to talk. You know.'

The sky which had been so overcast began to blossom into a dusky red sunset. 'Glad we're not driving into that,' Rachel murmured, adjusting her mirror. 'I expect it will be lovely from the house. Every night we've had these spectacular sunsets.'

'Hope Hillie remembers to look,' Natasha said. 'And poor old Tom too. He must be feeling a real fish out of water.'

'She'll see he's all right,' Rachel spoke confidently. She had taken a shine to Hilary. 'Oh, Jess is indicating right. Is this it?'

'It must be. Yes, those awful trees. It reminds me of a cemetery.'

'Only because you know what's been going on.'

'No. Honestly. I thought so before. And I noticed something strange. Maisie never called it home. She always called it one-four-eight.' Jess drove her car across the road and Rachel waited for another gap and then followed. 'Oh God.' Natasha hugged her cardigan around her. 'I wonder what the hell we can do here?'

'We're deputizing for Maisie. Just think of it like that. We don't advise at this stage. We just listen.'

'Is that part of the Westminster training?' Natasha asked sourly.

Rachel grinned. 'I suppose it is. Cheer up, Nash. This is the exact opposite to boredom.'

'Hm . . .' Natasha opened her door and climbed out. 'Perhaps I might opt for peace and quiet in future.'

Jess was nowhere to be seen but the front door stood open, so Rachel led the way inside. The hall, where just over a week ago Maisie had taken Natasha's first phone call, was heavy with oak and even sported antlers in the stairwell. The door on the left was also open and Jess's voice came from inside, raised and protesting.

'But I don't get it! How did it happen? When I left he seemed . . . docile!'

Rachel and Natasha followed the voice into the sitting room. Natasha remembered it well and disliked it more this time than when she'd seen it first. Mark and Jess were both standing by the fireplace; Mark was taller than Jess but otherwise could have been her twin. He had his arm across the mantelpiece and his head resting inside his elbow. It was very obvious he had missed a night's sleep. Jess was angry, hands clenched at her sides, her long plait over one shoulder. She had held back her feelings throughout the long day and now she seemed to be sparking with them. She said, 'And where are the boys? You don't know, do you? You went to sleep!'

Natasha and Rachel stood just inside the door, complete outsiders. Mark said, 'They're over with the Archers. I got Doc James in after you'd left. Dad started demanding to see Tom. Then someone called McEvoy. I said they were on their way and I rang Doc James . . . I couldn't cope, Jess. Sorry. Anyway he took the boys with him and rang later to say they were staying with the Archers. He gave Dad an injection and put him to bed. And – yes you're right as usual – I fell asleep. When I woke up about an hour ago, the house was empty. I've been searching ever since.' He looked up from the mantelpiece and saw Natasha and Rachel. 'Oh God . . . I'm sorry. I remember you – both of you – come and sit down.

You know what's happened of course. We're so grateful to you for taking Tom.'

Natasha liked him immediately used as she was to Hilary's brusque ways. Rachel thought privately that Maisie and Natasha had made a better job with their children than Duncan and Joy had with theirs. Even as she shook Mark's hand and took the seat he indicated, she was wondering how she could help with Rebecca and Janice. After all, they were Duncan's daughters as well as Joy's. She had always assumed she was hopeless with children but she seemed to be doing very well with Hilary . . . and now Mark.

Nash was gushing as usual. 'It must have been dreadful for all of you. And Mark – you've had to act as gaoler since yesterday afternoon. We want to help. If there's anything . . .'

Jess snapped, 'The only thing to be done now is to search for Dad as well as Mum!'

Rachel said, 'Have you reported his absence to anyone, Mark?'

'No. Somehow . . . I couldn't.'

'Not the police. No. What about asking your doctor if there is anyone who could help? He sounds sympathetic.'

Jess immediately made for the telephone in the hall. 'I'll do that. We should find out if the stuff he gave Dad might need to be repeated.'

Natasha looked at Mark's grey face. 'Why don't you go to bed? Jess is hating having to rope us in like this and she'll take it out on you. Go on to bed. We'll wake you if anything happens.'

Mark shook his head. 'I can't. I wouldn't sleep anyway.' He looked down at Natasha and said, 'It's not Mum's fault is it? This business about Tom's birth . . . I mean they must have settled that years ago.'

'They did.' Natasha glanced at Rachel who shook her head slightly. Natasha said firmly, 'Maisie found out something. Her loyalty to your father was . . . well . . . based on gratitude, I suppose. And then she found out that he had no sense of loyalty.'

Mark said quietly, 'I went through his stuff – to see if he'd packed anything. There were things there . . . handcuffs and – and . . . sort of . . . thongs—'

Natasha made one of her small distressed sounds and got up quickly to take his hands. 'Well then . . . now you know. Have faith in her, Mark. She's made mistakes like us all. But she didn't deserve . . . what she got.' She shook his hands gently. 'It's certainly not her fault that your father has become . . . ill.'

Jess, entering the room, said bitterly, 'I don't think it would have happened if she'd stayed put.'

Natasha dropped Mark's hands and turned to face the angry girl. But it was Rachel who said, 'For once in her life your mother has made a decision on her own, Jess. She is doing something for herself. For whatever reason, that has got be good.'

Jess suddenly sagged. 'I suppose so.' Her voice was helpless. She glanced at Mark. 'We didn't know . . . we had no idea . . . things had gone so horribly wrong here. We've always been at boarding schools and now right up in Edinburgh.' She looked fully at Mark. 'I'm sorry I was horrid. Let's go into the kitchen and have a hot drink or something. Then you might as well go to bed.' She glanced around. 'Doc James says Dad will come home. He'll wander around for a bit and feel groggy and come back to sleep off the injection. He said to leave the door open and wait for him. I'll do that. I'd like to.'

Rachel stood up. 'We'll stay with you, of course. But the kitchen and a hot drink sound wonderful. Lead the way.'

Jess did so and said over her shoulder, 'I told Dr James you were with us. He said – ' she hiccoughed loudly – 'he said that Mum had talked about you and he wasn't a bit surprised you'd rallied round and that you would look after her.' She laughed. 'As if Mum was the patient, not Dad at all!'

Natasha took in the dishevelled kitchen at a glance and began to clear a space on the table. 'Back home – in the States – we've got a doctor like that. He said to Hillie once that he called himself a family doctor and that was what he was. He treats one member of the family in particular and the rest of the family as a whole.'

'That's nice.' Jess smiled shakily. 'This sickness – ' she gestured with her arm around the kitchen '– is very infectious!'

They all smiled and Rachel, rummaging in the bread bin, said, 'Hold your breath, Jess. That usually gets rid of hiccoughs.'

Mark sat down at the table, giving up all pretence at helping. 'It's a family thing,' he said. 'Ian's the worst. When he's worried he just can't stop hiccoughing. Gives him away all the time.' He glanced up at Jess. 'By the way, sis. Steve phoned from Bristol. Sent his sympathy and love.'

'Oh?' Jess coloured immediately; it wasn't only the hiccoughs that gave away her feelings.

'He'll come up here if we need him. I thought that was decent. But of course I told him we could manage.'

'Oh,' Jess said again with a slightly disappointed inflexion.

Rachel stuck stale bread under the grill and switched on. She found tins of soup in a well-stocked larder and began to open some. Natasha reached down soup bowls and Jess, rather helplessly, supplied spoons and knives. Natasha went into the hall to ring Pru. The line was engaged.

They eventually sat down to the toast and soup. Mark's eyelids were drooping, and while he could still listen Rachel suggested some plans.

'I'm supposed to be the bossy one,' she smiled at Mark. 'But I think it might be good if you could go to bed with a feeling that something definite was in the pipeline. Have you got a tent anywhere? If not, we can buy one . . . I'm going to suggest that if, when, your father comes back, we ask Dr James to find him a place in a private nursing home. Just for a week or two, until he . . . calms down.' She looked across at Jess, who, after a moment's hesitation, nodded. Mark said or did nothing. 'And then we all – Ian and Simon too – go back to Prospect House. Have a holiday. Wait for your mother to turn up. What do you say?'

Mark said, his words already slurring, 'What if she doesn't? Turn up, I mean.'

'Then we shall have to start all over again. The thing is, you will love it in the hills. We've made a marvellous pool in the stream, so you can swim. You can have campfires – no-one for miles. You can walk, explore . . . and incidentally help Pru to smarten up the house a bit so that she can get a decent price for it!' She turned to Jess. 'Tom is in with Evie. Hilary is with Nash. You could come in with me if you like.'

Jess said, 'It would be marvellous to get away from here. I have to admit, this house feels . . . dreadful somehow. What do you think, Mark?'

It was obvious Mark did not really care. He said, 'Why not? If Mum comes back here she's got her key. We can leave a note for her on the hall table. It will be something a bit different for the boys to do.' He looked across at Rachel. 'There is a tent actually. In the loft.'

Rachel said, 'That's settled then. Now off you go, Mark. We'll clear up here and make ourselves comfortable in the sitting room.'

Natasha planned how she would recount all of this to Hilary. 'Rachel just took over. Makes me realize that Duncan Stayte didn't stand a chance.' Or perhaps not. Hilary was, after all, only fifteen. She went back into the hall and tried the Malvern number again. It was like giving Rachel a present to tell her afterwards, 'By the way, Duncan rang you earlier. Do you want to ring back?'

Rachel paused, tea towel held like a flag. Then she said, 'No. Let him sweat for a bit.'

Evelyn was a long time settling Tom. She found a bedside lamp for him so that he could read if he woke in the night; she put a glass of milk and some biscuits within reach in case he felt empty; she ran a bath for him and made some cocoa. When Pru went into Natasha's room to make sure Hilary was all right, she was met by a barrage of complaints.

'It's not fair, Pru! I am motherless – and fatherless – too. Just because he's a boy Evie is spoiling him completely! There's only enough water for one bath, so who has it?'

'You've been swimming and had a hose-down—'

'*And* I haven't got a bedside lamp! And where's the cocoa?'

Pru smiled amiably. 'Funny, I overlooked the fact that you

are still a little girl! Here, let me tuck you in – would you like a story?'

'Oh . . . shucks!'

'And old-fashioned too. Shucks? Something one hasn't heard since the days of Mickey Rooney.'

'I was going to say something else, then I remembered you're religious!'

Pru looked down at the beautiful heart-shaped face framed in dark hair. 'There's something your mother hasn't told you then,' she commented, picking up discarded clothing and folding it ostentatiously.

'What's that?'

'I'm not a bit religious. Not really.'

Hilary said, 'I could have told her that.' She peered over the sheet, forgetting her complaints for the moment. 'But you're spiritual. You're very spiritual.'

Pru laughed. 'And what does that mean, oh precocious one?'

'Well, you saw Evelyn's friend – the dead one – Edith. Didn't you?'

'Oh for Pete's sake, Hillie—'

'No, really. There are people who can sort of . . . get in touch.' Hilary fumbled, for once in her life at a complete loss for words. 'I don't mean you're one of those nutty crystal-ball women. But you kind of . . . feel your way around things. Kind of.'

Pru finished straightening the room and looked down again at this replica of Natasha Barkwith. Then, when Hilary was almost wriggling under her gaze, she said 'OK. You win. How do you like your cocoa? Milky? With sugar?'

Hilary, released, grinned. 'I hate cocoa. And Ma left me a big torch so I can read and see my way to the john in the night. And I love it here – being with you. And now with Tom.' She reached out a hand. 'Thanks, Pru.'

'My pleasure,' Pru mimicked her accent and took the hand and very gently kissed the knuckles.

'Wow . . .' Hilary's eyes were very bright. She cleared her throat and said in her usual tough voice, 'Listen, Pru. You're going to have to stop Tom calling you Miss Adair. OK?'

'OK,' said Pru and left.

Back in the kitchen, where it seemed they were going to live from now on, Evie had at last come downstairs and was washing up Tom's cocoa cup.

'Funny thing,' she said thoughtfully. 'Now the two children are here, we're . . . settled. Aren't we?'

Pru nodded, smiling; the phone rang.

'Goodness!' Evie flapped her tea towel. 'First Duncan, then Natasha and now . . . who?'

Prudence picked up the receiver in the hall. It was Rachel this time, expounding her plan to bring the remains of the Davenport family up to Prospect House. In view of Evie's comment Pru felt free to give her wholehearted support. She wished them luck with their vigil. 'Be careful,' she warned. 'Whatever the doctor says, he is potentially dangerous. I certainly would not leave the doors unbolted.'

'No,' Rachel agreed.

Pru had only just replaced the receiver when the telephone rang again. She picked it up, said 'Hello' and then stood there listening for a long time. Evelyn clattered to a halt in the kitchen and came to the door, eyebrows raised. Pru replaced the receiver very carefully.

'That was Meg's mother. Meg died this evening. An hour ago.'

Evelyn put her hand to her mouth and stared at Pru as she stood very still by the telephone, her head bent.

'Pru . . . my dear, I'm so sorry. This thing with Meg . . . it's hit you hard, hasn't it?'

Pru nodded dumbly and Evelyn faltered, 'Come and sit down. Have a cry. I'll make some tea.'

Pru nodded again and Evelyn returned to the kitchen. She heard Pru sit down and then the shuddering sobs. Tears came into her own eyes. The awfulness of being human descended on her as it so often did lately.

Pru controlled herself at last. 'I'm so sorry. Forgive me, Evie. It was momentary. This whole thing has been so sudden. Meg didn't tell us. We should have known something was wrong because she visited the doctor so often. But . . . some GPs haven't got much time for us. And I suppose we thought they were stonewalling Meg.' She put her hands to her face. 'Looking back . . . I could have helped her more. I have never committed myself properly to a relationship. I called it giving people space – but . . . but . . .' the sobs started again and Evelyn put down the teapot and held her closely. Pru gasped, 'She left me a note. It thanked me . . . thanked me . . . for making the last fifteen years so happy! I did nothing, Evie. Nothing.'

'My dear girl . . .' Evelyn's tears splashed freely on Pru's thick grey hair. 'Was she in the habit of telling lies?'

'Of course not! She was as straight as a die.'

'Then believe her. Whatever you did or did not do made the girl happy. Accept that, Pru. Be thankful for it.'

'Oh Evie . . .' Pru clutched the small woman to her and buried her face in the apron. 'You are such a comfort. I should have come to see you – I intended to after the funeral. But I didn't.'

'It's because you feel awkward with us, Pru. And there's no need.'

Pru lifted her head and stared at Evie's ordinary face. She whispered, 'Do you know?'

'Edith did. I didn't believe her. But when we arrived and saw Meg, then I thought she might be right.'

'I'm sorry, Evie.'

'Why? For making Meg happy? For being wise and good and true? Because you are those things. I knew that when you saw Edith. She wouldn't show herself to me or the others. But to you—'

'Evie, please. That was one of those strange coincidental things—'

'Call it that if it makes it easier to accept. I know what I know, Pru.' Evelyn withdrew herself and said, 'Tea. And then bed, I think. If the girls are bringing all the Davenports here tomorrow we shall need our strength.' She patted Pru's hand and said tritely, 'Life has got to go on, my dear. And now you've seen Edith, don't you realize that Meg is with us too?'

Pru said with a kind of humorous despair, 'Oh Evie . . .' But she drank her tea.

* * *

As soon as Jess was asleep inside her sleeping bag on the floor, Natasha and Rachel went around locking doors and windows and drawing curtains. They slept fitfully on the two pale cream couches and at six o'clock got up and reversed the process. Then they took a long look through the various windows, decided that in spite of the doctor's prognosis Ted Davenport had not returned in the night, and went into the kitchen to make tea.

'They won't want to come with us unless their father is in a hospital somewhere,' Rachel said gloomily.

'Shall we say he came back and we called the doctor and it's all done?' Natasha suggested wildly.

'Obviously your brain doesn't work without proper sleep.' Rachel sighed. 'I think we're in for another day here. Perhaps we could take it in turns to get some sleep.'

'Oh God, it's so ghastly here. Like being in a Gothic horror story. I could kill Maisie.'

Rachel said drily, 'Unless Ted does it for you, of course.'

'Oh shut up, Ray!'

'All right. What do you suggest then?'

'I think we should talk to this doctor. Without the kids.'

That proved surprisingly easy as neither Jess nor Mark were disturbed by the telephone, the door opening and closing, the kettle unexpectedly whistling. 'They make me feel so old,' Natasha moaned. 'I used to be able to sleep anywhere, any time. Now, even with that ghastly but comfortable sofa, I get two hours at the most!'

Dr James proved to be short and round, a Pickwickian figure. At his request they went outside to talk. 'I think the other two have had enough of talking about their father as a medical case. And anyway, I'd like to make certain he didn't come back last night.' He walked ahead of them peering at flower beds. 'No, there are no footprints. I'm amazed. He has an enormous sense of his possessions and this is his house. Always has been. His house, his wife, his kids.'

'Except for one,' Natasha murmured.

'Quite. You did the right thing getting that boy away. It is now just as important to keep Mrs Davenport out of harm's way.' He nodded at their shocked expressions. 'The two people who threaten his possessiveness. D'you see?'

'Oh God . . . there's no way out. We're stuck here, aren't we?'

'I shall advise Jess and Mark to go back to your house in Malvern with you. He won't go very far away. He might even be asleep in the garage . . . the garage!' They all looked at the pseudo coach house next to the kitchen door. The double doors were very slightly ajar. Dr James almost galloped across to them and peered inside. Then he turned back. 'The car has gone,' he announced. 'Of course that is high on the list of possessions. His car. How stupid of me not to think of it. And he's not fit to drive.'

'And we don't know where he's gone.' Natasha looked nervously at Rachel. 'Have we left any clues as to where Prospect is?'

'No,' Rachel replied definitely. 'Surely it is much more likely that he's parked around the corner fast asleep?'

The doctor nodded. 'But I'm afraid this means I shall have to call the police in. He's very much a loose cannon.' He stared at the garage, obviously thinking. Natasha fidgeted like a child. Rachel frowned at her. Then he said, 'It won't be pleasant for the kids. I'll delay calling in until you've gone.' He made for the kitchen door. 'Let's get them up and tell them what's happening. Then you can pack and collect Ian and Simon from the Archers' and skedaddle.'

The doctor talked to Jess and Mark alone while the other two assembled some kind of breakfast. They had no idea what he said but it certainly convinced Mark and Jess. They came into the kitchen and ate cornflakes and scrambled eggs in a subdued way but they did not question the doctor's advice, and after they had eaten they went to the attic to fetch the tent and begin packing.

Rachel said, 'This is awful. We're all acting as if once we're in Malvern we'll be safe. But he could be waiting in a side road to follow us . . . we simply do not know how his mind is working – or whether it's working at all!'

'Don't let them hear you say that.' Natasha said, 'I simply

feel we'll all be better when we get out of this place.' She stuffed socks into a pillowcase. 'Let Jess lead the way. We'll come behind. He doesn't know your car.'

So, in the end, after a great deal of what Rachel termed 'faffing about' they left one-four-eight, Mark's car loaded with the family, Rachel's with the luggage wedged around Natasha. Ian and Simon were apprehensive but also almost hysterical with excitement; Natasha said she could hear the hiccoughs over the roar of the morning traffic. Like Roly Jenkins before them, they had memorized the number of Ted Davenport's Rover, but nothing like it appeared in Rachel's mirror and Natasha felt as if her head must unscrew, the number of times she turned it to gaze down side roads. What they failed to notice was an ancient green Morris Minor which was at least three cars behind them; by the time they started up the long avenue to Great Malvern the Morris had disappeared. The man driving it was not Ted Davenport, but he had a wild look in his eyes and if he had had the same kind of power beneath the small green bonnet, he would have overtaken them immediately. As it was he got lost long before he got to Great Malvern, and ended up in a clearing overlooking the great Severn plain around Worcester.

Hilary and Tom spent all morning in the pool. Tom had grand ideas for tying a rope to an overhanging tree so that he could swing across to the deep-end of the pool and splash into it. He worked on that while Hilary continued to shore up the dam. Evelyn had taken some meat out of the freezer and was busy making an enormous stew; Pru was writing to Mrs Simmonds, Meg's mother.

When the cars arrived and disgorged six people and piles of luggage, it was mayhem. Tom insisted on doing huge Tarzan swings and splashes in the hope of thoroughly wetting Ian and Simon; Rachel wanted to take Jess to her room as soon as possible and get her settled. Mark, for some unaccountable reason, seemed to think he had to get the tent up before anything else. Hilary, crouched behind the dam, watched him secretly. He was grown up but still only four years older than she was. She looked at him, then at Tom acting like a fool. And then as Natasha called out, 'Pru, where's Hillie?' she scooped up two handfuls of water and hurled them at her mother. And then, as she screamed with laughter, she realized she was no better than Tom and turned on him to duck him as if all this – whatever it might be – was his fault.

Eventually order came from chaos. Pru pushed the dining room table against the kitchen table and all ten of them sat around and helped themselves to Evelyn's stew. 'Nothing like sharing a good hot meal to make people feel at ease with one another,' she said comfortably, fetching more potatoes and heaping plates willy-nilly. Tom and Jess were quiet but the others made up for it. Simon and Ian wanted to swim but Evelyn said not until at least three o'clock when their food would have been digested properly. So Hilary and Tom began to organize an expedition to find the combe Tom had described last night.

Rachel said, 'Washing-up first. You four younger ones will be taking on the washing-up. Is that all right?'

They looked up at Rachel. Natasha and Pru could both see the words 'unfair' forming on Hilary's lips. Then she thought better of it. 'Yeh. Fine,' said Ian. And no-one hiccoughed.

So it was that when the Morris Minor came chugging up the gravel drive, the four women were all in various relaxed attitudes between the stream and the newly erected tent. Mark and Jess had gone inside to make tea and doubtless to talk privately. Evelyn, lying in the only decent deckchair, was asleep, Rachel and Natasha were telling Pru about the sheer awfulness of one-four-eight.

'Who the hell is this?'

Natasha stood up and peered in the direction of the engine note. 'My God – is it him? What are we going to do?'

'It's not him.' Pru was standing too; her superior height gave her a better view. 'It's probably Bryn. I think he's got an old Minor.' She sat down again. 'Anyway, we know he won't let Ted Davenport through, so just relax, Nash.'

Natasha subsided too. The Morris crunched slowly up to the stream and stopped and a man got out. He was probably in his mid-forties, brown hair greying at the edges, mild blue eyes wide with anxiety, a very flushed face.

He looked at the four women and then his gaze settled on Natasha.

'What the hell are you doing here?' he said.

Natasha got up again. 'Ron!' She looked at him wildly. 'It's you! How did you find me?'

'I followed the Ford. With the kids in it. I didn't see you. I tried to stop them – overtake them – I kept flashing my lights and sounding the horn. But they didn't hear me.'

Natasha only half-heard him. She blurted, 'My God, Ron, I thought we'd said goodbye. You can't come here. I'm staying with my friends – you simply cannot come barging in like this.' Natasha had never had this trouble before. She looked at Pru and wailed, 'I'm so sorry, Pru!'

Pru said, as if she were a hostess at a garden party, 'You're a friend of Natasha's? We were going to have some tea. Would you like to join us?'

'Not really. What I meant was – I didn't know about Nash. It was the kids. The Davenport kids.' Ron came forward and looking at Pru, at last sat down at her feet. 'Look, I'm sorry. I didn't know what the hell was going on. But last week Ted Davenport came to see me. Looking for Maisie. She'd run off, you see.'

'Maisie?' Rachel leaned forward. 'Just who are you?'

'I'm Ron Jenkins. Well, Roland Jenkins – but that doesn't suit a plumber, does it? I'm Maisie's brother.'

Natasha gave one of her strange little yelps and Rachel said, 'Good God!' Pru said, 'Please sit down, Ron. We're hoping Maisie will join us at the end of this week. But meanwhile I'm afraid her husband, Ted Davenport, is suffering a nervous breakdown. So we've brought the family up here out of harm's way.'

'Good job too.' Ron Jenkins sat himself on the grass. 'Thing is . . . Davenport is crazy. He came to see me last night. He was raving mad. And then, when I was going to throw him out again, he collapsed on the floor of my kitchen. So I got him in the car and took him home. All the doors locked. No-one about. So I got him into his garage and put him in his car. He was coming round by then. Kept going on and on about killing her. Killing Maisie. My sister.'

Ron looked at Natasha. 'I thought if Maisie had wanted me to know all this stuff, she'd have come and told me herself. So I drove home. Then I got thinking. Maisie is missing. He's gone off his head. What if he's killed her already?'

Natasha said resentfully, 'You couldn't have knocked very hard last night. Rachel and I were asleep in the sitting room.'

'Well you are a heavy sleeper, old girl, aren't you?' He spoke without irony and Natasha felt her face redden. 'Anyway I thought about it all night and I came back this morning and the car that was parked by the front door was just driving away. So I followed it.'

Evelyn, apparently semi-conscious through all this, opened her eyes and smiled. 'Did you say you were a plumber? I think I remember you at my friend's house. Edith . . . Would you like a cup of tea before you start work?'

Ron looked around as if for escape. And Natasha started to laugh.

Sixteen

They were all agreed on one thing: Ron's hideous suspicions must be kept from the young Davenports. Pru quickly told Ron what Natasha flippantly called 'the present state of play'.

'So you see our object at the moment is to give the five children a sense of sanctuary and security. We're saying – and I still believe this – ' Pru cast a quick look at the others 'that Maisie will turn up here on Friday. So this is a little holiday until she arrives and they have a proper family conference and decide what to do about, about—'

Rachel supplied, 'Father.' She returned Pru's look. 'We mustn't forget that the man we see as a violent sadist is their father. They still love him.'

Ron said, 'Poor little devils. It was like this for Maisie and me when we were kids. We didn't know where we were. That's why we clung together.'

Natasha, still inclined to laugh foolishly now and then, said, 'I simply cannot believe this. I mean . . . it's so coincidental—'

'Not really.' Ron seemed to be taking that side of events quite well. 'I'm a plumber. I've done contract work for that swimming-pool firm before.'

'But that we should be linked through Maisie—' Natasha stopped speaking and put a hand to her mouth. 'What will Hilary say?'

'Hilary?' Ron frowned.

'My daughter. She knows about you. That rotten Mayhew woman—'

Ron was impatient. 'For God's sake, Nash! Stop acting like a drama queen! She never saw me – she was at school. She doesn't know my name. And as we're not going to tell the other children about me, I don't quite see how she can make any connection!'

Natasha reddened again, not enjoying being put down like that. Pru said, 'We must tell them that you are Maisie's brother. They know about you. In fact your presence will be reassuring. The only way you could have got here is if Maisie told you our address. So they will think she is in touch with you.' She sighed. 'I'm afraid we can't put you up. Unless you would like to sleep in the tent.'

'I'll have to get back. I'm working tomorrow. Besides, I might be more use to you back in Birmingham. He might even call on me again!' He looked up as the kitchen door opened and Jess appeared carrying a tray. He lowered his voice, 'I'm dead worried about our Maisie. If she's on the run why didn't she come to me – she knows I'd've helped her. It's all very well saying she'll turn up on Friday as planned. But where the hell is she now?'

Pru stood up again, smiling widely. 'Jess.This is your uncle! He's dropped in on the off-chance of seeing Maisie – never dreaming you'd all be here. Isn't it marvellous?'

Ron played along as best he could. 'Your mum and me lost touch years ago – I didn't even know she was married with a big family.'

Jess put down the tray and took his hand formally. 'She was with you – just like she told Aunt Evie!' Her face relaxed with relief. 'Where did she go afterwards?'

Ron fumbled for a moment. 'I forget, to be honest. She wanted to look up other friends in the city before coming up here.'

Mark joined them and they sat around with the tea and some biscuits and because the two Davenports were so delighted to see him, it was like a party. For a time they forgot the horrors of their father and simply rejoiced in Ron's obvious ordinariness; he was proof to them that Maisie was safe and well.

Eventually Ron said he could not wait for the younger children to turn up, he would have to get back. Jess tried to persuade him otherwise. 'The boys would so enjoy seeing you, Uncle Ron! And you could sleep in the tent—'

'I've got a business to go to, Jess.' But Ron was obviously

flattered. 'I'll give you a bell on Friday or Saturday. See if your mum would like to see me again.'

'Oh she will, she will.'

Pru said, 'I'll have a lift down to the farm if I may, Ron. Mrs Bryn bought some milk and bread for us this morning.' She smiled at Evelyn. 'Rather like feeding the five thousand at the moment, isn't it, Evie?'

Ron was courtier-like. 'A great pleasure.' He opened the passenger door for her and she folded herself into the little car. They drove off, waving through the windows.

Ron said, 'You wanted a word in private? Me too. I'm still worried sick about Maisie. One of the things he, Davenport, said to me was that she had everything money could buy. I know that doesn't count in the end, but . . . well, she's not used to roughing it. And you can be sure he's stopped all joint bank accounts. Unless she had cash on her, she'll be skint.'

'Yes.' Pru sighed. 'She had to borrow some money from Evie, so she is skint. But having said that, Ron, remember when she ran away before – from you incidentally – she found herself a room and a job and managed quite well. I think men tend to underestimate Maisie.'

He said, his voice strained, 'Do you know why she ran away from me?'

Pru looked at him calmly, then away. 'You made her sleep with you.'

He sucked in his breath as if she had slapped him. Then he said, 'It wasn't like that. I swear to you. Our foster dad – he used to beat her. I looked after her. Cuddled her up.'

'And took her into your bed,' Pru reminded him.

'Oh God.' He groaned. They had manoeuvred around the bluff and the farm was visible across the two fields. He switched off his engine and bowed his head to the steering-wheel. 'It happened. She let it happen. We comforted one another. I loved her – I really loved her. There was never anyone like Maisie.'

'Until you met your wife. And when she went . . . I suppose there were others before Nash?'

He lifted his head. 'Look, Miss Adair—'

'Call me Pru.'

He sat up, encouraged. 'Pru. I just wanted to be ordinary. I got married. It didn't work out – she found someone else. Yes, there were others before Nashie. But I felt something for her – Nash. I was sorry for her. She's got that much passion in her . . . I asked her to marry me.'

Pru almost laughed. She asked curiously, 'What did she say?'

'She said no. She made some crack about me wanting her money. We laughed about it. I laughed like that with Maisie. We were friends as well as lovers.'

'As well as brother and sister,' Pru said.

Ron looked round, frowning. 'We weren't really brother and sister. Brought up together, of course. But we were both taken from the orphanage. When we were small. I wouldn't . . . we wouldn't . . . at least I don't think so . . . if we'd been real blood relatives.'

Pru too was surprised. 'Did Maisie realize this?'

'Well . . . she must've done.'

Pru said, 'I'm not sure about that. You see, Ron, your foster parents told her that they knew she was sleeping with her brother, and if she didn't do just what they told her, they would tell the police and you would go to prison for a very long time. So when Maisie ran away, it was to protect you.'

Ron stared at her in horrified silence for a long time. Then he breathed, 'Those . . . bastards!' And then, 'That's why she never looked me up again. The threat was . . . permanent. And anyway, knowing our Maisie she would always carry her guilt around with her.'

'Quite.'

He turned and directed his stare through the windscreen. 'First her foster father, then her husband,' he said quietly.

Pru said again, 'Quite.' Then, suddenly, she put a hand on his arm. 'But, Ron, she is not dead. I promise you that. I think she is in danger – if he finds her he will go berserk probably. But she was alive last Wednesday. Because I saw her. In Corporation Street.'

He said, surprised again, 'Why didn't you say – back there?'

'I can hardly believe it myself. But . . . I am believing it now.' She smiled suddenly. 'Ron, I'm glad you appeared out of the blue today – thank you. And thank you for telling me what happened all that time ago. It's good that you're in Birmingham. You might see Maisie at any time.'

He swallowed. 'Yes. If I can find her before he does it would help, wouldn't it?' He fumbled in his map pocket and produced a pen. 'Can you write down your phone number? I'll give you a ring. Keep in touch. And here's one of my cards – will you do the same?'

She wrote the Malvern number and gave the card back to him. 'Of course. Drive on now, Ron. I must not be too long.' She gave him one of her steady looks. 'I am the only one of us who knows about Maisie and you. She gave your name as next of kin. And then once – when I suppose she needed some time off – she said her brother had flu. She was never any good at lying. I obviously got it wrong. I'm sorry.'

They drove up to the five-barred gate and she got out to open it for him and then waved him through the farmyard. She could understand why both Natasha and Maisie had slept with him. He was . . . reassuring.

Natasha was amazingly quiet for the rest of the evening. Nobody noticed, because the noise level was very high when all ten of them were inside the house. Once Mark shepherded Simon and Ian outside it was quieter, but still the kitchen was filled with the clatter of clearing up. Natasha sat on at the table with her hands around her coffee cup, staring intently through the window. The sky was violet and crimson, but it was obvious she was not looking at the dying sun.

Hilary said, 'Ma . . . you OK?'

'Sure.' Natasha produced a smile. 'How about you?'

'We had a great time. Tom remembered this place – like a little valley – a secret valley. Those bendy trees sort of overhung it and you could swing across from branch to branch like Tarzan.'

'Sounds wonderful.' Natasha looked up. 'You're enjoying yourself, Hills. Better than back home?'

Hilary nodded immediately. She said, 'The boys . . . the Davenports . . . you don't have to make an effort.' She shook her head, puzzled. 'I don't know what I mean.'

'You can be yourself?'

'Well, one bit of myself.' She sat down. 'There are about five hundred of me, Ma.'

Natasha smiled. 'That's what makes you so special, hon.' She took her daughter's hand. 'Don't be frightened about that.'

'Yeh. But there are five hundred of you too. And Harve . . . he understood that.' She made a funny little face. 'Not many people get it, Ma. So when you find someone who does . . . I mean who gets it . . . it's quite important.'

Natasha sighed. 'Yeh.' She squeezed the small, slim hand. 'I'll tell you something, baby. I wish I hadn't burned his blasted suits!'

In the hall, Rachel was talking to Duncan. She said sternly, 'As a matter of fact, it's not me who has done the disappearing act. I phoned twice and got no answer. Well . . . only that ridiculous answer-machine message from Miss Chambers.'

Duncan was contrite. 'Darling, I'm sorry. I had to take a couple of days off and drive Joy up to Soar Tops . . .'

'I knew it! I knew she'd go there! It's our home, Duncan!'

'Hang on, Ray. This is our home. London. You know you prefer it – you never liked Charnwood. Be fair. That's one thing – you've always been fair.'

She was conscious he was being conciliatory and she wondered why. There could be only one reason. He had slept with Joy. She wondered how she was going to bear this.

He said, 'Ray, the girls turned up here. Both of them. They'd heard that Joy had left Lucas Field and they thought there might be a reconciliation.'

Rachel could have screamed. She said coldly, 'And was there?'

'No. Something happened. I can't tell you until I see you. Joy became hysterical. She threatened to break us up, Ray. I couldn't face that . . .' He sounded utterly miserable.

'There's only one way she could break us up, Duncan. By sleeping with you.'

'Ray, don't joke. Please. I had to get rid of her – Joy, I

mean. I told her she could stay at Charnwood as long as she liked. If she'd just keep away from the press – and you.'

Rachel did not know what to say. She wanted to believe him.

She decided to leave the subject of Joy. 'What about Douglas?'

There was a pause. Then he said, 'So you know?'

'Know what? I haven't watched or heard any news today. What has happened.'

'Happened?'

She said impatiently, 'I'm assuming you're talking about the breakaway? Douglas has some inside information?'

'Oh. Oh yes. Yes, actually. There have been further moves from a certain lady and a certain Member of the Cabinet. Yes. I can't wait to see you about that, Ray. If it happens it could mean Government status for us. Shadow, of course. But in the frontline somewhere.'

Suddenly Rachel was uninterested in a possible breakaway Party. She said, 'What did you think I meant? Has something else happened with Douglas?'

'No, of course not. That ghastly girlfriend rang for you to go to tennis or something. Not your scene is it, Ray?'

'Not a bit.' She was still frowning slightly; she knew Duncan better than he knew himself.

And then, suddenly, endearingly, he said, 'By the way, the new chair arrived and Miss Chambers sat on it and it snapped off.'

They both laughed.

'But when are you coming home? You're not really staying away another ten days, are you? I don't think I can cope, Ray. I didn't realize how much I relied . . . and besides with you here, there can't be any gossip.'

She felt a sudden yearning for him; the thought of their bedroom . . . her satin nightgowns . . . the open window blowing a breeze across the river. She said with genuine regret, 'Duncan, darling, I just can't leave at the moment. Perhaps after the weekend. Things should come to a head then.'

'After the weekend? Promise?'

'Promise.'

He made some kissing sounds and she glanced around her and then made some back. She replaced the telephone and stood there for a moment, thinking how terribly important sex was to a marriage and thanking God that Duncan had found her so sexually satisfying. She remembered that first time: he had run his hands over her sturdy buttocks and the inside of her footballers' legs and had whispered, 'You're so strong, Ray . . . like a schoolboy . . . strong and direct and uncomplicated.' No-one had ever wanted her before. Her father had shown her what an exciting thing sex was but it was the one thing he had not been able to fix for her. Until Duncan.

Pru had worked like a demon all that Tuesday in an effort to come to some kind of acceptance of Meg's death. On Wednesday she telephoned Cornwall to tell them what had happened. She spoke to Margaret James.

'Mrs Simmonds, Meg's mother, thinks it would be better if none of us went to the funeral.' Margaret gave a cry of protest and Pru said very clearly, 'I can understand it, Margaret. And we'll have our own memorial service for her. It will be better.'

'Pru, I am so sorry. So very sorry. What about you? Are you coming home immediately?'

'No. Do you remember I told you I was meeting old friends here at Malvern? One of them is in trouble. I have to be here for at least another ten days.'

'It doesn't make sense. They were managing without you for . . . how long?'

'Fifteen . . . twenty years,' Pru supplied, acknowledging Margaret's point.

'You are always expected to solve people's problems, Pru. And now you have one of your own. You have a bereavement. Let someone help you for a change.'

Pru nodded. 'That is why I am hanging on.' She smiled slightly. 'There is one person who might help. I don't know whether she will be willing to. But she could, yes. It's worth hanging on.'

'Is she one of your friends?' Margaret asked curiously.

'Yes. But she is the one who has gone missing.' Pru sighed. 'For whatever reason, Margaret, I have to find her.'

'And then? Will you bring her to Telegraph House?'

Pru laughed. 'No. Never that.'

There was a pause. Then Margaret said heavily, 'I see.' She waited, and when Pru said nothing she added, 'Pru, in this day and age, is there any need for Telegraph House?'

'I don't know.' Pru stared through the window. Jess was slowly walking towards the stream. She wore a bathrobe and began to undo the belt. Mark came up behind her in swimming trunks. She dropped the robe where she was and they ran screaming towards the pool. Pru thought how young they were; and how easy it was when you were young. She said into the receiver, 'Perhaps that is something we should discuss. When I get back.'

'You are coming back? Definitely?'

'Of course. We must mourn Meg together.'

Margaret made a sound that showed it was not the complete answer she had wanted. And then she said goodbye and they rang off. Pru walked slowly through the kitchen where the other three were clattering dishes in the sink. Outside, the young Davenports were getting thoroughly muddy in the pool; Hilary was climbing precariously along the branch of a very supple willow with the end of a rope in her hand. 'She's trying to find somewhere to tie it so that they all can swing into the water,' Natasha explained unnecessarily. 'Have they found him?' she asked, glancing sharply at Pru.

'Ted Davenport? I don't know.'

'Sorry. I thought you were phoning the police. Perhaps we should do.'

Pru nodded but did not move. Evelyn said, 'Girls, Pru is finding it difficult to tell you. Monday evening . . . Mrs Simmonds telephoned. Meg died.'

Pru held up a hand against Natasha's instant cry of sympathy. 'I'm all right. Don't let's talk about it. I'm all right. I phoned Telegraph House to tell the others. We look after each other. We shall have a service when I get back.'

'You're not going to the funeral?' Natasha asked.

'There's too much to do here,' Evelyn said quickly. 'We can't spare her.'

Rachel, fidgeting, said, 'As a matter of fact, I was going to ask if I could have a day off. Would it be too much? There's something I should do . . . at home. If I could leave really early tomorrow, I could be back here by seven or eight in the evening.'

'Oh, Ray!' Natasha exploded. 'If you think an afternoon in bed can make him forget his first wife, you must be mad!'

Rachel's face flamed. 'We're not all like you, Nash!' she snapped back. 'Duncan has some news for me about . . . what I was telling you. He needs to discuss it properly.'

'For God's sake!' For some reason Natasha was furious. She turned to the others. 'The woman behind the throne indeed! It turns out she's got an informer in the enemy camp! Some of the Cabinet – yes the Cabinet, can you believe it – are about to defect and set up some crackpot Party all of their own—'

'Nash! I told you that in the strictest confidence!'

'And now we're being asked to believe it can't go ahead until Ray has put on her seal of approval! Bollocks! She's after a quick fix in bed – she's frightened the first wife will have got there before her—'

Rachel said coldly, 'Don't judge other people by yourself, Nash. My God – the plumber! And Maisie's brother too! You must have been bloody desperate. But then you always did like taking Maisie's boyfriends, didn't you? Have you slept with Ted Davenport?'

Pru and Evelyn were horrified. The row had blown up out of nothing. Evelyn said, 'I thought we were so close . . .' Pru said, 'Shut up. Both of you. Just stop speaking.' They did so and into the silence, suddenly and completely unexpectedly, came Natasha's sobs. Evelyn moved to touch her and then stood back. Rachel went over awkwardly and put a hand on the wracked shoulder. 'All right. I'm sorry,' she said in a stifled voice.

Natasha gasped, 'No, it's me. I'm poison, aren't I? Just because Harvey plays around I think . . . it's some kind of revenge you see . . . oh, Ray, I am sorry. Really. You are the power behind the throne – just like you always said. It's just that I don't understand politics and I'm, I'm,' her voice rose despairingly, 'I'm always bored by them!'

Rachel sat down next to Natasha and did not remove her hand. Everyone sat very still until Natasha's sobs abated. Then Evelyn spoke.

'Girls, a lot has happened. And we're working hard. We're tired and confused. This . . . sort of thing . . . is only to be expected.'

Pru seemed to collect herself. She said, 'Yes,' very definitely.

Evelyn seemed to be the only one able to make decisions. She said, 'Listen . . . Rachel must go and see Duncan. If she doesn't she will be trapped here. We don't want – any of us – to feel trapped here. This is our sanctuary, not a prison.'

Natasha looked up, her face sticky with tears. 'Oh, Evie, you're so bloody wise!' She turned to Rachel. 'Darling, you must go. Otherwise it will be all my fault.'

Rachel frowned and looked torn. She removed her hand from Natasha's shoulder. Pru smiled. 'Come on now, Ray. Listen to Aunt Evie. Tomorrow morning . . . leave really early. OK?'

Rachel said hesitantly, 'You're trusting me to come back?'

Evie put four mugs and a pot of coffee on the table. 'You won't be able to stay away. It would be like switching off a good play before the end.'

They all grinned. Rachel said, 'You don't even sound like Aunt Evie today!'

And Evie said happily, 'It's Edith. She keeps popping up in things I say.'

Pru turned her smile upside down. 'I rather hoped she was sticking with Maisie.'

'Oh, Pru . . . she's everywhere,' Evelyn reprimanded.

Rachel got on the M4 at Bristol and put her foot down. She had driven fast down the M5 but this last piece of motorway was familiar to her and she averaged eighty-five and hardly noticed it. She had phoned Duncan the previous day and had left a message on the answer-machine, but she would arrive far earlier than she had said. She wanted to be in time to take him a tray of tea in bed. And share it with him. She grinned as the wind whipped her hair across her face. Evelyn's little homily against any of them feeling trapped must have struck a chord because she felt as free as a bird. The weather was holding; tomorrow Maisie should turn up; she and Natasha had cleared the air in some obscure way . . . it was as if they had tapped into a shared root. Hadn't she herself thought just before the row that sex was vital to marriage? And, after all, promiscuous though Natasha might be, didn't Natasha know the truth of that better than most? She gave a lorry driver a blast on the horn to warn him he was encroaching onto the third lane and swept by him as they reached Maidenhead. In half an hour she would be with Duncan. She glanced at the clock on the dashboard. Seven forty-five. By eight-thirty she would be in bed with Duncan. She gasped with a sudden rush of sensation and pushed her hair off her hot face. They would have all day to talk and eat; this early-morning meeting was set aside for something else.

She parked the car outside the mews garage; it did not matter if she blocked in Duncan's car. She took off her sunglasses, picked up her bag and went around to the front door. Inside, one of her Chinese rugs was rucked up against the bottom of the stairs and the parquet looked as if it could do with some buffing; otherwise everything was as usual and very quiet. She went into the kitchen; not neat at all. It smelled strongly of whisky and there were glasses all over the place and two plates with the remains of a Chinese meal clinging to them. She put them to soak while the kettle boiled; laid a tray and carried it upstairs. And then, on a sudden whim, she placed it carefully on the landing table, went into the dressing room and slipped out of her slacks and T-shirt and into a satin nightdress. And then she went back to the tray, picked it up and turned the handle of the bedroom door as quietly as she could.

The one thought that stayed constant in her head after that was that she must not drop the tray. To drop the tray would be to announce her presence and her shock. Somehow she managed to hold it. To carry it to the top of the stairs and put it on the little table again. To go back and close the bedroom door with enormous care. To snatch up her slacks and T-shirt and bundle them under one arm. To pick up the tray and go oh-so-carefully back down the stairs and into the kitchen and replace everything as she had found it. Thank God she had not washed those plates and glasses; she had straightened her rug in the hall. Quickly she kicked that back to the bottom step, made for the front door, paused and returned to the office. There were seven messages on the answer-machine: she pressed the button labelled 'delete' and the numbers descended silently to a zero and then two dashes. She had doubtless erased six very important messages from Cabinet Ministers. She did not care. Her own message had gone with them. And then she was outside again, holding the door on the turned key, inching it close, releasing the key with terrible caution, tiptoeing – quite unnecessarily now – around the terrace and into the mews.

By the time she was back on the M4 the jumble of thoughts in her head had steadied into one definitive picture. Her bed. Next to the open window through which a breeze blew the curtains gently. The striped duvet cover . . . diagonal stripes in blue and black, daringly clashing. Two heads on the adjacent pillows. One, of course, Duncan's. The other, unmistakably, Douglas Maccrington's.

She could not believe it. Yet . . . was this why Douglas kept in such close touch? Was this what Joy had discovered and might tell? She had always known that Duncan had an enormous sexual appetite, hadn't she? And she had been away now for over a week.

She smiled tightly, the wind widening her lips and hurting her teeth. She had been frightened he would turn to Joy. Well . . . at least he had not done that.

She came to the interchange and forced herself to concentrate hard. And then she was roaring up the M5 towards Worcester, longing with all her soul to be back at Prospect House where, in spite of all that was happening, there was a feeling of innocence.

* * *

She turned off early and drove through Upton-upon-Severn. And it was then, negotiating the village street, that she realized she was still wearing her satin nightie.

Seventeen

It was mid-afternoon by the time Rachel reached Prospect House. Eight hours of driving had given her an unkempt raw look that warned everyone, even Ian, that she was unapproachable. She went to her room to find Jess lying on her inflatable mattress, reading a Danielle Steel. Rachel flung the satin nightgown onto her bed and herself after it. Jess sat up apprehensively.

'Is something wrong?'

'Why should something be wrong?' Rachel asked. 'I went to London to see my husband. I've seen him. He looks well and very happy and he is not sleeping with his ex-wife.'

Jess flushed. 'Well . . . that's excellent, isn't it?' She indicated her book. 'According to this, you're very lucky, Aunt Ray. Most men seem to need more than one wife.'

Rachel borrowed one of Natasha's phrases. 'Tell me about it.'

Jess, taking this as an invitation, said, 'Well, actually, I haven't said anything . . . well, to Mr Lavington perhaps . . . I don't remember now. But I think there might have been something between Dad and Mrs Donald.'

Rachel rolled onto her side and stared down at the girl. The young face was bright red and bent towards the book, a long finger traced the raised letters of the title. For the first time since leaving the house in Pimlico, Rachel wanted to weep. She said tightly, 'What the hell is the matter with men? And why the hell do we care?' She sat up and leaned over her knees. 'That's the answer, Jess. We must not care. You and me. We mustn't care.'

Jess lifted her shoulders. 'Sounds easy. I've already tried it actually. The trouble is, if we love them, then we care. It's that inevitable cause and effect thing.'

'And of course . . .' Rachel felt suddenly small and definitely petty. 'Of course you love your father.'

Jess looked up fleetingly. 'I'm not sure. He's not . . . actually . . . he's not like my father any more. In a way it's as if Dad is dead. I feel as if I'm mourning Dad?'

'Oh my God. Oh, Jess, I'm sorry.'

'Mark and I . . . we've talked about it a lot. Mrs Donald said our grandfather was mad as well. Which looks as if it's an inherited . . . thing. Weakness.' Her finger reached the last letter of the title on the book and trailed onto the pillow. 'I tried to show Tom that he was lucky not to be a full member of the family. Because, after all . . .'

'Don't be ridiculous, Jess!' Rachel found she was kneeling in front of the girl. 'With your medical training you must realize that the chances of this kind of thing running through generations are very rare.'

'I'm not worried for myself.' Jess looked up, her face now set. 'But I certainly can't have any children.'

Rachel was aghast. She sat back on her heels. 'Darling girl. You'll change your mind. When you meet someone . . .' She stopped speaking at the look on Jess's face. 'Oh God. You're already in love. Aren't you?'

'I don't know.'

'Who is it? God, you're only eighteen and a young eighteen in most ways! And your mother isn't here . . . oh God!'

Jess said, 'Calm down, Aunt Rachel! I only think . . .' She took a deep breath and began to talk. It was obvious suddenly that she had wanted to talk ever since she arrived. 'He, he sort of liked me. I know that. Even Tom thought that he liked me . . . And I liked him. He was so, so *competent*!' She rushed on: Langford Veterinary Hospital, the clock tower, the Somerset farm where the horse had been sick, the swim in Weston's muddy waters; even the Exmoor farmer who hung pictures in his barn. 'Mark wants everything to be scientific and neat. Steve . . . understands. Understands that beyond the science, bigger than any logic, is . . . is feeling.'

Rachel could think of nothing to say to that. Her knees were hurting and she straightened with some difficulty and sat on the bed. Her problems . . . Nash's divorce . . . they were all so tarnished compared with this young girl's idealistic discovery. She said quietly, 'I don't know what to say, Jess. You are so young and honest and good. You are very much like your mother. You've both got a kind of innocence—' she checked as Jess made a sound almost of contempt, then she went on. 'Jess, I'm not going to change that word. Innocence is what Maisie always had. It's been betrayed but from what your Aunt Evie says, it's still there. It's one of the reasons she had to leave your father, to keep it intact. Try to understand that. Try to hang onto your own innocence.' She put out a hand and touched Jess's fingers. 'Innocence has very little to do with virginity, my dear. Everything to do with your attitude . . . one's own nature.'

Jess looked up; her dark eyes were full of a longing to believe. 'You all stick up for Mum because she's your friend. But . . . well, she's driven Dad mad. Hasn't she?'

'I think he managed that by himself, Jess.' Rachel stood up. 'Come on. Let's go down and make some tea. Tomorrow your mother will be here and you can talk to her. I don't feel qualified to say much to you.'

'Because you never had children?' Jess uncurled herself and dropped the book onto her pillow. 'But, don't you see, that makes you perfect. You can talk to me like – like another human being. Objectively.' She squeezed her eyes as if to hold back tears. 'I mean, the way you told me that you had been worried about your husband . . . in case he, he, slept with his first wife. That's such a compliment. As if I'm old.' She shook her head and amended quickly, 'Older.'

Rachel laughed. 'I tell you what. I feel heaps better since seeing you, Jess.' She went ahead down the stairs. 'Now all I've got to do is to work out how I'm going to deal with . . . things.'

Jess managed a smile. 'The reunion, do you mean? All of us descending on you? I think the reunion is making you stronger. You're going back to when you were certain.' She stopped smiling and sighed. 'That's what I miss. Until this thing with Mum and Dad, I was so certain . . . so sure of my life and what I wanted to do.'

'You will be again.' Rachel said the trite words and meant them but her mind had seized on what Jess had said. The reunion was a nostalgic thing; a reminder of what they had been; how they had been. She knew suddenly what she must do; she must visit her father. When Maisie came back and they sorted everything out, she must go to Leyhill Open Prison and visit Eric. Duncan had made her promise she would never see her father again, but all promises to Duncan were now null and void. And anyway Duncan had no idea that her father had always fixed things for her. And he would fix this too.

Meanwhile the kitchen was overflowing with bodies. The children had thrown themselves into their activities a little too enthusiastically and now they were tired and argumentative. Hilary was sulking. Tom was awkward with Ian and Simon; his relationship as half-brother was too new to contemplate. Jess had stayed in the room she was sharing with Rachel. Mark, who had spent more time than anyone with his father, was secretly frantic about his mother. He vividly recalled the thickset body hunched on the leather couch, the dark eyes like coals in the white face. When Edward had spoken, he had said quite simply, 'She has to be punished, Mark. She has always had to be punished. This time it must . . . count.' Mark had always been proud of his girlish mother; the fair bubble curls and wide china-blue eyes. Now he remembered the violet bruise along one cheek and the time she had broken her wrist.

Aunt Nash's daughter, Hillie, said with her American twang, 'A penny for 'em, Mark.' And he stared at her and said, 'Worthless, I'm afraid. Why don't you see what's on the television? Settle the boys down for me, will you?'

But she was not interested in helping and said stubbornly, 'Why me? Because I'm a girl? Why don't you ask Tom to do your work for you?'

He stared at her, more surprised than annoyed. And then Aunt Rachel bustled in and took over. She was incredibly bossy but he didn't mind in the slightest. Jess was behind her and said, 'Come for a walk, Mark?'

'Let's.' He drew her arm through his and they went outside. Hilary muttered disgustedly, 'Not another case of incest!'

Evie said, 'Incense, Hillie? I can't smell a thing.'

And Natasha snapped, 'Just shut up, will you, Hilary?'

Hilary flounced into the sitting room where Tom was watching an old film on the telly featuring Doris Day. She wasn't surprised; he was so obviously a Doris Day person. But then he melted her heart by looking up and saying, 'Come and watch with me, Hillie. I don't seem to have seen you all day!'

She smiled beatifically and sat on the floor next to him. 'You see? You *are* in love with me,' she said comfortably. 'Thank God for that. I thought I was losing my touch!'

He laughed and put an entirely friendly arm over her shoulder. 'You're such a dope!' he told her. But his arm was warm on her bare shoulder and his touch seemed to connect several parts of her body in a similar sensation.

She said, 'You shouldn't be rude to me, Tom. Not only are you a bastard but I am much older than you.'

'How much?' he enquired with interest.

'My birthday is next month.'

'Mine is just inside next year. So . . . six months.' He paused but she said nothing because her voice might shake. He withdrew his arm and said in a low voice, 'Thanks for making it all right. About me being . . . illegitimate.'

She felt as if a cold wind blew across her shoulders but at least without his arm her voice would be OK, so she said sturdily, 'You can't be illegitimate. No-one can be born against the law. But you are a bastard.'

He laughed, delighted. She said, 'I mean it, Tom.' And she knelt above him and put her mouth against his. Their teeth grated uncomfortably. She sat back down, disappointed.

'What was that about?' he asked, suddenly not sure of himself any more.

'I was testing you. You failed actually, but I'll tell you anyway. I'm going to phone my father. Harvey. As soon as I can get the phone to myself. Ask him over. Try and get them together. Will you help me?'

Doris Day was singing. He ignored her and turned to look into Hilary's gypsy face. His eyes were intensely blue and his fair hair flopped almost into them. Hilary felt her heart squeeze very gently.

He said, 'You know I'll help you. With anything.'

She held her breath. Then she puffed it out and grinned. 'OK. You passed after all.'

On Friday Maisie did not come and it rained all day. The hills became grey and ominous. Pru and Natasha took a car load into Malvern to get food. Rachel and Evelyn helped Mark to bring in the sleeping bags and lay them on the dining room floor. The stream rushed into the pool and overflowed the dam wall. Everything became muddy and damp. Hilary, who had opted to stay at home, said she had asked Pru's permission to call her father. She used the extension on the landing and could be heard chattering away for over half an hour.

'Pru's not made of money,' Evelyn commented when she came downstairs smirking secretly.

'I promised I'd pay her.' Hilary looked at Evie beseechingly. 'Don't tell Nash I talked to Harve, will you, Evie? It would hurt her feelings.'

Evelyn's sympathy was instant. 'You're piggy-in-the-middle, aren't you?' she said. 'You know Rachel and I can be discreet.'

Rachel said, 'I've had a lot of practice in being discreet. My middle name.'

Mark called, 'Here they come – good Lord, the car's slipping almost into the stream!'

They gathered by the front door; sure enough as the car rounded the bluff the wheels were slipping sideways in the mud. And then they gripped on the gravel and the overfull car jogged sedately up to the house.

'We're really going to be marooned here!' Natasha greeted them without her previous excitement. 'The bloody field is a sea of mud and the farmyard, well, Bryn is using the tractor so you can tell!'

Everyone looked serious. The rain would keep them indoors; there were too many of them – ten people – for the four-bedroomed house. Pru ran in with the last of the shopping; the extended table space was already covered with plastic bags.

She gasped, 'We bought some asparagus. And some strawberries. And lots of fish for fish and chips. We'll have a slap-up supper and forget the rain!' She looked at their glum faces. 'We can play cards all afternoon.'

Ian said, 'But no swimming.'

Surprisingly, Hilary was also determinedly optimistic. 'Why not? What earthly difference does the rain make?'

Evelyn flapped her hands. 'All that mud indoors.'

'Not to worry, Aunt Evie. We'll change in the garage. Pru, don't put the car away just yet, OK?'

Simon said in a small voice, 'What if Mum turns up? Will a taxi be able to get through to us?'

Natasha said sternly, 'What did we tell you in the car?'

'You said that the taxi would get as far as the farm and then Bryn would bring her in the tractor,' Simon said.

'Well then.'

'It's just that . . . she's not *here*!' Simon's voice rose almost to a wail.

Tom said sensibly, 'I've been thinking. Maybe she thought the reunion started on Monday. Things often start on Mondays, don't they?'

Evelyn said, 'Of course. That's it. The last week in August, we said. That's Monday!'

No-one questioned this; Simon looked slightly comforted and Rachel herded them into the garage with towels and costumes. The costumes were still wet from the day before and there were groans from the boys. Jess and Hilary donned theirs behind an upturned wheelbarrow with some stoicism: Jess's mind was so permanently elsewhere that she hardly noticed what she was actually doing any more. Hilary simply felt that, as it had been her suggestion, she should keep her enthusiasm well-fuelled. Evelyn watched from the kitchen window as Rachel opened the garage door and ushered them out. Hilary ran up the bank and leapt for the rope, missed and splashed into the middle of the pool; Tom hurled himself after her. Ian and Simon capered on the edge, rain plastering their hair to their heads. Mark walked precariously along the submerged wall of the dam and dived neatly from it and Jess simply continued to walk until she was deep enough to strike out in a ladylike breaststroke.

Evelyn felt herself smiling and was amazed. If anyone had told her three weeks ago that she would be sharing a house with nine other people, practically cut-off from the world in the Malvern Hills, she would have been horrified. Yet here she was, pulling her weight, coping with all the small emergencies that arose, somehow ignoring the much larger emergencies that threatened, and actually enjoying it all.

As the girls came back into the kitchen she put the kettle on automatically. 'Shall we have a peaceful cup of tea?' she suggested. 'The swim and its aftermath will take up at least an hour and a half.'

The others gathered around and she fetched cups and milk and listened to them chattering and smiled again. Rachel had looked simply dreadful yesterday, but already she seemed to be getting hold of herself. Nash . . . dear, silly Nash . . . who was so close to her precocious and terrifying daughter, was temporarily under control, though what would happen to her in the future was anybody's guess. And Pru, less mysterious now, yet still full of mystery; Pru, bereaved yet unable to grieve properly, who seemed these last few days to be comforted by the fact that she had been allowed to see Edith . . . Pru was very special. When they had time, when all this business with Maisie was settled, they must concentrate on Pru.

Natasha poured milk into the cups. 'You're looking very solemn, Evie. Are you thinking what a hopeless lot we are?'

'I'm thinking how wonderful you are.' Evelyn spoke simply. 'And how much I love and admire you.'

The girls looked up, startled and touched. Rachel said, 'What a fool Maisie is to be missing this!' Natasha took the teapot and poured. She said, 'We're going to have to do something about Maisie, aren't we?' And, as if in response, the telephone rang and she went on, 'Well thank goodness the kids are all outside. What's the betting that's Dr James – or the police – to say Ted Davenport's been caught?'

But it was actually Ron Jenkins on the line and he asked to speak to Pru. Natasha handed over the receiver almost petulantly. 'I don't know why he won't talk to me,' she commented. 'My God, if he's trying to put me down again like he did on Tuesday afternoon, he'll have to try harder than this!' But as no-one had realized that Ron was putting Natasha down, they all looked at her blankly and she sat down again with unnecessary force.

Ron said quickly, 'Listen, I don't want to frighten anyone but I have to tell you. Whether you pass on the news or not is up to you. Ted Davenport has just left – I tried to stop him but he didn't let me get within two yards of him. He's driving – I've rung the police with the number of his car, but you know how it is with them. Until a crime is actually committed . . .'

Pru said, 'Thank you, Ron. He didn't . . . try anything?'

'He knows he's no match for me. But why I'm ringing. He searched the house – this house – and I let him because I thought it might calm him down. Then he whipped out onto the pavement – for a sick man he is moving fast – and he was muttering something about the next port of call. Lavenham. Have you heard of it? It's a village in Suffolk – I think it's Suffolk. I could go up there if you like—'

Pru interrupted with some dismay. 'Lavenham? No . . . I think he must have said Lavington. Oh dear . . . Sam Lavington is Evelyn's neighbour in Earlswood. He helped Evelyn when Ted Davenport was . . . well, unpleasant.'

Ron said, 'Oh . . . ah. Is he elderly? Yes? Can he cope? Is he on his own? What should we do?'

Pru looked at the others through the kitchen door. They stared back at her wildly. She said, 'He's elderly and on his own. I don't know about coping . . . not if Ted goes off the rails. I can telephone and warn him.'

Ron said, 'Give me his address. I'll drive there straight off.'

Pru dictated the telephone number and address and said, 'We'll keep in touch.' She immediately dialled Mr Lavington's number and said over the receiver's mouthpiece, 'He's doing the rounds again. He's just left Ron's. And he was obviously going to Mr Lavington's.'

Evelyn gave a cry of distress and Natasha put an arm around her. Rachel said, 'We must keep an eye on the kids. They mustn't know about this.'

Pru was already talking to Mr Lavington. Evelyn slid out from Natasha's arm and went to the phone. 'Let me speak to him.'

Pru stopped reassuring him about Jess and the others and handed over the receiver. Evelyn said, 'Mr Lavington? It's me, Miss Hazell. You can use my bungalow if you like. But better still why don't you go and stay with your son for a few days. Until this blows over?'

Sam Lavington said, 'Ah . . . my dear . . . Miss Hazell. How are you?'

'I'm very well – really very well. But this business, it's too bad pulling you into it. And now it seems you are in actual physical danger.'

'I was just saying to your friend that this might well be a blessing in disguise. If he breaks in, the police can nab him. And then maybe the doctors can get him put in some safe place.'

'Breaks in? But the damage, Mr Lavington! You've got everything so neat—'

'And I can get it neat again, my maid. Don't you worry your little head about that. The important thing is to get this man put into hospital.'

'Oh, Mr Lavington. You're so brave.'

'Sam.'

'Yes. Sam.'

'And you won't worry any more . . . Evie?'

'No. I won't, Sam.'

Pru said in a low voice, 'I think we should ring the doctor, Evie. As soon as possible.'

'Of course. I'll say goodbye then, Sam. And hope to see you next week. In happier circumstances.'

Rachel had taken Dr James's number and ran upstairs to get it. He was out but his wife promised to give him the message as soon as he returned. They gathered around the table again; the tea was still warm yet they felt an hour must have passed since Natasha poured it. From outside the screams of the younger children were no longer reassuring. Natasha said heavily, as she had said ten minutes before, 'We really are going to have to do something about Maisie, girls.'

Evelyn forced herself to sip her tea. 'But what? If the police manage to arrest her husband for breaking into Mr Lavington's . . . oh dear, poor Mr Lavington! And it was none of his concern, after all!'

Natasha said, 'He loves being part of it, Evie. You know that. Don't fret on that score.'

'But supposing he is hurt?'

'He'll have his son with him. And Ron – Maisie's brother – will be there in under an hour. Nothing will happen.' She glanced at Pru. 'This could be a blessing in disguise, actually. Couldn't it, Pru? Couldn't it, Ray?'

'Yes . . . yes . . .' the other two said in unison. Then Pru added, 'But Maisie is still missing. And if I did see . . . something last week, then perhaps I should go back to Birmingham and try to pick up the, the—'

'Vibes,' Natasha supplied. 'But that's all rubbish, Pru. You said so yourself. You were in a highly emotional state and Edith was on your mind—'

'She wasn't,' Pru refuted flatly. 'Meg was on my mind. Solely Meg.'

Rachel said, 'Well, that doesn't mean anything special, Pru. Nash is right. You can't go off on a wild-goose chase like that. Surely if Ted Davenport is taken into some kind of custody, that's all we need to worry about?'

'You mean, you don't want to see Maisie?' Pru asked, unusually truculent.

'Not a bit of it! I mean, our prime concern is for Maisie's safety. With her awful husband out of the way, we can assume she is at least safe from him. And as for coming here . . . this is entirely a voluntary reunion, Pru.' Rachel tried to smile. 'No-one forced us to meet up. And if Maisie's choice is to stay away—'

Evelyn said slowly, 'That's all true, Ray. But Maisie *did* intend to come. She talked me into it too. And it's been worth it. It would be worth it for Maisie. She could be with her children again. Properly.' She looked at Pru. '*I* don't think you imagined Edith, my dear. I think Edith let you see her so that you would know she was keeping an eye on Maisie. I agree with you that it would be worthwhile to go back to the spot where you saw Edith, and take it from there.'

Pru pushed her teacup away. 'You see, girls,' she said slowly. 'My mother has . . . contact . . . with a group of men who are quite powerful. In Birmingham. Rotarians, councillors, chairmen of corporations. Obviously the police won't look for a forty-year-old woman who voluntarily left home. But there are other ways of tracing missing persons. I could ask my mother to put the word around.'

Natasha said, 'I didn't think you had much to do with your mother since . . . since you bought Telegraph House.'

Pru acknowledged the truth of this with a quick nod but said, 'And I should do. And this could be an ice-breaker. She will adore the element of intrigue. And anyway,' Pru looked down. 'She should know about Meg.'

There was a silence broken by Evelyn who said tentatively, 'I would come with you except that with so many of us, I think I can be more useful here.'

'There's no point in anyone coming with me,' Pru looked up at last. 'To be honest, I'd rather do it alone.'

'When will you go?' Natasha asked.

Rachel said, 'Now. Why don't you go now? You can ring us tonight to hear what happened with Ted Davenport. Besides which, if this rain continues we might not be able to get the car around the bluff. Slip away now so that the kids don't have to know too much.'

Pru looked startled for a moment but when the others added their encouragement, she nodded. 'Yes. You're right. I can talk to Mother tonight and get out really early tomorrow morning. All right.' She levered herself up from the table; she looked tired and older than her years. 'I'll put some stuff in a bag.' She looked round. 'Girls . . . thanks.'

Down near the lakes in Earlswood, Ron Jenkins arrived at Mr Lavington's at the same time as Young Sam. They were ushered inside and made their own introductions. Mr Lavington suggested tea and Young Sam went to his car and produced a pack of beer from the boot. About an hour later a nondescript man, holding a large umbrella over his head, knocked and assured them that they were under surveillance. 'The family doctor has been in touch, and we are taking this seriously. You have no need to worry at all.' They took him at his word and sat in the little front room playing cards and watching the rain stream down the windows.

Sam Lavington said dourly, 'I don't envy them girls looking after a big family up there. Nothing to do, nowhere to go. Gawd.'

Ron Jenkins got up and peered through the rain; there was no sign of the Rover.

'They'll cope,' he said. 'Nash – the Barkwith girl – she's got enough energy for five ordinary mortals. And the tall one with grey hair—'

'Some sort of nun, isn't she?' asked Sam Lavington.

'Dunno. Could be. Plenty of common sense.'

Sam Lavington grinned. 'As for that Rachel. Bossy-boots if ever there was one. She'll tell 'em what to do!'

Young Sam looked at his father, who seemed to be shedding his years fast. 'Gives us all something to think about, I suppose,' he commented.

'Don't want you to forget about the pub, mind, our Sam,' Mr Lavington warned. 'When all this is over and done with, we don't want to be put back on the shelf and forgot, like.'

Young Sam said dourly, 'Not much hope of that when you're around.' He glanced at the mantelpiece. 'Bloody plastic ducks,' he said.

'Served their purpose,' Mr Lavington maintained.

Ron said, 'He isn't coming.' He came back to the table and picked up his cards, looked at them and put them face-down again with a disgusted snort. 'He's fooled us all. He isn't coming.'

The grey afternoon melted into a greyer evening. At ten o'clock Young Sam tucked his father into the passenger seat of his car and took him to his detached house with its lakeside garden. Ron struggled into a sleeping bag and lay on top of the bed. The police were still invisible.

But it did not matter because there were no callers.

Eighteen

The Honourable Mrs Adair was astounded by the whole story. 'Dear girl, things like that simply do not happen in this day and age! We're at the beginning of a new decade. My God, evil men in cloaks—'

'Mummy. Have I mentioned one evil man in a cloak?'

'But, darling, that's how it sounds! I remember Maisie Davenport. I simply cannot see her in the role of Trilby – and that is what you are saying, is it not?'

'Well . . . in a way. But I don't think she was ever enslaved to her husband in quite the way Trilby was. No, she was loyal to him.' Prudence sighed. 'There have been odder relationships as you well know.'

'You mean yourself and that girl at Telegraph House? Meg, was it?'

'Actually, I was thinking of you and your courtiers.' Pru stared steadfastly through the window. 'That's another thing I have to tell you. Meg died. On Monday evening. I took her home – to her own home with her parents. And she died.'

Constance Adair was sincerely grieved. 'Oh, Pru. Oh, darling, how simply dreadful. Oh I am sorry.' She looked into the face that was so like her own. 'Dear girl. Does this mean the end of the community?'

Pru lifted her shoulders. 'I don't know, Mummy. I love the place.'

'Yes, it is beautiful, I grant you that.'

'There is something I have to settle first. I have to find Maisie. Can you put out the word? One of your boyfriends might know something. She could have applied for a job with someone. I don't know. It's a forlorn hope, but I had to give it a try. Tomorrow morning, before the shoppers arrive, I'm going to walk up and down Corporation Street. There's just a faint possibility she was there a week ago last Wednesday.'

'Ten days ago? What are you, some kind of Indian tracker?'

'Don't be silly, Mummy . . . I told you it was a faint hope.'

'My God. One of your sightings.'

'What do you mean?'

'You remember. When you were a little girl. You used to pretend you saw Daddy. Of course, darling, you knew him only from photographs, so it was just ridiculous. But you were so sure about it that Edgar used to say you had second sight.'

'Did he? I've forgotten.'

'So this, this feeling about seeing your friend Maisie, was not a sighting?'

'No.'

'Ah well. You'll have to do what you think best. Try to be back for lunch and I'll ask Edgar to join us. He's so sensible. He might have a suggestion.'

'Yes. Thanks, Mummy. I'll do that.'

'I have to go out this evening, sweetie. Tickets for the ballet. Such a bore. But James fancies himself as a patron of the arts and he might sponsor them for a provincial season.'

'James?'

'Sir James Delingpole, Pru. You must remember him. I think he's the tiniest bit on the other side. And it does his reputation no harm at all to be seen out with me.'

'Oh God. You see yourself as a do-gooder for homosexuals, do you?'

'Why not, darling? It's why Edgar has remained so true. Why I always trusted him with you.'

'Edgar?' Pru started to laugh. 'Edgar and Delano? But Delano always made passes at all his typists!'

'Of course. He was trying to prove something.'

Pru said impulsively, 'I wish I'd known.' And then she remembered how Edith had implied that she slept with Mr Delano and she dissolved completely. 'Well, Edith, I know now!' she said aloud. 'You owe me one, remember!'

Constance opened her wonderful eyes wide. 'What on earth are you talking about, Pru?'

'Mummy, darling, don't be late for James. I'll see you tomorrow. For lunch.' Pru actually kissed her mother. Fondly. And then watched her go upstairs to change. She was well into her sixties and looked not much older than Pru herself.

Pru laughed again and went to the kitchen to make herself a sandwich before going to bed.

The weather was much better on Saturday but rain clouds menaced from the southwest and Evelyn's left shoulder ached persistently, which meant rain was on the way. Rachel was spending a lot of time on the telephone. First she rang the Adair house in Barnt Green, where a maid informed her Miss Pru was out and the Honourable Mrs Adair was still in bed. Then she rang Ron Jenkins's number and got no reply. Then she rang Mr Lavington and got Ron who told her that nothing had happened. 'Nothing at all?' she said, incredulously. They were used to non-events up here in the hills, so it seemed as if everything must be happening in Birmingham. 'Sweet effall,' Ron said succinctly. 'Old Lavington's son came round and we played cards all afternoon. Police reckoned they'd got an eye on the place but we haven't seen any signs of it. And Sam took the old man off to his place for the night. They're not back yet.'

'What are you going to do?'

'I've got a business to run. I'll have to leave 'em to it.'

'All right. Well, thanks for keeping in touch and everything.'

Then she rang Dr James and got hold of him personally this time. He was much more hopeful. 'I've convinced the police that Davenport must be hospitalized. So at least they'll apprehend him on sight. Before he can do anything silly.'

Rachel thought how much better it was to talk about Maisie's husband as a sick victim rather than a hunter. She replaced the receiver and looked down the hall. No-one was about. Natasha, who had been hovering nearby to share what was being said, had gone up to Evelyn's room to rub her shoulder. Mark and the boys were pitching the tent again on some higher ground; Jess was washing up. Hilary and Tom had been absent since breakfast. Rachel thought grimly that they had not washed up once.

She picked up the telephone again and dialled. A voice said, 'Prisoners' Welfare here. May I help you?'

She cleared her throat. 'I'm enquiring for Mr Eric Strang.' She gave a number and a date. She had not had to look up her father's particulars; they would stay with her always. Information came across the line with commendable speed. He worked in the library; had been in hospital last winter with pneumonia but had expressly forbidden anybody to contact her.

She asked about visiting times and made an appointment for two weeks' time.

'I must warn you, he might well refuse to see you. He has refused to see visitors for the past two years.'

She said curiously, 'He's had visitors then?'

'He could have had visitors,' the voice corrected.

She knew that one of the would-be visitors must have been Rosa Benson, Eric's secretary. She replaced the receiver slowly and stood in the hall remembering Miss Benson. She had indeed been the power behind Eric's throne, 'covering all the angles' as he put it and never aspiring to oust Denise. Rachel wondered how Rosa had felt about Eric's almost public sexual advances. She had always gone 'all unnecessary' as Eric had put it, blushing and giggling like a schoolgirl and never ever slapping him away. Rachel shook her head, quite unable to come to terms with the way she too had accepted the situation simply because her father had implied it was right. Eric had always known best; had been daring and masterful; calm when Denise was hysterical, always on top of the world when Denise was usually at the bottom.

Rachel went to join Jess. She wondered whether she would tell her father . . . anything.

It took Hilary and Tom half an hour to walk the mile to Bryn's farm. Hilary skidded flat on her back twice and was covered in mud; Tom had dared to laugh at her so she had cleaned her fingers in his hair. Mrs Bryn, feeding the geese, declared they looked like a pair of mudlarks and if they were going into Malvern they'd best come inside and have a bath.

'We're not going right into Malvern.' Tom did the talking because Mrs Bryn said she couldn't understand 'that American language'. 'We thought any taxi driver would not want to come through the mud. So we're meeting the taxi the other side of the farm.'

'More visitors?' Mrs Bryn threw up her hands. 'You'll be wanting more supplies then?'

'I think Pru and Nash brought enough stuff back yesterday,' Hilary said in her Chudleigh voice. Mrs Bryn was pleasantly surprised.

'Teaching you to speak proper,' she congratulated. 'What time are you expecting this batch then?'

Hilary looked at Tom and he said, 'We're not sure. We'll just walk up the lane and wait a while.' Hilary said, 'It's not a batch, Mrs Bryn. It's just . . . my father.'

'Oh!' Mrs Bryn smiled her pleasure. 'Well that will be nice for you and your mammy now, won't it?' She waited while Hilary recovered from a fit of coughing. Then she said, 'Will he speak English?'

Tom said quickly, 'I think so.' He turned to Hilary who was coughing again. 'Come on. We don't want to miss him.' And he lugged her through the gate.

It was strange to walk in the heart of the city when it belonged to postmen, newspaper boys and cleaners. Pru had brought her umbrella just in case, but the sunshine filtered through the buildings and warmed patches of the pavement; the sky that was visible between rooftops was feathered with cloud. A mackerel sky they called it in Cornwall. It meant rain later. She hooked the handle of the umbrella into the belt of her slacks and fumbled in her bag for sunglasses. Already a headache was nagging behind her eyes. Yesterday, up in Cheshire, Meg's family had buried her body and Pru had determined not to think about it. Today was another day;

the sun shone cruelly as if Meg had been forgotten. Life had to go on.

She came to Markhams' window and paused, looking at the grilled glass and wishing she did have the second sight her mother had mentioned so casually. How easy it would be if she could go into a trance and summon up Maisie's whereabouts. Not to mention Davenport's. She remembered seeing a film of *Blithe Spirit* when she had been quite young: laughing when the adults laughed and wondering why they laughed because to her it was quite normal to see people who weren't really there. Day-dreaming, her mother had called it. Perhaps then, in those far-off days of innocence and ignorance, she had known and accepted some kind of gift as normal. Possessed by everyone. Then, later, as she grew older and wiser, knowledge had bred cynicism and her gift had gone.

She moved to the left of the window, where, glinting through metal shutters, she could see a tiara. It could not be the tiara belonging to the marcasite Coronation Suite, surely? That particular line had gone out when she was still working for Mr Delano. But she could remember it very well, and how they had tried on the wonderful tiara and posed mockingly for each other. How beautiful Maisie had looked; the glittering grey marcasite becoming almost part of her fairness. Pru could visualize her now; yet not quite as she had been, thinner, smaller. Not really Maisie at all. Pru stared and felt her heart stand still as the reflection intensified. And then she spun around. But Meg was not there. She had known she would not be. She had known she was conjuring her out of the tiara, the reflections in the glass and her treacherous, sliding memories.

She straightened her back consciously and set off at a fast pace as if she knew exactly where she was going. If Edith really was around, keeping her usual sharp eye on all of them, she would take Pru to Maisie: Pru told herself this firmly, saying it inside her head over and over again so that there would be no space, not a crack, for doubt. Faster and faster she walked until she was almost running, and then, quite suddenly, the umbrella still hooked into her belt swung between her knees and sent her sprawling.

The pavement hurt some of her body; she identified the painful places as she checked herself over for serious injury. Her inner arms, reaching to save herself, were burning with grazes; her breasts and hips had hit the paving stones next and would hurt more later when the shock was over. Her chin and then her nose had arrived last. She lay still for a moment until the sound of coins rolling to the edge of the kerb and falling into the gutter made her lift her head. Her bag had swung off her shoulder and flown open. The contents were strewn everywhere.

Nobody had seen her; for that she was deeply thankful. She got to her knees with some difficulty, tried to stand and sat down with a bump. The world was dark and shadowy. She removed her sunglasses and blinked hard. She was in a patch of shade but beyond it the world was still bright and clear. There was a strange noise coming from somewhere. She identified it as a sobbing sound; she was making it herself. She reached out as far as she could and scooped her belongings towards her. Her fingers were numb and she was bleeding . . . her arms and her nose. She stretched her legs in front of her; nothing was broken. The sobbing intensified. She knew she must control it, get up, find a phone box and call a taxi, but for the moment she could do nothing but fumble with her handbag, trying desperately to put everything back.

And then, most unwelcomely, a lorry appeared all kitted up with road-sweeping apparatus. It roared and swept its way inexorably towards her. She wanted to get up and move off again purposefully, but she sat there staring at its approach, sobbing quietly. It stopped opposite her and the driver looked out of his window. 'You all right, miss? Took a toss, did you?'

She nodded. That's all it had been. She had taken a toss.

'Can I do anything? D'you want an ambulance?'

'No. I'm all right. Honestly.'

He got out of his cab and put his arms beneath her armpits so that she had to struggle to her feet when she would have much preferred to go on sitting there for another few minutes. He was a short, stocky man and she towered over him.

'Now you sure you're all right? Where was you going?'

What could she say? 'To see the Markhams.' She indicated the shop front with a nod of her head. 'They've got a town house round here.'

'That's right. Just down Coventry Street, innit? They're on my beat.'

'Yes.' She had forgotten, now it came back to her. 'It was a mews house. Rachel lived there once and she sold it to them. She had a red car in those days.'

'Did she now?' The small man peered up at her doubtfully. 'You sure you'm all right now?'

'Sure. I've got Edith with me, you see.'

He got back into his cab and watched her as she tottered around the corner. He wondered if she was on the vodka; you couldn't smell vodka.

Pru recognized the house immediately because it had a red door to match the red car, and the brass was the brightest in the whole street. She wondered if they would be up yet. Edgar would look after her. Telephone Mummy and organize a car back to Barnt Green.

She rang the bell and waited. And when she had given up hope, the door opened.

And there stood Maisie.

They ate prawns and bread-and-butter for lunch: Pru and Natasha had brought back huge bags of frozen fish yesterday and there had been no room in the freezer for the prawns. Ian described the lunch they had eaten last week in the hospitality tent at Edgbaston. Archer's mother had let them choose what they wanted from the buffet. Ian had had seven chocolate eclairs. Mark told him there was no need to boast about behaving like a pig. Ian said pigs did not like eclairs. Mark said pigs liked anything. Jess suddenly said, 'Shut up! Both of you! Just shut up!'

Simon finished making a sandwich of his prawns and surveyed it without pleasure. 'Saturdays were my favourite day. But this one is pretty awful.'

Rachel was surprised. 'Why? I thought, with the nice weather back, you'd be enjoying yourselves again.'

Simon lifted his shoulders to his ears. 'Tom's left. I suppose he thinks we're infectious. He doesn't want to catch anything.'

'What on earth do you mean – Tom's left?'

'He's been avoiding us ever since we arrived. He went off this morning and we haven't seen him since.'

Natasha frowned. 'I thought you were all out there putting up the tent again – I was just going to ask where the two of them had got to.'

Simon took an enormous bite of his sandwich. Evelyn looked at Mark. 'Is this right?'

'They went for a walk. Yes. The two of them. I didn't think I had to chain them to the place.'

Jess warned 'Mark, stop!'

'Sorry.' He glanced at Natasha. 'Sorry, Aunt Nash. It's just that . . . Hilary makes no bones about the fact that I have no authority over her. And Tom and she get on well . . .'

Natasha frowned. 'When did they leave for this walk?'

Jess said quietly, 'It was their turn to wash up the breakfast things. They'd gone then.'

Rachel nodded. 'It crossed my mind that you shouldn't be doing it.' She shook her head gently at Natasha. 'You're not worried, are you? She's really very sensible, Nash. She role-plays a lot, but underneath she's sound.'

Nash felt a stab of pleasure that Rachel had discerned so much. 'I'm not worried for Hillie. I'm worried for Tom.'

Rachel laughed and after a moment so did Evelyn. Jess said, 'As a matter of fact, Tom can look after himself. It's good that he's got Hillie. Simon's right, he doesn't want much to do with us any more.'

The three women were united in their protests but the Davenports looked unconvinced. Jess cut through it all again.

'There's the phone. It must be for you, Aunt Rachel.' Rachel went into the hall and Natasha said, 'Why? Why should it be for Rachel?'

Jess raised her brows. 'She's been on the phone all morning.

Or most of the morning. Politics, I think. Something about a man called Eric Strang.'

Before Natasha could take this in properly, Rachel – most uncharacteristically – screamed from the hall. 'Girls! It's Maisie! Maisie – is it really you? Oh my God – we've been frantic – where are you? What are you doing?' She listened and looked up after a while. 'She's been working for the Markhams. In their house in Coventry Street – remember where I lived?' She listened again. 'And Pru is *with* you?' She lifted her head. 'Pru is with her – at this precise moment!' She ignored the exclamations from the kitchen door and concentrated again. 'Oh Maisie, I'm sorry – tell Pru we're sorry. But she's not seriously hurt? Well, thank God for that. And you'll come back here together? When? Tomorrow? Well yes, of course. Make it tonight if you can – we can manage.' She looked up. 'They might arrive tonight! If not, Sunday, tomorrow!' Her voice softened. 'Oh, Maisie, it will be good to see you. The children are all here . . . you want a word . . . all right. We'll talk when you arrive. We'll talk all night. Thank God you are safe.' She beckoned Jess into the hall and handed her the receiver. 'Go to it, Jess. She's safe and well and everything is going to be fine.' The boys whooped their delight and had to be hushed so that Jess could hear her mother. The three women sat at the table again, suddenly so totally relaxed it was if they might fall to pieces.

'My God . . . all the time . . . it's so obvious now we know.' 'How silly of me not to think of it.' 'She said she was offered work in the shop but she couldn't afford to be seen . . .' Natasha, Evelyn and Rachel were speaking almost in unison, their words overlapping. The relief was intense enough to show them how worried they had been before.

'Nothing is really solved,' Evelyn reminded them. 'He's still out there somewhere. And the children . . .'

'But it feels wonderful, doesn't it?' asked Rachel. 'Poor old Pru was walking along the street – where she'd seen that person who was like Edith—'

'Who *was* Edith,' Evelyn corrected. 'And probably Edith led her straight to Coventry Street—'

'And tripped her over on the way! Apparently she had a

dreadful fall. Nothing broken but when Maisie opened the door she was pouring with blood and in tears.'

'In tears? Pru?' Natasha leaned forward. 'She must have been shaken to bits – she's so tall to fall over – it's a miracle she didn't break something. But the shock—'

'Maisie's put her to bed and she's sleeping it off right now.' Rachel glanced in the direction of the hall. The children were still talking to their mother. 'Did you know the Markhams were . . . odd?' she asked.

'No!'

'Maisie said that's why she went to them. She knew they would never hurt her or betray her to Ted. She said she'd always liked gay men. She felt safe with them. And they were kind.' Rachel frowned, thinking about it. 'Maybe . . . maybe it works like that with Pru's lot too.'

Natasha said, 'Oh for goodness' sake.' She stood up suddenly. 'D'you know, I'm so tired. I feel as if I've put down a heavy load. I'm going to have a lie-down. Is that OK with you two?'

'Of course.' Evelyn stood up. 'Let's all go upstairs and rest, girls. The children will amuse themselves. Come on. My shoulder is so much better since that rub, Nash. I think I could go to sleep now.'

So they trooped upstairs and lay on their beds. 'Like old ladies,' Nash said ruefully. And in five minutes she was asleep.

As Nash drifted off, so Pru came out of her deep sleep. She too had found Maisie's sudden appearance almost unbelievable. The shock and the relief had almost knocked her out then and there. Certainly it had been impossible to stop the tears. By the time Maisie had taken her into her small room at the back of the house, she was sobbing uncontrollably and Maisie had taken her in hand as if she were one of the children, bathing her grazed arms, smoothing on cream, calling to Mr Edgar to make tea and bring the aspirins. Mr Delano too had arrived post-haste from the bathroom and they had squashed just inside the door and expressed astonishment in a variety of words and gestures for some time.

Pru sobbed away her reserve and self-control and talked as she had talked to the road sweeper.

'I thought Edith would bring me to you and I was just wandering around while the streets were empty and I thought I saw Meg in the window of Markhams and of course it wasn't Meg . . . I imagined her, just as I imagined Edith. And I was walking fast to try to get away from imagining things and I got my umbrella caught . . . fell . . . the pavement was so hard.' Her voice rose into a wail. 'It was so hard, Maisie. And I lay there and thought I would never find you and now . . . now . . .'

Maisie said, 'And now you've found me. And I wasn't lost at all. I told Mr Delano that I would be coming to see you on Monday morning – first train – and he said he would drive me to the station—'

'That's what we thought!' Pru's voice rose yet another register. 'But we were so frightened Ted would get to you first. He's full of anger and, yes, hatred, Maisie. And we don't know where he is . . . a loose cannon. He's a loose cannon, Maisie.'

Edgar came forward. 'Pru . . . dear Pru. Shall I ring your mother, my dear?'

'No. She'll still be in bed. Ballet last night.' Pru's eyes were already closing. 'Knows I am looking . . . searching . . . no worries.'

'All right. I'll wait until lunchtime.' He straightened. 'Let her sleep, Maisie. Come down and have some breakfast.'

But Maisie was firm. 'No. I'm staying with her for a while.' She arranged her pillows and Pru sank into them. Maisie said almost sadly, 'She needs me.' And Pru slept. She slept better than she'd slept since leaving Telegraph House, as if she did not have a care in the world. And Maisie's unmistakable scent from the pillows seemed to soak into her head like balm.

Natasha woke to find the rain clouds had stacked themselves on top of Worcester Peak, dividing their world into two distinct sections. Behind the house night waited to empty its rain. In front and below, the sun was doing its usual spectacular late afternoon swansong but its light was not being absorbed by the rest of the sky. It remained intense and glaring; defiant.

Natasha put on the spotted dressing-gown and prowled around the house. Both Evie and Ray were still asleep in their rooms; Evelyn rolled into a ball like a dormouse; Ray flat on her back, mouth open, a slight snore trembling her top lip. Natasha clutched the dressing-gown around her – it was definitely chillier – and padded downstairs. Jess was in the sitting room, reading. She was half lying in an armchair, her legs propped high on the wall and she had to slew sideways to grin at Natasha.

'Isn't it marvellous? Everything is going to be all right now, Aunt Nash. Mother thinks Aunt Pru will be fit to drive up here either this evening or tomorrow morning! We won't have to spoil your reunion any more.'

Natasha was shocked. 'Darling, Jess! You haven't spoiled anything! You, you've bonded us together. I can't explain . . . you've been . . . *essential*!'

'Oh, Aunt Nash! Mother always says you are right over the top.' The grin grew wider. 'You're her favourite, you know. She thinks the world of all of you, but you were always her favourite.'

Natasha almost blushed. She said instead, 'For God's sake stop twisting your body like that, Jess! You're making my back ache!' She waited until the girl righted herself and then asked, 'Where's everyone? I know Ray and Evie are asleep . . . by the way I think you should drop the aunt business. Just call us by our names.'

'Oh . . . thanks. Nash.' Jess grinned again. 'It's such a silly name really. But still.' She pulled her sweater down. 'Ian and Simon are in the tent. They've regressed to playing Indians. And Mark spotted an otter. He's downstream watching.'

'What about Hillie and Tom?'

'Not back yet. They don't even know about Mum. Tom will be so pleased.'

'We all are.'

'Yes. But Tom will be specially pleased. I mean, we all

belong to Mum. So he won't feel he's an . . . outsider.' She saw Natasha's expression and went on, 'That's why Hilary has been so good for him. She doesn't mess about, does she? She's so *rude*!'

Natasha laughed. 'Yes. I know what you mean. She's in the business of breaking down barriers and taboos.'

Jess looked eager. 'Yes. That's it, exactly. Yesterday she said to me that I could always blame my craziness on Dad. She said "the rest of us have only got ourselves to blame"! See what I mean?'

'I think so. That's your particular bogeyman, is it? And she brought it out into the light of day and it looked a pretty poor specimen?'

'I suppose so. Anyway, she has been good for Tom. So don't get annoyed with her for staying out all day. He probably needed her.'

Natasha said, 'You're a nice girl, Jess. And I'm not seriously annoyed with her – a bit exasperated perhaps.' She looked out of the window. 'I wonder when the rain will come. I think I'll walk down to the farm. See if they're around. Bryn said they could help move the sheep some time. They might be doing that.'

She went back upstairs and put on jeans and a sweatshirt. It was four-thirty. She wondered what Maisie and Pru were doing now. Pru would be awake and ravenously hungry probably. They'd eat then they'd get a taxi to Barnt Green – or maybe Edgar would drive them. There'd be a lot of laughing and talking and then, probably about five or six o'clock, Pru would begin the drive back to Malvern. So they could be here by eight; unless it started to rain before then. Natasha began to plan supper, then smiled at herself. Two weeks ago planning menus had been the last thing on her list of things to think about.

It was good to be out and walking on her own. She loved company but the last couple of days had proved to her that it could pall quite quickly. The feel of the gravel under the thin soles of her pumps was comforting; she liked the noise it made too. It was a different story when she came to the bluff. Skid marks were much in evidence; it almost looked as if someone had fallen near the stream. She looked around for Mark but could see no-one. The hills appeared to be featureless, but they were pocked-marked with dells and copses. She must remember to inaugurate a grand game of hide-and-seek. The kids would love that.

She was panting heavily when she reached the five-barred gate. There was no sign of Bryn but the geese waddled towards her, splashing mud on their pristine breasts, complaining loudly. Mrs Bryn looked out of the door.

'Climb over!' she bawled. 'Save opening it!'

But Natasha was wary of the geese. 'Seen any of the children?' she bawled back.

Mrs Bryn jabbed with her hand. 'The old combe I do believe!'

Natasha looked down; no sign of a combe but she did recall Hillie saying something about a secret place. Tom had remembered it from coming here with Maisie.

'OK – I'll go and see.'

She skirted the farm boundary and crossed a trackless field to another stile. The land dropped abruptly in a natural terrace. She skidded down it and crossed another enormous meadow where sheep were nibbling their way to a corner by the hedge for the night. Another terrace and she could see the tops of trees apparently growing straight out of the ground. That must be the combe.

It took her half an hour of giant striding and skidding from terrace to terrace before she reached it. She could feel her temper rising with each scramble. It was almost six o'clock; it would take twice as long to climb back up to the farm, then another half an hour to the house. Maisie might have arrived . . . the rain might have started . . . 'Bloody kids!' she said aloud. 'Bloody, bloody kids!'

The next terrace was rock-strewn, practically bare of grass. And then the ground dipped suddenly; a huge cleft appeared, tree-lined, full of dampness and vegetation. She could hear water and smell leaves and flowers. It was like entering Eden. She hung onto the next rock and gazed down. She was on the side of a gorge; the ground dropped almost precipitously beyond the rock.

She could easily scramble from tree to tree but there must be an entrance and exit. No way was she going to trek further along the side of it looking for an easy way in. She leaned forward and lifted her voice. 'Hillie! Where the hell are you?'

The undergrowth moved halfway down the side of the drop. The little devils were hiding there.

She screamed, 'I can bloody well see you! Come here this minute – I'm simply furious with you! D'you hear? I'm not joking!'

Somone was using the tree to stand up. Male hands appeared on the trunk. It must be Tom. But it wasn't. Tom still had his boy's hands, white and slender. These belonged to a grown man. She put a hand to her throat. Was it Ted Davenport? Had he tracked across this rough terrain in his obsessive search for Maisie?

The figure lumbered to full height. She stifled a scream by pressing on her throat. The man was dark, like Ted Davenport; his shoulders were incredibly wide, just like Ted Davenport's. But he was taller. A different shape.

Then she removed her hand from her throat and the scream burst forth, outraged, furious.

'Harvey Nolan! I'm going to kill you! Then I'm going to kill Hillie! I might have guessed – where is she? What are you *doing* here? How could you do this to me?'

She wanted to turn and run back from rock to rock and over the next stile and the next and the next . . . but she was exhausted. Her treacherous feet were already plunging down the steep side of the miniature gorge. Harvey braced his back against a tree and held out his arms.

'Nash, baby, I love you, I can't keep away—'

And she was sobbing and screaming, 'Harvey, you son of a bitch! I hate you – d'you hear me? I hate you!'

And then she was in his arms and he folded her against him with the familiarity of fifteen years and their faces were pressed painfully together. And she could feel that he too was crying.

Nineteen

Pru sat on the side of the bed. Her hair hung in rat's tails around her face – which was still blotched with weeping – her nose and chin sported dressings as did both arms. She whispered, 'I look a mess, don't I? I am a mess . . . Maisie, when things – events – stripped away my outer layer, I find this underneath.'

Maisie was busy emptying drawers and packing things into the bag she had taken from one-four-eight. She looked up and smiled. 'That's how I felt two weeks ago. I don't any more. And neither will you. This whole . . . nightmare . . . is my doing. And I intend to put things right. Make everyone realize it is just a nightmare. You'll realize it too.'

'It's not just Ted going mad, Maisie. It's all this half-life I lead. I'm the tiniest bit psychic apparently, but not quite enough. I can love and lose Meg, but I can't make a stand and go to her funeral and publicly mourn her loss. I could make life easy for you – and the children. I've got money and a house . . . two houses now. But you're scared because I'm a lesbian and you think I want to sleep with you.'

Maisie looked startled for a moment, then laughed. 'Yes, I was scared, wasn't I? But not of you, dearest Pru. Never of you.' She stopped packing and sat in a chair opposite Pru. She picked up a hairbrush and began to brush Pru's tangled hair. 'Shall I take the pins out of your knot-thing at the back? Then we can start again. And before you know it, you'll feel better.'

Pru turned her head and suffered the brush as it snagged at her scalp. She said, 'I don't understand, Maisie. When we talked – after Edith's funeral – you actually flinched.'

Maisie smoothed another tress of hair onto the brush. 'I

did, didn't I? You see, Pru, I've always known *I* was a mess. For years I've known it. The children made me feel less of a mess – ' she giggled at the rhyme ' – so I put everything I had into them. But underneath . . . I must be rotten, Pru. I slept with my brother. I slept with a hippie who wanted a one-night stand. And I stayed with Ted who wanted . . . something else. And then you said something to me that showed just how much of a mess I was. You said something about you loving me and me loving Nash.' She began to twist the hair into its usual knot. Strands fell out and curled around Pru's scarred face. 'I knew instantly that you were right. I have always loved Nash.' She finished pinning the hair and turned Pru's head so that she could look into her eyes. 'I still do. And never, not in a dozen lifetimes, would Nash feel the same about me.' She very gently removed the dressing on Pru's nose. 'I've been promiscuous, Pru, dear. I've been looking for someone decent to love. And when I found that person . . . she wasn't interested in me.' She took the dressing from Pru's chin and sat back. 'That's better. You look halfway normal already.' She said seriously, 'You are not a mess, Pru. You don't know what it means to be a mess. Because you are true . . . true to what you believe in. I was not frightened of you. I was frightened of myself . . . what I saw in myself.' She drew back suddenly at Pru's choking response. 'Now stop it! If you cry again you'll start those places bleeding and I'll have to plaster you up again and you'll look worse than I did after Ted had punished me!'

Pru gave another cry at that and Maisie took her face again very gently and said, 'I'm sorry, Pru. I shouldn't have said that. Poor Ted. What will happen to him?'

'He'll go into a hospital I suppose.'

Maisie sighed deeply then stood up and began to pack again. She said quite calmly, 'I shall sell one-four-eight if I can. We can manage with three bedrooms – the boys can go in together and one for me and one for Jess. Tom can go to school with Simon and Ian . . . we can manage.'

Pru stared at her in astonishment. 'You've got it all worked out.'

'Yes. I've thought of it such a lot.' Maisie turned. 'My one fear was that Ted would recover and somehow – when he divorced me – he would get custody of the children. But there will be no question of that now, will there?'

Pru swallowed. 'No. I wouldn't imagine so.'

Maisie clipped her case shut and lugged it to the door. 'Did you really think I was helpless?' She smiled at Pru almost sadly. 'Don't be sorry for me, Pru. I have chosen to do – and to appear – the way I have done. But now . . . I think I've expiated my guilt. Don't you?'

Pru put a hand up to her hair and tucked it behind her ears. 'There should never have been guilt in the first place.' And she started to explain that Ron was not related to Maisie in any way.

The sun was an hour lower in the sky and the rain clouds were encroaching. Natasha lifted her head and whispered, 'We must go. Oh, Harvey, whatever we have done to each other . . . we're still in love. Do you realize that? It's been . . . like that first time.'

'And that was here. In these English hills,' Harvey could not stop kissing her. His mouth left hers and travelled around her chin to her throat. She tilted her head further still and closed her eyes. 'Darling, I'm so desperately sorry about your suits.'

'My suits?'

'You know. I burned your suits. Hilary said that was the last straw.'

'Oh baby.' He kissed her properly. 'Honey. What did I care about my damned suits. Except that I thought it meant you'd gone for ever.'

'You had Pressburger,' she murmured.

'I bet you had someone.'

'Oh God. Yes, but it was nothing. Boredom, that's all.' She felt guilt. 'He was such a nice man. He asked me to marry him.'

'I never asked Pressburger. She wanted to take me over. Look after me.' He kissed her eyes. 'You never wanted to look after me, honey.'

'Do you want me to? Is that why you had your bimbos?'

'No. I don't want you to look after me. And that wasn't the reason for . . . what I have done. Oh, Nash, how can I explain it to you? They were there. On a plate. And people like Lew Blum and that film guy who said you could be an actress . . . no-one could resist you, Nash. Christ, I knew that better than anyone. I suppose Jennifer and – what was her name?'

'Roslyn,' Natasha supplied promptly.

'I suppose they were consolation? God, I don't even know myself.'

Natasha was silent, letting him kiss her while she studied the sky through the tops of the trees. The air was hot and breathless. Thunder was on the way.

She pushed him gently so that they both sat up. 'Harvey. Hillie phoned you and you came straightaway. That must mean you want to try again.'

'More than anything.'

'Me too, darling.' She held him off when he would have taken her in his arms again. 'But, Harve . . . nothing is solved. I can't ask you to promise to be faithful to me, because then, when you broke your promise, it would be worse than ever.'

'You trust me completely,' he commented drily.

'Darling, it's the same for you! For fifteen years we've been together and apart and screaming at each other and staging these kind of violent reconciliations – I'm not grumbling, I've loved this,' she swept the steep combe with one hand and then cupped his face. 'But baby, what about Hillie? And what about us? Eventually we shall get too old for it, too tired.' She kissed him. 'Harvey, in the last couple of weeks I've got to know some real people again. I mean *real* people. And so has Hillie. And it's been good for both of us.'

'What do you want, Nash? I'll agree to anything. Just so we can be together. Not divorced. The three of us a family.'

'I don't know. I really don't know, honey. Look, will you stay with us? Here? Just for a while? The place is packed to capacity but you can share my single bed – should be fun! Will you stay and get to know everyone? You might decide – when you've seen us together – that I'm not the girl you thought I was.' He protested loudly at that and tried to kiss her again. She held him off. 'As you get to know them, so you will understand more about me. Because I can't find the words either, darling. I don't want to whitewash what has happened. I want you to know me – warts and all.'

'God, Nash, do you think I find you perfect or something?'

'Of course not. But all that flirting—' He laughed at the old-fashioned word. 'OK . . . seduction? The games we played, whatever you like to call them – they involve other people who have lives of their own. We had no right . . .' She shook her head. 'Like I said, it's so difficult to find words. Stay here, Harvey. Listen. Really listen. And then, perhaps, we'll talk.'

'I want to stay. You must know that. But how will your friend Pru feel about another house guest?'

'Fine. She's not here at the moment. But she'll be fine.' Something hit her hard on her bare shoulder and she looked up. 'That was rain. Come on, let's get back. Hillie will be pleased her little plan worked. Let her gloat for a while.'

They scrambled up the side of the combe and reached the first of the rocks. The sky was deep purple and the sun struck through like a theatrical spot. Harvey said, 'We're going to get soaked.'

She looked at him. His dark face was alight with excitement. He was goodlooking in an Irish way with bright blue eyes dominating his olive-skinned complexion; but it had always been his energy she had loved. She said, 'My God. You should have jet lag. You should certainly be starving. And you can relish the prospect of an hour's slog uphill in the pouring rain!'

'Only when I'm doing it with you,' he said. And, holding hands, just as they had done fifteen years before, they began to struggle back up the terraces towards the distant farm.

The rain arrived in Birmingham before Pru and Maisie had left. It came with a giant clap of thunder that shook the terraced house so that the glass rattled in the window frames. As it died away the telephone rang. It was Mr Delano.

'Don't think of going yet, Maisie dear,' he said. 'Pru is not fit to drive anyway and driving conditions are going to be appalling later on.'

There was a click as Mr Edgar picked up the other phone. Maisie could imagine them sitting side by side at the massive desk in the luxurious office just up from the showroom. Mr Edgar said, 'We can manage to put up Pru. Tell her I will take the sofa and she can have my bed.'

When it had occurred to Maisie to go to the little house in Coventry Street just over a week ago, she had never doubted that the Markhams would take her in. The bonus had been that their 'daily' had a dreadful summer cold and was off sick and, as they both said, it seemed 'meant' that Maisie should be looking for a job for a few days just at that precise moment. She, remembering that first dreadful weekend in Birmingham with hardly any money and nowhere to go, agreed with them wholeheartedly. It was almost as if she had been guided to them; she had looked through the shop window, decided they weren't there and automatically walked towards Rachel's old house in Coventry Street. She had felt, quite suddenly, full of confidence. She felt it now.

'Don't worry about us please, Edgar. We're going back to one-four-eight. I need some clothes and I want to check that the house is all right. We'll probably stay the night there.'

'Will you be able to face that, Maisie?' They were both anxious. She could hear Mr Delano twittering in the background.

'Of course.' She looked over at Pru and smiled. 'It's been my home for ages. I'd like Pru to see it before . . . it goes. I've left a casserole in the fridge here – you can pop it in the oven when you come in, can't you? And there's French bread and plenty of cheese. And I think your Mabel will be back on Monday, don't you?'

They reassured her and warned her they would be phoning number one-four-eight frequently throughout the evening. And then she reassured Pru who was also doubtful about going back.

'No-one's there, Maisie,' she said. 'You realize – I told you, didn't I – that the children are all at Prospect House?'

'Darling, I've spoken to them. When you were still asleep. Jess says they're having a wonderful time. Tom is coming to terms with . . . things.'

'Hilary is making sure of that. And Rachel is wonderful with your Jess. They're sharing a room. I think I had better go in with Rachel and let you and Jess have my room.'

'Well actually, Pru . . .' Maisie led the way downstairs. 'I rather think – in the circs – it might be best if they came back home. We can arrange another reunion later, can't we? It will be such a crowd of us at your place. And we need to be home once Ted is in hospital. We shall want to visit him.'

'Will you?' Pru said, surprised.

Maisie was just as surprised. 'Well of course, my dear. We're a family.' She saw Pru's expression and said, 'That doesn't mean we're exclusive, Pru! But . . . you must understand! Ted is still the father of four of my children!' Still Pru said nothing and Maisie, opening the door and seeing the taxi arriving, said quickly, 'We'll talk about it later. Perhaps . . . just for a few days . . . if the weather improves . . . we could all muck in somehow at your place.'

The rain was hitting down 'like stair rods' as the taxi driver put it when he loaded Maisie's case and bundled them inside. Enclosed in the big square car they were immediately cut off by the force of the rain on the windows and roof; Pru drew Maisie's inadequate cardigan around her shoulders. They had run for the taxi beneath an umbrella but even so everything smelled damp. Traffic and people wavered outside the windows; the shops were closing and it was a long slow drive out of the city. Pru, cold and still disorientated, could hardly believe that she had set out to find Maisie only this morning; and here she was with her, cut off from the rest of the world and going to Maisie's house. Her grazes stung as the rain found its way through the sleeves of her cardigan. She thought with sudden anguish of the kitchen at Prospect House; the children quarrelling and Evelyn calming them down; the warmth from the cooker; Nash and Rachel cutting sandwiches like dervishes. For a few days they had all been her family.

They negotiated a roundabout and Maisie leaned forward

and said, 'Just up here on the left. Can you see the trees?' She turned to Pru and pointed. 'That's where Dr James lives. He's been so kind to me. There was a time when I thought I might die . . . he was so reassuring.'

'Yes. I have spoken to him. On the phone. And Rachel and Nash . . . they've met him.'

'Have they? Oh of course . . . Ted. From what you say, Mark and Jess have taken a lot on their shoulders.'

'Mark especially.'

The taxi swept into the drive of one-four-eight and up to the front door. Maisie opened her door and prepared to dive beneath the porch. She said suddenly, 'I knew I should come back. I touched the gateposts when I left.'

Pru paid the driver and took the case and umbrella from him. Maisie fitted her key into the lock and then turned and waved him goodbye. The rain beat mercilessly at them, slanting beneath the porch roof as if searching them out. Pru said, 'Hurry up, Maisie. We shall get soaked.'

Maisie said, 'I can't open the door. They key is turning all right. The door won't open.'

Pru took over. She said slowly, 'I think it's bolted from inside.' She raised her voice against the beating rain. 'That means someone is indoors, Maisie. Could it be Ted?'

Maisie looked round for the taxi. It had gone, apparently swallowed up in rain. Pru said, 'I think we'd better go. Perhaps we can phone from Dr James's house?'

Maisie had actually started to put up the umbrella when she changed her mind. 'No!' She pushed past Pru. 'This is my house, Pru! If someone's in there, I want to know who it is!' And without waiting for a response, she rang the bell long and hard.

Nothing happened. Pru said, 'It could be squatters. They won't open the door to us.'

'Squatters are supposed to go for empty property – it's obvious to anyone that this house is fully occupied.' Maisie rang the bell again furiously.

And then they heard the bolts being withdrawn. A top one, then a bottom. The chain was put on and the door was opened to its length. Hilary's face was framed in the gap. Maisie squeaked, 'Who the hell are you?' and Pru said, 'Hillie! What are you doing here?'

Hilary spoke in a high voice, 'I'm sorry. We're not religious here.' Her face worked furiously.

Maisie simply stared. Pru whispered, 'What? What is it? Why can't we come in?'

Hilary said in her falsetto, 'Certainly not! We're simply not interested!' Her eyes rolled to the top of her head and then leapt sideways. It was a hideous sight.

Pru breathed, 'Is Maisie's husband with you?'

'I'm afraid so,' Hilary sang. Her eyes went up and out.

'In the dining room?'

'Certainly!' Hilary snapped.

'Has he got Tom? As a sort of hostage?'

'Absolutely. Yes!'

Maisie said, 'Oh God.' Then, 'I'm Maisie. Tom's mother. I want you to take the chain off as quietly as you can and leave the door ajar. Go back to Tom. Try to separate him from Ted. Toilet. Anything. We'll give you two minutes.'

Hilary's eyes seemed to bc popping out but she nodded and began to close the door saying, 'You'll have to go, I'm sorry.' She slammed the door loudly, then after a second opened it again very quietly.

Maisie put her ear to the crack. Pru said, 'What shall we do? Shall I go for the police?'

'When we get inside you can phone.' Maisie glanced upwards. 'I had to see him some time, Pru. Best to get it over and done with now.'

The rain still poured. Somewhere it was overflowing a gutter and dripping insistently onto the gravel. Pru, thoroughly damp now, shivered uncontrollably. If only Rachel were here; she could cope with this.

Maisie glanced up again, 'I think she's done it. I'm going in. Use the phone in the hall.'

She slid through the door and Pru followed. The large square hall was before them, lined with doors, the staircase angling out of it at one side. Tom was making for the back door where the downstairs lavatory was. Ted Davenport, dishevelled, the sleeve of his suit jacket torn almost out of its seam, was close behind.

Tom glanced over his shoulder at the sudden draught and increase in rain noise; he gasped involuntarily. Ted followed his gaze and roared like a bull. Maisie advanced quickly.

'All right, Tom. Off you go to the loo. See you in a minute.' She turned left into the dining room. Hilary stood by the window, trying to see through the rain-washed panes. She turned and gripped at her throat like an old-fashioned heroine as Maisie strode purposefully into the room.

'Come in here, Ted,' Maisie called over her shoulder. 'It's the lightest room in the house and we can talk better.' She went to the gas fire and stooped to light it. Ted entered with a rush and then pulled up as she said very normally, 'Whatever is this young lady doing here, Ted? And Tom too. Have you kidnapped them or something?'

He stood two yards from her, clutching the mantelpiece. He was dribbling.

'Little bugger hid in the car.' He had not responded to anyone coherently since last Sunday. He sounded surprised by his own words. 'Trying to get Tom away from me. He's my son, Maisie. I've brought him up, you can't deny that. I had to bring them here.'

Maisie smiled. 'They said you were mad. You're not mad, Ted. You were very sensible to bring them here. It's your home. It's Tom's home.'

He roared again and quite suddenly swung his arm and cuffed Maisie's head. Pru, invisible until then, screamed, Hilary shouted. They both started forward.

Maisie said, 'Don't be silly, girls. I'm all right. I swing with the punches. Don't I, Ted? You like to think you're going to kill me. But there's only been once, or twice, when you've done any real damage. So you don't have any real intention of killing me. I know it and you know it. And if I roll with the punches, I'm usually all right.' She smiled and went towards him. Pru and Hilary looked wildly at each other. Maisie said, 'Hilary dear, will you go into the hall and – and look after your . . . friend.' Hilary hesitated and Maisie said forcefully, 'If you have half the sense of your mother you will know exactly what I mean.' Hilary looked from Maisie to Pru. She had heard a great deal about Maisie in the last few days; none of it tied in with this forceful woman. Pru was similarly amazed, but she nodded at Hilary who obediently went outside.

'That's better.' Maisie smiled at Ted but was obviously talking to Pru. 'Clearly the mention of a name set that one off. Otherwise, you're fine. Aren't you, Ted?' She was close to him now but she did not touch him. 'Shall we sit down, my dear? The sofa is just behind you. And you must be terribly tired. I don't expect you've had much sleep, have you?' He must have felt the edge of the sofa at the back of his knees and he sat down abruptly. She perched sideways on the other end. 'I've been working for Mr Delano and Mr Edgar, Ted. Before I went on holiday with the girls. Just to get some pocket money. Do you remember when you came to Markhams first to measure for the new display cabinets? Do you remember I brought you a cup of tea and a doughnut and we sat on the cellar steps and talked? You said it was like going to a birthday party and no-one had ever invited you to a party. Edith came and asked if you'd like more tea and you said no, you wanted a paper hat. And she found one from somewhere and brought it. She was always one for a joke, was Edith.'

Pru felt tears gathering in her throat. She watched as Ted relaxed slightly against the cushions on the garish sofa. He did not take his eyes from Maisie.

She said, 'You thought of me like that, didn't you, Ted? The little girl at the party who was looking after you. And when I told you about Chamberlain Street and you told me about your father and how you hid under the floorboards . . . it was a bond. I wanted to make it up to you for that time. And you – you told me you didn't mind that I'd done . . . what I'd done. You forgave me. You looked after me, Ted. When I knew I was pregnant I thought you'd throw me over. But you forgave me that too. And you married me. You were good to me, Ted. I did everything wrong and you always forgave me.' Almost imperceptibly, he nodded. She smiled. Her face was like a girl's again, pretty, insouciant. Her week with the Markhams had done her good; her curls, dampened by the rain, hugged her head like a 1960s hat. Her eyes were huge and densely blue. He could not look away from her.

'We must try to forget everything else, Ted. We've had some good times . . .' Suddenly her perspective changed, her eyes narrowed, she was talking to herself now. 'I must remember the good times, Ted. When Jess and Mark were still tiny, you used to drive me up to Malvern so that I could have a few hours walking with the girls. You would look after them for me. And we've had lovely days at Luddington, haven't we? First with Mark and then with . . . the younger one.' She smiled again but tremulously. 'We're so proud of them, aren't we? Mark and Jess . . . imagine them both being vets! Such a hard job for a lovely girl like Jess. You were right about boarding school . . . it's made them independent and strong. Like you really. They're not like me, are they?'

There was a sound above the constant drumming of the rain. Pru glanced through the window. Three figures huddled beneath a huge black umbrella. She recognized Tom and Hilary. The third one was a man, a stranger.

Maisie said calmly, 'Here is Dr James, Ted. Do you remember how kind he was when I had to have my sterilization? Was that when you really . . . turned away from me?' She took a deep breath and Pru could hear it catch in her throat. 'We must not remember that, Ted. If we died for each other then, well . . . so be it. The times before were good. They were good, Ted. We must remember that.' There was that faint movement of his head again. He had relaxed into the sofa entirely now. She nodded too. 'Go to sleep, Ted. You are very tired.'

Dr James came into the room alone. Pru could see the hypodermic held to one side. He came close to Ted; but there was no need for any urgency. The dark, heavy face was sagging into sleep already. As the doctor rolled up the sleeve of his shirt, Ted reached out with his free hand. Maisie looked at it, extended towards her. For a moment Pru thought she would ignore it. And then, she took it between both of hers and held it while the drug did its work and he slept.

Dr James said in a low voice, 'Well done, Maisie. We didn't want a lot of fuss for the sake of the children. I've left them in the hall.' He glanced at Pru. 'You are

Maisie's friend? Could you stay here while I telephone for an ambulance?'

Pru nodded dumbly. He went into the hall and Hilary and Tom appeared. Tom went to his mother and they held each other. Pru put an arm around Hilary and led her to the window.

'Well done, Hillie. I don't know what has happened – you will doubtless enjoy telling us very much indeed. But for now, shall we find the kitchen and make some tea? And then you can phone your mother and put her mind at rest.'

Hilary was suddenly aghast. 'Oh my God! Pru! I'd forgotten but Tom and I – we sort of set up an assignation for Nash and Harvey! In the combe about a mile downhill from the farm! And we were supposed to go back to the house and get Ma to walk that way! Poor Harvey is probably still in the combe soaked to the skin!' Her face was totally woebegone. 'Oh, Pru – it was such a good plan! And now it's gone all wrong and they'll never forgive me!'

And for the first time since she left Prospect House, Pru started to laugh.

When Harvey and Natasha reached the house they were indeed soaked to the skin. They were also very hot. Harvey was lugging a large zip-bag which made him hotter still. They stood in the garage, exhilarated and tingling with sheer exuberance. Evelyn, investigating the shouts of laughter, stood aghast at the sight of them.

Natasha spluttered, 'Oh, Evie – don't look like that! It's Harvey! My husband wot-was!' She glanced at him. 'And what is going to be again, I do believe!' She went towards Evelyn with open arms, only to be fended off.

'Nash! You are dripping – don't touch me! And where did he *come* from? My God, you've been cooking this up and haven't breathed a word and we've all been so worried – you really are the giddy limit, Nash! No, I'm serious, just stop that giggling and pay attention!'

Harvey, still handsome with his wiry curls already springing back to life, came forward. 'It's my fault, Miss . . . er . . .' 'Call her Evie,' Natasha advised. 'Yes. OK. Evie. Hillie rang me and I went along with this crazy plan to surprise Nash out of her socks – and it worked—' 'Not only my socks,' muttered Nash, dissolving again.

Evelyn said sternly, 'Natasha, that is not funny. I'm sorry, Mr . . .' 'Call him Harvey,' Natasha advised, quite unable to collect herself. 'Well, all right. Harvey. I really don't understand what is happening but obviously if Nash is pleased to see you, then so will everybody else be. And when Hillie turns up she will be absolutely delighted. Well, naturally, as it appears to be her plan that has brought you here.' She looked around. 'Hillie and Tom not with you then? I suppose they're frightened to face me. And Rachel.'

Natasha sobered suddenly. 'They're not here?' She looked at Harvey. 'Honey, did you hear that? They're not here.'

'Sure I heard it.' Harvey frowned. 'Look, can we get inside? I've got dry clothes in this bag. And you should change too, baby. We should try to get sorted out. Maybe the other kids you were telling me about . . . maybe they'll know something.'

But Natasha's mood had inverted completely. 'They've got lost. Fallen in a river somewhere. All these little hill streams will be bursting their banks . . . it's like a mudslide around by the bluff. Oh, Evie, Hillie is so impetuous – well, you know—' she indicated Harvey. 'She probably decided to explore some more and—'

'She's not on her own, Nash. And Tom is a very sensible lad.'

Harvey said, 'Now look, Nash, you're going over the top again. And we can't do a thing here. Let's go inside, for Pete's sake.'

Evie turned and led the way across the yard. The rain was driving in almost horizontally. They got inside the kitchen which was blessedly empty. 'Typical English weather,' Natasha gasped.

And Evie reminded her ironically, 'Straight from America, isn't it, Nash?'

Harvey laughed appreciatively and at the unmistakably male sound Rachel put a startled head round the door. She said, 'I wondered where you'd got to – God you're wet – serves you right! Harvey?' She shook hands and then grinned suddenly. 'This is what Hillie has been up to, isn't it? That long phone call, Evie. When the others were shopping in Malvern. D'you remember?' Rachel laughed. 'She's a great person in spite of having you two for parents!'

Natasha did not join in the general bonhomie. 'Ray, we can't find her. She's gone. I simply know something awful has happened. I just know it!'

And then the phone rang. Natasha snatched at it. Pru spoke clearly and slowly. 'Nash, my dear. We're all safe. Hillie and Tom and Maisie and me. We're at Maisie's house waiting for the ambulance to come and take poor Ted Davenport to hospital. Can you hear me, Nash? What's that noise?'

'It's me gibbering.' Natasha was crying openly. 'I don't know what has happened, but oh, Pru, thank God you're all safe. And Maisie too. Oh my dear . . . oh Pru . . . Harvey is here . . . Hillie arranged it all behind my back. I think he and me, I think—'

Pru said, 'She told us. She was worried Harvey might still be down in the combe waiting for someone to rescue him!'

'Oh God. I just can't believe it. Why is she at Maisie's house? What happened?'

'We don't know ourselves yet. Maisie and I came here to get clothes and things. And the three of them were already in residence. Ted, Hillie and Tom. I think he had some crazy idea of holding them hostage or something. Anyway, Maisie dealt with it.'

'Maisie? Maisie dealt with it? With Ted?'

'She had him calmed down in ten minutes, Nash. She was in complete control of the situation the whole time.' Pru's small laugh was rueful. 'We don't know Maisie. I don't think we've ever known her. I stood here wishing to goodness Rachel was with us. And Maisie just took over.' She filled in what details she could then asked if Nash would like to speak to Hillie. Nash, waiting for her daughter to come on the line, lifted her chin away from the receiver and reported to the others.

Harvey said, 'You didn't tell me she could be in danger from some maniac, Nash! What the hell's been going on up here? Are you girls on the run from this man? Was that the real idea behind your reunion? Christ if I'd realized you were taking my daughter away—'

Nash said, '*Me* take *her* away? God, Harvey, she ran away! And from you! Didn't you even miss your bloody credit card?' A voice said in her ear, 'Oh, Ma! Not already? I can't leave you a minute before you start rowing, can I?' And Nash subsided and smiled tremulously.

'Honey, I'm sorry. Harvey thinks I've led you into imminent danger here.'

'Ma, I am OK. Got that? I wouldn't have missed a minute of what has happened since I came back last week. Listen, I'll tell you everything when we get back. Just tell me that you and Dad . . . are you? Is it going to be OK?'

Natasha took a shaky breath and looked at Harvey. 'She wants to know if it's going to be OK. It is, isn't it?'

And Harvey relaxed and smiled unwillingly. 'Tell her yes. I guess so. Though why I want anything to do with a couple of crazy females like you—'

Hillie said, 'Let me speak to him, Ma.' And then, 'Hello, Horrible Harve. So she found you, did she? I just hope you had had time to get cold and hungry and really worried.' And then she put down the phone.

It was much later, after a white- faced Jess and Mark paused in their constant questioning, that they came to some conclusion about what they would do. The rain still hammered relentlessly on the shallow-pitched roof of Prospect House and Rachel reported a leak on the landing and placed a strategic bucket.

They sat around the kitchen table; occasionally one of the Davenport children would go into the hall and telephone their mother as if to reassure themselves that she was there, back home, and was coping.

'She sounds so . . . ordinary,' Simon said almost complainingly. 'As if nothing special had happened.'

Jess tried to make some sense of it. 'She knows that a great deal has happened, Si,' she said. 'But she has dealt with it. Dad's had . . . well, like an accident. And she's looked after him and got him into hospital. And now she wants us to know it's settled.'

Harvey said, 'She sounds like some kind of woman! I guess I'm beginning to understand why this reunion was so important to all of you. But, well, it can't go on, can it?' He was holding Natasha's hand and he moved it up and down as if to emphasize his point. 'It's just not big enough. And the cooking arrangements . . . fine when the weather holds. We've had some great times in these hills. But now' he looked at Mark, 'your mother won't want to be too far from that hospital I guess. And you must have things to do.'

It was Ian who said brightly, 'Why don't we all go to one-four-eight? There are loads of bedrooms, especially now Mrs Donald has left. And we could take you to the cricket ground, Uncle Harvey. And Jess could invite her boyfriend.' Jess flashed a furious look at Mark, and Ian said quickly, 'Tom told us.' He looked around. 'It would be great. We'd miss the pool here, of course. It's been such fun – it's a pity Uncle Harvey can't have a go on the rope. But we could go to the baths. And things.'

There was a little silence. Harvey raised his brows at Natasha, who shrugged. 'I'd like to have a few more days with the girls, of course. But I don't mind where it is. Not now.' She squeezed Harvey's fingers.

Rachel said, 'I feel the same.' She shrugged. 'It doesn't look as if Duncan will miss me, does it?'

Jess said stoutly, 'Well, we should miss you a lot, Aunt Rachel.' She turned to Evelyn. 'What about you, Aunt Evie? Will you come with us?'

'We're a family of sorts now.' Evelyn ran her fingers through her hair; it had long since given up the ghost on its permanent wave and clouded her small head like an Afro cut. 'We should stick together for a while, I think.'

Natasha's eyes filled with sentimental tears. 'Oh Evie . . .' she said.

'Now, now, honey. Come on,' said Harvey.

Rachel rolled her eyes at Jess who rolled hers back. Mark

said with unexpected humour, 'Can we take two lots of cow-eyed lovers? These two and Jess and Steve?'

Jess threw a cushion at him. The little party broke up then, the boys camping out in the sitting room, the others going upstairs.

Harvey was stupidly pleased to find his dressing-gown behind the door; Nash was suddenly delighted that Hillie was in Birmingham. 'Isn't this the biggest stroke of luck?' she murmured into his ear. 'And a single bed too. We haven't slept in a single bed together for yonks.'

'Yonks?' Harvey was starting to kiss her again and she had to gasp out her reply.

'Ages.'

Rachel and Jess undressed with their backs to each other. The rain rattled the ill-fitting window and a monotonous drip fell into the bucket on the landing.

Jess said, 'After what Hillie has done, I wonder if I ought to try and do something for you, Ray. I honestly think you should try to make your marriage work. If I invited Duncan to one-four-eight . . . we could have a big homecoming get-together or something and—'

'Jess. Stop.' Rachel wriggled out of her jeans and looked down at her legs. They were thick. There was no getting away from the fact that she was no-one's idea of beauty. 'Don't worry about it, please. I'm letting it all mull. Thursday was a shock, I grant you that. It helped to talk about it. But I'm certainly not going to do anything irrevocable.'

'Good.' Jess struggled into her serviceable pyjamas and leapt into the other bed. 'The good thing about all this is that you and me . . . we're friends. I hope. Aren't we?'

Rachel felt herself flush with sheer pleasure. 'Oh I hope so, too. I'll write to you in Edinburgh. Will you find the time and energy to write back?'

'Of course.'

'I'd like some advice about how to deal with my step-daughters. I think it's about time I took an interest in them as well as their father.'

'That would be nice.' Jess sighed deeply. 'Isn't it surprising how we go on living when there's a mess? I mean we go on eating and sleeping and getting meals and clearing them away . . .'

'Yes.' Rachel thought of how it must have been for her stepdaughters, Rebecca and Jan, five years ago. She said again, heavily, 'Yes.'

Evie finished creaming her face and neck and went onto the landing to spread an old towel over the top of the bucket to absorb the sound of the rain. She crept downstairs to check on the boys. Then she tapped on Rachel's door and asked if they were all right.

'Fine.' Rachel grinned over the top of her sheet. 'I wouldn't bother asking Harvey and Natasha if they are comfortable, Evie!'

Jess giggled and Evelyn said with dignity, 'I had no such intention, Ray dear. And I don't think you should make those kind of remarks in front of Jess.'

Jess giggled more, then said quite seriously, 'I've grown up a lot since all this business with Dad, you know, Evie.'

'Yes,' Evie sighed.

'And it's good. It's really good!' Jess said stoutly.

It was two o'clock the next morning when Mark came upstairs and raised the alarm. The boys came after him trailing sleeping bags and books and cushions and anything else they could carry.

'It's the swimming pool,' Mark announced. 'I went for a drink of water and it's coming under the kitchen door – the water, I mean. So I looked out. Nash's dam wall is a bit too good. The pool is pouring over the bank this side and will soon be running through the house! There's nothing we can do.'

They gathered on the stairs, peering over the banisters. At two-thirty, Mark paddled across the hall, opened the front door then went back and opened the kitchen door. By the time he came back he was up to his knees in rushing water. They stood, huddled together above this new indoor river; it was an awesome sight. The straw mats from the kitchen floor bobbed past, followed by shoes and a half-open umbrella.

Suddenly Natasha began to laugh and once started she couldn't stop.

'Honey, stop it! This is no time for hysteria—'

'Darling, it is! Don't you see? The great baptism for our reunion! It's washing away all our sins – don't you feel that? We've found Maisie and she is all right and she is strong and can deal with whatever happens next! And I've found you and you've found me! And Pru will be all right after Meg. And, and—'

Rachel said drily, 'And Evie and I will certainly survive.'

'The thing is . . .' Evie pulled her dressing-gown cord very tight. 'The real thing is . . . we know we haven't lost anybody. Especially Edie.'

The boys watched as their sister and the three women hugged each other delightedly. Harvey clasped them in his big arms. 'Who the hell is Edie?' he asked.

Mark said gloomily, 'She's a dead person, Harvey. A dead person.'

Harvey waited for something else. Ian and Simon started to laugh and even Mark half grinned.

Harvey said, 'Ah. Well then. That's OK, I guess.'

And everyone laughed.

Twenty

Some time when it was still dark, the rain ended; there was a lull, a few splutters and it was gone. By that time the people at Prospect House had rearranged the sleeping arrangements. Evie was sharing Rachel's bed, shrinking herself against the wall and eventually falling asleep with her head on Rachel's shoulder. Mark, Ian and Simon used Evie's room, and Mark, flinging himself on her bed, slept better than he had done since the return from Bristol. Natasha and Harvey continued their ecstatic and very private reunion. And Jess and Rachel, whispering together after Evie had gone to sleep, eventually drifted off when the rain ceased.

The sound of Bryn's tractor woke them about eight-thirty. Natasha, ebullient to bursting point, leapt out of bed, flung up the window and surveyed the steaming and brilliant view.

'My God! The pool's gone! Absolutely gone! No sign of my dam at all. I wanted you to see it, darling. It was an engineering miracle, almost.'

Harvey joined her and looked at the line of pebbles which disappeared through the kitchen door. 'Looks as if it was also the direct cause of our personal flood,' he commented. 'I know we were all laughing about it earlier this morning, honey, but why was it such a great thing?'

'Like I said, it washed away a lot of . . . muck.' Natasha spoke soberly. She turned in Harvey's arms. 'It was a symbol for our clean start, darling. You and me. Maisie . . . an entirely new life for Maisie. Maybe some solution for Rachel – I don't know. And, who knows, perhaps something for Pru as well. And Evie.' She giggled. 'Evie has a beau. He's a real character. Keeps plastic ducks.'

'Is he all there?' asked Harvey doubtfully.

'Very much so. He'll look after Evie. If she'll let him.'

Harvey kissed her cloud of dark hair. 'You smell nice. I'd forgotten how good you smelled. And you're caring about these people—'

'Instead of myself? Is that what you mean?'

'Now don't get miffy—'

'Darling, I'm not getting miffy. I agree with you. Entirely. It's been good for me, all this.' She looked up at him. 'Have I asked you to promise me you won't get involved with other women? I – I'm sort of accepting that there are no solutions. Only – only serious endeavours!'

Harvey laughed. 'Oh baby, baby. You are wonderful. D'you know that?'

'Of course I know that.' Unwittingly she used Hilary's words. 'And I know something else. You're in love with me. And whatever happens, I think you always will be.'

He held her close. 'I think you're right,' he said.

They kissed and then looked down. Bryn's tractor had chugged around to the back door and he was standing on the footplate, cap pushed back, scratching his head at the sight of the mess. Natasha leaned out of the window.

'Bryn! Hi! Don't worry – we'll all set to and clean up! And it's a wonderful morning!'

The others began to appear, looking through windows and crowding down the stairs. Mark had worn wellingtons the night before and he put them on now to wade through the mud to the kitchen. 'It didn't get as far as the fridge,' he yelled back. 'Food is intact!'

Bryn met him. 'You'm all right, all of you? We had no idea this had happened. I brought the tractor round because of the state of the fields around the bluff. When I saw the mud course and realized it had gone right through the house, I was worrit to death! How about the little 'un – the old lady?'

The 'old lady' appeared on the stairs in her dressing-gown. 'She's all right, thank you,' she said frigidly. 'And if you'll pass me those wellingtons, I'll come and begin to get us some breakfast.'

They congregated in the dining room which had luckily escaped most of the water. Rachel, Natasha and Evelyn between them made toast and passed it through. Ian and Simon thought it was all great fun; suddenly they were released from the necessity of being serious; they grabbed each other's toast and shouted and purposely slithered into the hall on the mud and generally behaved very badly. Jess made one or two half-hearted attempts to control them, then joined Mark with a broom. Harvey fixed up the hose they had so recently used as a shower and sluiced down the hall. The boys dodged in and out of the spray. Eventually Harvey turned it on them full force to calm them down.

It was surprising how quickly they cleared up. The water was not dirty; they pulled up the old hall runner and threw it outside. The boards scrubbed almost white and smelled sweetly of elm. Bryn chugged back and forth bringing newspapers to mop up the wet, and fresh milk, some pasties made by Mrs Bryn, some beer for Harvey and Mark. He took the boys with him so that they could help put some sheep through a dip. 'They're wet enough to go through themselves! Bit more damp won't hurt them,' he said.

By mid-afternoon the house was its basic respectable self again. 'Good enough to lock up and leave?' Natasha asked Evelyn.

'Certainly.' Evelyn poured tea. 'The only thing is, shall we get the cars out of here?'

Harvey said, 'It's drying fast. And Bryn will give us a tow if necessary. Nash and me'll walk down to the farm and order a cab. OK, honey?'

'Whatever.' Nash took her tea. 'Oh . . . lovely. Lovely, lovely English tea.' She looked around. 'Girls, I think Hillie and Harvey and I might be going back to the States quite soon. I just want to say to you . . . thanks.'

Evelyn leaned forward and took her free hand. Natasha put down her teacup and reached for Rachel. And it was Rachel who scooped Jess into the ring. Harvey and Mark stood outside it, grinnning indulgently. And Harvey said, 'Listen, old man – ' he made the term ironical '- it could be that in twenty years' time you will be back here. Meeting up with my daughter and this Tom of hers and your Jess. What d'you think?'

Mark said, 'Not me.'

Jess looked over, her eyes very bright. 'You'll be here, or else!' she said.

That night Hilary took the floor. They were in the living room of one-four-eight, their stuff strewn over chairs and coffee tables. They had made the house their own. Hilary stood on one of the sofas and sat herself on its back. She surveyed everyone, beaming.

'It's been better than Swiss Family Robinson – or anything! I mean, Mr D. was batty – he could have done anything!' She looked at Tom defiantly. 'That was why I came along! Nothing to do with not wanting to be left out as you so nastily put it—'

'You would have been more sensible to whip back to the farm and phone for the police,' he said, but smiling at her, already knowing that they would probably spend the rest of their lives together.

'I couldn't leave you – it would have been desertion in the face of the enemy—'

Tom said, 'Get on with it. And remember you are talking about the man I thought was my father.'

'Sorry. Sorry, Ian. Simon. Mark. Jess.' She flapped her hands. 'But you know what I mean. You of all people—'

Mark said flatly, 'You could not leave Tom in the hands of my father. I don't like that – I hate it. But I, we all, have to accept it.' The others gave subdued nods. Hilary blushed.

'Well, yeah. I guess that's how it is.' She gathered herself and went on, 'Anyway, we'd met Harve at the top of the lane and told him the plan and taken him down to the combe. And we came back to try to get Nash to go down to the combe—'

'How were you going to do that?' Natasha asked curiously.

'Tom was going to say I was sulking and wouldn't come back home. Some nonsense or other.' Hilary made an airy gesture. 'Any more interruptions? No? Well . . . we were only halfway back to the farm when Mr D. popped out from behind one of those huge boulder things and grabbed Tom.' Hilary forgot to be theatrical and suddenly shivered. 'It was horrible! Really horrible! I thought he was going to kill him there and then. I shouted and screamed—'

'She ran at him with a rock and tried to hit him,' Tom put in, 'And she caught me across the shin—'

'I didn't mean to! I told you in the car how sorry I was.'

Tom said soberly, 'It made Dad worse actually. He started to drag me up the terraces left of the farm. He'd got his car on a track which led straight to the road junction. He kept saying that those women were not fit to look after his children.' He frowned. 'He reckoned he'd seen someone in a nightdress. And then not in a nightdress . . . in the buff I suppose.' Rachel hoped no-one was looking at her.

Hilary said, 'We gradually got the message that he'd been watching the house for some time. He must have slept at least one night in the car. He looked . . . awful.'

'You just tagged along, did you, honey? Minding your own business as usual?' Harvey was only half joking. The realization of the danger his daughter had been in was hitting him hard.

'Not quite like that, Harve. I was arguing with him. Talking to him, the whole time. I expected him to hit Tom.' She looked at Maisie. 'He didn't. Not once.'

Maisie said, 'Thank you for telling me that.'

'He got to the car and flung Tom into the passenger seat. Tom was fighting like a maniac. It was so easy for me to get in the back. I got most of my body under Tom's seat. I honestly think Mr D. forgot I'd been there. He had some sellotape and he stuck Tom to the seat – no, don't laugh, that's what he did. Didn't he, Tom?' Tom nodded. Hilary swept on. 'Then he just got in the car and drove.' She rolled her eyes. 'God, it was awful. I was sort of tangled up with the bar that slides the seat back and forth. Ever time we went over a bump, the weight of Tom's body came down on my legs – I thought they'd be broken in fifty places.' Tom snorted and Jess said, 'Did he say anything? What was he going to do?'

'He said that once Mum knew he'd got me, she'd come home.' Tom looked at his mother. 'And the amazing thing for Dad was that she did. I'm sure that's why you could talk him round, Mum. He was so . . . surprised. That at last one of his plans had succeeded.'

Maisie's eyes were full of tears. Pru said warningly, 'Maisie, stop it.'

Hilary was contrite. 'Do you want me to stop too?'

'No.' Maisie was emphatic. 'I want to hear everything. Every detail.'

Hilary nodded. 'The rain had started by then. It hammered down. His driving was terrible – but anyway we made it. He put the car in the garage and shut it down and got Tom out and through the door to the house. It took me ages to get out from under the seat. I wasn't quite so worried about Tom by then, because if he needed him as a kind of hostage he wasn't going to hurt him. Even so I *was* worried. I thought I'd sneak in and use the first phone I came to. But of course he was going round pulling them out and throwing them into a box. He saw me – he didn't seem a bit surprised – perhaps he'd known I was there all the time. Anyway he ignored me. Pushed Tom into the living room and ripped off the tape. Tom was really great. He just walked over to the sofa and sat down and asked me if I would sit down too.' She looked at him. 'What did you say?'

Tom shrugged. 'Dunno. Something about making ourselves comfortable for the evening.'

Hilary grinned. 'It was great anyway.' She sighed. 'But when you rang the bell, Pru, it wasn't so good. He nearly jumped a mile and then he rushed behind the sofa and got Tom's throat. I tried to bite his fingers and he pushed me off—' she winced slightly as she got to this part. Maisie sucked in her breath; she could imagine how Ted had pushed Hilary away.

'Anyway, he said to me to get up straightaway and answer the door and get rid of whoever it was.' She glanced at Maisie. 'So you see he wasn't really expecting you. Not then.' Maisie said nothing and after a short pause Hilary went on. 'Well, you took over then. I mean . . . you took over. You were in control. We all thought he was. But it was you.' Still Maisie said nothing and Hilary said, 'What I don't get is . . . how did Dr James know we were there? I mean, there were no phones.'

Pru said, 'He didn't think it was worth taking out the one in the living room. He might have needed it anyway. I dialled the James's number and left the phone on the table. He must have heard Ted roar and go for Maisie.'

Harvey said, 'Oh God . . .'

Maisie said, as she had said the night before, 'He didn't hurt me. I rolled with the punch. No damage done.'

Hilary got off her perch and crossed the room to squeeze herself between her parents. The others began to talk, commiserating with Maisie, congratulating her. Hilary said in a low voice, 'I don't mind if you shout at each other. Just be together, will you?'

Natasha was right; they did not stay very long at Maisie's big house in Edgbaston. Maisie herself had to go to the factory and go through the books, see the foreman, talk to the ancient secretary. Leo Barkwith went with her and between them they transferred the management of the place into her hands. The workforce, all qualified carpenters and joiners, seemed pleased with the new arrangement. They knew Maisie simply as the boss's wife, but some of the older men remembered now that she had had a hard time of it with Ted Davenport. They made sure that the younger ones did not take advantage of her inexperience. And she drew on her small knowledge of bookkeeping, gleaned years ago from Edith, out of date now but a good basic foundation. Ted had kept a tight rein on his paperwork; Maisie said after only a few days, 'My God, we are very comfortably off, Mr Barkwith. Tom says he wants to stay on at Luddington . . . well, he certainly can.'

'Call me Leo, my dear. And perhaps your other two boys would like to go there? It would give you the time for this place. If you intend to run it yourself?'

'For a while, I would like to. Then I can report to Ted on visiting days.'

'Very . . . laudable.'

Maisie, sensing sarcasm, said quickly, 'He's my husband, Leo. And I did promise to stick by him in sickness and in health.'

Leo said mildly, 'I was under the impression that you had left him, Maisie.'

'I had. I considered he had broken all the vows in the book. His illness makes things . . . different.' She did not dwell on it. 'I think you may be right about Ian and Simon. Tom misses them. And they miss Tom. Yes, I think you are right. I'll see about getting them places at Luddington.'

Leo Barkwith looked at Maisie and saw what everyone else saw: the curls and blue eyes and round face. He had known Ted Davenport as a difficult man, but until Nash had confided in him, he had not realized how difficult. He wondered what had become of the dour and peculiar Mrs Donald. Two sides of Ted Davenport's particular coin, light and dark.

He braced himself and said, 'If there is any way I can help, please telephone. About anything.'

She looked back at him and for a moment he could see sadness in her eyes. Surely she wasn't hankering after her husband?

'Thank you, Leo. But as you probably know, there is nothing. Nash would be horrified if she knew how I felt.'

'Nash?' He was completely bewildered.

'Sorry. Nothing. One last thing. This order book. There's quite a list of jobs, but when they are done, what then?'

He pointed to the first firm listed. 'That's the biggest department store in the Midlands. They would keep you going for ever – stick with them. And others will come. Davenport Shopfitters have a good reputation. Did you know that Ted was considering having his own glassworks?'

'No. We never talked about work. Was it a good idea, d'you think?'

'Not really. I thought at the time it was a touch of the megalomanias.' He realized what he was saying and apologized profusely.

Maisie shook her head. 'Don't worry. Ted was always like that. You should see the furniture at one-four-eight. I thought I'd sell it and buy something that's already been used. Homely. You know.'

'I know.' He smiled and took his leave. As he said to

Natasha later, 'She'll be all right, your friend Maisie. Pretty tough underneath.'

On the strength of that, Natasha consulted Pru, Rachel and Evelyn.

'Maisie would probably be happier if we weren't around. And I think Harvey is itching to get back home.'

Rachel said lightly, 'So it's what you want to do, is it? You've had enough of the reunion so let it be over.'

Evelyn tried to mediate. 'Steady on, Ray. Nash is probably right about Maisie. She has to get on with this new life and we're almost an interruption.'

Rachel said bitterly, 'I agree, but it's just the perfect excuse for Mrs Nolan. She wants to get back to her life of luxury where she doesn't have to wash up and cook and do . . . any bloody thing!'

The other three looked at her in surprise. Natasha said, 'Ray, it's not like that, honestly! I have to admit I wouldn't mind breaking the party up quite soon. For Hillie's sake.'

'Hillie?' Rachel stared. 'My God, Hillie doesn't want to go back to the States. Not while Tom Davenport is in this country!'

'That's it. Exactly. And Hillie is so damned persuasive – I mean I trust Tom completely and in many ways he's still a kid. But Hillie . . . I'm never sure about Hillie.'

Pru smiled. 'No-one will ever be sure about Hillie. That's why Tom loves her.' She nodded at Natasha. 'You're right. You should go. For Hillie's sake.' She paused then added, 'And for Maisie's as well.'

Evelyn said, 'I must admit I wouldn't mind getting back to the bungalow. Houses need to be lived in, don't they?'

'Nothing to do with a certain gentleman who keeps ducks?' Natasha teased.

Rachel did not laugh with the others. Unexpectedly she felt . . . petulant. She said, 'All right for Nash then. And you too, it seems, Evie. And Pru will want to dash back to Telegraph House of course! That leaves me. No husband, no role, no nothing.'

Pru said impulsively, 'Come with me, Ray! Please. I don't particularly want to go back – but I have to. Things to do. Pots to throw. People to see. I'd love it if you would come and keep me company.'

Rachel looked taken aback. The other three were all looking at her. She could not forget the moment of total disorientation . . . disgust . . . that she had felt at the sight of Duncan's and Douglas's heads so close in her bed. And now Pru was suggesting she should spend time with a lesbian community. It was impossible to dissociate the two.

She said hesitantly, 'Pru . . . it's just that . . . I don't know whether I could . . . sort of . . . take it. I mean, I'm so totally heterosexual . . . I can be very broad-minded in theory. But I have discovered that when it comes to . . . to . . . anything else . . . I just can't seem to . . . take it.'

Pru laughed. 'Oh, Ray. Thanks for your honesty. I can imagine. And if you can't – well, you can't. But think about it, will you? I mean, you'd have your own room. You'd never see anything personal. We're quite private individuals.' She paused and added mischievously, 'And wouldn't it give Duncan a suitable shock if he heard where you were staying?'

Rachel opened her eyes wide. Everyone else laughed. And after a while, so did she.

'OK. I'll think about it. But first I have to go to Bristol. Business. Can you wait until I come back?'

'Of course.'

Maisie came in then and they told her what they had decided. She nodded.

'I've mucked up this reunion, girls. But next year . . . I promise.' She smiled at Pru. 'Why don't you keep Prospect House? Instal a few mod cons? You could let it – I bet between us we could find people only too glad of a couple of weeks total seclusion. Then the five of us could use it each year. What do you say?'

Pru said with unaccustomed emphasis, 'Done!'

Natasha said, 'Wow, I can build my dam again! And this time, I'll include a sort of plug. One of the stones I can remove when there's any sign of rain.'

Everyone groaned. Maisie said, 'I wish I'd seen your pool,

Nash. You really are amazing, aren't you? Everything you put your hand to, you jolly well succeed!'

'Not a bit of it,' Nash turned her mouth down. 'I've got the divorce papers to prove it.' She brightened. 'But I've got a second chance, girls. And I'm going to succeed! And my God, I'm telling you, luxury apartment I might have, but this is going to be damned hard work!'

Maisie glanced at Pru. 'But worth it, yes?'

'Yes.' Nash spoke definitely.

Evie left the next day. In the morning she went with Maisie to visit Ted Davenport. Strangely his troubled mind had thrown up some memory and he had asked to see 'Edie'. When Maisie passed this on, Evie was adamant. 'He means me.'

'He definitely said Edie's name.' Maisie looked troubled. 'I don't think you should visit him, Evie. He can be . . . strange.'

'Even if he meant Edie, that will be all right. Edith is never far from me these days, so in a way . . .'

Maisie, who had been unwillingly impressed by Pru's experience, said, 'Well, all right. But if he reacts badly, you must go, Evie. Promise me.'

'Of course.' Evie shivered. 'I remember the last time I saw him . . .'

'Oh my God, I didn't realize – don't come, my dear!'

'That's why I have to come.' Evelyn shook her newly set hair. 'It's like getting back on a horse when you've been thrown.'

So they went to the day room at the mental hospital on the outskirts of town. Perhaps because of its inauspicious outside it was particularly relaxed and comfortable inside. The wards had been partitioned into single rooms; there were tea-making facilities in the day room and one of the patients was handing around tea and coffee as they arrived. Evelyn, nervous and fidgety, was particularly impressed with the flowers. Surely, if anyone were going to start throwing things around, there would not be so many magnificent arrangements? And the television – wouldn't that be smashed in? She glanced around and saw that everyone looked bored but quite normal.

Maisie said sadly, 'Padded cells are out, Evie. Drugs are in.'

Evie felt a rush of pure compassion. She took her coffee and said impulsively, 'The flowers are just beautiful.'

'I do them,' the woman patient said simply. 'I do them three or four times every day. I'm obsessional, you see. And the staff thought it was a good idea to find something useful for me to be obsessional about.'

Evelyn's cup rattled in its saucer but she said politely, 'What a good idea. Isn't that a good idea, Maisie?'

Maisie nodded. She had already seen Ted sitting by himself at the window. Gazing out. She shivered slightly. 'There's Ted,' she said brightly. 'Shall we go over, Evie? Or perhaps I'll go first and tell him you're here.' She smiled and Evie suddenly noticed that her front tooth was chipped. Had Ted done that? Evie too shivered. 'Finish your coffee and then come across. All right?'

'All right.' Evie sipped at her cup as if her life depended on it and wished she hadn't insisted on coming in the first place. Everyone looked so normal, but they weren't, and Ted Davenport was a violent man. A terrible man. And what was she going to say to him? She rehearsed several opening gambits then decided she would say nothing; he must make the first approach.

But when her turn came to approach his chair she went forward bravely and held out her hand. 'Hello, Mr Davenport. How are you feeling today?' It was a ridiculous thing to say somehow, but it seemed to be the right thing too.

He managed the semblance of a smile. 'Not too bad thank you, Miss Hazell. And how are you?'

It was as if they were at a party. Small talk. She nodded and smiled. 'Very well.'

'You enjoyed your holiday in Wales?'

She recalled that Mr Lavington had told him that she was going to her sister's in Wales. She was about to continue the fable and then, quite suddenly, decided against it.

'You know I didn't go to Wales, Mr Davenport. I was in Malvern with Pru Adair and Rachel Stayte and Natasha Nolan. We were waiting for Maisie to join us. You must remember because you watched us for a couple of days.'

Maisie said quickly, 'And you had a nice time, didn't you, Evie?' She looked at Ted. 'They enjoyed themselves a great deal, Ted. The weather was grand.'

But Ted was looking at Evie; and he was frowning darkly. Maisie said something else; something about the unique countryside. Neither of them heard. It was as if they had locked into each other's thoughts.

And then, when Maisie ran out of platitudinous nonsense, Ted said, 'I want to apologize. That was why I asked you to come. I want to apologize for – for anything I did. Which upset you.' He waited. Evelyn said nothing but her gaze did not waver from his. At last he looked away and back through the window. He said something.

Maisie leaned forward. 'What was that, dear?'

He said, 'I'm glad she's not frightened of me any more.'

Afterwards Maisie said, 'That was the first time he's faced up to what happened, Evie. I can't thank you enough. It was a risk you took but it worked.' She smiled. 'You're not usually one for taking risks, Evie Hazell. It was Edie who always did that.'

Evelyn lifted her shoulders. 'There you are. That was why he asked to see Edie.'

'Perhaps.' Maisie hugged the older woman. 'Are you sure you want to go back home now?'

'Yes please, Maisie.' Evelyn suddenly grinned. 'Nash was partly right. I would like to see the man who keeps ducks. He deserves to know what has been happening. You don't mind, do you?'

'I don't mind. He saw the worst of Ted after all.' Maisie sighed. 'You were right, Evie. I never loved Ted properly. But we've been together for so long. When you tell your duck man about him . . . be as kind as you can.'

'Oh, Maisie . . .'

* * *

Natasha lay in the double bed that had been Ted's and Maisie's, then just Ted's. She had her hands behind her head, her eyes half-closed; but she was not sleepy. She was watching Harvey as he dressed after his morning shower and she was wondering whether it was just sex that held her to him and him to her, or whether there was something else. She badly wanted there to be something else. She had enjoyed sex with many men: Tom McEvoy, Ron – who, thank God had turned out not to be Maisie's brother – and one unforgettable time with Lew Blum on the counter of Mabs's laboratory-like kitchen which had involved some sunflower-seed cooking oil. But sex was all it had been. There must be something else with Harvey, otherwise why had she been so damned glad to see him in the combe? And why should he come over for her if he hadn't felt the same?

He was struggling into jeans and she opened her eyes wider to admire his still-flat stomach and muscly thighs, then immediately closed them again because that was all to do with sex. Even so her treacherous mind retained a picture of him and assured her that he had just enough hair on his chest to be manly without looking like a werewolf. And his hands were good too; not long and slender and effete like Tom McEvoy's had been, nor stubby like Lew's, but certainly short-fingered, broad and . . . capable. Yes, if Harvey had been with them at Malvern doing the Swiss Family Robinson bit, he would probably have made a campfire and had cook-outs with the boys. She smiled behind her closed lids, remembering his face; she loved his face; it was a determined face. He wasn't a stubborn man, but when he thought something was right and necessary, he went for it. My God, how he had gone for her that summer of sixty-four! She had been twenty-four and fairly experienced, but she had been flattered. Oh yes, she had been very flattered by the flowers and the telephone calls and the dinners and the presents. And then, when he had just popped out of the ground in Malvern when they were doing one of their hikes . . . had Hillie known about that? Was that why she had made such elaborate arrangements to secrete her father in the combe?

Picking up her thoughts as he so often did, Harvey said, 'Hey, Nash. How did Hillie know about that first time we made out in the hills? Did you tell her?' He hopped to the bed, one leg still not in its trouser. She opened her mouth to prevaricate and he grinned. 'You did. Didn't you? She's fifteen and you told her how I seduced you in that heather. You probably told her about the time you told me you were pregnant and I yelled at those backpackers . . . My God, you did!' She was blushing helplessly and trying to explain that it had all been done so jokingly, but by that time he had fallen on to the bed and was rumpling the sheets and tousling her hair and rolling her over so that he could bite her earlobe.

She gasped, 'I don't want to do anything now, Harve! Please! I'm serious!' He let her surface and rested on an elbow, staring at her, surprised. 'I was just working out what we had that was so . . . so . . . powerful. And it's more than sex. And then you start all over again—'

He knelt above her. 'Are you telling me we're not going to have sex any more?'

'Of course not! Idiot! I'm simply trying to work out what else there is between us. And you . . . doing that' – she slapped his hand away – 'interferes with my train of thought!'

He smiled suddenly. Then he lifted her to a sitting position and held her against his chest.

'Nash, never analyse anything that is good. It might disappear, honey. We love each other. That's it. We love each other.'

'You make it sound like a mantra,' she said, her voice muffled against his shoulder. He smelled good and she sniffed luxuriously.

'Yes. You've got it, honey. It will be our mantra. And when there's rows – when you're not speaking to me and I'm thinking I hate you – we'll say it. Come on, say it now – we love each other.'

She pulled back to look at him; her eyes filled with tears. 'You know, darling, for an idiot, you're quite . . . wise,' she whispered. And then she said, 'I love you. And we love each other.'

He kissed her and said, 'Who is going to tell Hillie that we're going home tomorrow?'

'You?' She shook her head at her own reply. 'No. Me.

I'll tell her. But I have to be able to promise that we'll come back.'

'There's my brave girl.' They both laughed. And then he kissed her, and then it all started again.

That evening they ate in the garden; the weather was good again but the nights were already drawing in and dusk softened the formalized lawn and shrubs. Everything had a new lease of life since the heavy rains. As the boys finished the last of the sausages from the barbecue they played a kind of game of identifying the various smells.

'Smoke . . . sausages . . . after-shave . . . no, snapdragons. Mum, do snapdragons smell?'

Maisie was scraping plates into a plastic bag. 'I don't think so.' She sniffed the air. 'Isn't it the tobacco plants around the kitchen window? They're the ones that smell at night, aren't they?'

'That's night-scented stock. I think we're smelling those early chrysanths in the centre bed.' Pru collected the plates and prepared to go indoors. 'Evie would know. I wonder how she's getting on?'

Maisie followed her with the empty salad bowls. 'I felt dreadful leaving her alone in that tiny bungalow. She looked so small when she stood by the door and waved me off.' She opened the dishwasher and began to pile in the plates. 'Golly, Pru, what would I have done without her that Friday night? I didn't even think – plan – anything! I'd thought Ted was loyal to me, I'd thought Mrs Donald was too. And they were doing such *things* . . .' She crouched over the sink and Pru placed a tentative hand on her shoulder. She turned immediately and put her head on Pru's shoulder and held onto her fiercely. Pru said nothing. Above the yellow curls her eyes closed.

After a moment Maisie withdrew. 'Sorry. Sorry, my dear. I shouldn't have done that, I know it's hard for you.' She took a deep breath and turned back to the sink. 'It's just that I have longed for you to hold me and comfort me. Just as a friend – a dear friend. My life is so upside down . . . completely changed. I need a dear friend.'

'I am that friend, Maisie,' Pru said steadily. 'I don't ask anything more than friendship.'

Maisie turned her head and smiled. 'Thank you.' Then she switched on the dishwasher and above its hum she went on, 'Pru . . . I have a suggestion. You know I am tied here for a while. I want to take control of the business before I consider selling it or putting in a manager – whatever. And I want to be able to visit Ted regularly too.' She ignored the protest from Pru and added almost casually, 'Until he dies.'

Pru was startled. 'Do you envisage that being . . . soon?'

'Apparently so. It seems his blood pressure is at bursting point and he could have heart failure any time.' Maisie took a cloth and began to wipe over the surfaces. She could have been talking about the weather.

Pru said, 'My God, Maisie! All that rushing around—'

'Quite. Looking for me. That is why I have to continue to visit him while he is alive. He found me – or I found him – and he must know that I am still around. His wife. But when he is dead, I shall be free. Free to make a home where I want – where the children will be happy. Where friends will come to visit me. Dear friends.' She stopped wiping and rinsed out the cloth, then folded it neatly on the edge of the sink. 'I would like to live at Prospect House, Pru.'

Pru said, 'A-a-a-h. I thought you might be going to say you would come to Cornwall.'

'There are the children, my dear. I cannot throw in my lot with a group of lesbians – my kids, Ted's kids – are very conventional. But at Prospect House – which they know better than I do – if my friend who, incidentally, was the previous owner, is often there . . . well, that is something quite different. They know already that we are dear friends.'

There was a long silence. Outside, the children were screeching into the dusk like owls. Pru said, 'You know whatever I have is yours, Maisie. You could learn to drive and live in Prospect House. Of course. I am not sure of my own plans as yet.'

Maisie beamed. 'That makes two of us. How do I know what is going to happen? The factory could go bust. Ted could make a recovery. In which case, of course, I would divorce him immediately and would probably be penniless! The world is wide open and full of possibilities. But we both know that if we continue to live, then neither of us will become attached to a man. And though I cannot speak for you, I know that I will not become attached to anyone except that maniac out there.' She stopped speaking and listened. Natasha was giggling hysterically. Rachel said loudly in a bored voice, 'Oh for God's sake, Nash. Just shut up!'

Maisie and Pru smiled at each other.

Pru said, 'Yes. OK. So we might well end up together?'

Maisie said, 'Who knows?' She picked up a tray and made for the door. 'Let's collect everything else and come inside. There's a programme Ray wanted to see. Duncan might be on it.' She paused by the kitchen door and looked back. 'Thank you for holding me.'

Pru followed her. She thought incredulously that there might be some kind of a future for her after all. She wondered whether she could build a pottery at Prospect House; whether her stuff would sell in Great Malvern. She breathed in the cooler night air, then wondered whether Edith and Meg were smiling at her. Somewhere.

One of the children came screaming up. 'There's fireflies, Pru! Behind the garage – we saw some fireflies! Come *on!*'

Behind the garage but at the bottom of the garden, Hilary and Tom were in Tom's old tree house watching the fireflies dance. Hilary had been weeping, and she sniffed now, disconsolately, like a child, and spoke like a child. 'Tom, make me pregnant. Then they'll have to let us be together. Come to my room tonight – tell Ian and Si you're going to the can—'

He had his arm across her shoulders and he shook her gently but firmly.

'Shut up, Hillie! When you talk like that you sound like a ten-year-old!'

'You don't want to!' she accused, pulling away from him and wailing. He clapped a hand over her mouth.

'Shut up! Of course I want to. But – what are you talking

about – don't you think when I didn't come back, Simon and Ian might come looking for me?'

'But you would go back! It doesn't take five minutes—'

He interrupted with a stifled laugh. 'You really are such a kid, Hillie Nolan! It would probably take us ages! Anyone would think it's like taking a pill or something. And anyway, we don't want it like that.' He pulled her back and put his cheek against her dark hair. 'We're in love, Hills. Didn't you know that? We don't want some sordid one-night-stand thing. That's what put me off being a vet – when I was in Bristol seeing the mating arrangements. No thanks.'

She wasn't soothed. 'You don't care that I'm leaving. You won't miss me.'

'I shall miss you. You'll be in my thoughts all the time. But, like your mother said, we're getting heavy . . . that's a funny American phrase, Hillie, but it makes sense. I feel heavy with my love for you. And she's got a point – what can we do with this love of ours unless it's go to bed together?'

'Well, just be together, that's what!' she said, exasperated.

He sighed. 'We could go on like this all night. You know what she means and so do I. She's said you can still go to Chudleigh next term. So you can come to Luddington with my mother when there's anything on. We'll see each other. Often.'

'You're so *reasonable!*'

'I don't want to spoil this last evening arguing. We're here. Now. We've had an amazing time. There will be more amazing times.' He kissed her pleadingly. 'Please let's watch the fireflies now.'

'Oh, Tom. You're younger than me too. To think I actually considered going for Mark.'

'He wouldn't have had you.' Tom held her very close. 'He only loves animals.'

They could hear Ian and Simon screaming to the others to come and see. Jess replied that the midges were biting and she was going indoors. Rachel said she would go too and they could watch *Westminster Tonight.* Natasha said worriedly, 'Where are Hillie and Tom? Harvey, you don't suppose they've skipped off somewhere?'

Suddenly Hilary turned and kissed Tom on the mouth and this time their teeth did not clash. She slid down the tree.

'I'm here, Nash!' she called. 'Is there any more food?'

Natasha smiled into the darkness. She was, after all, still a little girl.

Twenty-one

The Nolans left early the next morning. There was much kissing and hugging but no more tears. It was suddenly a point of honour with Hilary to keep a British stiff upper lip; she imagined Tom would consider her more mature for doing so. When he gently punched her upper arm and said, 'Well done, old girl,' it was as if he'd given her the Victoria Cross for gallantry. She punched him back and said rallyingly, 'Well done yourself, old fruit!' And they both managed a grin.

Harvey pumped everyone's hand and promised Ian and Simon he would keep practising 'in the nets' back home so that next year he could give them a decent game. Natasha couldn't stop thanking everyone.

'Ray, you were just marvellous. A tower of strength. The best of luck with whatever you decide to do.' She reached up to Pru's shoulders. 'As for you. You always were wonderful. You are still. And you always will be.' She drew the greying head down and kissed the wide mouth. 'Will you make me a special pot? A sort of commemorative pot?'

Pru gave her gentle smile. 'Commemorating our reunion?'

'Make another one for the reunion. This one – this one is for me. I'll tell you why later on. Perhaps.'

She made a backward movement of her head to where Harvey was talking to Mark. Pru nodded, understanding.

And then Natasha went to Maisie. 'You missed out, Maisie.' She put her arms right around the small figure and held her close. Black wiry hair spilled over blonde curls. Maisie stood very still. 'Yet you didn't. You were the hub, the calm centre of the storm. You got on with things while the rest of us went slightly crazy.' She breathed a laugh into Maisie's ear. 'When you came back into the action, you simply took over. And we all thought you were helpless!' She withdrew slightly. 'I'll have to phone you often, honey. I'm going to need your advice. Is that OK?'

Maisie's full lips opened slightly. She whispered, 'That's OK.'

And at last they were gone. They were calling at Earslwood to say a final farewell to Evie, then going to Thatch End to pick up the rest of Natasha's stuff and some text books for Hilary. Their flight left Gatwick at nine o'clock that evening.

Rachel went next. She was driving to Bristol to the open prison just off the A38. And then she was meeting Pru at the Berkeley Arms by the Severn and after lunch she would follow Pru's big car all the way down to Cornwall and Telegraph House.

She dressed carefully for her visit: a navy-blue trouser suit and a silk shirt. Her thick hair, paler since the Malvern holiday, was kept off her face by a wide green bandeau. She was looking better than she had for ages; her eyes weren't such a fishy blue, the colour of the bandeau made them hazel; her skin was good and her feet, revealed in strappy sandals, might be plump but they were also small and neat.

She stacked her case on the back seat and settled herself with sunglasses.

'Where's the hat?' Pru asked, smiling.

'My sunhat?' Rachel fished it off the floor of the car. Someone had used it for mopping up the water in Prospect House. 'It'll dry. I shall wear it in Cornwall perhaps.'

'Good old Ray.'

Jess said, 'Don't forget to write, will you? Did I give you my address?'

'You did. I'll send you mine when I know where I'm going to be living.'

'Don't be too . . . judgemental,' Jess warned.

Rachel patted the hand resting on top of the driver's door. '"From the mouths of babes and sucklings",' she quoted.

Everyone waved the green car away and Pru went indoors to get her stuff. Her car, still smelling slightly of Cornish cauliflowers, was waiting outside the garage. She put her case in the boot and slung her bag on the passenger's seat. Something was protruding from the outside pocket; she leaned across to push it safely inside and saw it was the letter from Meg. She sat down sideways and took the letter out and held it between her palms as if she were praying. She had already thought she might make some kind of sculpture in memory of Meg, to stand in the garden overlooking the Atlantic. Now she knew what form it would take. It would be a mermaid. Everlastingly young, strangely sexless yet always alluring. She closed her eyes and imagined the turn of the shoulder, the eyes gazing out towards . . . America? Towards Nash perhaps? Another member of the group, like Edith, invisible but there.

Mark's voice, tentative and therefore tender, said, 'Are you all right, Pru?'

She opened her eyes. He was leaning on the open door of the car looking down at her. His dark eyes were concerned and . . . caring. Did he know about her? Did he find that interesting? Mysterious?

She said, 'I was thinking, Mark. Planning a sculpture.'

'Of your friend?'

So he did know. He was not repelled.

'Yes. But more . . . *for* her . . . I mean it doesn't have to look like her. In fact I thought . . . a mermaid.'

'Oh.' Suddenly his face was transformed by a smile. The likeness to his father disappeared. He said, 'How lovely!'

'I hope so.' She turned and replaced Meg's letter then stood up. Mark did not move and they were very close. She thought suddenly: oh my God, he thinks he is in love with me . . . he thinks he understands . . .

She said, 'I must say goodbye to your mother and the others. I'll say it here and now to you, Mark. Thank you for being there when we needed you. You're still needed here. You know that, don't you?'

'Yes.' He smiled. 'I couldn't have done much without you. Do *you* know that?'

She was going to pass it off, disclaim all responsibility, treat him like a child. And then she knew she could not do that.

She said, 'I didn't know. I know now. Thank you.'

She said no more but walked past him and into the house.

The three boys were making a picnic. Tom looked a bit distant but Ian and Simon were back to normal, quarrelling and pushing and making a mess. She organized them as best she could, ruffled their heads, said goodbye.

Tom said, 'I won't wave you off. D'you mind? I thought I'd go and sit in the tree house.'

'I don't mind. We'll see each other soon I expect.'

Jess and Maisie were nowhere downstairs; she found them in Ted's old bedroom. Natasha had forgotten the red, spotted dressing-gown. Jess was folding it ready to pack. Maisie was staring at her helplessly.

Pru said, 'I wouldn't bother, Jess. It was Harvey's anyway.' She smiled slightly at Maisie. 'I think your mother should take it on. Just to show she was part of our reunion although she wasn't there!'

Jess laughed and immediately draped it around Maisie's shoulders. It engulfed her. She held it closely for a moment, then slid out of it, laughing. 'I'll keep it for Nash.' She looked at Pru and there was a complete understanding between them. Pru knew that Maisie would often hold the dressing-gown to her face and weep into its folds. She accepted that. After all, there was the sculpture of the mermaid to think about. She must remember to tell Maisie about the sculpture.

She said, 'I'm off. Give Evie a hug from me next time you see her. And . . . before winter comes, shall we go to Prospect? See what kind of improvements you might need?'

Maisie nodded. Jess said, 'What's this? Mum? Are we moving?'

Maisie smiled. 'Maybe. Not yet. I have to be near your father. But I've always wanted to live in the country.'

Jess shrieked. 'Mum! It's wonderful out there! Proper country. The boys loved it in spite of . . . well, in spite of what was happening. Oh, Mum!'

'We'll see. Don't get too excited.'

Jess grinned at Pru. 'One of Mum's stock sayings. Don't get too excited. The original wet blanket.'

They trailed out to the car and Pru settled herself behind the wheel. All she had to do was to switch on, start the engine, press the clutch and engage first gear then drive slowly out onto the Edgbaston road. If she took each small operation step by step, she could do it.

Jess leaned in and pecked her cheek. 'Thanks for everything, Pru. You took us on as a ready-made family and we all appreciate it.'

Maisie said quietly, 'Can you put up with having all of us on a more permanent basis, Pru?'

Jess looked round, surprised. 'We're sharing Prospect House? Better still! Oh do say yes, Pru! Please!'

Pru smiled obediently and said, 'Yes.'

Maisie leaned through. 'Thank you, Pru. I think we can learn to live together, don't you?'

'Yes,' Pru said again.

Maisie chuckled in her throat and kissed her on the lips. Just for a moment Pru registered Maisie's full soft mouth on hers; the smell of her; the feel of her curls. And then she was engaging first gear without any recollection of switching on the engine. She was sliding down the gravel drive, waiting for an opening in the traffic, waving through the window and . . . leaving.

Evelyn had her best coffee set laid out on the garden table and there were chcolate biscuits sweating slightly in the shade of the umbrella. Best of all, Sam Lavington was approaching from his bungalow carrying two extra garden chairs to accommodate all of them.

Hilary and Harvey hung back slightly but Sam was not one to stand on ceremony.

'Here. Take these.' He thrust the chairs at them. 'Let the women have a minute together.' He indicated a place for the chairs just inside the front door. Natasha and Evie were completely blocking the hall. 'Leave them there. I want to show you something.'

Hilary got rid of her chair with alacrity. 'Is it the ducks? Nash has told us about the ducks.'

'Probably painted me as a crazy old man, eh?' Sam cocked a bushy eyebrow. Harvey laughed but Hilary said earnestly, 'Not at all. She thinks you're marvellous. Just what Evie needs too.'

'Oh she does, does she? I think that had better be left to Evie and me!' The old man looked at Harvey. 'You Americans don't believe in letting things take their time, do you?'

'Hillie. Shut up,' Harvey advised.

Hilary apologized. 'I hoped it would be the ducks. Everything is a bit solemn at the moment,' she explained.

Sam led the way into the middle of the green area. 'Well, it is about the ducks, so you're lucky.' Sitting in a circle under a willow tree were the plastic ducks. 'They're marking where the pond is going to be,' he said, describing a rough circle with his boots. 'The whole duck-thing was to soften the warden up for a pub. I suppose your mum, Nash, told you that too, did she?'

'Well. Yes, she did say that was the kinda overall scheme.'

Sam was triumphant. 'We're going to get both. Village duck pond. Village pub. What do you think about that?'

Hilary thought of Tom coming to visit Evie with his mother and maybe helping Mr Lavington with his plans. She wished . . . oh how she wished . . .

Harvey said, 'Great. I like English pubs. But I bet you won't get Evie inside it.'

'Don't be too sure. She tells me she went swimming in that pool your mother made.' Sam looked at Hilary. 'She's a reserved little lady is your Aunt Evie. But that's what makes a woman interesting. Gives her a bit of mystery. Makes it exciting when she lets some of the reserve go. Wouldn't you agree, young lady?'

Hilary knew he was getting at her because of her American brashness. She didn't care. She said, 'That's how English women play it. Yes. But just 'cos we seem to be like an open book, doesn't mean you can read us! Sometimes you need to have a code.'

He looked surprised. She was surprised herself. Harvey said, 'Well done, Hillie.' He turned his grin on Sam. 'I'm not sure I know the code for my women yet, sir. But whichever way they play it, there's never a dull moment!'

And Sam, looking at the precocious young girl before him, shook his head and smiled a slow, unwilling smile. Then he gathered up his ducks and they went across to where Natasha and Evie had lugged the chairs through the bungalow and into the back garden.

Rachel stared across the table at the man she had not seen for almost three years. Eric Strang was not so much thin as shrunken. His head seemed to have dropped between his shoulder blades, his nose was more prominent because his cheeks had caved in. His hair had gone, not only from his head but from the backs of his hands. He wore the bottle-green prison trousers, but a check overshirt.

She hardly knew how to greet him; Duncan had made it clear that any contact with him would be picked up unfavourably by the press but in any case she had had no wish to see her father in prison. The whole point of Eric had been that he could fix anything. He had not been able to fix prison. And he had not been able to fix Denise's suicide.

He smiled slightly at her obvious discomfort and said, 'Hi, baby. Long time no see.'

She just stopped a gasp of incredulity. It was how he had always talked, but she hadn't realized before that he was acting a part: was it Humphrey Bogart or Robert Mitchum?

She said, 'Hello, Eric. How are you?'

'Well. Fit and well.' He looked around, pretending to be surreptitious. 'This place is a doddle, honey. The screws try to be friends.' He barked a laugh. 'There's classes for everything under the sun. Creative writing. Carpentry. Cooking. Gardening.'

'Are you taking any of them?'

'Writing. Cooking. Anything indoors.' He laughed again.

She thought: he's nervous . . . he's nervous . . . of me! She said seriously, 'Well, the writing will keep your mind active. Help you to . . . to . . . get started again. Not much longer, is it?'

'Six months if I continue to behave myself!' Another of those unnatural laughs. 'And that's no problem.' He leaned forward confidentially. 'I'm getting through it by treating it like a holiday, honey. I'm here because I was working too hard.' He noticed her widening eyes and became defensive.

'It's true, baby. I had too many irons in the fire and couldn't keep a proper eye on all of them. If that's not overwork, I don't know what is!' He sat back. 'Things weren't good between Denise and me – well, you know that. Don't let anyone kid you it was my fault she topped herself, Ray.' He leaned forward again: the effect was as if he were sitting in a rocking chair delivering words of wisdom. 'She'd have done it years ago if I hadn't stopped her.'

Rachel tried to make a stand. 'How did you do that, Eric?'

He grinned. It was the grin he had given her when she caught him and Miss Benson on the bed together. 'You know how I did it, baby. With the magic touch.'

She gripped the edge of her chair.

'And when you weren't there to give the magic touch . . .'

'You're saying it's my fault for getting banged up?' He made a little boy's face. 'Come on now, honey. D'you think I chose to end up here?'

She stared at him for a few more seconds and then looked away. He had argued a full circle, rather like politicians did. She had heard it before. The complete and total failure to take any responsibility for personal actions.She took a deep breath and let it go. He had leaned back again and was telling her how long he slept each night, what the meals were like and how he got a regular supply of cigarettes and whisky. She glanced around the room; it was full of flowers and the windows looked out on gardens. But the chairs and tables were steel-framed and beneath the scent of stocks lay the unmistakable smell of disinfectant.

She waited for a pause and said abruptly, 'What do you think of homosexuality, Eric?'

He said, 'Not much. We do it, of course. Go mad if we didn't. But it's not as good.'

For a dreadful moment she thought she might faint. She had never fainted and had imagined it was simply a sudden lack of consciousness. The nausea that swept her, and drained the blood from her head and heart, warned her it was worse than that. She stiffened her spine, breathed deeply, forcing her ribcage out as far as it would go.

He said, with just a hint of concern, 'You OK, babe?' He rocked towards her again. 'Listen. You don't have to feel bad about staying away. I was glad. I worked hard to get you where you are today, honey. I'd hate to see your house come tumbling down. I mean that.'

She gasped ironically, 'Gee. Thanks, Eric.'

'Well, what is it then? You're asking questions as if you're some kind of reporter. Is it the sex part? For Christ's sake, Ray, don't get things out of proportion. I'm in here with men. What else would I do?' He registered her expression and flung himself back in his chair. 'Haven't you ever masturbated?' He came back towards her to look into her face. 'Well then. What's the difference?'

'It's just . . . sensation then, is it? A physical sensation?'

'Oh we're on to that old thing about women and love . . . spiritual, eh?' He barked his laugh, relaxed back again. 'Don't get me wrong, baby. I was fond of Denise. I still love my little Rosa. And I'm crazy about you – I always was. That's why I tried to teach you . . . things.'

'I see.'

'Of course you do.' He reached for her hands which were now clenched in her lap. 'Baby. I am you. And you are me. It was always that way – you knew it when you were a kid. Don't forget it now.'

She fought the faintness again, clutching his hands to stop herself sliding backwards. He mistook her grip and smiled with a kind of smugness.

'That's right, honey. You and me. I won't see much of you, I know that. But I'm there for you when you need me.' He shook her hands and gave a different laugh, almost a chuckle. 'You obviously needed me today, babe. And here we are. The master and his apprentice. Eh?'

'I'll have to go, Dad—'

'I know. He's waiting for you somewhere and you mustn't make him wait too long, eh? Just long enough.' He released her hands. 'That's the first time you've called me dad in ages. I don't think I like it.'

'Sorry, Eric.'

She stood up and so did he. And suddenly he came around

the table and put his arms around her and kissed her. It was somehow a moment of poignancy and she knew that she would not see him again, ever. And then he spoiled it.

'Lose a bit of weight, baby. I know men like big breasts, but it's still just possible to have too much of a good thing.' He breathed a laugh in her ear and moved away. She held the back of the chair until the room steadied around her.

For some reason she thought of the typist's swivel chair which apparently had broken beneath Miss Chambers's weight. She smiled and straightened. She was, after all, Rachel Stayte now and she was on her way to meet a friend at the Berkeley Arms.

When the Nolans had gone, Evelyn cleared away her coffee set while Sam took his chairs back and returned to dry her precious bone china. She kept an eye on him as she swilled the sink and polished the taps. He did it beautifully, poking a curled end of the tea towel between the handles and giving the teaspoons the sort of buffing that brought out the shine.

She felt bound to ask him to stay for lunch.

'Just a salad and some cold meat,' she said. 'I shall have to do some shopping this afternoon. I'm running out of everything.'

'I'm seeing young Sam at the Three Tuns at one o'clock. The Trust has been negotiating with a brewery about building a small pub on the green. Young Sam will tell me the latest.'

'Oh. That's nice.' Evelyn still wasn't convinced about the pub and she definitely felt rejected about her lunch invitation. She carried the crockery through to the cabinet in the tiny dining room.

'Don't bother with shopping this afternoon.' He followed her, looking suddenly rather helpless. 'Have a good rest. Let's go out for a meal tonight. I haven't been to a restaurant for a meal for . . . well, since Young Sam took me at Christmas. The Three Tuns is only round the corner. I'll book us in, shall I?'

She was going to say no. Nicely of course, but evenings were not her best time and the Three Tuns sounded like the thin end of a wedge to her. Then she glanced up and saw that he was nervous. He leaned on the edge of her dining table and moved from one foot to the other. He reminded her of Tom, completely uncertain as to what Hilary might say or do next. And, more recently, he reminded her of Mark when he looked at Pru.

She said, 'I'd love that . . . Sam.' She smiled. 'Actually I could do with a nap this afternoon. I've loved being with everyone, but it's very tiring.'

He straightened; really he had quite a military bearing.

'Course it is. But makes you appreciate being on your own after, doesn't it? You've got to vary things a bit, see. If you're on your own too much then you get . . . lonely. But if you . . .' He was looking down at her and somehow petered out of words.

She swallowed. 'Exactly.'

There was a most embarrassing pause. Then he said, 'I'd better go. Evie. Thank you for . . . everything.' He grinned suddenly. 'D'you know, you've completely changed my life.'

'Me?' She was incredulous. She had never changed anyone's life before.

'Yes. You.' He moved into the hall, skirting the umbrella stand neatly. 'I was working away at trying to make something happen around here. And suddenly, there you were. Bam!'

'I've been here ages, Sam.'

He sighed. 'I know. What a waste of time. Eh?' He opened the front door, turned and took her hand. 'We won't waste any more, Evie. Will we?'

She was going to withdraw; her face reddened. And then she said quietly, 'No, Sam. We won't waste any more.' She closed the door and leaned against it and thought of what this declaration could mean. Certainly it would mean going to pubs. Certainly it would mean getting a committee together to arrange digging the pond. And . . . her face became so hot she had to press it against the wood of the door . . . it might even mean . . . going to bed. And she wasn't like Edie who was a spinster but not an old maid. She was that awful word, a virgin.

And then she thought of Nash and Harvey; and she thought

of Maisie and the terrible Ted and she thought of Duncan Stayte who slept with men and Pru who slept with women. And she straightened with determination and marched into the kitchen.

'If anyone is going to make me not a virgin,' she said aloud, 'then it must be Sam Lavington. No-one else will do!'

And she began to cut a lunchtime sandwich.

The Nolans settled themselves in their business-class reservations. Hilary was unusually quiet as the great plane took off. She pressed her face to the glass and watched the patchwork countryside below and very obviously fought to hold back her tears. Harvey kept his hand on her shoulder as if trying to inject a constant flow of sympathy. Natasha, who would normally have dealt with the situation very vocally, was also silent.

'Going to miss the old place too?' Harvey asked. 'You know – both of you – we'll be back in the fall. It's not the end of the world.'

Natasha nodded mutely. Hilary said in a choked voice, 'We wanted it this way. It was me fixed it. Remember?'

'Sure, honey.' Harvey drew a breath as they levelled out and the pilot's voice began to tell them about height and cloud formation. 'How about something to eat? Or drink?'

Both women shook their heads and Harvey pretended incredulity. 'Neither of you? Both refusing food? Nash, come on. You had coffee for breakfast, coffee at Evie's place and tea at your mother's. You haven't eaten anything.'

Natasha still shook her head. Hilary sat back and undid her seat belt. 'I wouldn't mind a Coke. And some of those little cracker things. What's the video? And what's the dinner menu?'

Harvey laughed and removed his hand. 'My God. Miserytime over for you, Hillie? See what you can do with your mother.'

Hilary pulled her mouth down. 'I don't think you understand the British attitude, Harve. Our feelings run deep but we put a good front on. Isn't that so, Ma?'

Natasha looked at them both with big eyes then, at last, spoke.

'I've got something to tell you. I wasn't sure. Then I was. And now . . . you might be . . . horrified. I just don't know.' She coloured slightly. 'I do hope you won't be. Because it could be just wonderful.' She swallowed. 'Or, maybe, not.'

Hilary looked. Harvey said, 'Christ. You're not ill are you?'

'No. Not ill. I'm . . . we're . . . the three of us. *We* are having a baby.'

Harvey said nothing. Hilary squeaked, 'But Pop's been here two weeks! Just two weeks!'

'I know. But I was certain . . . that time in the gorge . . . I was certain then. And . . . and . . . yesterday I went to the chemist and got one of those kit things. And . . . it was positive.'

Hilary said a word that was banned even in the Nolan household. Her parents did not reprimand her. Harvey was still silent. Natasha said pleadingly, 'Darling, I know we're older. But it will be all right. I promise. I want this baby so much. Please . . .'

Hilary said brutally, 'He thinks it's someone else's. Tell him, Ma. Tell him that's impossible.'

Natasha did not reply. She continued to look at Harvey. And then, very slowly, he undid his seat belt and stood up. He looked around the business section. It was not full and the seats were occupied mostly by men.

He said loudly, 'Listen, everyone!' One or two startled faces looked up from newspapers. 'Can you all hear? I'm forty-five. This is my beautiful wife. This is my wonderful daughter.' He looked at them both. Then his face split in an enormous grin. 'We're having a baby! Another baby! Got it? The Nolans are having another baby!'

Even Hilary squealed and put her hands to her face. Natasha let her eyes overflow and held out her arms to him.

The Berkeley Arms was dark with beams and prints and hanging mugs and antlers. Pru, looking like a retired film star with her greying fair hair straying out of its knot and feathering her aristocratic face, carried two glasses of lager and lime from the bar to a table in the window. Rachel sat there, staring unseeingly at the view of the village street.

She took her drink and sipped it carefully. 'Thanks, Pru. Thanks for the drink. And for being here.'

'I said I would be.'

'I don't mean here. I mean *here*!' Rachel gestured wildly to describe the world, perhaps even the universe.

'Was it awful?' Pru asked.

Rachel lifted her shoulders, sipped again and said, 'Do you know how Edward the Second was murdered in Berkeley Castle?'

'I saw the play.'

'Did it scare you? I mean in a personal way?'

'People – some people – are scaring. Terrifying. Yes.'

'He scared me. Eric. My father. He terrified me. And the awful thing is, I am his daughter. He told me that he is me and I am him. Or he. Whatever.'

'We all have that . . . awfulness . . . in us, Ray. But we can control it. We can face up to it, consider it, deal with it.'

A boy of about sixteen came to their table bearing two ploughman's lunches. He said something about the weather and had they come to see the Severn Bore. Pru answered him. Rachel took some cutlery from a paper napkin and spread the napkin carefully across her knees.

Pru did likewise and then said, 'I am gay. But that doesn't automatically cut off my other feelings. None of them. If Duncan is bisexual you should talk to him. Seriously, Ray. You must talk to him.'

Ray cut a tomato in half. 'I thought we were talking about Eric.'

'We were. But everything you say is related to Duncan. You are in love with him, Ray. Surely you know that? If you were not, none of this would matter.'

'Wouldn't it? Eric has been having sex with other men in prison. Because he can't manage without it.'

Pru buttered a roll and took a bite. After a while she said in a neutral voice, 'That's got nothing to do with Duncan, has it?'

'No.'

Rachel sighed and began to eat. Pru left some of hers. Rachel said, 'I'm going to eat everything. As a defiant gesture. Because Eric advised me to lose some weight.'

Pru laughed. 'Sometimes I am quite glad I never knew my father. And I admire Mummy too. D'you know, I don't think she has ever slept with another man. Isn't that amazing?'

Rachel said, 'It's wonderful. I haven't slept with anyone except Duncan.'

'And he was married to Joy. And now sleeps with his colleague.'

Rachel looked up, surprised. 'That was pretty . . . direct.'

'I want you to look at the facts. They're not so terrible then.'

Rachel sighed again. 'Oh, Pru. I'm glad I'm coming down to Cornwall with you. I don't know what the hell to do. D'you think all the magical mystery of the place will give me an answer?'

'I think you already know the answer.' Pru smiled. 'It won't pop out of the sand or the rocks. Eric couldn't give it to you. It will be your decision. No-one else's.'

'You're a hard woman.' Rachel smiled suddenly. 'I always modelled myself on you. Did you know that? But now . . . I can't do that!'

'You don't need to model yourself on anyone, Ray. You never did. You are efficient and clever. You are a complete, capable woman. That's what you are and how you look. Don't try to change that. It's utterly . . . fulfilling.'

'Aw . . . shucks!' Rachel said in Hilary's voice. And they both laughed.

Maisie sat on the garish sofa where so recently Ted had sat. She was wearing the spotted dressing-gown over her nightdress and she dug her hands deep into the patch pockets and held it to her. The boys were in bed and Mark and Jess were sharing a phone call with their friend in Bristol. Just for half an hour Maisie was alone.

She did not dare let her thoughts go free; they jumbled

somewhere at the back of her mind, some of them fighting to get full consciousness, others rather drearily nudging at her . . . don't forget . . . don't forget. Some specifications for a new display area at a shop in Bristol lay on the coffee table. She had some costings for a similar set-up from two years before and could work out a price for the job. She had managed to give estimates for two such jobs already and they had both been well within her price. She had always known that figures were her strong point; figures made sense, they were stable, reliable. It was like the house number: one-four-eight. You touched the figures; they were always there. Doc James had said, 'Keep working, my dear. It is therapeutic in itself. And, frankly, it is all you can do for your husband just now.' With a sigh Maisie leaned forward and picked up the first 'spec'. She did not feel like working; she felt like sitting and dreaming about Nash but if she did that she found her mind would let some of the other thoughts escape. Ted. Ted and Mrs Donald. She squeezed her eyes tightly shut, then opened them and began to read from the paper.

There was a sound behind her and she turned quickly. It was Tom. She dropped the paper, smiled, held out an arm and scooped him to her.

'Oh, darling. How nice to see you. Couldn't you sleep?'

'No. Sorry, Mum. You were working. Do you have to work – I mean to get enough money for all of us?'

'No. Not at all. If I sold the business, we could live on the income from capital . . . well, investments I suppose. But we could live well. As it is, Ian and Si can join you at Luddington – which they're all for and I think you are too.'

'Rather! But . . . why don't you sell up? Take it easy?'

'Well for one thing, it's Dad's business. Not mine to sell. And it's something I can keep going for him. And . . . I like to feel, after all these years, that I can actually do something useful.'

'Oh, Mum!' They smiled at each other. Maisie thought it was almost like looking in a mirror. His eyes and hair and skin were like hers. Even his ears . . . the shape of his face.

He said abruptly, 'Mum . . . sorry . . . but can you tell me about my father?'

She blinked. This was not even one of the many jumbling thoughts at the back of her head; this was something new. And it shouldn't be. Surely it was natural that after all that happened in the past months Tom would want to know about his real father?

She said, 'I can talk about it – him – if that is what you mean, darling. But I can't actually tell you much. He never knew about you. I never saw him again.' She took a breath and looked over the top of Tom's head. 'He was dark-haired – not black like Dad, but dark brown. His hair was very long. Like John Lennon's. Everyone tried to look like John Lennon in those days.'

There was a pause. Tom said timidly, 'What was he like? What was he . . . actually . . . like?'

'He was nice. He must have been nice because I wouldn't have . . . you know.'

'He—' Tom swallowed audibly. 'He seduced you.'

'You have to let yourself be seduced. He offered me freedom, Tom.' Maisie spoke seriously. 'Freedom from all responsibility – responsibility for my own actions. And for the actions of others.' She almost told him about Roly, about her weakness, her inability to say no. But she didn't; he was, after all, only fifteen. Hilary had made him sentient, that was all. She said, 'I knew it would never be anything more than summer madness. I had Mark and Jess at home. I could never have left them.'

'He was a hippie?'

'Yes. There were four of them. They had an old van. Two other girls. It was an early spring and they were going around the fairs. Busking. Plaiting necklaces and anklets. They were going to Spain in the autumn. Tom spoke Spanish.'

'Tom?'

'That was his name. The least I could do was to give it to you.' She sighed. 'Sorry, my love. It was just another of my many mistakes. I did the best I could about it.'

Tom was silent and after a while she went on, 'When you leave school, would you like us to trace him?'

'Perhaps. I don't know. I'm so happy now . . . I feel guilty about being happy when Dad is . . . well, like he is. Let's leave it for now, Mum.' He hesitated and added, 'Unless you want to . . . see him again?'

Maisie laughed. 'No, darling. You can banish that thought. Later . . . much later probably . . . I think I shall live with Aunt Pru. In the Malvern house.'

'Mum!' he pulled away to stare at her. His blue eyes were alight. 'That would be wonderful – just wonderful! There would be somewhere for us to come to. All of us.'

'By all of us I expect you mean Hilary,' Maisie said gravely.

'Oh, Mum. Yes.' He stood up. 'I mean Hilary.' He smiled shakily. 'Thanks for not laughing about it. It's so . . . terribly serious.'

'I know.'

'It's right too. Do you see that, Mum? It joins us. You and Nash. Hilary and me.'

For a moment she was startled, wondering whether he knew. And then she realized there was nothing to know. She nodded. 'I've always wanted to be linked with Nash in some way,' she said simply. 'And you're arranging it for me.'

After he had gone she held the dressing-gown close again, then released it and reached for the papers.

Twenty-two

Rachel had not been prepared for the sheer beauty of Telegraph House and its adjacent cove. As she followed the Ford out of Penzance, through lush lanes lined with flowering walls, she was assailed by the scent. Cut grass, sand, sea and flowers combined to make a heady perfume, and she sniffed the air like a cat and waved to Pru, who waved back through her window and then put up her thumb.

They came up on to the barren tops of Penwith where the thin soil barely provided hold for the grass, and enormous boulders thrust their way into the middle of fields. And there, suddenly, was Buryan Church, menacing and dark on the skyline, threatening death in the midst of all that abundant life. Rachel shivered slightly and was thankful when they were through the village and onto cliff roads which climbed again and then began to pitch downwards. The sea spread out before them, glittering in the early evening sun, and the Ford took a left turn onto a track not unlike the one leading to Bryn Farm. Rachel braked slightly and followed. Huge umbrellas of cow parsley almost met in a tunnel, but, below and ahead, the sea was always there and she could now see over her windscreen the tiny sandy cove far below them. She changed right down and chugged closer to Pru; the track leaned around a bend and there was the house, sunk in its own garden, the granite walls glinting crystalline in the sun, the steeply pitched roofs perched like jaunty party hats half hiding the upper windows. It should have been completely out of place. But rhododendrons and ivy provided a bodice and crinoline, the glass was turned into red rubies by the sun, the enormous door stood open and a motley collection of deckchairs was assembled on the lawn, clothes flapped from a line strung between apple trees, a conservatory leaned out from the house full of tangled vines. It was a home.

Both Rachel and Pru were more than ready for the warm welcome awaiting them. They were helped out of their cars, their luggage whisked off. They were eased into deckchairs and plied with tea and scones. Rachel, terrified of inadvertently catching sight of any overt sexuality between the women, gradually relaxed in the garden-party atmosphere. Someone called Margaret said she had seen Duncan on the television only last night and really what he said made absolute sense.

'Last night?' They had watched the television in the living room at one-four-eight, flipping through the channels for news and weather. Rachel had known Duncan's itinerary better than he knew it himself. Surely there had been no television appearances?

Marion Jeffort, who had made the scones, nodded. 'He's down this way, isn't he? Plymouth. There are quite a few Liberal voters in Cornwall.'

Rachel felt her heart jump. Unexpectedly she suddenly yearned for the terrifying excitement of the hustings. She remembered sitting in her car, microphone to her lips, intoning, 'Vote for freedom. Vote for liberalism. Vote for Stayte.' And as she had come through one of the Soar villages her voice had risen uncontrollably. 'Vote for Stayte – the man with ideals as well as ideas! Vote for Duncan Stayte and know that you have struck a blow for your country!' It had been unforgivably jingoistic and her co-driver had giggled and looked at her, amazed. But by then Rachel had meant what she said. She was not only in love with her boss, she admired and respected him. And . . . somehow there had always been the understanding between them, that if he got into Parliament he would also get into her bed.

She took a shaky breath. Had Eric fixed that for her? Had Eric actually said in the man-to-man blunt way he had, 'Take on my Rachel and she'll make sure you get your seat. And if you do, I think you should reward her. Don't you?'

Marion said, 'Have another scone, Rachel. You're looking rather pale around the gills.'

Margaret, who had dealt so expertly with the cesspit,

laughed. 'It's the thought of seeing her husband! Don't worry, Rachel. We're all here to get away from men. And we've succeeded. No reason why you shouldn't!'

One or two laughed. Thank God Pru did not. Instead she said, 'Rachel is here for a rest. We've all had quite a busy time. She more than most.'

Margaret accepted the implied reprimand amiably. 'Sorry, Rachel. I can understand politics are a nerve-wracking business. You've come to the right place. No stress here.'

It seemed to be true. As the days drifted by, Rachel gradually relaxed. Apart from a few of the women who paired off occasionally, the little commune could have been any group of unusual people wanting to make separate lives for themselves. She fitted into their routine with surprising ease. Duncan was never far from her thoughts, but the whole problematic situation seemed separate and easily shelved. This was a time for her; a sort of recuperation. And in any case she was terribly interested in the way Pru lived. Pru's mystery was still there, but this was part of it; this was why she had never really related to any of the men at Markhams.

Meg's death was the first bereavement the commune had suffered. So there was an aura of sadness about the place which, for Rachel, fitted in well with the September days of golden sunshine and shorter evenings. Pru was arranging the private memorial service and had asked everyone to write a paragraph about Meg which would be read out. During the evenings, after supper, they discussed their tributes and talked about Meg. Pru and two others remembered her as a young girl arriving at Telegraph House for the first time.

'She was Catholic and had been expelled from her school for adoring one of the nuns.' Pru looked at her hands. She had been sketching all day; thinking about materials. She wanted the mermaid's hands to be outstretched, so perhaps a metal would be the best medium.

Rachel said, 'How did she discover this place?'

'I'd bought it the year before.' Pru looked up, smiling. 'Alison and Sarah came to my mother's house one day.' Her smile grew. 'Oddly enough, Edwin brought them.' She looked over to two elderly women sitting by the window. 'D'you remember that evening?'

The older of the two spoke. 'How could I forget it?' She addressed Rachel. 'We'd lived together for years. Lots of women did. Halved the rent . . . company . . . you know, all the usual reasons. And we were looking for a retirement cottage. We talked a lot about it. Pru came to see us. Sarah used to make delicious lemon pancakes—'

Sarah interrupted. 'She didn't come for the pancakes, Ali. She came because she wanted the company of like minds.'

Pru nodded. 'True. And I'd just had a legacy. A big one. And suddenly I realized what it could mean. I could live separately. I could make pots. Others could come too . . .' Her face shone. 'It was a wonderful time, Ray. I tried to get Maisie to come too . . .' She shook her head. 'Anyway, we're talking about Meg.' Her voice dropped. 'Meg was wildly unhappy. She'd run away and she was part of the little hippie group. Tom McEvoy and Co.'

'My God!' Rachel exclaimed blankly.

'Quite. Maisie fell for Tom McEvoy and I fell for Meg.'

'Just like that?' Rachel said, still amazed at such a turn of events.

'Just like that. So when we discovered that Nash's little fling with Ron the plumber had actually been with Roly, Maisie's foster brother . . . well, it seemed all of a piece.'

'My God.' This time Rachel sounded awed.

And Pru said again, 'Quite.' And then she stood up briskly. 'Listen, I know it's late but I have to finish a sketch I'm doing, Ray. Tomorrow, let's have a swim first thing. This last little piece of summer won't last and the tide is in at eight . . . what d'you say?'

'Yes.' Rachel smiled. 'Thanks, Pru.'

So they began their swims. Sometimes Rachel would go alone. Once during her second week it poured with rain and she still swam, lifting her face between each stroke to feel the bullets of water on her head. It was a lotus existence; she hardly knew how she felt any more; whether she could ever face Duncan again. She gardened with Margaret; she cooked with Marion; she watched Pru begin her first models of Mermaid Meg; she swam and walked through the heavy sand of the cove; and she climbed the cliffs and visited the amphitheatre at the top and watched a seal lie on its back and consume its evening meal of mackerel. Pru often asked her, 'All right, Ray?' And she would smile and nod and tell Pru what a wonderful place this was and she could stay here for ever.

'You know you can. We've had a number of single women come here.'

'But they don't stay?'

'No. A lot of couples don't stay either. It satisfies them completely for a time, and then they know they have to join the world again.'

Rachel frowned. 'Do you feel that, Pru?'

Pru nodded. 'Yes. I have to do this piece of work. But I think it will be the last I do down here.'

'And then what?'

For a moment Pru looked utterly forlorn. Then she shrugged. 'I'm not sure. It depends on someone else. But I am going to renovate the Malvern house. That's my next project. I hope to move there after Christmas. Early spring perhaps.'

'But it's as cut off as this place,' Rachel protested.

'Not quite. And it's near big cities. Worcester, Bristol, Birmingham. Anonymous places where prejudice isn't so obvious. I could sell stuff there. And I'd be more accessible to my friends.' Pru smiled. 'I'd insist on the reunion every year. And more than that. I'd want you all to visit me often.'

She saw Rachel's expression and said quickly, 'You could live there with me, Ray.'

'Oh come off it, Pru. You'd have your pots. What would I actually do? All right, keep house for you. But . . . oh God, I'm sorry, but I need more.'

Pru smiled slightly but she offered no more solutions.

At the end of Rachel's second week at Telegraph House, when the October winds were beginning to whip the Atlantic into a frenzy, Pru had a telephone call. Rachel and she had been trying to tame the vine in the conservatory so she used the phone there. It was where she had first spoken to Natasha over two months ago.

'Maisie!'

Rachel, busy with twine and scissors, glanced around and noted the way Pru's face lit up. It immediately settled into its usual calmness but it had been enough to inhibit Rachel from exclaiming and joining her at the receiver. She cut another length of twine and started to tie in a trailing stem.

Pru listened for some time, then said hesitantly, 'I don't know what to say. How do you feel? Is it too early for any reactions?'

Another long pause during which Pru made little sounds of understanding. Then she said, 'Of course. Naturally. There is no hurry, my dear. A year at least. You have to make sure the boys settle at Luddington with Tom . . . yes, the business. I would imagine Nash's father would be of immense help . . . yes. Yes. Of course. Anyway, it will give you time to be certain . . . yes.'

Rachel dealt with a branch heavy with fruit. There were already six enormous baskets of grapes. She wondered whether the little community made wine.

Pru said, 'I thought next spring. I need good weather – couldn't get workmen out there in the winter. Besides I shall be busy here for a while.'

Rachel put a grape into her mouth. It was juicy but not sweet; she chewed it determinedly and her eyes watered slightly.

'She's here. D'you want a word? Of course I shall tell her – of course she'll be pleased! You've missed out on getting to know Ray now. She's strong. Very strong.' Pru caught Rachel's eye and grinned. 'No, all right. Yes, I'll pass on your best wishes.' And then her tone sharpened. 'Maisie, listen, just a moment. Are you sure about this? I mean, what about Nash? Yes, yes, I accept that.' There was another pause and then Pru said, 'Is she? Really? My God . . . Hillie is sixteen!' She listened and then said, 'How do you feel about it . . . really? What do you mean you told Tom about his father? You think he understood . . . yes he is very sentient at the moment.' She made more sounds, nodding. Then she said, 'All right. We'll talk again. If Nash rings – oh.' She removed the receiver from her ear. 'She's hung up. Someone was at the door. Apparently the house is a hive of activity.' She picked up the scissors and began to snip grapes into the basket. 'She sent her love. Did you gather that Ted has died?'

'I wondered.' Rachel still chewed her grape. She said, 'The skins are so bitter.'

'What? Oh, the grapes. Yes. We use them for wine.' Pru glanced at her. 'He died yesterday. In his sleep. Maisie was with him.'

Rachel made a face.

'Yes, quite. She's coping very well actually. Evie is going to help her with the funeral. Mary Barkwith, Nash's mother, has offered her help too. It's not until next week.' Rachel said nothing. Pru snipped a bunch of grapes and said, 'The better news is that Nash is pregnant. She phoned Evie who phoned Maisie. Apparently she told Harvey and Hilary almost as soon as they took off in the plane. She must have been all of two weeks. And Harvey turned round and announced it to the rest of the passengers!' Still Rachel was silent. Pru said quietly, 'What is it? Ted's death? Are we going to the funeral?'

Rachel forced herself to swallow. She was going to nod, still not trusting her voice, then some demon made her say bitterly, 'Well, it seems you won't want to miss a chance of seeing Maisie.'

Pru stopped cutting. She stared at Rachel and noted the damp eyes and high colour. She said, 'So. You gathered most of what was said.'

Rachel said defensively, 'It's not as if I were eavesdropping, Pru! My God, no wonder you were so damned anxious when Maisie disappeared! How long has that been going on?'

Pru put the scissors on a scrubbed deal table and sat down in front of them.

She spoke slowly and clearly. 'I have loved Maisie from the moment I saw her at Markhams. I knew she was looking for someone special . . . her brother, Ted Davenport, Tom McEvoy . . . none of them were right. I hoped the someone special would be me. It was Nash.'

Rachel's indrawn breath was very audible but she continued to pull the grapes off willy-nilly and drop them into the basket.

Pru said, 'Meg and I . . . we grew together. We became interdependent. She was happy. She knew about Maisie but she was happy. And I was infinitely comforted. I hope . . . one day . . . I shall be as happy and Maisie will be comforted. Does that make sense?'

'Perfect sense.' Rachel pushed the basket aside with one foot and went to the door. Outside, a sudden squall of rain hit the conservatory glass and shook it. She paused, her fingers on the door handle. 'You'll grow old together like Sarah and Alison. You'll live in Prospect House and make pots and Maisie will be the perfect housewife. We shall all come and see you every summer. Some of us will come in the winter too so that we can walk in the hills. Nash will descend on you at intervals and Tom and Hillie will often be there because you'll be understanding and caring and they'll be completely happy with you. And at Christmas you'll go into Worcester and buy your presents and laugh as you pack them up and . . . and . . .' she was weeping freely now and opened the door with a jerk. The wind rushed in and blew the vine everywhere. She scrambled through into the rain, shut it behind her and began to run through the garden to the field path leading to the stile to the cove.

Pru found her crouched between two rocks, huddled into a foetal position, crying like a child. She threw caution to the winds and gathered her up, holding the strong, straw-coloured hair with one hand, feeling Rachel's tears slide unchecked into her own neck.

'My dear, my dear Ray, I'm sorry, sorry. I didn't realize it would be such a shock to you. You seem so openminded . . . forgive me.'

Rachel could not speak but she moved her head from side to side.

'Not that?' Pru tried to draw back so that she could see Rachel's face but Rachel clung like a limpet. 'All right. You'll tell me in a minute. Let it cry itself out.' Pru made some of her sounds, then she murmured right into Rachel's ear, 'D'you know, when I was driving back from Chester that terrible, terrible day, I had to stop three times to cry as you are crying now. And when I found Maisie in your old house looking after Edgar and Delano I simply could not stop crying!' She stroked the rough hair. 'Perhaps that's what our get-together was all about, Ray. Letting go.'

Rachel sniffed mightily and lowered her head so that she was butting Pru's shoulder. She spoke haltingly to the sand so that Pru had to strain to hear her words.

'I'm angry, Pru. Angry as well as unhappy. Don't you see that? I'm unhappy because I'm not loved. I'm wanted – Eric wanted me for his own even when he was fixing it for me to sleep with Duncan! When he let me watch him making love to his secretary, I knew he was really doing those things to me. I knew it. And Duncan . . . it's just sex with him . . . I'm good at sex you see. Because of Eric.' She wriggled her shoulders almost irritably as Pru tried to gather her closer and went on in a stronger voice, 'And now you. You and Maisie. Real love . . . I don't know about the sex bit – I don't care! All I know is that you live happily ever after – people will be happy when they are with you because you are happy! Oh, I'm sorry, Pru! I'm glad you are going to be happy and I'm glad Maisie is too . . . but there's nowhere for me, not really. Nash is all wrapped up with Hillie and Harvey and this new baby. And Evie is having her wonderful late romance with Sam Lavington. And you and Maisie . . .' Her sobs redoubled. 'It's self-pity, isn't it? That's all it is. And it's despicable. But . . . I can't help it, Pru! I know you'd let me share Prospect with you and Maisie – you'd teach me how to make pots and you'd probably make me your marketing manager . . .' she tried to laugh. 'But, don't you see? I had to start in your shadow, Pru. At Markhams. I can't do that again – I just can't!'

Pru did see because she said nothing; she stroked the nape of Rachel's neck and stared out to the rough sea with her far-seeing grey eyes, but she said nothing.

After a while Rachel sat back and leaned against the rock, exhausted. Her face was blotched and swollen, her eyes slits of blue. She opened her mouth to speak and Pru said quickly, 'Don't dare to apologize, Ray. This is hard enough to bear without you apologizing.' She held up her hand. 'I feel awful. Completely selfish. But I'm not going to apologize either. I told Maisie – the day I found her – that I had been stripped of all my layers . . . but this one was still there. This blind spot, this assumption that because you are capable, have had a successful marriage, were able to make things work for you . . . I assumed that you could cope with anything. How stupid!' She sighed. 'I still feel that heterosexual people are the lucky ones.' She shook her head and said again, 'How stupid!'

Rachel drew up her knees and clutched them to her chest.

Pru said, 'Shall we go back to the house now? We could have some tea in the conservatory and watch this storm.'

Rachel closed her eyes. 'You go on, Pru. I need some space. Give me half an hour. An hour.'

Pru hesitated. 'Are you sure?'

Rachel nodded and after a while Pru got to her feet. 'All right. But no more than an hour.' She moved around the rock and then she came back. 'Ray, listen. I have to tell you this. I've been in touch with Duncan.' She paused at Rachel's exclamation, then went on levelly, 'He's speaking in Truro tomorrow night. He'd like to come here afterwards. Will you see him?'

'I don't know. I don't think so. I still have no idea how I feel.'

''Don't you see, you have been coming to a decision through a process of elimination. Just now . . . you realized that yet another option was closed to you – to share a house with Maisie and me. It's a valid option, Ray, whatever you say. It could work if you wanted it to work. But you don't, so you turned it down. Just as you turned down a permanent place at Telegraph House. And Jess's invitation to stay with all of them in Birmingham.' She bit her lip. 'Now another option is coming up. To meet Duncan again. Are you going to turn that down too?'

She did not wait for an answer but turned and pushed herself into the wind and across the sand. Rachel sat on, hunched over her knees, the occasional whips of wind gradually drying her face. She had not cried like that for years; not since Denise had taken the overdose; not since the night of the election when Duncan had come to her room.

She stood up at last and looked out at the sea. Beyond the arms of the two headlands the white horses rode tempestuously, but inside the cove it was still calm, the swell rising into a wave and crashing on the shoreline in a flurry of spray. She watched it for a while and then suddenly decided to go into it. She peeled off her sweatshirt and unhooked her bra, then kicked off her trainers and stamped out of her jeans and pants. She ran down to the water, conscious as ever of her own heaviness; more so now that she was naked. She did not hesitate at the water's edge but plunged into the spray and struck out beyond the breakers where she could lie on her back and soar upwards as light as a feather, despite her breasts and thighs. She watched the grey sky as if expecting it to lower itself gently upon her. Smother her. Make it easy to sink underneath and drown. She rolled over and struck out again and knew how Denise had felt. Another pill, another drink, another pill . . . Her arms moved in time to the mantra. The water caressed her clumsy body, making it sleek and otter-like.

And then she heard the shout from the shore and knew that Pru had come back for her. She sighed and trod water, staring out to where the white horses reared. She wouldn't have done it of course; but she could have gone a little further. Just a little.

The shout came again. She turned and looked towards the shore. Duncan was waist deep; the swell was lifting him, soaking his shirt. As it lifted her too she could see his discarded suit above the tide line. But he still wore a tie. And he couldn't swim.

She sobbed and rolled into a powerful crawl and was with him in ten seconds. He was floundering, splashing with his arms, helpless when the swell lifted him off his feet. She put her arms around him and used the wave to carry them both to knee-depth. The wave receded and they lay in the shallow water; he was blubbing. She did not know whether it was terror or relief or anxiety. Or what.

She scrambled to her feet and hoisted him up. 'Come on! Stand. Otherwise the next one will wash us back!'

They staggered up the shore together and when they were ankle-deep he stopped and held her to him.

'I thought you were going to kill yourself! Oh God, Ray. Pru said she'd left you in some distress, but I never thought . . . how the hell could she have just left you? Oh, Ray, don't leave me – please don't leave me!'

He clung to her, his hands slipping on her wet body, kissing her wherever he could. She thought bleakly that in a moment they would go behind the rock and make love. He wanted her and heaven knew she wanted him. And once they'd done that she would go back to him and the old struggle would begin all over again. Fighting for him . . . all the time fighting for him the only way she knew how.

He gasped, 'Ray. Listen. I love you. I thought it was . . . you know . . . just when we were in bed. But . . . but . . . things have happened, Ray. And I found out something very important. I don't think I can function properly without you. That's got to be love, surely? I don't know any more. I thought I loved Joy and the girls. And I did. And I still do in a way. But I can manage without them. I can't manage without you. Say you'll stay with me, Ray. Please.'

She looked at him. His face was ravaged, his hair, slicked to his head by the water, revealed a bald spot, his legs – she had never noticed before – were very thin and bowed. Of course he'd done so much horse-riding up in Leicestershire.

She said, 'I'll stay with you, Duncan.'

He sobbed. 'I'm so much older than you, darling. You're young and strong and fearless.' He stared at her. 'Look at you. You look wonderful. Oh God . . .'

She said, 'Let's get that wet shirt off you. Come behind these rocks. Come on, my dear. I'll warm you . . . come on . . .' She led him out of the water and onto the dry sand, picking up his suit and piling it with her own clothes. Then she held him to her and eventually made love to him. And she knew he was right: she was strong. Pru had told her as much, so had Nash and Evie. It had taken Duncan's weakness to prove it to her. She had to be strong; strong enough to bear the pain of his weakness.

She dressed him in his suit and bundled his wet shirt and

tie under her arm. He tried to tell her about Douglas but she spared him that.

'I know. It will be all right. We'll get through it.'

She began to walk back through the sand towards the stile. He said, 'Ray . . . I promise you . . . I promise you it won't happen again—'

'Don't promise.' She managed to smile at him. 'No need. I won't let it happen again.'

'It was his price for all the bits of information.'

'I know. We can do without them. Come on. This wind is cold.'

'I haven't told you everything. Joy is still at Charnwood. She won't leave.'

She drew him to the stile and kissed him. 'Let her stay there for a while, darling. Perhaps Becky could have a word with her stepfather. I remember Becky was very persuasive.'

He straddled the stile and looked down at her adoringly. 'Ray. Prudence told me that you've been a tower of strength all the time at this house in Malvern. When she phoned . . . she said you'd dealt with everything . . . I realized then, that's how it is. At home. You deal with everything.'

'Not quite, sweetheart.' She smiled the rallying smile again. 'I didn't do very well with the typist's chair. And I interfere with things that are in your province.' She helped him down and wrapped her arms around him. The rain cut across the sea and tore at them. She gasped a laugh, still trying to lighten him up. 'Let's be . . . a bit more careful. Shall we?'

'Oh yes. Yes.'

And they walked back to the house, leaning on each other, like an old married couple. And Rachel had a sudden, wonderful thought. She and Nash were the same age. And Nash was having a baby . . .

That night Pru began the plaster cast of the mermaid. Somehow her sketches, her ideas, had grown to include many women. The mermaid would, of course, have Meg's vulnerability. But it would have Rachel's strength too. Nash's effervescence; the revelation that was Maisie and the tentative emergence of Evie supported by the invisible Edith.

As she worked she began to smile. She thought incredulously, I'm happy again . . . how can that be? It must be because her life had a new purpose; her dream of living with Maisie was going to come true. But it was more than that and she could not think what it was. She did not realize that the combination of all the women in her mermaid comprised a mystery that was herself.

And in New York, where the fall was arguably the best time of the year, Harvey and Natasha, and sometimes Hilary, would walk in Central Park before breakfast and Natasha would join the t'ai chi practitioners and feel her limbs stretching towards the sun. Hilary dreamed of returning to England at half-term where the Chudleigh staff would doubtless draw down their mouths in disapproval of her late arrival. It wouldn't matter of course. She would be within fifty miles of Luddington where Tom was. He had written her a poem last week. She had almost shown it to Nash and then known that she must never do that.

And in Earlswood, near Birmingham, in a small estate built for retired people, work was beginning on a new building. It was to be a public house with an inner courtyard and lots of mock Tudor beams. A competition was being run to find its name: Mr Lavington had recently seen a film about a land where elderly people were made young and he thought that Cocoon would be a good choice. Evelyn had put her entry in without telling anyone. She wanted The Village Inn. The brewery had already agreed to excavate a pond on the green, so her suggestion might be very well received.

Maisie, who without actually being at the reunion of Markhams staff had somehow become its hub, attended her husband's funeral in a very suitable grey dress and hat. She mourned, genuinely, for what might have been. When she saw Roly Jenkins standing on the edge of the mourners around the open grave, she was able to greet him without guilt or terror. He came back with everyone else to one-four-eight and nibbled at the crustless sandwiches and made friends with the boys.

The next day Maisie talked to Leo Barkwith about selling the shop-fitting business, and she took Pru to see some of the unsold units which would make excellent storage space for Prospect House. The day after that she packed the spotted dressing-gown in tissue paper and then an enormous bag, and she took it to the post office and sent it off to Natasha by airmail. She had always believed in living in the present and making the best of everything. She began to look forward very much to moving to Malvern with Pru.

Markhams continued to thrive genteelly. Mr Delano and Mr Edgar, thrust into the periphery of the drama of the reunion, had a new and fascinating topic of conversation that winter. The 'girls' became their property; surely they had contributed a great deal to the wonderful characters who had burst in upon them that hot August of 1980? Mr Delano remembered with a forgiving, nostalgic smile, his frantic advances on Edith Manners and then Prudence Adair. 'What was I trying to *prove*?' he asked his brother, spreading his hands humorously. Mr Edgar, who still visited the Honourable Mrs Adair, shook his head helplessly. 'They are such delightful creatures,' he murmured. 'When all is said and done, they are delightful.' 'Mind you, the staff we have at present are surprising,' Mr Edgar placed his fingertips together and leaned across the table. 'Did you know that Miss Matthews has two children by different fathers?' Jane Matthews was Mr Delano's present secretary and, though very efficient, had an unfortunate way of answering the telephone. Mr Delano had once emerged from the lavatory to hear her say, 'Hang on a minute, I'll see if I can dig him out of the coffin.' However, it now seemed that she was as mysterious as Miss Adair had been.

He nodded. 'You surprise me in one way. Not in another. As you said before, they are all delightful. All of them. In one way or another.'